（傣族）刀兴平 岩温扁 搜集整理
张昆群 张立玉 英译

兰嘎西贺

"十三五"国家重点图书
中国南方民间文学典籍英译丛书
丛书主编 张立玉 丛书副主编 起国庆

THE
TEN-HEADED
KING
OF LANGA

出品单位：
云南省少数民族古籍整理出版规划办公室

·汉英对照·

武汉大学出版社

图书在版编目(CIP)数据

兰嘎西贺:汉英对照/刀兴平等收集整理;张昆群,张立玉英译.—武汉:武汉大学出版社,2021.11
中国南方民间文学典籍英译丛书/张立玉主编
"十三五"国家重点图书
ISBN 978-7-307-22644-9

Ⅰ.兰… Ⅱ.①刀… ②张… ③张… Ⅲ.傣族—叙事诗—中国—汉、英 Ⅳ.I222.7

中国版本图书馆 CIP 数据核字(2021)第 214261 号

责任编辑:郭　静　　责任校对:李孟潇　　版式设计:韩闻锦

出版发行:武汉大学出版社　　(430072　武昌　珞珈山)
（电子邮箱:cbs22@whu.edu.cn　网址:www.wdp.whu.edu.cn）
印刷:湖北恒泰印务有限公司
开本:720×1000　1/16　印张:56.75　字数:683 千字
版次:2021 年 11 月第 1 版　　2021 年 11 月第 1 次印刷
ISBN 978-7-307-22644-9　　定价:120.00 元

版权所有,不得翻印;凡购我社的图书,如有质量问题,请与当地图书销售部门联系调换。

丛书编委会

学术顾问

王宏印　李正栓

主编

张立玉

副主编

起国庆

编委会成员（按姓氏笔画排列）

邓之宇	王向松	艾　芳	石定乐	龙江莉	刘　纯
陈兰芳	汤　茜	李克忠	杨　柳	杨筱奕	张立玉
张扬扬	张　瑛	和六花	依旺的	保俊萍	起国庆
陶开祥	鲁　钒	蔡　蔚	臧军娜		

序

近年来，民族典籍英译捷报频传，硕果累累。韩家全教授等人的壮族系列经典翻译陆续出版，王宏印教授等人的系列民族典籍英译研究著作已经问世，李正栓教授等人的藏族格言诗英译著作不断在国内外出版，王维波教授等人的东北民族典籍英译著作纷纷付梓，李昌银教授等人的"云南少数民族经典作品英译文库"于2018年年底出版，其他民族典籍英译作品也在接踵而至。

近日，中南民族大学张立玉教授传来佳音：他们要出版"十三五"国家重点图书——"中国南方民间文学典籍英译丛书"。虽叫民间文学，其实基本上都是民族典籍。这一系列包括十本书，它们是《黑暗传》《哭嫁歌》《哈尼阿培聪坡坡》《彝族民间故事》《南方民间创世神话选集》《十二奴局》《召树屯》《娥并与桑洛》《金笛》《梅葛》。其中，好几本是云南少数民族的。只有一本是汉族典籍，即《黑暗传》。很有意思的是，这些典籍展示了不同民族的创世史诗或诸如此类的东西。

《黑暗传》以民间歌谣唱本形象地描述了盘古开天辟地结束混沌黑暗，人类起源及社会发展的历程，融合了盘古、女娲、伏羲、炎帝神农氏、黄帝轩辕氏等众多英雄人物在洪荒时代艰难创世的一系列神话传说。它被称为汉族首部创世史诗。《哈尼阿培聪坡坡》是一部完整地记载哈尼族历史沿革的长篇史诗，堪称哈尼族的"史记"，长5000余行，以现实主义手法记叙了哈尼族祖先在各个历史时期的迁徙情况，并对其迁徙各地的原因、路线、途程，各个迁居地的社会生活、生产、风习、宗教，以及与毗邻民族的关系等，均作了详细而生动的辑录，因而该作品不仅具有文学价值，而且具有重大的历史学、社会学及宗教学价值。《南方民间创世神话选集》包括一些创世神话，主要是关于世界起源和人类起源的神话。《十二奴局》是一部在哈尼族广泛流传的民间诗歌，它通过"哈尼"（传统歌）的形式在民间演唱，世代流传。"奴局"是哈尼语，相当于汉族著述中的"篇"、"章"或汉族曲艺中的曲目。"十二奴局"即十二路歌的意思。译著表现了远古哈尼先民奇特的想象，涉及天体自然、人类发展、哈尼历史、历法计算、四时季令、农事活动等各个方面的知识，完整地反映了哈尼先民对天地形成、人类起源、民族迁徙的认识，具有创世神话与英雄史诗的合集之性质，可以说是哈尼族最为重要的文学经典之一。《梅葛》是彝族的一部长篇史诗，流传在云南省楚雄州的姚安、大姚等彝族地区。"梅葛"本为一种彝族歌调的名称，由于人们采用这种调子来唱彝族的创世史，因而创世史诗被称为"梅葛"。

其余几本书展示了一些少数民族的风俗习惯、恋爱故事、斗争故事等。《哭嫁歌》是土家族文化典籍。土家族姑娘在出嫁时用歌声诉说自己在封建买办婚姻制度下的不幸命运。《哭嫁歌》是土家族姑娘演唱的一种抒情歌谣，富有诗韵和乐感，融哀、怨、喜和乐为一体，以婉转的曲调向世人展示土家人独特的"哭"文化。《彝族民间故事》是一部以流传于云南楚雄彝族自治州彝族人民中间的民间故事为主体，同时覆盖全省包括小凉山等彝族地区的民间故事集。这些故事丰富多彩，从中能看到民族民间故事的各种形态和生动、奇妙而颇具彝族民族特色的文化特征。《召树屯》是傣族民间长篇叙事诗，叙述了傣族佛教世俗典籍《贝叶经·召树屯》中一个古老的传说故事。这部叙事诗一直为傣族人民所传唱，历久不衰。《娥并与桑洛》是一部优美生动的叙事诗，一个凄美的爱情悲剧。《金笛》是一部苗族长篇叙事诗，富于变幻性和传奇性，尽情铺叙扎董丕冉与蒙诗彩奏的悲欢离合，热情赞颂他们在与魔虎的激烈斗争中所表现出来的坚贞不屈、英勇顽强的精神，许多情节含有浓郁的民族特色。

这些故事都很引人入胜，都很符合国家文化发展需求，向世人讲述中国故事，传播中华文化，并且讲述的是民族故事，充分体现了党和国家对各民族的关怀。

民族典籍英译是传播中国文化、文学和文明的重要途径，是中华文化"走出去"的重要组成部分，是国家战略，是提高文化"软实力"的重要方式，在文化交流和文明建设中起着不可或缺的作用，对提升中国国际话语权和构建中国对外话语体系以及对建设世界文学都有积极意义。

中国民族典籍使世界文化更加丰富多彩、绚丽多姿。我国各民族典籍中折射出的文化多样性极大地丰富了世界多元、特色鲜明的文化。人们对多样性形成全新的认识角度和思维方式，有助于开阔视野，丰富思考问题的角度，挖掘这些经典中的教育价值和文化价值，对世界其他民族都有指导和借鉴意义，并且有助于建设我国的文化自信。

民族典籍翻译与研究事业关乎国家的稳定统一，关乎民族关系的和谐发展，关乎世界多元文化的实现。在中国，民族典籍资源极为丰富，有待进一步挖掘、翻译，仍有许多少数民族典籍亟待拯救，民族典籍翻译与研究工作任重而道远，民族典籍翻译事业大有可为。

李正栓[①]

2019 年 7 月 19 日

[①] 李正栓，中国英汉语比较研究会典籍英译专业委员会常务副会长兼秘书长；中国中医药研究促进会传统文化翻译与国际传播专业委员会常务主任委员。

前　言

　　《兰嘎西贺》是一部影响广泛的傣族神话叙事长诗，被誉为傣族"五大诗王"之一。主要叙述的是勐沓达腊塔王子召朗玛与勐甘纳嘎公主南西拉的爱情故事。整部史诗，情节曲折，语言优美。作为傣族"五大诗王"中的一部、傣族文学经典，《兰嘎西贺》是傣族文化体系中非常重要的一部分。它吸收了傣族传统文学的精髓，但它的重要意义不仅仅在于它具有较高的文学价值，还在于它反映了傣族的原始文化观念，展现了傣族古代社会生活的方方面面。它对傣族社会、历史、宗教等方面的研究提供了丰富的资源。

　　《兰嘎西贺》之所以引起学者的关注，一个重要原因是它取材于印度最著名的史诗《罗摩衍那》。这部史诗可以说是中印文化交流的结晶。《兰嘎西贺》虽然与《罗摩衍那》有一定的渊源，但绝不是照搬照抄或原文翻译，作者对内容和主题思想上都重新建构，其人物形象和故事发生的场所都是以西双版纳地区傣族人民生活为原型，展现了傣族古代社会生活的方方面面。作品具有浓郁民族特色和地方特色。因此几个世纪以来，《兰嘎西贺》一直深受傣族人民的喜爱。

　　该史诗目前还没有英译本出版。对本书进行英语翻译，将有助于世界了解我国丰富多彩的少数民族文化尤其是傣族文学、促进中华多元文化走向世界，对于国内外傣族文学研究、诗学研究将具有积极意义。

目 录

第一章　勐兰嘎 …………………………………… 4
第二章　十头王 …………………………………… 32
第三章　继位 ……………………………………… 68
第四章　肆虐 ……………………………………… 106
第五章　勐沓达厝塔 ……………………………… 148
第六章　择婿 ……………………………………… 190
第七章　婚礼 ……………………………………… 228
第八章　让位 ……………………………………… 260
第九章　出走 ……………………………………… 310
第十章　勐基沙 …………………………………… 340
第十一章　遭难 …………………………………… 394
第十二章　结盟 …………………………………… 446
第十三章　阿努曼 ………………………………… 482
第十四章　战前 …………………………………… 558
第十五章　初战 …………………………………… 604
第十六章　破敌 …………………………………… 634
第十七章　决战 …………………………………… 694
第十八章　凯旋 …………………………………… 762
第十九章　冤 ……………………………………… 806
第二十章　团圆 …………………………………… 854

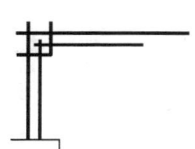

Contents

Chapter 1	Meng Langa	5
Chapter 2	The Ten-Headed King	33
Chapter 3	Succeeding the Throne	69
Chapter 4	Havoc	107
Chapter 5	The Kingdom of Dadalata	149
Chapter 6	Choosing a Son-in-law	191
Chapter 7	Wedding Ceremony	229
Chapter 8	Abdication	261
Chapter 9	Exodus	311
Chapter 10	The Kingdom of Jisha	341
Chapter 11	Sufferings	395
Chapter 12	Alliance Formed	447
Chapter 13	Anuman	483
Chapter 14	Before the War	559
Chapter 15	The First Battle	605
Chapter 16	The Enemy Defeated	635
Chapter 17	The Decisive Battle	695
Chapter 18	Return in Triumph	763
Chapter 19	Injustice	807
Chapter 20	Reunion	855

千万朵荷花呀，一齐绽开，
千万团彩云呀，从天降落。
行走的月亮也悄悄钻进竹楼，
听我吟唱动人心魄的《兰嘎西贺》①

这故事宛如涓涓的泉水，
我要让它流进傣家人的心头。
这故事犹如芬芳的缅桂，
我要让它薰香傣家人的竹楼。

我的故事像滔滔的江水，
我的故事像浩瀚的海洋。
请你们细心地听吧，
沁人肺腑的《兰嘎西贺》源远流长。

---

① 兰嘎西贺：兰嘎，地名；西贺，十个头。兰嘎西贺即兰嘎的十头王。

Tens of thousands of lotus are blooming together,
Tens of thousands of colorful clouds flying down from heaven.
The moving moon secretly crept into the bamboo house,
All listening to me chanting the thrilling story of *Langaxihe*①.

The story is just like trickling spring,
I wish it would flow into the heart of the Dai people.
The story is as fragrant as magnolia,
I wish it would fill the bamboo house of the Dai people.

My story runs like billowy river;
My story surges like vast ocean.
Please be patient and listen attentively to me telling you
The heartwarming story of *Langaxihe* lasting for ages.

---

① Langaxihe: Langa, the place name; xihe, ten-headed. So it means the ten-headed King of Langa.

第一章　勐兰嘎①

一、兰嘎

在辽阔无际的海洋里，
有一个富饶美丽的岛国兰嘎。
它是商船来往停泊的地方，
它是东西方交通的枢纽。

岛屿上有宽阔的平坝，
居住着勤劳善良的百姓。
他们种的谷子像黄金，
他们养的牛羊如繁星。

蜿蜒逶迤的大山底下，
埋藏着丰富的矿藏。
金银铜铁锡和铅，
取之不尽，用之不完。

---

① 勐兰嘎：勐，区域，国家。勐兰嘎即兰嘎国。

第一章 勐兰嘎 Chapter 1 Meng Langa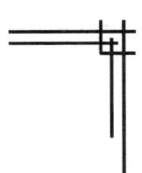

Chapter 1　Meng Langa①

I　Langa

On an island in the vast and boundless ocean,
There was a rich and beautiful island kingdom named Langa.
Commercial ships berthed here to refresh their supply.
It became a transportation hub connecting the west and east.

There were wide plains on this island
Where hardworking people lived for generations.
The gleaming rice they planted looked like gold.
The cattle and sheep they raised were numerous as stars.

There were mountains meandering along the island.
Beneath the mountains rich minerals were buried.
Gold, silver copper, iron, tin and lead,
Their deposits were abundant and inexhaustible.

---

① Meng Langa: Meng means area or country. Langa is the name of a place. Therefore Meng Langa means the Kingdom of Langa.

岛屿上生长着茂密的森林，
栖息着斑斓的蜥蜴和巨蟒。
飞翔着美丽多姿的白鹤、犀鸟和孔雀，
漫游着成群凶猛的虎豹、野牛和大象。

浩瀚无边的汪洋呀，
紧紧把绿色的兰嘎岛环抱。
波涛万顷的大海呀，
蕴藏着绚丽的珊瑚、珍珠和玛瑙。

兰嘎宛如一颗海上的明珠，
又像一颗宝石烁烁闪光。
它终年不断的花香随风向远方飘散，
它富饶美丽的名声天下传扬。

在兰嘎与大陆之间的海底，
居住着一个斑壳长脚的大蟹。
就像一个巨大的暗礁石，
守护着兰嘎宽阔的水域。

巍峨的城池肃穆壮观，
各色旗幡在城墙上迎风飘扬。
闪耀着霞光的缅寺、佛塔，
矗立在允兰嘎①的四面八方。

---

① 允兰嘎：允，城的意思。允兰嘎即兰嘎城。

第一章 勐兰嘎 Chapter 1 Meng Langa

Dense forests grew on the vast island
Which were the habitats of colorful lizards and python.
And the white cranes, hornbill and peacock flew in the woods,
Wild tigers, leopards, buffaloes and elephants roaming.

The green island of Langa was nestled
By the surrounding vast and boundless ocean.
Under the endless waves and billows of the sea
Colorful corals, pearls and agates were hidden.

Langa was just like a pearl in the sea,
And it also looked like a shining precious gem.
Its everlasting fragrance of flowers drifted with the winds,
And its abundance and beauty were known to the world.

Under the sea between Langa and the continent
Lived a giant crab with colorful shell and long feet.
It was like a giant submerged rock
Guarding the wide water channel surrounding Langa.

On the island stood the solemn and awesome city wall;
On the city wall colorful flags danced against the wind.
Temples and pagodas were everywhere in Yun Langa[①],
They glinted under the sunlight at dawn and dusk.

[①] Yun Langa: Yun means city. Therefore Yun Langa means the City of Langa.

雄伟的宫殿建在城中心，
红墙黄瓦高达二十层。
宫殿的梁柱施漆加彩涂上金粉，
宫殿的壁画千姿百态栩栩如生。

有威望的国王是叭①兰巴，
美丽的王后叫南②安嘎嫡。
国王万里挑一把她选上，
她和国王犹如星星伴月亮形影不离。

南安嘎嫡协助国王管理国家，
每天接受臣民百姓的朝拜。
每天处理大事小事千万件，
就像把一团团乱麻理成细纱。

勇敢的士兵骑着膘壮的战马，
手持长矛弓弩守卫着边关要卡。
健壮的水兵驾驶着庞大的舰船，
劈波斩浪在辽阔的海上巡察。

百姓们在勐兰嘎安居乐业，
国王和王后的美名传遍海角天涯。
一百零一个勐都来称臣纳贡，
森林的妖鬼也接受他们的管辖。

---

① 叭：傣语词，音近于帕雅的合音。一般冠于国王、官员和头人的名字前面，以示尊敬。
② 南：对公主和尊贵的妇女的称呼，冠于名字前面。

第一章 勐兰嘎 Chapter 1 Meng Langa

The magnificent palace towered in the center of the city.
It was twenty stories high with yellow tiles and red walls.
The beams and columns were painted with gold powder;
On the frescoes were pictures which were so true to life.

The king ruling the country was prestigious Ba① Lanba,
And the beautiful Nan② Angadi was his queen.
The king had selected the queen from thousands of beauties.
They were inseparable as star always accompanying the moon.

The King, assisted by Nan Angadi, governed the kingdom.
Everyday subjects and officials paid them their respect.
Together they solved thousands of problems, big or small,
It was like weaving thread out of balls of messy jute.

Brave soldiers were mounted on stalwart war horses,
With spears in their hands they guarded the frontiers;
Strong sailors steered gigantic warships,
Scouting the territorial waters on the vast and wavy sea.

Common people lived a happy life in the Kingdom of Langa;
The reputation of the king and queen spread all over the world.
One hundred and one kingdoms came to pay their tribute;
The ghosts and spirits in the forest were also under their rules.

---

① Ba: in the language of the Dai, Ba is used before the name of the King, officials or chieftains to show respect.

② Nan: used before name to address the princess or honourable woman.

勐兰嘎的威望比山高,
国王和王后的权力比地大。
他们有享不尽的荣华富贵,
但也美中不足,白璧有瑕。

大好的日子年复一年过去,
他们身边还没有添过一个儿女。
勐兰嘎的王室怎能没有后继,
国王对王后说出了自己的心意:

"我们身边没有一棵出土的笋苗,
为此事我内心受尽了煎熬。
希望你去缅寺滴水赕佛,
祈求天神恩赐给我们一个孩子。"

丈夫的话像一碗澄澈的清水,
点点滴滴洒进妻子的心里。
王后选择了一个吉祥的时日,
宫女们簇拥着她到缅寺求子。

天神有感于王后的虔诚,
让漂亮的南安嘎嫡怀了身孕。
国王高兴地叮咛宫女尽心护理,
要像雌燕孵蛋那样的细心。

第一章 勐兰嘎　Chapter 1 Meng Langa

The authority of the Kingdom of Langa was higher than mountain;

The power of the king and the queen was greater than the earth.

While they enjoying endless prosperity and luxury

There was still one tiny flaw in their perfect life.

Good days were passing by year after year,

But they hadn't got any son or daughter.

How could the king rule on without an heir?

The king spoke out his mind to the queen,

"There isn't one baby like bamboo shoot around us.

I have been suffering much affliction because of this.

Please go to the temple and worship the Buddha,

Please pray to heavenly gods to bless us with a child."

The remarks from the king were like a bowl of clear water,

And they dripped drop by drop into his wife's heart.

The queen chose a propitious day to start her journey,

Accompanied by maids she went to the temple for a child.

The heavenly gods felt the piety of the queen,

And they blessed beautiful Nan Angadi with pregnancy.

Excitedly, the king ordered the maids to take good care of the queen,

Asking them to be as careful as a female swallow hatching her eggs.

兰嘎西贺 The Ten-Headed King of Langa

在一个星星闪烁的夜晚,
月亮像美丽的少女披着纱巾。
王后怀胎十月分了娩,
漂亮的公主在寝宫里降生。

像初一到十五的月亮天天长大,
公主长得恰似雨露中的缅桂花。
国王请来智者帕麻纳①,
为公主取了个美名古蒂提拉。

鲜艳的凤凰花开了十六回,
南古蒂提拉长到了十六岁。
长大了的公主焕发着青春的光华,
池塘里的荷花没有她的颜色滋润。

天真烂漫的公主古蒂提拉,
宛如勐兰嘎的一颗明珠。
国王和王后疼爱女儿,
就像对眼珠那样珍重爱护。

鹦鹉要有栖息的地方,
凤凰要有居住的金窝。
国王为使女儿过得如意,
特地为她建盖了一座漂亮的塔楼。

---

① 帕麻纳:主管宗教、祭祀的官。

第一章 勐兰嘎 Chapter 1 Meng Langa

On a starry night with the moon
Like a beauty veiled with pretty shawl,
The queen labored after ten month's pregnancy,
And a beautiful princess was born in the palace.

As the moon changes its shapes from a crescent to a full one,
The princess grew up like a magnolia bathed in dew and rain.
The king sent for the wise official Pamana① to name her,
Who gave her the beautiful name of Guditila.

The flamboyant phoenix flower bloomed for sixteen times,
Now beautiful Nan Guditila was sixteen years old.
The grown-up princess was radiant with her youthful spirit,
And she outshone even the blooming lotus flower.

The innocent princess Guditila,
She was like a pearl to the kingdom of Langa.
The king and the queen loved their daughter dearly,
Cherishing her as they did to their own eyeballs.

A parrot needed a perch to rest on;
A phoenix needed a gold nestle to live in.
The king wanted her daughter to live a happy life,
And he had a pretty tower specially built for her.

---

① Pamana: the official in charge of religion and ritual of sacrifice.

高高的塔楼有九个屋顶,
美丽得就像出土的花笋。
塔楼矗立在御花园中,
公主住在里面如居仙境。

二、古蒂提拉出走

叭兰巴眼看自己年过半百,
就像一棵苍老的大青树,
尽管树干粗壮,绿叶成荫,
也难以经受严酷的风霜雨露。

心情沉重的国王日夜思索:
"自己年迈没有儿子,
像大海明珠般的岛国啊,
总该有个后继人来掌握。"

他经过慎重仔细的考虑,
决意冲破传统的规矩,
让独生女古蒂提拉继承王位,
再招个女婿辅佐她把国家治理。

公主听到这个消息,
立即到父王面前表明心迹:
"我尊敬的父王啊,
女儿的终身大事请你不必操心。

第一章 勐兰嘎 Chapter 1 Meng Langa

The high tower had nine layers of roof,
And it was as beautiful as a flower sprout.
Standing high in the royal garden,
The tower was a fairyland for the princess to live in.

II Guditila Ran away from Home

Ba Lanba now was in his fifties,
And he felt like an old evergreen tree.
Although it still had solid branches and green leaves,
This old tree couldn't stand harshness ahead any more.

The overwrought king kept worrying and thinking,
"Now I am old and have not got a son.
But there should be an heir who can go on ruling
My island kingdom which was like a pearl in the sea."

After careful and discreet consideration,
The King decided to break up the tradition.
He would choose his only daughter to succeed to his throne,
Then find her a husband to assist her in ruling the country.

At hearing the news,
The princess went to her father and bared her heart,
"My dear father, the Majestic King,
You don't have to worry about my marriage.

"女儿嫌弃堆积如山的财宝,
女儿厌烦喧哗嘈杂的凡尘,
女儿不愿做兰嘎明珠之主,
女儿向往着到深山老林去修行。

"女儿的要求违背了父王的心愿,
乞求父王一定要对女儿宽恕。
女儿的话绝不是随便说出,
它是女儿深思熟虑的结果。"

国王听了气得翘起胡子,
他强忍怒气把女儿劝说:
"父亲已经年迈体衰,
已承受不了繁重的宫廷政务。

"你没有哥哥和弟弟,
你不承袭王位谁承袭?
招婿辅政是可行良策,
父王的苦衷你一定要体恤。"

国王企图说服宝石般的女儿,
南古蒂提拉越听越不顺耳。
她就像叫唤不已的小鸡,
向父王跪下再次坚决表示:

第一章 勐兰嘎　Chapter 1 Meng Langa

"Roomful treasure is despicable in my eyes;
I am also tired of the hustling and bustling world.
I don't want to become the ruler of this kingdom;
I long to practise Buddhism in the deep mountain forest.

"I know what I request is against your wish,
So I beg you to forgive my disobedience.
I am not saying it for fun,
It was a decision I had considered over and over."

The king became furious at hearing this.
In smothering anger he tried to persuade his daughter,
"I am too old and fragile now
To handle the tiresome state chores anymore.

"You don't have any brother elder or younger,
Who will inherit the throne if you don't?
It is workable to get you a husband to help with governance,
Please think it over for the sake of your old father."

The king tried to talk his jade-like daughter out of her idea,
But what he said was increasingly displeasing to Guditila.
Like a little chick keeping chirping,
She knelt in front of her dad and pleaded resolutely,

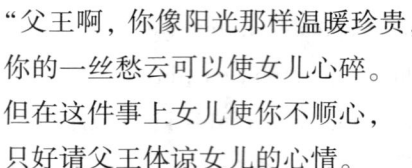

"父王啊，你像阳光那样温暖珍贵，
你的一丝愁云可以使女儿心碎。
但在这件事上女儿使你不顺心，
只好请父王体谅女儿的心情。

"父王啊，兰嘎国家这么大，
不要以为只有你的女儿才行。
臣僚中不乏聪明干练之才，
你可以在他们当中选贤任能。

"国王也可以来自百姓，
百姓里也有治国的能人。
只要你相信他们的才华和本领，
你可以将王位禅让给他们。"

至高无上的国王叭兰巴，
听到女儿这番叛逆的话，
急得心头颤抖话都说不出，
气得满脸煞白肺都要爆炸。

南古蒂提拉没有再与父王争辩，
心里却坚定了到森林修行的意念。
拜别父王母后回到塔楼，
一个人悄悄地准备出走。

第一章 勐兰嘎 Chapter 1 Meng Langa

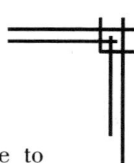

"My dear father, you are warm and precious sunshine to me,
One whiff of your anxiety will break my heart.
I am sorry that I made such decision against your will,
But what I can do is pray that you will forgive me.

"My dear father, Langa is such a big country,
Please stop thinking only your daughter is the right person.
There are many capable officials in your court,
You can pick out the most suitable one to run this kingdom.

"A king can also be selected from the common people.
There must be a capable one who can rule the country.
As long as you have faith in their capability and skills,
You can surely hand over your throne to those people."

Hearing the rebellious remarks from his daughter,
The supreme King Ba Lanba was out of his mind with fury.
He felt his heart throbbing and could not speak out a word;
He was so shocked that he felt his lungs seem to be burst.

Nan Guditila stopped arguing with her father
But she was more resolute with her decision.
Returning to her tower after saying goodnight,
She secretly made preparation for her leaving.

星星在寂静的天空眨眼，
月亮已隐藏到天边。
公鸡已经放开喉咙啼鸣，
南古蒂提拉只身离开了宫廷。

公主披荆斩棘走过千山万壑，
经历了长途跋涉的困苦艰辛。
昼行夜宿整整走了七天①，
来到了遮天蔽日的伊麻板②森林。

芳香的花瓣撒满林间，
清新的微风吹拂粉面。
太阳像金子般光彩明亮，
气候温和，空气新鲜。

绿树丛中掩映着巴朗③，
房里干干净净宽宽敞敞。
这里是年老的隐者居住的处所，
这里是帕拉西④修身养性的地方。

---

① 七天：泛指多天。
② 伊麻板：泛指原始森林。
③ 巴朗：在深山老林修行的和尚居住的茅屋。
④ 帕拉西：在深山老林里修行的和尚，有高深的法术和渊博的知识。

第一章 勐兰嘎 Chapter 1 Meng Langa

The stars were blinking their eyes in the sky;
The moon was hidden behind the horizon;
Roosters were singing to welcome the new morning;
At this moment Nan Guditila alone left the palace.

The princess cut her way through thistles and thorns in the mountains;
She suffered unspeakable hardships dragging herself through valleys.
After seven full days and nights① of long treks,
Finally she reached the dense forest named Yimaban②.

Fragrant flowers were dotted all over the wood;
Fresh and gentle wind drifted between the trees;
The sunlight was bright and brilliant as gold;
It was such a nice day with warm and fresh air.

A cottage of Balang③ was hidden among the green woods.
It was clean, tidy and spacious inside.
This was the shelter for the old hermits to stay in;
It was where Palaxi④ retreated for practising Buddhism.

---

① Seven days and nights: a broad term for many days.
② Yimaban: a broad term for primitive forest.
③ Balang: the cottage of a monk who practices Buddhism in deep forest.
④ Palaxi: the monk who practices Buddhism in deep forest and are erudite and expert in magic arts.

公主怀着十分虔诚的心，
走进巴朗朝拜正在坐禅的帕拉西。
她的话语犹如小溪的流水，
声声句句说得轻柔熨帖：

"慈祥的圣者帕拉西，
黑眼珠的古蒂提拉问候你。
我有心在你身边服侍你，
请收下我这姑娘做养女。"

"你这美丽娇嫩的荷花呀，
你的家乡在什么地方？
为什么来到这深山老林？
这里可不是抚养你的池塘。"

"我是兰嘎王国的公主，
是父王母后的独根笋苗。
我今年刚满十六岁，
父亲就要我继承他的王位。

"女儿已经看破红尘，
不喜欢人世间的混沌，
在那复杂肮脏的人世，
充斥着压榨、欺骗和纷争。

第一章 勐兰嘎 Chapter 1 Meng Langa

Princess walked into the cottage with her devoted heart.
She approached Palaxi who was sitting like a Buddha.
With a voice pleasing as flowing creek,
She spoke to him gently and sweetly,

"Dear Palaxi, the kind and Saint,
Guditila with black pupils says hello to you.
I wish I could stay here to serve you,
Please be kind to adopt me as your daughter."

"You are as pretty and tender as a lotus flower,
Where did you come from?
Why are you here in this remote forest?
Here is not a pond where you can live an easy life."

"I am the Princess of Langa Kingdom,
The only daughter of the King and the Queen.
I just turned sixteen this year,
But my father wants me to succeed to his throne.

"I am disillusioned with the mortal world,
And I am sick of the chaos of this earth.
In this complicated and squalid society
Flooded exploiting, cheating and fighting.

"我不愿陷入黑暗的泥潭,
更不愿陷入权势的争战。
我要像池塘里的荷花,
一身洁净,出淤泥而不染。

"女儿无心为王也不想当王后,
唯一的愿望是脱俗离凡。
恳请慈父发发善心,
答应我在此和你同福共难。"

帕拉西听了公主的表白,
为有人同他一起修行而高兴。
当即应允收她为养女,
但对她是否虔诚还不放心:

"姑娘啊,你要修行的心意可钦可佩,
可这里吃的是野果,喝的是泉水。
在这里苦苦修行一辈子,
你是否熬得过这么长的年岁。"

"慈父啊,我来修行的决心已定,
就是再苦再长我也能忍受。
今天托你的洪福庇荫,
我才有缘在你的身旁修行。"

第一章 勐兰嘎 Chapter 1 Meng Langa

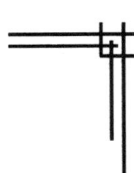

"I don't want to sink in the dark muddy pit;
I hate to get involved in the plots and schemes.
I wish to be the pure lotus flower in the pond
Coming out of the dirty mud unsoiled and pure.

"I have no intention to be a king or a queen;
I only wish to be free from the world of mortal.
Dear Father, please be kind to me.
Let me stay here going through the good and bad with you."

Hearing what the Princess had told him,
Palaxi was glad someone could practise Buddhism with him.
At once he agreed to adopt her as his daughter,
But he still had doubt about her faith and piety,

"My girl, your determination is admirable,
But here you can only eat wild fruit and drink spring water.
So I am wondering whether your will is strong enough
For you to enduring all the hardship in the rest of your life."

"My dear father, I have made up my mind.
I can endure whatever hardships or sufferings.
Now it is only with your permission and blessing that
I can have the honor to practise Buddhism by your side."

帕拉西听了十分高兴：
"这里的果子你可尽情吃，
任何东西都有你的一份。
从此你就把我当作亲生的父亲。"

帕拉西为公主盖了一间茅屋，
让南古蒂提拉独自居住。
父女俩互敬互爱与世无争，
相依为命苦度光阴。

再说公主出走的那天清晨，
宫女们走进公主的内房，
她们轻轻掀开蚊帐，
不见公主睡在金床上。

宫女们分头奔出去，
像蝴蝶四处把花王找寻。
找遍宫殿、花园和河边，
都不见公主的身影。

国王和王后听说女儿失踪，
一下子就昏倒在地。
王后的眼泪像溪水流淌，
国王苏醒后把大鼓擂响。

第一章 勐兰嘎 Chapter 1 Meng Langa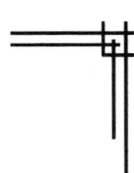

Palaxi was happy to hear what she said.
"Help yourself with all the fruits here,
You have share of everything in this cottage.
From today on I will treat you as my own daughter."

Palaxi built another thatched cottage,
So that Nan Guditila could live all alone by herself.
The Father and Daughter respected and depended on each other.
And they lived a harsh but happy life free from the earthly world.

Let's come back to the day when Princess left the palace.
In the morning, the servant maids went into her bedroom.
They drew the mosquito net open to help her up
Only to find the princess was not in her bed of gold.

The maids rushed out to look for her around
As butterflies trying to seek the queen of flower.
They searched the garden, the palace and the riverside.
Nowhere could they find a trace of the Princess.

At the news of the disappearance of their daughter,
The King and the Queen fainted and fell onto the ground.
The tears of the Queen fell like flowing creek;
Coming back to life, the king pounded on drums.

平时狮子般威武的国王，
突然变得像衰老的大象。
他用微弱缓慢的声音，
说出公主失踪的不幸消息。

他对大臣和头人们宣布：
"我那明珠般的公主，
今天像风一样突然消失。
宫殿里外都找不到她的踪迹。

"是不是因为她长得美丽，
贪色的贼人把她窃去？
还是我昨天刺伤了她的心，
她想不开出走去自尽？

"不管公主出了什么事情，
你们一定要想办法找寻。
谁找到了我的女儿，
我一定赏他万两黄金。

"不管公主走到哪里，
只要打听到她的消息，
再遥远再偏僻的地方，
我都要用金鞍大象去迎接。"

大臣们遵照国王的命令，
带着队伍分几路出发。
有的到各勐去寻找，
有的到森林去搜查。

第一章 勐兰嘎 Chapter 1 Meng Langa

Usually the king looked powerful as a roaring lion,
Now suddenly he turned debilitated like an old elephant.
He spoke in a feeble and dragging voice to his officials
Of the sad news that the princess had disappeared.

He declared to his officials and the chieftains,
"My peal-like daughter, the Princess,
She disappeared as a sudden gust of wind today.
There was no any trace of her in or out of the palace.

"Is it because she is too beautiful
That a lusty thief has taken her away?
Or she was so much hurt by me yesterday
That she went out to commit suicide?

"No matter whatever happened to my daughter,
You must try your very best to find her.
Whoever can find and bring my daughter back,
I will offer him ten thousand kilos of gold as reward.

"No matter wherever the Princess is,
No matter how far or remote she is,
As long as there is information of her whereabouts,
I will send elephants with gold saddle to get her back."

All of the officials followed the king's order immediately.
They led the searching groups setting out in different directions.
Some went to the neighboring kingdoms;
Some went to search in the deep forest.

兰嘎西贺 The Ten-Headed King of Langa

找遍村村寨寨，旮旮旯旯，
从芒果开花时找到芒果成熟时，
从禾苗种下时找到收割时，
一直没有找到公主的下落。

国王和王后找不到公主，
就像母牛失去了小牯，
就像母兔失去了小兔，
就像钢刀刺心一样的痛苦。

欢乐的宫廷再也听不到歌声，
高大的塔楼也变得凄凉孤寂。
憔悴的王后天天呼唤古蒂提拉，
见到别家的姑娘就想到自己的女儿。

椰子树开花又结果，
时间像浮云飘过。
国王和王后天天祈祷，
祝愿女儿消灾免祸。

第一章 勐兰嘎　Chapter 1 Meng Langa

Each corner in each village had been searched.
From the time mango flowers bloomed till mangoes ripened,
From the time the rice was planted till rice was harvested,
Still there was no news of the whereabouts of the Princess.

The king and the queen could not find their Princess,
They were like cows that have lost their calves,
Like mother rabbits that have lost their little ones,
They were as painful as their hearts were stabbed by knives.

No more happy songs could be heard in the palace.
The tall tower became desolate and deserted.
The haggard queen murmured Guditila's name all day long.
She thought of her daughter each time she saw other girls.

The coconut flower bloomed and coconut grew on the trees.
Time flew like drifting clouds.
The king and the queen prayed each day,
Praying their daughter were safe and sound from disasters.

第二章　十头王

一、魔王出世

南古蒂提拉在幽静的森林里，
像亲女儿般勤侍候帕拉西。
每天砍来柴火、挑来泉水，
找来各种野果和山药充饥。

她就像蜜蜂那样辛勤，
她遵循佛规无限虔诚，
她皈依佛法修身养性，
不觉过了七个月光阴。

她的虔诚感动了天神叭英①，
叭英为兰嘎国王叭兰巴担心，
担忧年迈的叭兰巴一旦升天，
勐兰嘎的王位无人继承。

---

① 叭英：在傣族神话里天堂共十六层，主管一至六层天的天神叫叭英。

第二章 十头王 Chapter 2 The Ten-Headed King

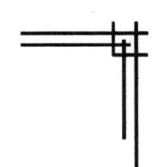

Chapter 2　The Ten-Headed King

Ⅰ　The Birth of the Devil

Nan Guditila lived in the tranquil forest.
She took care of Palaxi like his own daughter.
She gathered firewood and fetched spring water,
And she collected wild fruits and yam for food every day.

She worked hard like a diligent bee.
She followed the rule of Buddhism with great piety,
Practising Buddhism teachings and purifying her soul.
Now seven months passed before she knew it.

Her devotion touched the heavenly god of Baying①.
Baying began to worry about the King of Ba Lanba.
He feared that when senile Ba Lanba passed away,
There would be no heir to the throne of Langa.

---

①　Baying: There are sixteen levels of heaven in the myth of the Dai. The heavenly god in charge of the first level to the sixth level is Baying.

33

叭英请最高天神玛哈捧下凡，
到森林与古蒂提拉幽会，
诱惑公主婚配怀孕，
使勐兰嘎的王位后继有人。

南古蒂提拉见到玛哈捧十分高兴，
忙向玛哈捧合掌询问：
"像缅桂花一样美的召①啊，
你是天神还是凡人？

"你像阳光一样灿烂夺目，
你像十五的明月一样皎净。
你的光临使大地增添异彩，
你的光临给森林带来光明。

"看你是心地善良神态文雅的男子，
你一定具有崇高的灵魂优美的品质。
你到森林里来有何贵干？
你的家乡在哪里？

"我这在森林修行的姑娘，
热忱欢迎你的到来。
有福气的人啊，
请你到我的寒舍少憩。"

---

① 召：对国王、王子和尊贵的人的称呼，一般冠于名字前面。

第二章 十头王　Chapter 2　The Ten-Headed King

Pleading to Mahapeng, the heavenly god of the highest level,
Baying asked him to come to meet with Guditila in the forest.
Mahapeng would charm the princess and impregnate her,
So that there would be an heir to the kingdom of Langa.

Nan Guditila was very happy to see Mahapeng.
With folded palms, she came forward to him,
"Honorable Zhao①, you are charming like a magnolia flower,
Are you a human being or a god from heaven?

"You are as bright as the sunlight;
You are as pure as the moonlight.
Your arrival has brightened the earth;
You have brought sunlight to the forest.

"You look like a kind and graceful gentleman,
You must have a noble heart and character.
Why are you here in the forest?
And where did your come from?

"I am a girl practising Buddhism in the forest.
I would like to give you my warmest welcome.
You, the blessed one,
Would you please be my guest in my humble cottage?"

---

① Zhao: used before one's name to address King, Prince, or distinguished guests.

美貌标致的天神玛哈捧,
好似闪着亮光的玻璃。
他用软如棉花的声音,
对古蒂提拉说出甜言蜜语:

"像斑鸠一样美丽的姑娘啊,
感谢你的热情邀请和赞美。
你娓娓动听的话语像糖水,
每一句都是那样香甜和清脆。

"我不是世间凡人也不是叭英,
我是天神玛哈捧。
也是我与你有缘分才得相会,
我来执行一个神圣的使命。

"手臂像莲藕般的姑娘啊,
有件事我要对你讲明,
要让你心中像湖水一样明亮,
要让你心地像大地一样坦然。

"你放弃荣华富贵到森林修行,
一生奉守着神圣的信念,
遵行着崇高的美德,
你的心愿一定会实现。

第二章 十头王 Chapter 2 The Ten-Headed King

Mahapeng, the charming and handsome heavenly god,
He was as shining as a piece of precious glass.
With a voice as soft as cotton,
He spoke to Guditila most sweetly,

"My young lady, you are beautiful like a dove.
Thanks for your compliment and your invitation.
Your pleasing words are like honey,
Each of them sounds so crisp and sweet.

"I am neither a human being or heavenly god of Baying.
I am the heavenly god of Mahapeng.
It was destiny that brought you and me to meet.
I am here to fulfil a holy and sacred mission.

"My beautiful girl with arms as white as lotus roots,
I need to explain one thing to you
So that you can keep your heart as clear as water of lake,
And you can accept what I will do without any embarrassment.

"You forsook worldly wealth to practise Buddhism here;
You hold on to the holy belief in your heart,
You have been doing what noble virtues dictate,
So your wishes will be fulfilled because of your devotion.

"可是你的出走给父母带来无限忧愁,
你可想过兰嘎王国不能一日无主?
你要为勐兰嘎的前途着想,
不能没有人继承你父亲的宝座。

"如果你不想使兰嘎王位断线,
你就得向天神祈求儿子。"
天神玛哈捧的一番话语,
像明镜一般使公主受到了启示。

公主回想起自己的身世,
担心父亲的王位没人承袭。
她按照玛哈捧的旨意,
摘来十个芳香的芒果准备求子。

她用清水把芒果洗了又洗,
又把芒果放在圣洁的供盘里,
举过头顶敬献给玛哈捧,
祈求天神恩赐一个儿子。

清香的芒果甜如蜜,
玛哈捧吃了还想吃。
公主古蒂提拉又去摘,
恰巧树上掉下个象牙芒果。

第二章 十头王 Chapter 2 The Ten-Headed King

"But your departure has brought endless agony to your parents.
Have you ever thought Langa can't go on without a king someday?
For the sake of the future of the Kingdom of Langa,
Someone must succeed to the throne of your father.

"If you want the blood of your royal family to continue,
It is time that you prayed to heavenly gods to have a son."
The Princess was enlightened by the heavenly god.
With his words as bright as a mirror.

The Princess recollected her life story in the palace,
And she came to worry nobody was there to inherit the throne.
So she did as Mahapeng suggested,
Plucking ten fragrant mangoes to make the preparation.

She cleaned all the mangoes with water again and again,
Then she put them in the holy plate of sacrifice.
She raised the plate above her head offering to Mahapeng,
And she prayed to the heavenly god to bless her with a boy.

The mangoes were sweet like honey,
Mahapeng ate up all of them and still wanted some.
So the Princess of Guditila went out to get more.
Then an ivory mango happened to drop off the tree.

象牙芒果沾满灰尘和污泥，
公主忘了用清水冲洗，
慌忙拿来献给玛哈捧，
玛哈捧吃了全身舒畅又轻松。

南古蒂提拉又突然想起，
床头还有个熟透的金芒果。
她细心地用清水洗干净，
捧在手心献给玛哈捧。

公主默默向玛哈捧祷念，
向他索取有福气的子嗣。
玛哈捧在公主的肚皮上抹了三下，
完全满足了南古蒂提拉的心意。

玛哈捧轻言细语宽慰公主：
"不久你定会生下有福气的儿子，
他们会像你供奉的仙果一样纯洁，
长大了的儿子会大有出息。

"你第一次敬献的十个芒果，
天神首先赐给你男孩一个。
这孩子长着十个头颅，
无比英俊又相貌奇特。

"你第二次敬献的象牙芒果，
生下的孩子有野象那么魁梧。
他的肤色像乌鸦那么漆黑，
力气能移山，本领能堵河。

第二章 十头王 Chapter 2 The Ten-Headed King

The mango was smudged with dust and mud,
But the princess forgot to clean it with water.
She hurried back to offer it to Mahapeng;
Mahapeng ate it and felt relaxed and comfortable.

All at sudden it occurred to Nan Guditila
That she had another ripe golden mango beside her bed.
After cleaning it carefully with water,
She held it in her palms and offered it to Mahapeng.

The princess prayed to Mahapeng in her heart,
Asking him to bless her with a son.
Mahapeng touched her belly for three times,
And he promised her prayer would be answered.

Mahapeng told the princess in a soothing voice,
"Very soon you will give birth to blessed sons
They will be as pure as the fruits in the offering plate,
They will be ambitious and accomplished when they grow up.

"For the ten mangoes you gave to me the first time,
You will be bestowed with a boy.
This boy will have ten heads,
And he will be unique and extremely handsome.

"For the ivory mango you gave to me the second time,
The boy you will have is as strong and stalwart as a wild elephant.
He is tanned and dark like the black crow and he is so strong
That he can easily move a mountain or block a river.

"你第三次敬献的金芒果，
生下的孩子俊秀善良。
他才学渊博、聪慧正直，
他的名字将流芳百世。"

玛哈捧说完便驾着云霞飞回天庭，
漂亮的公主古蒂提拉仍住在森林。
不久她浑身酸软没有气力，
经常阵阵恶心、想吃酸冷的东西。

南古蒂提拉整天心神不宁，
就像随风逐浪飘动的浮萍。
身体发生了从未有过的变化，
她意识到自己已经怀孕。

她忐忑不安地将情况告诉父亲，
帕拉西听了高兴万分：
"你和天神玛哈捧结合，
这是天赐良缘、命运注定。

"有缘天上人间来相会，
这是你修行得来的福气。
你不必担忧害怕，
你要好好保重身体。"

鲜艳的俊腊皮花缀满枝头，
绽开的花朵送走寒雾冷烟。
双双归来的沙燕快活地飞翔，
用它那欢乐的歌声迎来春天。

第二章 十头王 Chapter 2 The Ten-Headed King

"The third mango you gave to me
Will bring you a kind boy of delicate beauty.
He will be a wise scholar and a man of integrity,
And he will be remembered throughout the history."

Mahapeng flew back to heaven on clouds after the remarks.
The pretty Princess of Guditila still lived in the forest.
Soon she felt sore and weak all over her body;
She felt like throwing up and preferred something cold and sour.

Nan Guditila was agitated and restless each day,
Feeling like a leaf blown away in the wind.
After noticing the changes in her body,
She began to realize that she was pregnant.

She told her adopted father her situation uneasily,
Palaxi was thrilled to know the good news,
"Your union with the heavenly god of Mahapeng,
It is a union destined and blessed by fate.

"Destiny brought you two from different worlds to meet here.
That's also because of your devoted practice of Buddhism.
You don't need to worry or get scared,
What you should do is take good care of yourself."

The colorful Lapi flowers were blooming on the branches;
And the blooming flowers sent off the chilly fog.
The sand swallows returned and flew joyfully in pairs,
They were greeting the spring with their lovely songs.

兰嘎西贺 The Ten-Headed King of Langa

黄雀在矮小的草丛中筑巢，
针线鸟在高高的吊窝里孵蛋。
南古蒂提拉怀胎已经十个月，
在温暖的森林里分娩。

一个有福气的儿子平安降生，
是个十个头的奇特的怪婴。
左右肩上各有三个头，
正中间四个头又白又嫩。

四个头像节节砌高的金塔，
最大的一个头才会说话。
刚刚才脱离母体，
嘴里已长满洁白细密的乳牙。

二十只眼睛像星星，
二十只耳朵多么灵敏；
十个丰满红润的脸庞，
像十五圆圆的月亮。

孩子的名字应符合他的福分，
天神玛哈捧是他的父亲，
孩子的名字应跟着父名，
帕拉西给他取名捧玛加。

第二章 十头王 Chapter 2 The Ten-Headed King

Orioles built their nests among the low groves of grass;
Needle birds hatched their eggs in the nest high in the trees.
It had been ten months since Guditila got pregnant.
Then she laboured in the warm season in the forest.

A blessed son was born safe and sound.
It was an eccentric baby with ten heads.
Three heads stood on each shoulder,
Four heads in the middle were tender and fair.

The four heads were like layers of golden pagoda.
Only the tallest and biggest head could speak.
After only seconds out of his mother's womb,
His mouth was already full of white and tiny teeth.

His twenty eyes were like twinkling stars;
Twenty ears were sensitive to any voice;
His ten faces were round and red
Just like the full moons in the sky.

The baby should have a name matching his great blessing.
Since the heavenly god of Mahapeng was his father,
He should be named after the heavenly god.
So Palaxi named him Pengmajia.

刚刚落地就会走路,
刚刚落地就会说话。
十个头的捧玛加啊,
像雨露中的竹笋娇嫩挺拔。

南古蒂提拉第二次怀孕,
生下的二儿子黑如乌鸦。
怪模怪样谁见了都害怕,
帕拉西给他取名衮纳帕。

衮纳帕生下就像魔鬼,
不到三个月就长得有小象大。
他独自一人睡在岩洞中,
天天在岩石上滚爬。

南古蒂提拉第三次怀孕,
生下的三儿子健美又文雅。
他的身体就像金子熔铸,
帕拉西给他取名彼亚沙。

他的眼睛如水晶般明亮,
他的脸颊像吸饱阳光的香瓜。
他的性情温良又沉静,
他的肤色胜过日月的光华。

年老的爷爷和年轻的妈妈,
用木薯、芋头、野果和香瓜,
抚育三个孩子成长壮大,
三兄弟经常在森林一起玩耍。

第二章 十头王 Chapter 2 The Ten-Headed King

He could walk soon after he was born;
He started to talk once he walked on the ground.
Oh, the ten-headed Pengmajia,
He was like a tender and straight bamboo shoot.

The Princess of Guditila got pregnant again.
She gave birth to another son as tanned as black crow.
He looked so odd that he would frighten everyone.
And Palaxi named him Gunnapa.

Gunnapa looked like a little devil.
In just three months he grew as big as a calf elephant.
He slept in the cave by himself,
And he climbed up and down the rocks everyday.

Nan Guditila was pregnant for a third time.
This time the son she labored was elegant and handsome.
He was as fair as a figure of gold,
So Palaxi named him Biyasha.

Hie eyes were pure like crystals;
His face was like the ripe melon immersed in sunshine.
He was always calm and gentle.
And his skin is fairer than the light of the Sun and the Moon.

The old grandpa and young mom worked together,
Feeding the babies with wild fruit, cassavas, taro and melons.
The three brothers were brought up tall and strong,
And they always played together in the forest.

就像会飞的鹦鹉，
就像会跑的小鹿，
就像调皮的猴子，
三兄弟一天也闲不住。

三兄弟唱啊跳啊，
他们天真烂漫多快乐。
三兄弟经常谈天说地，
就像一起吃米的小鸡。

三、父子相见

日子一天一天过去，
三兄弟已长大懂事。
他们不满足森林的天地，
天天缠着母亲问东问西。

他们就像闹着吃奶的羊羔，
紧紧缠着母亲撒娇；
又像顽皮的鹿崽，
偎依在母亲的胸怀。

他们一齐询问母亲：
"为什么来到这深山野林？
怎么从不见父亲的面？
谁是我们的父亲？

第二章 十头王 Chapter 2 The Ten-Headed King

Just like the parrots with wings,
Like the deer that run very fast,
Also like the naughty monkeys,
The three brothers couldn't stay quiet for one day.

The three brothers sang and danced all the time.
They were innocent kids living a happy life.
They always talked about everything around them,
Chattering like three chicks pecking grains of rice.

Ⅲ The Meeting of the Father and Sons

Day by day time flew fast, and now
The three brothers were old enough to understand the world.
They wanted to know things out of the forest,
And they clung to their mother asking endless questions.

Like lambs anxious to be milked,
They teased their mother all day long;
Like naughty baby deer nudging their mother
They buried themselves in her arms.

They three asked their mother together,
"Why are we here in this remote forest?
Why have we never seen our father?
Who, on earth, is our father?

"父亲如今在哪里？
是不是就是慈祥的帕拉西？
是不是父亲把你赶走？
还是他早早就离开人世？"

南古蒂提拉沉默了很久，
才从头到尾诉说自己的经历：
"我眼珠般珍贵的儿啊，
听我把实情告诉你们。

"母亲不是在森林里生，
也不是在森林里长大。
我是国王叭兰巴心爱的公主，
我的故乡是辽阔美丽的勐兰嘎。

"你们的外祖父老年无子，
我才十六岁就要我继承王位。
还要给我招赘纳婿，
共同把广阔的勐兰嘎治理。

"我不稀罕高贵的王位，
也厌烦豪华的宫廷。
我不愿与父王发生争执，
悄悄逃到这里来修行。"

三个儿子打断母亲的话，
焦急地想知道父亲的情况：
"我们的父亲住在何方？
他的皮肤是黑是白还是黄？

第二章 十头王 Chapter 2 The Ten-Headed King

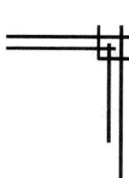

"Where is our father now?
Is the kind Palaxi our father?
Did our father drive you out of his house?
Or he has been dead for quite a long time?"

Nan Guditila kept silent for a long while,
Then she told them her whole story,
"My precious sons, you are like my own pupils.
Listen to me for I will tell you all the truth.

"I, your mom, was not born in the forest.
Neither did I grow up here.
I am the princess of the king of Ba Lanba,
The big and beautiful Kingdom of Langa is my birthplace.

"When your grandpa got old and still had no son,
He wanted me to succeed to his throne when I turned sixteen.
He also planned to find a husband for me
So that my husband and I could govern the kingdom together.

"The noble crown is nothing to me,
And I also got tired of the luxurious royal palace.
I would rather not quarrel with my father,
So I sneaked out to practise Buddhism here in the forest."

Anxious to know more about their father,
The three sons interrupted her talk,
"Where is our father living now?
Is his skin black or yellow or white?

"他是一棵挺拔的大榕树,
还是一棵瘦小的槟榔?
他像大象那样威武,
还是像瘦马那样窝囊?

"他的模样到底怎么样?
他的本事到底强不强?
我们能不能见到他?
让我们见一面又有何妨?"

南古蒂提拉连忙回答:
"你们的父亲是天神玛哈捧,
他的面孔像洁白的月亮,
他的心肠像柔软的棉花。

"他具有天下最善良的品质,
他像一颗纯洁的宝石。
他精通各种超群的武艺,
他掌握许多深奥的知识。

"你们如想见到他,
就要像母亲一样虔诚修行。
父亲知道儿子有诚意,
就会下凡来会晤你们。"

三个儿子听了心领神会,
就像绿叶盛着泉水那样清晰。
他们多么渴望见到亲生的父亲,
就跟着爷爷学艺、修行。

第二章 十头王 Chapter 2 The Ten-Headed King

"Is he like a gorgeous and straight banyan tree?
Or he is like a small and thin betel nut tree?
Is he mighty like an elephant?
Or weak and timid like a skinny horse?

"What exactly does he look like?
Is he mighty and capable?
Will we have any chance to meet him?
What harm does it do if we could see our father?"

Nan Guditila answered them hurriedly,
"Your father is the heavenly god of Mahapeng.
His face is like the bright moon;
His heart is as tender as the cotton.

"He is the most kind-hearted one in the world.
He is as precious as a pure gem.
He is a master of all kinds of martial arts,
And he knows everything under the sun.

"If you really want to meet him,
You need to practise Buddhism as piously as I.
When your father knows and feels your devotion,
He will come down to the earth to meet you."

The three sons understood their mother now.
Their minds were as clear water held in green leaves.
How they longed to meet their father!
They began to learn things from their grandpa.

孩子们朝思暮想的心愿，
感动了在天庭里的父亲。
五年后一个晴朗的日子，
玛哈捧下凡来到森林。

太阳给森林镀上异彩，
草地披上了霞光烟霭。
玛哈捧一个个会见儿子，
先向捧玛加身边走来。

从没见过父亲的捧玛加，
见眼前来的人红光满面，
以为是有福气的圣哲来巡察，
忙用有礼貌的语言问他：

"福气广大的圣人啊，
你像天神光临森林。
你有何贵干？
请问你的尊姓大名？"

身披霞光的玛哈捧，
亲切地对大儿子说明：
"我就是你日夜思念的父亲，
阿爹也时刻思念着你们。

"阿爹眼珠般心爱的儿啊，
你想要点什么本领？
想要什么你随意提出，
我当尽量满足你的要求。"

第二章 十头王 Chapter 2 The Ten-Headed King

They kept the wish in their heart day and night.
Their father in the heaven was so much touched.
On a clear and sunny day after five years passed,
Mahapeng came down from heaven to the forest.

The sunlight coated the forest with brilliant colors;
The colorful clouds and mist shrouded the grassland.
Mahapeng came to see his sons one by one,
And firstly he walked towards Pengmajia.

Pengmajia had never met his father before.
Seeing a man with bright and red face approaching him,
He thought that was a saint patrolling the forest.
So he asked him with good manners,

"Your saint with great blessings,
You came down to the forest like a heavenly god.
Why are you here today?
May I have the honour to know your great name?"

Mahapeng was bathed in the morning sunshine.
He explained to his eldest son genially,
"I am your father that you have missed so much,
I want you to know that I miss you too all the time.

"My son, you are as precious as my pupils to me.
What kinds of skills or talents you want to have?
Just tell me whatever you want,
I will manage to grant your wishes."

捧玛加听了格外高兴，
急忙合掌拜见父亲。
他提出了各种要求，
玛哈捧都一一应允。

赐给他高超的本领和武艺，
不惧怕水淹火烧，
能战胜毒蛇猛兽，
锋利的刀箭杀不死。

玛哈捧严肃地告诫大儿子：
"阿爹已全部满足了你所要的一切，
但你不可能天上地下全无敌，
有三样东西不许你征服。

"一是一个正义善良的王子，
他即将在人间出世，
他有最高贵的命运和品性，
他有绝顶的聪明和才智。

"他是人类的一颗明星，
他有征服宇宙的本领。
他像麂子一样善良，
你却不可能把他战胜。

第二章 十头王 Chapter 2 The Ten-Headed King

Pengmajia was thrilled to hear this. Hurriedly
He paid respect to his father with folded palms.
He asked for many things that he desired for,
And Mahapeng promised to fulfil his dreams.

He was bestowed super martial arts skills and power.
He would never be afraid of disasters of flood or fire.
He could conquer all kinds of wild beasts or venous serpents.
He would survive sharp knives, swords or arrows.

Mahapeng told his eldest son solemnly,
"I have given you all that you desired for.
But you are not invincible in this world.
There are three things that you can't conquer.

"One is a prince of integrity and kindness.
He will be born to this world very soon.
He is noble and he stands for justice,
He will be a wise scholar full of wisdom.

"He is the bright star to lead the human being;
He has the power to conquer the universe.
He is as kind as a muntjac,
And you can never defeat him.

"不允许你向他挑战,
狂妄自大冒犯他。
要是你不听我的警告,
必定惨败在他的手下。

"二是神圣的弓阿沙尖①,
当年叭捧②赠给人类开天辟地。
神弓有一万五千斤重,
能拉开它的只有一个王子。

"三是森林里的白猴,
它们是人类的好兄弟。
无论何时何地,
你对它们都不能轻视。"

玛哈捧还警告大儿子:
"切莫贪婪地追求安乐,
奢望有时会带来灾难,
忠实与虔诚才是应当遵循的美德。

"阿爹告诫你的一切,
要当作神圣的天规不许违背。
否则就要受到惩罚,
招致毁灭的厄运。"

---

① 弓阿沙尖:一种神弓。
② 叭捧:七层天以上的天神。

第二章 十头王 Chapter 2 The Ten-Headed King

"You are forbidden to challenge him;
You shouldn't offend him out of arrogance.
If you choose to neglect my warning,
You are doomed to be destroyed by him.

"The second is the holy bow of Ashajian①, given by
The god of Bapeng② to mankind to conquer the world.
The bow weighed ten thousand and five hundred Jin.
There is only one prince who is capable of drawing it.

"The third is the white monkeys in the forest.
They are the friends of human beings.
Under whatever circumstance
Should they be despised or insulted by you."

Mahapeng again warned his first-born son,
"You shouldn't indulge yourself in debauchery.
Greed and wild wishes might invite disaster;
Loyalty and integrity are the virtues you should pursuit.

"Remember everything that I told you today,
They are the sacred bottom line that you mustn't break.
Otherwise you will be punished severely,
Great disaster and bad fate are surely to befall you."

---

① Bow of Ashajian: a bow with magic power.
② Bapeng: the heavenly god living on the seven layer of heaven.

最后玛哈捧给他一把神弓，
就是神圣的弓赛宰①。
附上七支锋利的神箭，
捧玛加的生命之弦就系在弓箭里面。

玛哈捧语重心长特别告诫：
"这是一件天下无敌的武器，
你要身不离弓心不离箭，
千万千万不可丢失。

"有了这把弓赛宰，
什么战争你都能打赢。
即使乌云遮黑了天空，
你也能射开乌云现光明。

"雨点般的利箭射来，
你可以不必闪身。
蚂蚁般的敌人攻来，
你可以纵横驰骋。"

捧玛加万分高兴，
保证遵从天父之命，
双手接过弓赛宰，
对父亲合掌拜了再拜。

---

① 弓赛宰：生命之弓。

第二章 十头王　Chapter 2 The Ten-Headed King

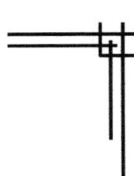

Mahapeng gave his son a magic bow as his last gift.
It was the holy Bow of Saizai①
Together with it were seven sharp arrows.
The fate of Pengmajia was attached to the bundle of arrows.

Mahapeng told his son gravely and earnestly,
"This is an invincible weapon in the world,
Take them with you wherever you go,
And you must never get them lost.

"With this Bow of Saizai by your side,
You will win whatever the battles.
Even when the dark clouds covered the sky,
You can shoot and split them to let out the sunlight.

"When the arrows fly to you like raindrops
You even don't have to dodge them.
When enemies as countless as ants attack you
You can still dash about in the battlefield."

Pengmajia was very excited to hear this.
He promised he would follow his father's advice.
He took the holy bow with both hands and
Bowed to his father with folded palms again and again.

---

① Bow of Saizai: means the bow of life.

彩霞萦绕的玛哈捧，
告别大儿子捧玛加，
径自走向峭壁上的岩洞，
会见了二儿子衮纳帕。

神采奕奕的玛哈捧对衮纳帕说：
"大象般威武的孩子啊，
我是你的天父玛哈捧，
你有什么要求尽管讲吧！"

衮纳帕高兴得连忙双膝跪下说：
"天神父亲呀，可把你盼来了，
儿思念你已有十二年，
十二年我想见到你望眼欲穿。

"孩儿现在只想美美睡一觉，
请赐给我长眠的本事。
让我一觉睡上十二年，
让我睡个够，无事不再起。"

有福气的天神玛哈捧，
满足了二儿子的心愿。
答应让他饱饱睡足十二年，
还把一杆宝镖给他留在身边。

"这是一杆神奇的宝镖，
是一件万斤重的武器。
百掷百中，降魔杀妖，
你要好好掌握不要丢失。

第二章 十头王 Chapter 2 The Ten-Headed King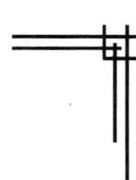

With the colorful clouds surrounding him
Mahapeng said goodbye to his eldest son.
He walked straight to the cave under the cliff,
There he met his second son Gunnapa.

Mahapeng said to Gunnapa energetically and joyfully,
"My son, you are as strong as an elephant.
I am your father, the heavenly god of Mahapeng.
You can ask for anything you want from me!"

Instantly, Gunnapa knelt down in front of Mahapeng,
"My dear father, you are here with me at last.
I miss you every day in the last twelve years;
I have waited longingly to see you for all the time.

"Now I only want to have a very good rest.
Please teach me the knack of long sleep.
So that I can have a sleep of twelve years,
With nothing being able to disturb me."

The blessed heavenly god of Mahapeng,
He granted his second son's wish.
He promised his son a sweet sleep of twelve years,
And he also left a magic flying dart with his son.

"This is a precious dart with magic power,
It is a weapon weighing five thousand kilograms.
It can hit any target and kill any devil and monster.
You must keep it safe and never get it lost.

"宝镖最忌沾染腐臭，
不能碰到脏物和尸体，
无论你闻到多么恶心的腥味，
都不能吐出唾液。

"你一定要保持宝镖的纯洁，
它才会有巨大的杀伤力。
不然宝镖就会失去威力，
出去就不会返回你的手里。"

衮纳帕接过心爱的宝镖，
向天神父亲连连磕头。
玛哈捧前脚刚跨出岩洞，
衮纳帕就倒下地呼呼大睡。

玛哈捧来到彼亚沙的住地，
会见了乖巧可爱的小儿子。
彼亚沙与两个哥哥生性不同，
说出了金玉般的话语：

"日月般光辉的天神父亲啊，
孩儿日夜把你思念。
今天你像太阳一样出现，
请倾听孩儿至诚的心愿。

"你的儿子彼亚沙，
不喜欢人间挥戈动武，
向往世界无灾又无难，
祝愿人类生活美好幸福。

第二章 十头王　Chapter 2　The Ten-Headed King

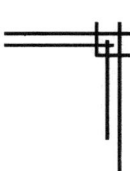

"The dart should be kept from anything filthy or stinky.
It can't touch upon corpse or sordid items.
No matter how disgusting the fishy odour you smell,
You can't spit out your saliva.

"You must keep the dart pure and clean,
Then it can maintain its great destructive power.
Otherwise it will loss its magic,
Once it flies out it will never return to your hand."

Gunnapa took the magic dart from his father,
He kowtowed again and again to give his thanks.
The moment Mahapeng stepped out of the cave,
Gunnapa fell down to the ground and slept sound.

Mahapeng then came to the place where Biyasha lived.
There he met his youngest son who was clever and lovely.
Biyasha was different from his two elder brothers,
The words came out of his mouth were like gold and jade,

"My dear father, heavenly god with light of the sun and moon,
I have been missing you day and night.
Today you appear in front of me like the Sun,
Please let your son tell you his most sincere wishes.

"I am your son Biyasha.
I don't like any kind of violence in the world.
I wish the world were free from war or disaster.
I pray for the mankind to live a happy and beautiful life.

"如果你有什么赏赐,
我需要的是聪明才智,
精通天文和地理,
能预卜未来的凶吉。

"儿愿掌握丰富的知识,
有拯救黎民百姓的本事。
儿愿远离灾难的祸根,
身居高位不与豺狼为伍。"

玛哈捧心中格外宽慰,
小儿子的心愿像一片黄金。
便交给彼亚沙天书和神笔,
传给他高明的知识。

"天书和神笔孕育着人类的知识,
它像广阔的蓝天无所不包,
它像浩瀚的海洋无所不在,
你要时时顶礼经常拜读。"

玛哈捧满足了三个儿子的要求,
分别授予他们不同的本事。
最后依依不舍与儿子告别,
驾着祥云飞离大地。

第二章 十头王 Chapter 2 The Ten-Headed King

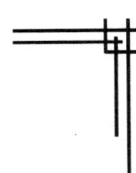

"If you have anything to grant me today,
Please bless me with intelligence and wisdom.
I long to be a master of all kinds of knowledge,
So that I am able to predict the unknown future.

"I want to learn as much as I can,
So that I can save the lives of common people.
I would rather stay away from all the banes,
I wish to live nobly without wicked people around."

Mahapeng felt proud and comforted hearing his words.
The wishes of his youngest son were like a piece of gold.
So he gave Biyasha a holy prophet book and magic brush,
And he also passed on his wisdom and knowledge to him.

"The book and brush contain all the knowledge of the world.
It is all-embracing as the vast sky covering everything.
It is all-compassing like the boundless ocean.
You must read it over and over to master the essence."

Mahapeng fulfilled his three sons' wishes;
They were bestowed with different kind of talents.
At last he said good bye and left them reluctantly.
On the clouds he flew back to his home in the heaven.

第三章　继位

一、特殊的使臣

玛哈捧走后月亮又圆了十二次，
十四岁的捧玛加长得十分威武。
二十只眼睛闪闪发光，
犹如海底捞出的一把明珠。

十三岁的大力士衮纳帕，
长得比妖怪还可怕。
头颅像一口大铁锅，
身子比老象还要大。

肉色像木炭一样漆黑，
力气抵得上一千匹骏马。
有时拔起大树做烧柴，
有时抱起房大的石头玩耍。

十二岁的彼亚沙，
长得聪明又文雅。
每天在巴朗苦读天书，
世上的奥秘他都能解答。

第三章 继位 Chapter 3 Succeeding the Throne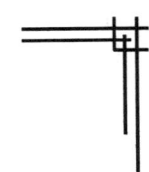

Chapter 3   Succeeding the Throne

I   The Special Envoy

The moon became round for twelve times after Mahapeng left.
At the age of fourteen, Pengmajia grew strong and powerful.
When he opened his twenty eyes, they were shining
Like white pearls taken from the bottom of the sea.

Gunnapa now was thirteen years old.
He looked more ferocious than a monster.
His head was as big as a pot,
His body was larger than an old elephant.

His skin was tanned like charcoal,
He was more powerful than one thousand horses together.
Sometimes he uprooted a big tree for firewood;
Sometimes he held and played with a stone as big as a house.

Biyasha was now twelve years old.
He was a clever and elegant boy.
He buried himself in the books in Balang,
And he had answers to all things under the sky.

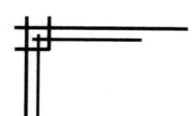

兰嘎西贺 The Ten-Headed King of Langa

椰子树一年年长高,
三兄弟一天天长大。
他们渴望回到母亲的故国——
美丽富饶的勐兰嘎。

一天三兄弟找到母亲,
提出久压在心头的要求。
他们要继承外祖父的王位,
解除外祖父的忧愁。

三兄弟对母亲说:
"像孔雀一样温和的妈妈呀,
我们有话要对你讲,
说得不对请你原谅。

"就像公鸡盼望着黎明,
外祖父一定想念着女儿。
就像鸟儿的羽毛已经丰满,
孩儿们现在都已经长大。

"孩儿们都学了一套本事,
像鱼儿不怕风急浪大,
像金鹿不怕山高路滑,
都想回去治理自己的国家。"

第三章 继位　Chapter 3 Succeeding the Throne

Coconut trees were growing taller year by year,
And the three brothers grew up stronger day by day.
They longed to return to their mother's homeland,
The rich and beautiful Kingdom of Langa.

One day, the three brothers went to their mother,
Expressing their deeply-buried wish.
They said that they wanted to succeed to the throne
To relieve the burden from their senile grandfather.

The three brothers said to their mother,
"Our mom, you are as tender as a peacock.
Now we would like to have a word with you.
Please forgive us if we say something wrong.

"As the rooster waits eagerly for the dawn,
Our grandfather must be missing his daughter.
Your sons have grown up and become strong
As the young birds have become full-fledged.

"All your sons have acquired some kinds of skills,
Now we are like huge fishes not afraid of strong wind and waves,
And we can run as fast as deer on high and slippery mountains.
It's time for us to go back and govern our own kingdom."

兰嘎西贺 The Ten-Headed King of Langa

仿佛阳光驱散了乌云，
南古蒂提拉的眼前一片明亮。
孩子们的话如同一碗清水，
洗去了她心坎上久积的忧伤。

她答应孩子们返回勐兰嘎，
但得先派人向父王讲明心愿。
此事关系十分重大，
应派聪明懂事的人前往。

妈妈一眼看准了彼亚沙，
让他去见外公最为合适。
彼亚沙带着母亲的书信，
接受母亲的重托立即启程。

彼亚沙走了整整七天，
穿过了浓密的原始森林，
才看见了绿莹莹的田坝，
来到了宽阔的勐兰嘎。

他边走边东张西望，
迎面遇上了一群美丽的姑娘。
姑娘们大方又活泼，
上前对异乡人把话讲：

"星星那样明亮的哥哥啊，
你一定是远方来的稀客。
我们是山旮旯里的凤尾竹，
从来没见过这么挺拔的椰子树。

第三章 继位　Chapter 3 Succeeding the Throne

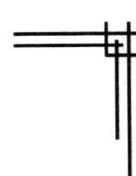

As if the sunlight broke through the dark cloud,
Nan Guditila saw a bright world in front of her.
The words from her sons were like a bowl of clear water.
They washed away the sorrow buried deep in her heart.

She agreed upon the request of her sons,
But someone should be sent first to explain it to her father.
This matter was of such great significance
That she needed an intelligent envoy to accomplish it.

She cast her eyes on Biyasha,
She was sure he was the most suitable candidate.
With his mother's letter in hand,
Biyasha hit on the road to the Kingdom of Langa.

It took him many days
To trek through the dense forest.
When he saw the flatland full of green crops,
He knew he had arrived in the huge Kingdom of Langa.

He looked around himself while walking,
Then he met a group of pretty girls on the road.
The girls were warmhearted and lovely,
And they came up and talked to the stranger,

"Our distinguished guest, you are as bright as a star,
You must be from somewhere very far.
We are the fern leaf bamboo in the village among mountains,
We have never seen someone so straight as the coconut tree.

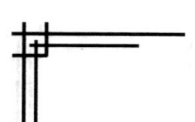

兰嘎西贺　The Ten-Headed King of Langa

"阿哥不嫌弃的话，
请到妹妹的竹楼上坐一坐。
尝一口阿妹栽的香瓜，
喝一口阿妹泡的香茶。"

彼亚沙感激姑娘们的好客，
热情地做了回答：
"缅桂花一般香的姑娘啊，
请你们别这样把我夸。

"我来自远方的深山老林，
有福气才能走到你们的身旁。
但现在我有要事不能耽误，
等以后再到阿妹的竹楼上看望。"

他告别了姑娘们继续赶路，
一直走进繁华的都城允兰嘎。
他在王宫外面逗留徘徊，
面对辉煌的殿宇惊叹发呆。

"喂，哪里来的小伙子？"
他的行动引起了卫兵的怀疑。
"赶快离开王宫禁地，
这里不是普通人游玩的地方。"

彼亚沙见王宫戒备森严，
心想，若要进殿必须"口出狂言"：
"我是召捧玛加的使臣，
前来向你们的国王索取江山和宫殿。"

第三章 继位 Chapter 3 Succeeding the Throne

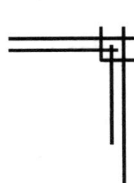

"Our dear brother, do we have the honour
To have you as our guest in our bamboo house?
Take a taste of the melon we have gathered;
Have a cup of fragrant tea to quench your thirst."

Biyasha was grateful for girls' hospitality,
And he answered them most friendly and politely,
"Girls, You are as pretty as magnolia flowers,
Your compliments are making me feel flattered.

"I am from the deep forest afar.
It is my honor to have met you here.
But I am now occupied with very important things,
I will come back and pay you a visit sometime later."

Saying goodbye to the girls, he continued his journey,
Till he arrived in the prosperous capital City of Langa.
He lingered outside of the palace wall,
Amazed and shocked at the grandeur of the palace.

"Hey, you the lad, where are you from?"
His wondering aroused the suspicion of the guards.
"Stay away from the forbidden area of the palace.
It is not a place of sightseeing for common people."

Seeing the guards keeping a strict vigilance over the palace,
Biyasha decided to act impudently to attract attention,
"I am the envoy sent by heavenly god of Pengmajia,
I come to ask the King for his land and throne."

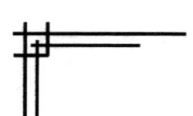

卫兵们听了像晴天下大雨,
一个个惊愕得瞠目结舌。
让彼亚沙在宫外稍等片刻,
急忙进宫将他的话原原本本禀告国王。

叭兰巴听了十分惊讶,
立即传令接见异国"使臣"。
彼亚沙被引着来到宫殿,
叭兰巴见了先即发问:

"像秋天云朵般洁白的孩子,
你从哪一个勐来?
你有什么事要见我?
快说吧,我不会见怪。"

彼亚沙合掌拜见国王,
请求国王原谅他的鲁莽。
他呈上妈妈的贝叶书信,
并向外公把经历讲。

国王读着信双手颤抖不停,
听着外孙的诉说他悲喜交集。
往事的回忆使他心潮翻滚,
老泪纵横犹如塘坝决堤。

第三章 继位 Chapter 3 Succeeding the Throne

The sentries were dumbstruck to hear this,
As if they were thrown into a storm on a sunny day.
Asking Biyasha to wait outside for a moment,
They rushed into the palace and reported it to the King.

Ba Lanba was surprised at the report from the sentry.
And he ordered to send for the foreign "envoy".
As soon as Biyasha was escorted to the court,
The King Ba Lanba posed him the question,

"You look like as clean and white as the autumn clouds.
My kid, from which kingdom did you come?
And why you wanted to see me?
Just tell me and I will not take it as an offence."

Biyasha paid his respect to the King with folded palms,
And he asked for forgiveness for his imprudence.
Then he presented her mother's letter to the King,
And told his grandpa what had happened for all those years.

The old king's hands trembled violently while reading the letter.

His grandson's story put him in a mixed feeling of sadness and joy.

When all the memories of the old days flooded in his mind,

His tears poured down as water rushing out of the broken dam.

王后更是忍不住放声恸哭，
把外孙紧紧搂在怀中。
她想起骨肉分离十五载，
问国王现在是否在做梦。

国王悲痛地对外孙说：
"我的孙儿啊，我的眼珠，
自从你妈妈悄悄出走，
我就陷入极度的不幸和痛苦。

"我问你呀小外孙，
你妈妈的身体是否健康？
遇到过什么灾难和疾病？
有没有野兽伤害过你们？"

"外祖父呀！由于有天神庇护，
我和妈妈哥哥都很幸福。
只有一件事要向你提出，
免得你为我们牵肠挂肚。

"我们远离故国和亲人，
都不愿再生活在深山老林。
我们多么想回到你的身边，
不知外公答应不答应。

"假若外公不同意，
宁肯让无价之宝付诸流水，
我就马上离开宫殿，
住在荒林永不返回。"

第三章 继位　Chapter 3　Succeeding the Throne

The queen could not hold herself but cried out loud.
She held her grandson tightly in her arms.
Thinking of the miserable separation for fifteen years,
She asked the king if she was in her dream.

The old king said to his grandson in tears,
"My grandson, my precious pupils,
Ever since your mother left without a word,
I have sunk into great misfortune and agony.

"My dear grandson, let me ask you.
What is going on with your mother's health?
Has she been through disaster or ailment?
Have you ever been hurt by any wild animals?"

"My grandfather, thanks to God
My mother and us are all living a happy life.
Could I make a request to you
So that your won't worry about us any more?

"We stayed so far away from our hometown and our families.
Now we don't want to live in the remote forest any more.
We long to come back and stay by your side,
And we are wondering if you agree or not.

"If you refuse our request,
And would rather discard treasure with flowing water,
I will leave the palace right now
And we will never come back from the deep forest."

外孙的话啊,
就像一碗酸涩的凉水。
外祖父的心啊,
就像射进一支竹箭般痛楚。

叭兰巴诚恳地告诉彼亚沙:
"亲爱的小外孙啊,
你们是外公心上的宝石,
你为什么要说这样的话?

"自从你妈妈离开宫殿,
外公两眼望穿心欲碎。
今天你回来报告喜讯,
外公是多么幸福和高兴。

"外公已经像衰老的枯树,
勐兰嘎的朝政要由你们弟兄来继承。
我要按照兰嘎王国的礼仪,
亲自到森林把你的妈妈和哥哥迎接。"

二、出迎

国王亲自擂响宫殿的大鼓,
鼓声回荡在兰嘎都城的上空。
众臣僚和头人们纷纷赶来,
俯首聆听国王的旨意。

第三章 继位 Chapter 3 Succeeding the Throne

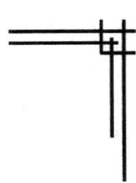

What Biyasha the grandson said
Was like a bowl of icy water.
It was also like a bamboo arrow
Piercing into the heart of the old king.

Ba Lanba spoke to Biyasha sincerely,
"My dear grandson,
You are like a diamond in my life,
Why did you say such heart-breaking words?

"Ever since your mother left the palace,
My heart has gone out of my body with her.
Now I am so happy and feel so blessed
Because you return with the good news.

"I am like an old, frail and dry tree
And you are to inherit the throne and govern the country.
I will go myself to get your mother and brothers back
With the most honorable etiquette of my kingdom."

II The Welcoming Ceremony

The king beat on the big drum himself in the palace,
And the sound of drum echoed in the sky of the capital city.
The tribe leaders and ministers gathered up
Bowing down to receive the orders from the king.

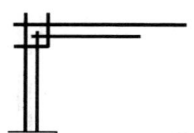

兰嘎西贺 The Ten-Headed King of Langa

"你们都没有忘记吧,
我那黑眼睛的女儿失踪十五年。
十五年中没有哪一日哪一天,
我们不痛苦地把她怀念。

"由于我的福荫浩荡无边,
兰嘎的明珠仍未熄灭光焰。
公主现在已经有了下落,
天神保佑她还在人间。

"昨天我的宝贝外孙来了,
他好比一颗明星降落宫廷,
他好比闪光的金水流出熔炉,
他们给兰嘎王国带来了光明。

"他带来了公主的亲笔信件,
他带来了兰嘎后继有人的喜讯。
天神玛哈捧赐福于她,
公主的三个儿子已长大成人。

"我的外孙都想离开森林,
回国把兰嘎的王位继承。
我已经答应了他们的要求,
让他们回国来主持朝政。

"我要劝说公主高兴地离开森林,
我要让外孙体面地回到兰嘎。
你们快去准备好象骑和骏马,
我要亲自到森林去迎接他们。"

第三章 继位 Chapter 3 Succeeding the Throne

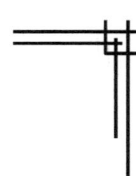

"I am sure you all remember it has been fifteen years
Since my black-eyed daughter got lost.
We have been missing her each day painfully
In the last long, long fifteen years.

"Thanks to my boundless benediction,
The pearl of Langa is still glowing.
Thanks to the blessing from the Gods above
Now I know the whereabouts of my Princess.

"My dear grandson came to see us yesterday.
Like a star descending to our palace,
Like melted gold flowing out of the furnace,
He brought light and hope to the kingdom of Langa.

"He brought me the letter from our princess,
And the good news that we have successors to my throne.
Protected by the blessings of heavenly god Mahapeng,
The three sons of the princess have grown up.

"My three grandsons want to leave the forest,
They are to return and succeed to the throne.
I have agreed to their request,
And they will come back home and run this country.

"I will persuade my Princess to leave the forest happily,
And my grandsons will return to Langa in great dignity.
You go and get ready the elephants and good horses,
And I myself will go to the forest to welcome them back."

兰嘎西贺 The Ten-Headed King of Langa

王宫的礼炮隆隆轰鸣，
惊天动地响了九声。
它们向全勐臣民宣告，
有威望的国王要出发远行。

国王叭兰巴走下殿阶，
后面跟着王后和外孙。
他们在文臣武官簇拥下，
金伞遮阴登上了象骑。

国王叭兰巴下令出发，
礼炮隆隆又响了三声。
象脚鼓、锥锣齐响，
出迎的队伍浩浩荡荡。

一头跟一头的大象，
一匹随一匹的骏马，
一辆接一辆的彩车，
一把连一把的金伞。

勇猛的武士在前面开路，
魁梧的武官殿后保护。
欢乐的人流走进了森林，
踏出一条宽阔的大路。

第三章 继位 Chapter 3 Succeeding the Throne

Solute-guns were fired resonating like thunders,
Nine solutes shook the earth and the sky trembling.
They sent the message to people all over the country,
That the dignified king would now start his journey.

Ba Lanba the King stepped down the stairway of the court,
He was followed by the queen and the grandson.
Escorted by a crowd of the officials and generals,
They mounted the elephants shaded by umbrellas of gold.

The King Ba Lanba gave the order to depart,
With the solutes fired another three times.
Mingled with echoing gong, drum and harp sounds
The welcoming procession marched forward mightily.

One elephant followed another,
Horses galloped one by one,
Colorfully-decorated floats moved one after another,
A thread of golden umbrellas moved in the procession.

The brave soldiers cleared the path in the front,
The stalwart warriors guarded as the rear troops.
With the joyful throng swimming into the forest
A wide road was left behind after the procession passed.

彼亚沙带着队伍晓行夜宿，
涉水爬山来到了幽静的伊麻板。
喧嚷声中拥来密密麻麻的兵马，
惊动了正在修行的南古蒂提拉。

她急忙叫来两个儿子：
"森林还从来没有这样热闹，
是大祸临头？
还是吉星高照？"

两个金子般的儿子安慰她：
"亲爱的妈妈不要担心，
有我们兄弟俩保护你，
不会发生什么不幸。

"母亲呀你再仔细观察，
这不像是歹徒的兵马。
队伍欢乐而有秩序，
说不定是弟弟来接我们回勐兰嘎。"

再说彼亚沙不到巴朗就下了象，
他招呼后面的队伍停下：
"外公外婆啊，前面就是我们的家，
队伍就暂时歇在这里吧！

第三章 继位 Chapter 3 Succeeding the Throne

Biyasha led the procession and they travelled day and night.
And finally they reached the quiet forest of Yimaban.
The clamour from the crowded soldiers and horses
Disturbed Nan Guditila who was practising Buddhism.

She sent for her other two sons and asked,
"The forest has never been so boisterous,
Is it the danger approaching
Or a good sign of blessing?"

The two gold-like sons comforted their mother,
"Please do not worry, our dear mother
Nothing will happen to you when we are here.
We two will stand beside to protect you.

"Please take a closer look,
The throngs do not look like robbers.
They are happy and marching in order
Maybe it is our brother coming to get us back to Langa."

Biyasha disembarked from the elephant before reaching.
He signaled to the throng after him to halt and said,
"Grandparents, our home is just ahead of us.
It is better if the procession could rest here temporarily!

"森林里一下来了这么多的人马,
妈妈不了解真相会害怕。
产生误会会引起冲突,
让我先回去告诉哥哥和妈妈。"

国王和王后下了象骑,
命令欢迎的队伍就地休息。
他们随彼亚沙来到巴朗房前,
南古蒂提拉见了一阵惊喜。

见到了离别多年的父母,
南古蒂提拉激动得昏了过去。
看到久别重逢的女儿,
父王母后悲痛得不省人事。

见母亲和外公都如此悲戚,
弟兄三人慌得没了主意。
连忙上前一个人扶着一个长辈,
陪着他们伤心流泪。

醒来互相问寒又问暖,
倾吐十多年怀念的情谊。
女儿问父母身体可安康,
父母说想女儿想得日夜焦急。

南古蒂提拉见父母黑发变白发,
象牙般坚硬的牙齿已经脱落。
灵敏的耳朵已听不到低声言谈,
辛酸的眼泪又如雨洒水泼。

第三章 继位 Chapter 3 Succeeding the Throne

"So many people and horses poured into the forest,
My mom might be scared not knowing what is happening.
Misunderstanding might lead to conflict. I think,
It's better for me to inform my mother and brothers first."

The king and the queen disembarked from the elephants,
They ordered the procession to stop and take a rest.
Then they followed Biyasha to the doors of Balang,
Nan Guditila opened the door and gasped with surprise.

Meeting the aging parents who she had not seen for years,
Nan Guditila got so excited that she almost fainted.
Seeing their daughter after so long a separation,
The old king and queen fell into a coma out of grief.

The three brothers became dumbfounded
When seeing their families drown in sorrow.
They rushed to hold up their loved ones,
And tears dropped down off their cheeks.

After pulling themselves out of sorrow,
They bared their hearts to each other.
The daughter asked about her parents' health;
The parents talked about their worries out of missing.

Nan Guditila saw the hair of her parents had turned gray;
Their teeth, once as solid as elephants tusks, had fallen out.
Their ears, once so sharp, could hardly hear others clearly.
Again, her tears of regrets gushed out as pouring rain.

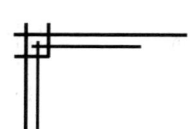

慈爱的叭兰巴和蔼地说道：
"聪明伶俐的女儿啊，
你出走这些年勐兰嘎风调雨顺，
还没有出现过遮天蔽日的乌云。

"但还有一件事使父母担心，
勐兰嘎的明珠还掩埋在森林，
现在勐兰嘎的王位有人继承，
勐兰嘎就像镜子一样明净。

"父母年迈已是风烛残年，
人老体衰已力不从心。
我们升天时，
亲生的女儿不在身边怎么行。

"受惊的麂子逃出山涧，
狩猎人走后它就返回老窝。
带箭伤的白鹤飞离沼泽，
等日子平安又会原地降落。

"你要接下百姓的花盘、黄蜡和米花，
跟随父母返回故国勐兰嘎。
让我们了却一生夙愿，
无忧无虑地安度晚年。"

第三章 继位　Chapter 3　Succeeding the Throne

The kind King Ba Lanba said to his daughter,
"My lovely daughter, for all those years since you left
The Kingdom of Langa had been blessed with good weather,
There had been no time when dark clouds covering the sky.

"But there is still one thing that distresses us.
The pearl of Langa is still hidden in the forest.
But now we have got heirs for the throne of Langa,
The kingdom will be as bright and peaceful as a mirror.

"We are at the end of our days as a candle in the wind,
We are too old and fragile to do the things we want to do.
We could not even think about the possibility
That our daughter is not with us when we breathe our last.

"The agitated deer would run away from the cave,
But it will return to its den once the hunter leaves.
The injured crane would fly away from the swamp,
But it will come back when there is no danger any more.

"You are to accept the wreath, honey bars and rice from my people,
And come back with us to your homeland the Kingdom of Langa.
Please grant us our long-cherished wish,
So that we can enjoy our remaining years peacefully."

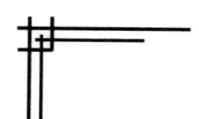

宛如屋檐的雨水涓涓下滴，
南古蒂提拉将心愿重向父母倾诉：
"眼珠般的父母啊，
请你们把女儿饶恕。

"你们可以带去我宝石般的三个儿子，
让他们协助外公把王国治理。
到时候再让他们把王位承袭，
女儿决心要在森林里终身修行。"

老两口抑制不住内心的悲怆，
哭诉着再把女儿劝说：
"菩提树叶般的女儿啊，
你是我们唯一的一颗宝石。

"如果你不顾我们之间的骨肉之情，
好说歹说都横着心不回去，
如果你不看父母跋山涉水远迎之意，
那我们就葬身在森林里。"

年迈体衰的父母哭肿了眼，
南古蒂提拉也阵阵心酸。
不忍心再让父母经受骨肉分离的痛苦，
只得听从父母旨意接下花盘。

第三章 继位 Chapter 3 Succeeding the Throne

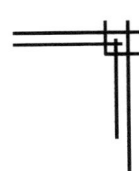

Tears from Nan Guditila were falling like raindrops,
She said to her parents repeating her wishes,
"My dear parents, your are precious to me as my eyes,
Please forgive me your disobedient daughter.

"You may take my three precious sons with you.
They will help you govern the kingdom.
They can succeed to the throne when the time comes,
But I am determined to stay in the forest all my life."

The old couple could not hold back their sadness,
They persuaded their daughter with tears again and again,
"My dear bodhi-tree-leave-like daughter,
You are the only emerald that we have.

"If you do not care about our family kinship
And still refuse to get back no matter what we say,
If our painstakingly effort to find you means nothing to you,
We would rather be dead and buried in this forest."

The fragile parents cried their eyes red and swollen,
Nan Guditila felt sorry for them deep in her heart.
She couldn't bear to see her parents suffer the painful separation,
So she obeyed her parents and accepted the welcoming wreath.

南古蒂提拉答应返回宫廷，
父王母后喜泪汪汪。
迎接的队伍也一片欢腾，
象脚鼓和铓锣敲个不停。

慈爱的母亲取出绸缎衣裳，
穿在女儿南古蒂提拉的身上。
它的颜色比彩虹还鲜艳，
它比凤凰的羽毛还漂亮。

她又取出薄薄的纱巾，
披在女儿南古蒂提拉的双肩。
它的线条比蛛丝还纤细，
它比攀枝花蕊还柔软。

南古蒂提拉换上筒裙，
上面织着斑斓的花朵，
莲叶托荷花衬着湖水的微波，
飞燕在彩虹下来往穿梭。

外婆又给三个外孙细细打扮，
捧玛加戴上纯金的帽子，
穿上彩色锦缎的衣服，
体态匀称，英俊威武。

衮纳帕穿戴上熊皮衣帽，
光滑黑亮就像乌鸦的翅膀。
彼亚沙穿上素雅的绸缎衣服，
举止文静，潇洒自如。

第三章 继位　Chapter 3 Succeeding the Throne

Nan Guditila agreed to return to the palace,
The eyes of her parents were full of happy tears.
The procession cheered for the good news,
And they played the drum and gong joyfully.

The amiable mother took out silk clothes.
She would like to get their daughter dressed up.
The clothes were more colorful than a rainbow,
And more flamboyant than the feathers of phoenix.

The mother took out a gauzy shawl again,
And she draped it on her daughter's shoulders.
The threads were thinner than the spider silk.
It was more tender than the silk cotton flower.

Nan Guditila changed her clothes and put on sarong,
On which the colorful flowers were embroidered.
Lotus flower and leaves swaying with the soft ripples,
Swallows flying back and forth under the rainbow.

Grandma again dressed up her three grandsons.
Wearing a hat of pure gold,
Dressed in colorful silk clothes,
Pengmajia was handsome with his elegant figure.

Gunnapa put on his bear skin hat and clothes,
The silky darkness was like the wings of the crow.
Biyasha was in his simple but elegant silk clothes,
Standing out with his gracious and casual manner.

三兄弟并排站在一起，
比月亮星星还有光彩。
美丽的姑娘见了都非常爱慕，
一个个目不转睛看着不想走开。

感谢天神保佑女儿安康，
感谢天神赐给三个外孙，
丢掉了十多年的无穷忧虑，
国王下令在森林里赶摆祝福。

伊麻板就像天上的乐园，
人们就像到园内游玩的天仙。
大家尽情地欢乐歌舞，
在森林里整整热闹了三天。

尊贵的国王和王后，
带领公主和金笋般的三个外孙，
置备了花盘、蜡条和鲜花，
来向圣洁的帕拉西辞谢。

"尊贵的帕拉西啊，
感谢你的善良和恩赐。
是你收养了我的女儿，
是你抚育了我的外孙子。

第三章 继位 Chapter 3 Succeeding the Throne

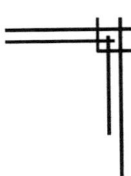

The three brothers stood side by side.
They were brighter than the moon and stars.
Those pretty girls were so much attracted
That they could not take their eyes off them.

To thank heavenly gods for their protection over his daughter,
To express his gratitude for their blessing of the three grandsons,
And to cast away dozen years' worries and agony,
The old king ordered a grand fair of celebration in the forest.

Yimaban was like a carnival in heaven;
People were like the fairies walking around.
And they sang and danced on and on.
It lasted for three whole days and nights.

The majestic king and queen, leading the princess
And the three golden-bamboo-shoot-like grandsons,
Offered wreathes, honey and flowers to the holy Palaxi
To express their gratitude and to bid their farewell to him.

"Our most distinguished Palaxi,
Thank you for your benediction and kindness.
It was you who adopted and took care of our daughter;
It was you who helped bring up our three grandsons.

兰嘎西贺 The Ten-Headed King of Langa

"今天我们像要远走高飞的鸟儿,
要把女儿和外孙带回去。
祈求你的金口玉牙,
赐给我们良好的祝福。"

帕拉西点头表示赞许,
说出了珍贵的祝词:
"爷爷心爱的孩子们啊,
你们就安安心心地回去。

"愿你们像井水洗过的宝石,
更加纯净和美丽。
抛弃忧愁和苦恼,
快快乐乐地生活在人世。

"愿疾病和灾难远离你们,
永葆荣华富贵的岁月,
祝兰嘎王国日益繁荣昌盛,
百姓在国王福荫下安居乐业。"

南古蒂提拉和三个儿子,
也向帕拉西惜别辞行:
"如果过去有违背佛规之处,
恳请你为我们忏悔祝福。"

帕拉西安慰他们母子:
"孩子们放心去吧,
神佛决不会责备你们,
爷爷为你们承担一切。"

第三章 继位 Chapter 3 Succeeding the Throne

"Today we are leaving here like birds flying away,
And we will take our daughter and grandsons back home.
We beg you to open your mouth,
And give us your blessings and best wishes."

Palaxi nodded his head for approval,
And gave them his best wishes,
"My dear children,
You may go back home with a peaceful mind.

"Bless you to be like gems cleansed by water,
And you will be more beautiful and pure-minded.
Sadness and sorrow will stay far away from you,
And you will live a happy and carefree life in the world.

"May you be free from disaster and disease,
May glorious days linger around you all years ahead.
May the Kingdom of Langa be more prosperous,
People will enjoy their life under the blessing of their king."

Nan Guditila and her three sons
Also came to make their farewell to Palaxi,
"If we had done anything against the rules of Buddhism,
Please pray for our repentance and give us your blessing."

Palaxi comforted the mother and the sons,
"You may depart with no guilt in your hearts.
Gods and Buddha will not blame or punish you.
I will shoulder all the responsibilities for you."

慈祥的帕拉西说完,
向他们一一洒了圣水。
收下花盘、蜡条和鲜花,
又祝福他们一路平安。

国王率领队伍离开伊麻板,
林间响起马嘶和象吼。
喧嚷的人群往回走,
欢欢乐乐来到了兰嘎坝。

喜讯像春风吹来,
人群像潮水澎湃。
威武的象队走到哪里,
哪里就是一片人山人海。

允兰嘎男女老少倾城出动,
欢迎国王叭兰巴归来。
矮个子在人墙后面踮起脚尖,
都想看一看公主和王子的风采。

三、捧玛加继位

国王接回了女儿和外孙,
命宫廷大臣传下意旨,
由大外孙召捧玛加继承王位,
选择吉日举行登基典礼。

第三章 继位 Chapter 3 Succeeding the Throne

After finishing his words,
The kindly Palaxi sprinkled holy water over them.
He accepted the wreath, wax of honey and flowers,
And blessed them to have a safe journey back home.

The king led the procession out of Yimaban,
Roars from the elephants and horses echoed in the forest.
The boisterous throng went onto the road leading to home,
Joyfully and cheerfully they arrived at the city of Langa.

The good news spread like spring breeze.
People rushed to the procession as tides,
Wherever the groups of mighty elephants were,
A sea of people would swarm around them.

Everyone went out of the capital city of Langa,
They joined the crowds to welcome back the King Ba Lanba.
The short ones had to stand tiptoeing among the crowds
So they could have a look at the majestic princes and princess.

Ⅲ Pengmajia Succeeding to the Throne

After the king welcomed back his daughter and grandsons,
He announced his decision to all of his officials.
The eldest grandson Zhao Pengmajia would claim the throne,
And an auspicious day should be chosen for the inauguration.

为庆祝召捧玛加登上王位，
全国上下忙得像沸腾的开水。
村村寨寨挂上彩旗神幡，
宫殿重新施漆彩绘。

把全勐最有名的能工叫来，
为召捧玛加修建三足鼎立的笋塔。
把全勐最能干的巧匠找来，
为新国王制作装珠宝的银匣。

用鲜花编成芳香艳丽的花环，
用棉花做成洁白多姿的动物，
用银盘装着蜡条和米花，
还准备了最珍贵的黄蜡和香水。

广场搭起了绿叶凉棚，
大路铺上了粗沙细石，
太阳像闪光的珍珠照亮大地，
隆重的登基典礼宣布开始。

尊贵的老国王叭兰巴和王后，
护送着威武的召捧玛加，
缓缓走下金色的宫殿，
来到笋塔接受登基的洗礼。

第三章 继位 Chapter 3 Succeeding the Throne

To celebrate Zhao Pengmajia's succession to the throne,
People all over the kingdom were hectic like boiling water.
Each village was decorated with the colorful banners;
The palace was repainted till each corner shone brilliantly.

The most talented builders were called together.
They were to build a tripod-like tower for Zhao Pengmajia.
The best craftsmen were summoned to the court
To make treasure case for the new king to keep his jewelry.

The wreathes were made of freshly plucked flowers,
Pure white animals statures were made of cotton,
Popcorn and wax of honey were served in silver trays,
The most precious perfume and wax were prepared too.

Shelters made of green leaves were set up on the plaza,
Roads leading to the palace were paved with fine sands,
The sun was shining like pearls on the ground,
Then grandiose inauguration was announced to start.

Escorting the mighty Zhao Pengmajia,
The respected old King Ba Lanba and the Queen
Walked slowly down the stairway of the golden palace.
Together they came to the tripod-like tower to start the inauguration.

臣民们一齐合掌下拜,
米花像雨点般撒出,
香花像彩虹般飘荡,
召捧玛加接受人们的祝福。

十个头的新国王穿起礼服,
文臣武将前呼后拥。
人们不断欢呼"水水水",
召捧玛加继承了勐兰嘎王位。

天神地祇和龙王都来了,
甫萨乐低①也从地下冒出。
他赐给新国王一辆飞车,
英达②的风火轮也赶不上它的速度。

召捧玛加立即跳上飞车,
飞车像闪电一样飞起,
上天入海飞行一圈才落地,
人群欢声雷动齐呼稀奇。

黑夜在欢乐中过去,
黎明在祝福中来临。
人们尽情地唱啊,尽情地舞,
祝福勐兰嘎江山万年春。

---

① 甫萨乐低:地神的一种。
② 英达:泛指天神。

第三章 继位 Chapter 3 Succeeding the Throne

The officials knelt down with their palms folded;
Rice flowers were sprinkled into the air like raindrops,
Colorful flowers were drifting like rainbows
And the new kings received blessing from his people.

The ten-headed king was dressed in his new outfit,
He was escorted and surrounded by the high officials.
"Water! water ! water!" was the chorus from his people.
Thus Zhao Pengmajia became the new king of Langa.

Gods of heaven and earth all showed up.
Pushayuedi① emerged from underground too.
He bestowed a flying cart to the new king,
Which is faster than the fire-and-wind wheel of Yingda②.

Zhao Pengmajia jumped onto the flying cart.
The cart flew with the speed of lightening
Soaring into the sky and diving into the sea,
Then it landed among the shouting crowds.

Dark night passed in the joyful cheers,
A new dawn came with all the blessings.
People sang and danced on and on,
Praying for the everlasting prosperity of Langa.

---

① Pushayuedi:one god of the Earth.
② Yingda:a broad term for all gods of heaven.

第四章 肆虐

一、娶妻

勐兰嘎的房子啊,
要数王宫的最高。
勐兰嘎的权力啊,
要数召捧玛加的最大。

召捧玛加统治勐兰嘎已经两年,
他治国的才能四方传扬。
但十六岁的年轻国王啊,
没有心爱的王后在身旁。

有了田就得种谷,
有了水就得养鱼。
一个国家有了国王啊,
就得有王后伴随。

羽毛丰满的斑鸠,
如果身边没有伴侣,
不会安心在原地憨睡,
它会在森林里乱飞。

第四章 肆虐 Chapter 4 Havoc

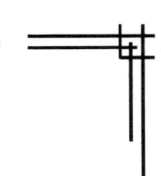

Chapter 4　Havoc

Ⅰ　Pengmajia Getting Married

Of all the houses in the kingdom of Langa,
The highest one is the magnificent palace.
Of all the people in the kingdom of Langa,
The most powerful one is Zhao Pengmajia.

Two years had passed since Zhao Pengmajia ruled the country.
His capability of governance is known to the world.
The young king was already sixteen years old,
Still he was single without a queen by his side.

Where there is paddy field, there is rice.
Where there is water, there is fish.
When a country has a king,
There must be a queen to accompany him.

Once a wild pigeon grows full-fledged,
If there is no mate by its side,
It would not perch in its nest with ease,
And it would fool around all over the forest.

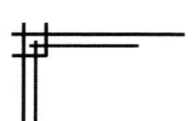

小麂子蹄硬角满了，
就要去寻找随身的伙伴。
没有伴侣的麂子啊，
一天要串几座山。

孩子长大了也是一样，
假若他没有找到如意的妻子，
年轻人的心啊，
就会像天上的浮云一样飘来飘去。

年迈的叭兰巴唯恐外孙不安心朝政，
整天为召捧玛加的婚事焦心。
他派官员带上珍贵的礼品去到树那，
向魔王叭干塔的女儿求婚。

美丽的公主南苏婉妮，
嫁给了年轻英俊的捧玛加。
可他有了一个王后还不满足，
心里翻腾像猫抓。

他还想再娶王妃，
到处物色绝代佳人。
好色淫荡的召捧玛加啊，
不满意与南苏婉妮的婚姻。

自从见过漂亮的龙女南苏甘塔，
他天天心神不定。
想龙女想得他饭菜不香，
想龙女想得他颠倒晨昏。

第四章 肆虐 Chapter 4 Havoc

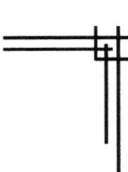

When the hooves of a deer started to harden,
It would set out to search around for its mate.
If a young deer hasn't got a mate by its side,
It would run over mountains to look for one.

It is the same story with a young adult,
Before he could find a wife that he likes,
He could not get his heart settled down,
Which would wander like floating clouds.

For fear that his grandson could not be focused on governance,
The old Ba Lanba worried about Zhao Pengmajia's marriage.
He sent for his high officials to Shuna with precious gifts
To ask for engagement with the daughter of the demon king Ba Ganta.

The beautiful Princess Nan Suwanni
Married the handsome King Pengmajia.
But he was not happy with just one queen.
His heart was disturbed like being scratched by a cat.

He wanted to get several concubines,
So he started to search for more pretties.
Zhao Pengmajia was so greedy and licentious
That he was not satisfied with his marriage to Nan Suwanni.

Ever since he had met the pretty girl of Nan Suganta,
He became fidgeted and restless every day.
With her in his mind, he lost his appetite to any food,
He missed her so much that he could not sleep at night.

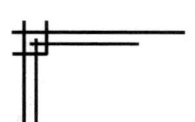

他穿上金丝织的衣服，
穿上有荷花瓣的套衣，
戴上纯金做的王冠，
驾上飞车潜入勐埃森。

荷花般的龙女南苏甘塔，
见召捧玛加到来惴惴不安。
"漂亮英俊的十头美男子啊，
你是哪里来的，有何贵干？"

召捧玛加被龙女的美色迷了心窍，
呆呆地望着龙女答话：
"海底的花王啊，
你就像池塘里美丽的荷花。

"我来自耸立海洋的兰嘎岛国，
我是威镇四海的兰嘎国王。
你是名传四方的美丽姑娘，
我慕名前来拜望。

"虽然哥哥身为一国之主，
但还是一只孤独的孔雀。
我坦率地对妹妹把话说透，
这次专程而来就为寻求佳偶。"

南苏甘塔微笑着说：
"哥哥的话犹如花蕊般芳香，
但高贵的国王怎能是孤独的孔雀，
你是不是专程前来取笑我？

第四章 肆虐 Chapter 4 Havoc

He put on his golden silk clothes
And his outfits decorated with lotus flower,
With his crown of pure gold on his head,
He sneaked into the Kingdom of Aisen on his flying cart.

Nan Suganta was as beautiful as a blooming lotus flower,
She felt uneasy to see Zhao Pengmajia.
"You handsome young man with ten heads,
Where are you from and why are you here?"

Bewitched by the beauty of the dragon's daughter,
Zhao Pengmajia stared at her and answered,
"The queen of flowers in the sea world,
You are like a beautiful lotus flower in the pond.

"I am from the island Kingdom of Langa,
I am its king holding the world in awe.
The reputation of your beauty has spread to each corner,
And I come to pay you a visit out of admiration.

"Although I am the lord over a country,
I am still single like a lonely peacock.
Let me tell you directly my intention.
I come here to ask you to marry me."

Nan Suganta answered with a smile,
"Your remarks are fragrant like flowers,
But how can a majestic king be a lonely peacock?
Or you are here just to make fun of me?

"我是凋谢了的花朵,
蜜蜂见了都不落。
我是干瘪了的槟榔,
已失掉了鲜红的颜色。

"你知道我已离过婚,
是年纪比你大的女人。
有福气的年轻国王啊,
我们结婚定会成为人们的笑柄。"

召捧玛加当面对天发誓:
"海莲般的妹妹呀,
我说的全是真心话,
丝毫没有骗你的意思。

"哥哥从小就在森林里修行,
从来没有接触过姑娘。
犹如露水没有沾着灰尘,
不信就让苍天大海为我作证。

"有缘分我才从异国来找你,
我对你的爱就像攀树的野藤。
我娶你就不怕嘲讽和打击,
不和你结成佳偶我不死心。"

召捧玛加的誓言感动了龙女,
南苏甘塔接受了他的爱情。
龙王慨然应允他俩的请求,
为公主举办了盛大的婚礼。

第四章 肆虐 Chapter 4 Havoc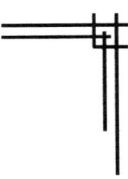

"I am a withered flower
Even a bee will not land on me.
I am a dried betel nut
That has lost its color of fresh scarlet.

"You know that I am divorced
And a woman older than you,
While you are a blessed and young king.
Our marriage will be a laughingstock."

Zhao Pengmajia vowed to the heaven,
"My dear sea-lotus-flower-like sister,
What I said was from the bottom of my heart,
There is no way that I would lie to you.

"I had practised Buddhism in the forest since my childhood,
I have never had the chance to get in touch with girls.
I am as pure as a drop of dew never touched by dust.
I would ask the sky and the sea to be my witnesses.

"Destiny drove me to come to you from a foreign country,
My love for you is like the vine clinging to a tree.
My determination can not be thwarted by irony or blow,
I will never give up the idea till I finally get you as my wife."

Dragon's daughter was moved by his oath,
Nan Suganta accepted the king's proposal.
Dragon King the father approved of their request,
And held a grandiose wedding ceremony for his princess.

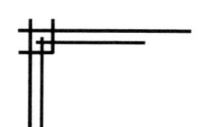

召捧玛加眷恋温柔多情的龙女，
在龙宫寻欢作乐了四个月。
然后带着漂亮的南苏甘塔，
浮出海面飞回勐兰嘎。

贪吃麂子的老虎，
永远满足不了它的食欲。
贪色好淫的召捧玛加，
有了两个妻子还不满足。

他才把龙女安顿在塔楼，
又乘上飞车来到勐纳嘎。
就像蜜蜂见了鲜花那样殷勤，
他见了南曼达公主说着甜蜜的话：

"美丽多姿的花王啊，
你的芳香飘满天下。
是你的芳香把我吸引，
我特意来向你求婚。"

刚会飞的小斑鸠，
不知道鹞鹰的凶狠。
很少出门的南曼达公主，
哪知道召捧玛加的品性。

第四章 肆虐 Chapter 4 Havoc

Zhao Pengmajia was obsessed with the affectionate Dragon girl,

He indulged in their union for four months in the dragon's palace.

Then taking the beautiful Nan Suganta with him

He flew out of the sea and back to the Kingdom of Langa.

Just as an insatiable tiger

Which was never satisfied with the deer meet at its hand,

Even after having two wives,

The licentious Zhao Pengmajia was not content at all.

As soon as he got his new wife settled down in the tower,

He flew to the Kingdom of Naga in his flying cart.

Just as a bee so attentive to fresh flowers,

he seduced the Princess of Nan Manda with sweet words,

"The most beautiful queen of flower,

Your fragrance wafted all over the world.

It was your fragrance that attracted me here.

I came specially to make a proposal to you."

Just like a fledgling turtledove

Which never knows how atrocious hawks can be,

How could the innocent Princess of Nan Manda

Know what a person Zhao Pengmajia really was.

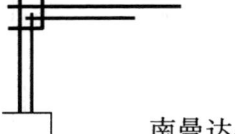

南曼达心上泛起一团疑云:
"亲爱的哥哥啊,
你的话就像清泉在林间流淌,
但不知是不是发自内心?

"我是干了的黄瓜叶,
已没有鲜嫩的色质,
妹妹没福气和你相配,
你还是快离此返回家去。"

召捧玛加微笑着回答:
"哥哥就像孤独的野鸭,
我说的话一片真情,
字字句句发自内心。

"哥哥是乘骑大象的一国之主,
要是我有一句谎话,
就让哥哥的二十只眼睛,
像黑夜一样失去光华。"

天下虚情假意的人啊,
骗了多少姑娘的心。
美丽的南曼达仍不大相信,
又将召捧玛加紧紧追问:

"哥哥真的没有情人?
哥哥真的爱恋妹妹?
你是不是用蜜水来迷住我,
可不要蜜淡水干又把我丢弃。"

第四章 肆虐 Chapter 4 Havoc

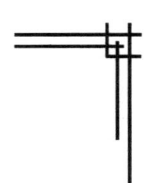

Doubtful cloud rose in the heart of Nan Manda,
"My dear brother,
Your words sounded like the spring flowing in the woods.
I am wondering if they came from the true lover's heart?

"I am the dried yellow leaves of cucumber
Which had lost its tenderness and lustre.
I don't have the luck to be a match to you,
You had better turn and go back home at once."

Zhao Pengmajia answered her with a smile,
"I am like a lonely wild duck.
I really mean what I have said,
And each word was from the bottom of my heart.

"I am the king that rides on an elephant,
If there were any trace of lie in my words,
My twenty eyes would lose their light,
As darkness befalls when night comes."

There were too many innocent girls in the world
Who had been cheated by the gullible womanizers.
Pretty Nan Manda still didn't buy his words,
So she kept asking Zhao Pengmajia,

"Do you really have no lover?
Are you really in love with me?
Or you are charming me with your sweet promise,
And you will desert me when you feel tired of me."

"哥哥不是水上的泡沫,
哥哥不是天上的浮云。
哥哥爱你完全是真情实意,
就像雄鹦鹉求爱那样忠诚。

"我是至高无上的国王,
不是游手好闲的花花公子。
要是我说了假话,
我怎么有脸回去见臣民?"

南曼达的疑云被大风吹散,
召捧玛加的话使她动心。
他俩就像一对相爱的斑鸠,
手拉手去朝见父母亲。

父王母后同意他们的婚事,
召捧玛加娶到了南曼达。
又在纳嘎王国欢度了四个月,
才领着新王后回到勐兰嘎。

漂亮的三个王后啊,
侍候着十个头的召捧玛加。
他整日在宫廷荒淫无度,
好心的三弟相谏他也不采纳。

衮纳帕不习惯城市的喧嚣,
又搬到悬崖峭壁去住。
找到一个六百米宽的岩洞,
一倒下就呼呼睡熟。

第四章 肆虐 Chapter 4 Havoc

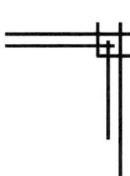

"I am not the foam on the water,
I am not the cloud in the sky either.
My love for you is all out of my heart,
I am faithful like a parrot courting its lover.

"I am a majestic king,
Not a playboy fooling around.
If I told lies and cheated on you,
How could I have the face to go back and meet my people?"

The doubtful clouds of Nan Manda were blown away,
She was moved by what Zhao Pengmajia said.
Like a pair of the turtledoves deeply in love,
Hand in hand, they went to see her parents.

Her parents, the king and the queen, approved of their marriage,
Zhao Pengmajia got married to Nan Manda.
They spent four happy months in the Kingdom of Naga,
Then Zhao Pengmajia took his new queen back to Langa.

The pretty three queens lived in the palace.
They served Zhao Pengmajia the ten-headed king.
Indulged himself in the carnivals in the court,
He turned a deaf ear to the advice from his yourgest brother.

Gunnapa was not used to the chaos of the city,
He moved back to the mountain with cliffs and precipices.
There he found a cave as wide as six hundred meters,
And he fell asleep as soon as he lay down.

时间一年年过去，
三个王后都生了儿子。
召捧玛加高兴万分，
请高贵的智者帕麻纳命名。

龙公主南苏甘塔分娩之时，
勐兰嘎黑云密布下着倾盆大雨。
山摇地动就像天崩地塌，
帕麻纳给大儿子取名米卡。

接着小王后南曼达也怀孕生子，
由于他的外祖父是叭团①，
又根据他的生辰年月，
帕麻纳给他取名叫菲玛兰敢。

大王后南苏婉妮生的儿子，
力气像老象一样巨大，
性子像大火一样暴烈，
帕麻纳给他取名叫歪亚拉。

三个王子一天天长大，
个个都像森林中的猛虎，
个个都像顶天立地的柱石，
他们幸福地生活在宫廷里。

---

① 叭团：魔鬼的头人。

第四章 肆虐 Chapter 4 Havoc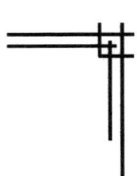

Time passed year after year,
All the three queens gave birth to a son.
Zhao Pengmajia was extremely happy,
And he sent for the wise man Pamana to name them.

When the Princess of dragon Nan Suganta labored,
The Kingdom of Langa was covered with dark clouds.
Heavy rain poured down shaking the mountains and earth.
Therefore, Pamana name the first-born son Mika.

The youngest queen Nan Manda also gave birth to a son.
Since his grandfather was Batuan①, the head of devils,
And also based on the time of his birth,
Pamana named him Feimalangan.

The son from the first queen Nan Suwanni
Was as strong as a big elephant.
He has a temper as hot as fire,
Thus Pamana named him Waiyala.

Three princes grew up as time went by.
Each of them was as mighty as tiger in the woods.
They stood upright as pillars holding up the heaven.
Together, they lived a very happy life in the palace.

---

① Batuan: the head of devils.

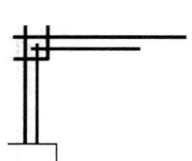

二、骄纵

海底的龙王巴拉麻，
原来是一个天神。
他自恃本领高强藐视天法，
酗酒闯祸弄得天庭不得安宁。

叭英见他闹得太不像样，
就把他从天堂贬到海洋。
他落在勐埃森，
后来叭英就封他为龙王。

他念念不忘天国生活的清闲舒服，
怨恨叭英把他贬得官职卑微。
他心中时时翻腾着这份夙仇，
一想起这些羞辱气愤就涌上心头。

他不能容忍叭英让他失去了天国的地位，
不甘心在叭英脚下忍辱求生。
他带着水将水兵冲上天庭，
要和叭英拼个你死我活报仇雪恨。

第四章 肆虐 Chapter 4 Havoc

Ⅱ Arrogance and Indulgence

Balama was the dragon King at the bottom of the sea,
And he was once a god living in the heaven.
He was conceited and contemptuous of the rules of heaven.
In his continuous drunkenness he turned heaven into a mess.

Seeing that Balama had gone too far,
Baying relegated him from the heaven to the sea.
He was settled down in the Kingdom of Aisen,
And Baying granted him the title of King of dragon.

Balama missed the good old days in heaven.
He hated Baying for the humiliated relegation.
With the deep hatred seething in his heart,
He felt unbearable indignation getting him mad.

He could not bear Baying for driving him out of heaven.

He was unwilling to live a humiliated life under the feet of Baying.

Leading his generals and soldiers, he broke into the palace of heaven,

He launched a life-or-death war against Baying to take his revenge.

叭英不容龙王侵犯神圣的天庭，
率领天兵出来应战，
双方兵马展开激烈的厮杀，
直杀得雷电交加天昏地暗。

双方势均力敌僵持对峙，
龙王难以攻进天宫，
叭英难以打退水兵，
整整七个月不分胜负。

龙王眼看难以取胜，
便派使臣来找女婿速发援兵，
召捧玛加立即命令儿子米卡，
率领大军乘战车直上天庭。

米卡站在天门外高声叫骂：
"可恶的叭英你听着，
我是龙王的外孙米卡，
亲率勐兰嘎士兵前来将你讨伐。

"我的祖父是天王玛哈捧，
我的父亲是十头王捧玛加，
哪个不慑于他们的威望？
我劝你还是赶快投降吧！"

米卡骂完就带领将士猛攻，
叭英边指挥抵抗边思忖：
"召捧玛加依仗天王的神威一向狂妄，
这次他儿子来也是气势汹汹。

第四章 肆虐 Chapter 4 Havoc

Baying would never tolerate dragon's intrusion,
He confronted Balama and his army with his own.
The two sides fought against each other so ferociously
That it was totally dark after fits of lighting and thunder.

The fight resulted in a stalemate due to their equal strength.
It's difficult for the dragon king to conquer the heaven;
It's impossible for Baying to drive the enemy off.
The war dragged on for seven whole months.

The dragon saw it's impossible to win the war,
So he sent envoys to his son-in-law asking for help.
Zhao Pengmajia immediately ordered his son Mica
To lead the army and rush to the battlefield in chariots.

Standing out of the gate of heaven, Mica shouted,
"You, damned Baying, listen to me carefully,
I am the grandson of the dragon King.
I am here with the armies of Langa to ask for your life.

"My grandfather on my father's side is the god of Mahapeng.
My father is Pengmajia, the king with ten heads.
No one in the world would not be in awe of them,
So take my advice and surrender to us in no time!"

After the shouts and curses, Mica started the attack.
Baying commanded his army to resist while thinking to himself,
"Pengmajia has always been arrogant because of his father,
This time his son was also so aggressive and overbearing.

"如果天兵迎战惹怒十头王,
天庭会遭到更大的祸殃,
还是避其锐气不战为好,
我们暂时撤退到上一层天堂。"

于是叭英下令打开天宫城门,
让龙王和米卡的队伍进城,
他率领天兵天将不战而走,
大队兵马向上一层天堂撤退。

米卡带领将士冲上天宫,
占领了金碧辉煌的宫殿,
威武的米卡坐上叭英的宝座,
胜利的欢呼声响彻蓝天。

祖孙在天庭住了七个月,
满怀喜悦班师回国,
勐兰嘎到处传颂王子米卡的战绩,
称赞他本领高强天地无敌。

第四章 肆虐 Chapter 4 Havoc

"If we fight back, the ten-headed king would be provoked,

Maybe more damage will be done to the palace of heaven.

It is better for us to shun from their edge at this moment,

We could temporarily retreat to the higher level of heaven."

Then Baying ordered to open the gate of the heavenly palace,

And the Dragon king and Mica with their army advanced in.

Baying led his generals and soldiers to retreat without a fight,

And the large group of troops withdrew to the upper level of heaven.

Mica with his soldiers rushed into the court of heaven,

He occupied the grandiose and glorious palace.

Sitting majestically on the throne of Baying,

Mica enjoyed the cheers for victory resounding in the blue sky.

The old dragon and grandson lived in heaven for seven months.

Then they triumphantly returned to their own country.

The great feat of Mica was celebrated all over the Kingdom of Langa.

He was praised as an invincible fighter incomparable in martial arts.

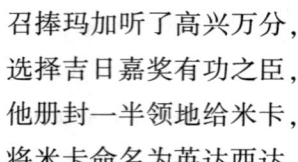

召捧玛加听了高兴万分,
选择吉日嘉奖有功之臣,
他册封一半领地给米卡,
将米卡命名为英达西达。

他还下诏命英达西达主持朝政,
要全勐臣民都拥戴他儿子,
他又送菲玛兰敢到龙宫,
向外祖父学习高超的武艺。

从此兰嘎王国更加威震四方,
到处听到的是奉承和赞扬,
从此远近各勐都来朝贡,
耳边响着的是阿谀和歌颂。

召捧玛加如豺狼更加贪婪,
傲慢和狂妄达到了顶峰,
外祖父母的话他听不进去,
众臣僚的忠告他当耳边风。

召捧玛加到处大兴土木,
城墙加固了又高筑,
御花园修建得无比阔气,
百姓们担负着沉重的劳役。

第四章 肆虐 Chapter 4 Havoc

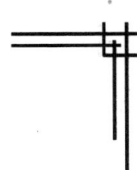

Zhao Pengmajia was happy to get the news.
And he chose a good day to honor the generals of credit.
He granted Mica half of his kingdom,
And the glorious name of Yingdaxida.

He issued an edict that Yingdaxida was to run the country,
Asking people all over the country to support his son.
He then sent Feimalangan to the dragon's palace
So that he could learn fighting skills from his grandfather.

Ever since then the Kingdom of Langa became more powerful.
In each corner of the country was flattery and praise to the king.
The neighboring kingdoms came to pay tribute to him,
All he could hear was endless blandishments and adulation.

Zhao Pengmajia became more greedy than wolf;
His arrogance and conceit went beyond reason.
He wouldn't listen to his grandparents at all,
He also turned a deaf ear to the advice from his subordinates.

Zhao Pengmajia started architectural projects everywhere,
He had the city wall built higher and more consolidated.
His imperial garden was reconstructed more luxurious.
But his people suffered from the heavy forced labour.

召捧玛加贪酒好色,
任意凌辱良家妇女,
他乘飞车成天游逛,
在龙国天堂到处寻欢作乐。

百姓被逼得纷纷逃亡,
守护勐兰嘎大坝的帝巴①,
也搬到远方异国的森林去住,
富饶的勐兰嘎一片凄凉。

三、调戏南西拉

召捧玛加驾驶飞车像老鹰一样,
飞到很远很远的伊麻板地方,
在这个原始的深山老林里,
各色各样的鲜花竞相开放。

成群的蜜蜂和蝴蝶啊,
来回在花朵上奔忙,
伶俐的野鸡和孔雀啊,
徘徊在花树下寻找食粮。

在百花争艳的花丛中,
有一棵花树名叫纳里本,
它的形态完全像一个人,
它的神采就像妙龄的姑娘。

---

① 帝巴:泛指管海洋、土地、森林的神,级别低于叭英。

第四章 肆虐 Chapter 4 Havoc

Zhao Pengmajia wallowed in wine and beauties.
He wantonly harassed good and decent girls.
All the time he fooled around in his flying cart
Enjoying the parties in the palace of the dragon King.

His people had no other choice but to flee to other places;
The heavenly god of Diba① who protected the dam of Langa
Also left to live in the remote forest of a foreign country.
The rich and beautiful Kingdom of Langa became desolate.

Ⅲ Nan Xila Was Harrassed

Zhao Pengmajia was flying in his chariot like an eagle;
He flew to the remote place named Yimaban.
In the primeval forests hidden in the remote mountain,
All kinds of flowers fully bloom to vie with each other.

Swarms of bees and butterflies were quite busy,
Flying back and forth among the colorful flowers.
The agile peacock and pheasants were wandering,
Foraging leisurely under the blooming trees.

Among the blooming flowers
There was a flower tree named Naliben.
It looked exactly like a human being;
It was glamorous as a pretty young girl.

---

① Diba: the god in charge of the sea, the land and the forest, inferior to Baying.

它周身散发出沁人的芳香,
它身上的颜色犹如白色的月光,
它红润的脸颊好像饱含金水,
它的姿容只有神仙美女才能欣赏。

有一个漂亮的帝巴姑娘南西拉,
在伊麻板森林修行,
她每天随着黎明来到,
坐在纳里本花树下祈祷。

像公猪一样的召捧玛加,
闲游来到纳里本花树下,
见树下坐着一个美丽的少女,
便凑上前去说出甜蜜的话语:

"像宝石一样闪闪发光的姑娘呀,
连日来哥哥到处在找你,
哥哥见你如同吃下香甜的蜂蜜,
今天要接你回去做妻子。

"亲爱的妹妹呀,
你别闭着眼睛不搭理,
鸟语花香谁还有心来修行?
现在是谈情说爱的好时机。

"你睁开眼睛看看我吧,
我从来没有串过姑娘,
你点着火把找遍天下,
也难找到像我这样的小伙子。"

第四章 肆虐 Chapter 4 Havoc

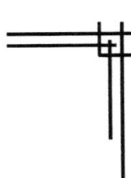

It gave off a special fragrance so refreshing;
It was milky white like moonlight;
Its pinkish face was as radiant as golden water.
Only a fairy lady had the chance to take a glimpse of its beauty.

There was a pretty girl from Diba named Nan Xila.
She practised Buddhism in the forest of Yimaban.
Every day she came to the forest with the rising sun,
And she meditated and prayed under the tree of Naliben.

One day, the boar-like Zhao Pengmajia
Strolled to the flower tree of Naliben.
Seeing a pretty girl sitting under the tree,
He approached her with honeyed words,

"My girl, you are like a sparkling diamond,
You are the one I have always been seeking.
Meeting you is sweet to me as honey,
Today I will take you home to be my wife.

"My dear girl,
Please don't even take a look at me.
Who cares to practise Buddhism in such season?
It is the best time to talk love with blooming flowers around.

"Please open your eyes and have a look at me,
I had never laid my hand on a woman.
Even if you search the world with a torch at hand,
It is impossible for you to find a lad like me."

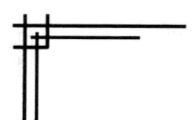

南西拉无动于衷地回答：
"我不愿做谁家的妻子，
我一心只想修行积德，
请你快快离开这里。"

贪色的召捧玛加不死心：
"薄眼皮的姑娘啊，
难道你要一辈子苦修，
年轻时不行乐更待何时？

"你老了变成一块干巴，
哪个小伙子会要你。
你还是听哥哥的话吧，
跟我一同回去过好日子。"

召捧玛加说着就动手动脚，
紧紧拉着南西拉的手指，
南西拉甩脱他的纠缠，
站起来迅速飞向天边逃避。

召捧玛加跳上飞车追赶，
像狂风一样追到天际，
南西拉转身逃到龙国，
他又追着钻进海里。

他狂笑着向南西拉扑去，
就像老鹰抓小鸡一样凶狠，
惊恐万状的南西拉一闪身，
摆脱十头魔王又钻进森林。

第四章 肆虐 Chapter 4 Havoc

Nan Xila answered nonchalantly,
"I don't want to be anyone's wife.
My whole mind is on practising Buddhism.
Please leave me alone now at this minute."

The wanton Zhao Pengmajia wouldn't gave it up,
"My girl with thin eyelids,
How can you live your whole life so ascetically?
You need to enjoy life when you are still young.

"You will get weathered when you are old.
Till then, no young lad wants to marry you.
You had better take my advice.
Come with me to enjoy a good life."

Zhao Pengmajia then began to take liberties with Nan Xila.
He stepped forward and held her fingers tightly.
Nan Xila managed to get away from him,
And she stood up and flew to the sky escaping him.

Zhao Pengmajia jumped onto his flying cart,
Chasing her to the sky like wild wind.
When she turned around and dived into the sea,
He followed her into the Kingdom of dragon.

He threw himself onto Nan Xila with hideous laughter,
He was ferocious as an eagle diving down for a chick.
Nan Xila got terrified but still managed to dodge aside.
Being free from the ten-headed demon, she fled to the forest.

召捧玛加紧追不舍，
直累得南西拉筋疲力尽，
直追得南西拉无处藏身，
只好又回到原地伺机逃遁。

召捧玛加哈哈笑着说：
"世间罕见的美人儿呀，
还是乖乖地服从我吧，
你再逃也是白费精神。"

南西拉的心像被烈火烧烫，
她大声斥责召捧玛加：
"你这无耻的十头魔王，
你想占有我是痴心妄想。

"你想玷污我纯洁的身躯，
就好比蜻蜓想歇在凤凰头上，
今天你这样欺负我，
将来你会得到恶果报偿。

"你这遭雷劈的国王，
竟如此荒淫无道伤天害理，
你将给你的国家带来祸殃，
你的十个头将像花一样凋谢。

"我的心像箭一样直，
宁愿折断也不弯曲，
我的身躯像泉水一样纯洁，
宁死也不让你玷污。

第四章 肆虐 Chapter 4 Havoc

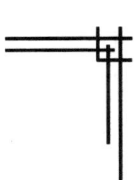

Zhao Pengmajia kept chasing
Till Nan Xila became exhausted.
Now She had nowhere to hide,
So she stopped to wait for another chance to flee.

Zhao Pengmajia said in a triumphant smile,
"You are truly a rare beauty in the world.
You'd better be a good girl who obeys me.
You are just wasting your energy in trying to escape."

Nan Xila's heart was seething with fire.
She reproached Zhao Pengmajia loudly,
"You, the shameless ten-headed devil,
It is only your daydream to get my body.

"You dream to take my body and smear my reputation,
That is like a dragonfly trying to land on the head of phoenix.
If you today have the nerve to blemish my purity,
You will surely be doomed with the fruit of revenge.

"I curse you to be split by lightening and thunder,
You are licentious and have committed unforgivable sins.
You will incur fatal disaster to your kingdom,
And your ten heads will fall off like withered flowers.

"My heart is as straight as a flying arrow,
It can only be broken instead of being bent.
My body is pure like spring water,
I would rather die than get stained by your dirty hands.

"天神呀，投下大火来吧，
让烈火把我焚烧干净。
我宁愿毁灭身躯和生命，
也不容十头魔王贴近我的身子。"

得到天神叭英的帮助，
树下霎时冒出一团烈火，
南西拉毅然跳进火中，
炽烈的大火立刻把她焚毁。

生平第一次见到这惊人的奇迹，
召捧玛加不觉目瞪口呆，
无处逃遁的美人突然隐没，
他只好招来天神地鬼交代：

"我命令你们守在这里，
假如南西拉复活重生，
你们抓住她后速来报告。"
说完跳上飞车愤愤而去。

四、挑衅巴力莫

召捧玛加来到干塔巴塔那山上空遨游，
俯视茫茫森林一片绿油油，
一只白猴在林间十分显眼，
正在向光辉的太阳合掌叩首。

第四章 肆虐 Chapter 4 Havoc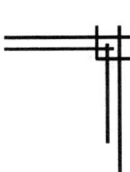

"Dear god of heaven, please cast down holy fire,
So that I could be burnt into ashes in the flames.
I would rather destroy myself and give up my life,
Than let this ten-headed devil draw near my body."

Thanks to the help from the heavenly god of Baying,
Suddenly burning fire appeared under the tree.
Nan Xila jumped into the flame without hesitation,
And the fierce fire burnt her into ashes in a blink.

It was the first time for him to witness such a miracle,
Zhao Pengmajia became totally dumbfounded.
The cornered beauty suddenly vanished into thin air,
He called upon the local deities and gave them an order,

"I order you to keep vigilant over here.
If Nan Xila came back to life again,
You have to catch her and report to me immediately."
After that he jumped into his flying cart and left furiously.

IV Balimo Was Provoked

One day flying over the Mountain of Gantabatana,
Zhao Pengmajia overlooked the deep green forest.
A white monkey stood out well in the woods,
He was bowing to the shining sun with palms folded.

白猴是勐基沙猴王巴力莫,
他信奉太阳神十分虔诚,
天天都来大山上,
向着至高无上的太阳顶礼膜拜。

召捧玛加又看到一只白猴在河里沐浴,
便从云隙里向下窥伺,
巴力莫瞥见气愤地说:"你不要脸,
怎么偷看我洗澡的妻子。"

召捧玛加轻佻地说:
"你这白毛长脸的猴子,
看看你女人洗澡有什么要紧,
你这爬树钻洞的东西也配讲什么廉耻。"

巴力莫顿时血涌心头:
"你这下流的无赖,
竟敢在勐基沙国王面前如此放肆,
你有能耐就下来和我比试比试。"

狂妄的十头王哈哈大笑,
他哪里把猴王放在眼里。
"你可知道我是顶天立地的天王,
你这小小白猴算什么东西?

第四章 肆虐 Chapter 4 Havoc

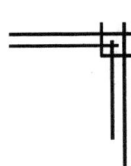

The white monkey named Balimo is the King of Jisha.
He worshiped the God of Sun piously.
Everyday he would climb up to the top of the mountain,
And worship the supreme God of Sun with all his heart.

Zhao Pengmajia saw another white monkey bathing in the river,
He watched it stealthily from the clouds.
Seeing what he was doing, Balimo said angrily,
"Shame on you, how dare you peek my wife bathing?"

Zhao Pengmajia said frivolously,
"You, a monkey with long face and white hairs,
What does it matter that I watched your wife bathing?
Does a despicable creature like you have sense of shame?"

Balimo got furious with blood surging to his head,
"You are a dirty and shameless rascal.
How dare you act so presumptuously in front of the King of Jisha?
Do you have enough nerve to get down and fight with me?"

The arrogant ten-headed king laughed out loudly,
He would never take the monkey king seriously.
"Do you know that I am a mighty god of heaven?
You little white monkey mean nothing to me."

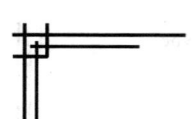

"我在空中等着你,
你有没有飞天的本事?
有种的就上天来吧,
比一比谁有高强武艺。"

巴力莫一气冲上十五约①高空,
就像狂风那样迅速,
召捧玛加还来不及看清楚,
巴力莫已把他的飞车抓住。

他把十头王紧紧掐在手里,
就像掐着一片干树叶,
他猛烈地挥手甩动,
甩得十头王气喘吁吁几乎气绝。

十头王无法忍受苦苦告饶:
"我求你不要再甩了,
请求你饶恕我的罪过,
从今以后愿意听从你的教导。"

巴力莫听到他如此哀求,
一边教训他一边放开了手:
"只要你真心不再欺负人,
我就放了你不记前仇。"

---

① 约:长度单位,人的视线所及为一约。

第四章 肆虐 Chapter 4 Havoc

"I am here waiting for you in the sky.
Can you fly into the sky?
Come up if you are not a coward,
Let us fight to see who is more powerful."

Balimo jumped up fifteen Yue① high into the sky,
And he moved as fast as hurricane.
Before Zhao Pengmajia had time to see clearly
Balimo had already snatched his flying cart.

He throttled the ten-headed king tightly in his hands
Just easily as he clenched a piece of dry leave.
He swung him violently left and right,
The ten-headed king almost got choked out of breath.

The ten-headed king couldn't bear it and begged for mercy,
"Please stop swinging like this,
Please forgive me for all my sins.
I will follow your instruction from today on."

On hearing his begging and petition
Balimo loosened his hands while preaching,
"If you really mean what you say and stop sinning,
I will let you go and forget the wrongs you have done."

---

① Yue: measure unit for length, which is about the distance how far a person can see.

召捧玛加又气又羞,
垂头丧气返回勐兰嘎。
俗话说江山易改本性难移,
不久他的老毛病又复发。

五、天怒人怨

十头魔王更加荒淫无道,
他的罪孽惹得天怒人怨,
勐兰嘎的守护神邀约众神仙,
到英达面前把他控告。

英达爱莫能助只得告诉他们:
"我们都身居天宫最下层,
都是在玛哈捧福荫下生存,
十头王的事须由他亲自过问。"

英达率领众神仙升到第三层天空,
在达来捧天宫参拜了玛哈捧,
"我们头上的玛哈捧啊,
你儿子召捧玛加的罪恶实在难容。

"他比猛虎还凶残,
他比恶魔还作恶多端,
天神地祇也整日惶惶不安,
百姓更处在水深火热之中。

第四章 肆虐 Chapter 4 Havoc

Zhao Pengmajia felt angry and shameful,
And he returned to his Kingdom of Langa despondently.
But as the old saying goes "A leopard never changes his spots",
Not long before he turned back to his old way of debauchery.

V Indignation of Gods and Grievance of People

The ten-headed king became more degenerated,
And his crimes infuriated both gods and his people.
The guardian god of Langa asked the other heavenly gods
To go to heaven together and impeach him in front of Yingda.

Yingda who would like to help but couldn't told them,
"We were gods at the lowest rank in heaven,
We could only live in heaven under Mahapeng's grace,
And only he could make the conviction of the ten-headed king."

Yingda led those heavenly gods to the third level of heaven,
After paying respect to Mahapeng in Dalaipeng Palace, they said,
"Your majestic Mahapeng, the one on top of our heads,
Your son Zhao Pengmajia has made hideous crimes.

"He is more vicious than fierce tiger;
He has done more evils than devils.
Even gods of the heaven and earth lived in panic,
The common villagers are suffering too much more.

"你给了召捧玛加高超的本领,
使得他毫无顾忌地到处横行,
主宰天宫的神王啊,
请你告诉我们制服他的办法。"

玛哈捧回答说:
"我对过去的许诺并不反悔,
我也曾用神圣的语言谆谆教诲,
让他切记不可胡作非为。

"我不允许他战胜三样东西,
善良正直的王子,
神圣的弓阿沙尖,
森林里的白毛猴。"

英达和众神仙心中有了底,
一起回到最下层天宫商议,
如果十头魔王要征服这三样东西,
命运将使他遭到毁灭性的打击。

第四章 肆虐　Chapter 4 Havoc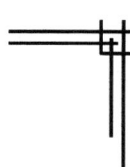

"You have bestowed him too much super power,
Which enabled him to do evils without any scruple.
You are the god in charge of the heaven,
Please tell us what we can do to bring him under control."

Mahapeng answered them,
"I could not take back my promises.
I have also taught him with sacred words,
Asking him to remember them and never do wrongs.

"There are three things that he could never conquer.
The kind and righteous Prince,
The holy bow of Ashajian,
And the white monkeys in the forest."

Yingda and the other gods felt at ease hearing this.
They returned to the under level of heaven to discuss.
If the ten-headed king wanted to defeat such three things,
He was doomed to be defeated and suffer fatal destruction.

第五章　勐沓达腊塔

一、沓达腊塔国王

辽阔无际的勐沓达腊塔，
多么富饶、多么壮丽，
它是文化知识的宝库，
它是人口稠密的国家。

宽广的土地居住着千千万万百姓，
平坦的坝子里村寨像繁星闪光，
翠绿的竹林掩映着幢幢竹楼，
俯视远望就像密密麻麻的蜂房。

繁荣昌盛的勐沓达腊塔呀，
都城立在国土的中央，
巍峨的城墙用石块砌成，
成千的将士戍守得固若金汤。

城中矗立着富丽堂皇的宫殿，
居中的正宫威严如山，
正宫里面有神圣的宝座，
威武的国王高高坐镇在上面。

第五章 勐沓达腊塔　Chapter 5 The Kingdom of Dadalata

Chapter 5　The Kingdom of Dadalata

I　The King of Dadalata

The vast and boundless Kingdom of Dadalata
How rich and magnificent it was.
It was a treasure house with brilliant culture,
And also a country with dense population.

Tens of millions of people lived on the vast land.
The villages on the flat plain sparkled like stars.
Among the green bamboo forest hid the bamboo houses.
Overlooked from above, they were like a densely-dotted hives.

The prosperous and thriving Kingdom of Dadalata,
Its capital was situated in the center of its territory.
The towering walls were made of stone.
Thousands of generals and soldiers guarded it from invaders.

In the city stands the magnificent palace.
The central main palace was as majestic as a mountain.
The sacred throne was housed in the main palace.
On the throne sat high the mighty king.

149

左面是一层比一层高的阁楼,
和正宫、塔楼三足鼎立,
登上最高一层阁楼瞭望,
平坝和森林尽收眼底。

右面是竹笋般的塔楼,
一节连一节耸入云天,
塔楼镀上金粉闪耀着金光,
国王和王后就住在塔楼里面。

治理这个国家的国王,
勐名就是他的名字,
召沓达腊塔的威望传四方,
勐沓达腊塔的盛名天下扬。

召沓达腊塔有三个王后,
大王后叫南苏甘嫡,
二王后叫南苏米达,
小王后叫南洁西。

她们就像麂子那样心地善良,
她们就像金鹿那样温柔伶俐,
她们就像来自三个地方的金孔雀,
各具妩媚姿色又都俊秀美丽。

第五章 勐沓达腊塔 Chapter 5 The Kingdom of Dadalata

On the left of the main palace was the attics going higher and higher.

Together with the main palace and the tower, they stood like a tripod.

Climbing onto the highest tower to look far into the distance,

One could have a full view of the plains and the forests.

On the right of the palace was the several-stored tower,

One after another they grew high into the sky like bamboo shoots.

The gilded tower glittered under the sun,

In which lived the king and the queen.

The kingdom was under the governance of the king,

And it also took after the king's name.

The reputation of Zhao Dadalata spread far,

And the Kingdom of Dadalata was known to the world.

Zhao Dadalata had three queens.

The first one was named "Nan Sugandi",

The second was called "Nan Sumida",

And the last one was "Nan Jiexi".

The three queens were kind-hearted as muntjac,

And as gentle and clever as golden deer.

They were more like golden peacocks from three places,

And they were charming and beautiful in their own ways.

缅桂花般的南苏甘嫡,
她的皮肤像闪光的金子,
她说话柔声细气像蜂儿展翅,
听她说话像喝进蜜水一样惬意。

洛金花般的南苏米达,
她的皮肤像鲜嫩的洛桑花,
她的眼睛像宝石闪光,
比夜空的星星还明亮。

荷花般绚丽的南洁西,
她的皮肤白里透红,
她的脸庞像开放的睡莲那么红润,
她在三只金孔雀中最娇艳迷人。

成百名宫女簇拥着三个王后,
三个美丽的王后伴随着亲爱的丈夫,
国王关怀王后无微不至,
王后承欢陛下无忧无虑。

国王拥有无数的武器,
——镖、箭、刀、矛,
国王拥有无数的战具,
——骏马、大象和车辆。

国王还有飞鞋一双,
是天神叭英赐赏,
飞鞋光彩夺目闪闪发亮,
它神奇的威力不可估量。

第五章 勐沓达腊塔 Chapter 5 The Kingdom of Dadalata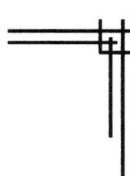

Magnolia-like Nan Sugandi,
Her skin was fair as shining gold.
She spoke in a soft voice like a bee spreading its wings.
Listening to her was as pleasant as drinking honey.

Luojin-flower-like Nan Sumida
Her skin was as tender as fresh Lausanne flower.
Her eyes sparkled like jewels,
Brighter than the stars in the night sky.

Nan Jiexi was as brilliant as a lotus flower.
With her delicate skin pink and white.
Her face looked like a blooming red lily.
She was the most charming of the three golden peacocks.

Hundreds of palace maids surrounded the three queens.
Accompanying their beloved husband,
The three queens are taken care of by the king in every way.
The majestic king and queens lived happily and carefree.

The king possessed countless weapons,
——Darts, arrows, knives and spears,
The king had innumerable equipment for war,
——Horses, elephants and chariots.

The king also had a pair of flying shoes.
Which were bestowed by God of Baying.
Flying shoes shone brilliantly,
whose magical power was immeasurable.

飞鞋只听从国王使唤，
国王经常穿起它到处游逛，
下能潜入海底龙国，
上能腾升云霄天堂。

召沓达腊塔和叭英交谊深厚，
他俩曾经喝下神圣的盟酒，
他俩经常相邀同游叙谈，
他俩经常商讨治国良方。

在一个阳光明媚的新年，
那是全民欢度的泼水节日，
和叭英素有宿仇的勐埃森龙王，
又兴兵作乱闯入天堂。

龙王率领成千上万的水兵水将，
抱着复仇决胜的信心，
团团围住了叭英居住的天宫，
叭英岂肯让龙王如此猖狂。

叭英骑上九牙宝象，
率领天兵天将出城迎敌，
叭英身先士卒冲在前，
无数水兵水将刀下命亡。

第五章 勐沓达腊塔　Chapter 5　The Kingdom of Dadalata

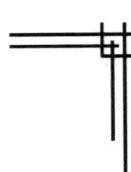

Flying shoes only obeyed the order of the king,
Who often wore them wandering around.
He could dive deep into the underwater Kingdom of Dragon;
He could also soar up to the heaven above the clouds.

Zhao Dadalata and God of Baying were close friends.
They once drank the sacred wine as a token of brotherhood.
They invited one another to get together for bosom talks,
And they often discussed the best way to govern a country.

On a sunny New Year Day,
All people were celebrating the Water-Splashing Festival.
An ages-long enemy of Baying, the Dragon King of Aisen
Once again stirred up his soldiers to break into the heaven.

Leading his tens of thousands of soldiers and generals,
With the confidence of his revenge victory, the Dragon King
Had the the heavenly palace of Baying surrounded seamlessly.
How could the God of Baying let the Dragon King be so rampant?

Baying mounted onto his cherished elephant of nine tusks,
Leading the heavenly armies out of the palace to meet the enemy.
Charging toward the enemies at the very front of his army,
Baying killed numerous soldiers of the Dragon King with his weapon.

155

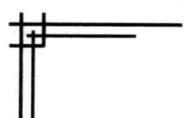

龙王巴拉麻毫不示弱,
怒吼一声迎了上来,
水兵水将蜂拥而上,
把叭英紧紧围在中央。

叭英高举手中神斧,
发出隆隆雷电轰击水兵水将,
龙王拿出怀中宝石,
射出能溶化雷电的耀眼红光。

雷电还击宝石发出巨响,
轰隆隆震撼了万里苍穹,
召沓达腊塔仰望长空猜想,
难道天庭又遭祸殃?

召沓达腊塔立即穿起飞鞋,
持刀直向天庭腾飞而上,
叭英见挚友前来助战,
喜出望外越战越强。

第五章 勐沓达腊塔　Chapter 5 The Kingdom of Dadalata

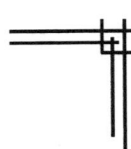

　　The Dragon King of Balama would not admit his defeat,
　　Growling angrily, he rushed forward and fought back.
　　Following him, his army flocked up,
　　And they swarmed around the God of Baying.

　　Baying raised his magic axe high sending off thunder and lightning,
　　Which struck the army of the Dragon King heavily.
　　The Dragon King took out from his chest his precious stone,
　　Which emitted brilliant red lights dispelling the thunder and lightning.

　　The thunder and lightning hit the gemstone making a deafening noise.
　　The crashing rumbling shook the heavens of thousands of miles.
　　Looking up into the sky, Zhao Dadalata was wondering,
　　Something terrible happening again to the kingdom of heaven?

　　Zhao Dadalata immediately put on his flying shoes.
　　Holding a knife, he flew straight up to heaven.
　　When Baying saw his best friend coming to help him fight,
　　He was so happy that he fought more and more bravely.

召沓达腊塔挥舞宝刀冲进战场，
和叭英并肩作战打击龙王，
龙王毫不畏敌愈战愈勇，
左右迎击斗志更旺。

龙王杀出包围跳上飞车，
勇猛地冲向天兵天将，
水兵水将紧紧跟随，
挥戈舞刀胡乱冲闯。

雷声隆隆、刀声当当，
电光闪闪、乌云乱翻，
天神、国王和龙王鏖战在一起，
天兵和水兵混战成一锅汤。

心狠手辣的龙王巴拉麻，
举刀砍向沓达腊塔国王，
眼明手快的国王连忙闪避，
不幸左手小指被龙王砍伤。

鲜血染红了召沓达腊塔的衣裳，
叭英见此情景奋力营救国王，
天兵天将一齐举起弓弩，
雨点般的神箭嗖嗖直响。

第五章 勐沓达腊塔　Chapter 5　The Kingdom of Dadalata

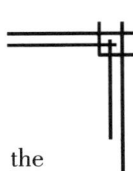

　　Brandishing his knife, Zhao Dadalata rushed into the battlefield,

　　He fought shoulder to shoulder with Baying against the Dragon King.

　　The Dragon King, not fearing his enemies, fought more courageously,

　　And he attacked left and right with a stronger will of fight.

　　Dragon King cut his way out and jumped onto his flying chariot,

　　And he charged toward Heavenly generals and soldiers of Baying,

　　His generals and soldiers following him closely,

　　Brandishing their weapons, they dashed and barged wildly.

　　The thunder rumbling and the knives clanging,

　　Lightning flashing and dark clouds tumbling,

　　Heavenly god, King and Dragon King fought fiercely,

　　Soldiers from heaven and from the sea were in a dogfight.

　　Balama, the ruthless and tough Dragon King,

　　Raised his knife and swung it at the King of Dadalata.

　　The agile King saw it and dodged quickly.

　　Unfortunately, the little finger of his left hand was wounded.

　　Blood stained the clothes of the King of Dadalata.

　　Seeing the scene, Baying came striving to rescue the king.

　　Heavenly soldiers lifted their bows and crossbows together,

　　The arrows swished down like raindrops.

水兵水将只顾招架箭矢，
叭英趁势带兵杀向敌阵，
整个水兵阵脚顿时大乱，
勇敢的国王也从侧翼扫荡。

龙王的队伍被摧垮，
勐埃森的水兵四散逃亡，
就像冲出堤坝的洪水，
龙王带着残兵败将逃回海洋。

在历时七个月的神龙战争之中，
召沓达腊塔英勇地援助了叭英，
天堂的和平与安全得到了保障，
龙王落得个彻底失败的下场。

叭英打了胜仗高兴万分，
把一把弓塔弩和三支宝箭送给国王，
为了保卫自身的安全，
国王随时把它们佩戴在身上。

召沓达腊塔凯旋回到王宫，
三个王后一一前来拜望，
国王向她们叙述了激战的经过，
最后又谈到了自己的受伤情况。

第五章　勐沓达腊塔　Chapter 5　The Kingdom of Dadalata

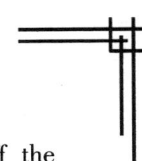

Soldiers from the sea could do nothing but ward off the arrows.

Baying took the chance to lead his troops to kill the enemies.

The troops of the Dragon King were at once in a state of turmoil.

The brave king also attacked their enemy from the flank.

The Dragon King's troops were destroyed.

Soldiers from the sea fled in all directions.

Like a flood breaking out of a dam,

The Dragon King fled back to the sea with his defeated army.

During the seven-month long war between god and Dragon,

The heroic Zhao Dadalata rescued heavenly God of Baying.

Then peace and security in heaven were restored,

And the Dragon King had been defeated completely.

Being so delighted to have won the battle,

Baying gave the king a magic crossbow and three precious arrows.

In order to safeguard his own security,

The king always took them with him.

Zhao Dadalata returned to the palace triumphantly.

The three queens came to visit him together.

The King recounted to them the fierce war.

Finally, he told them his own injury.

小王后听了连忙安慰国王:
"贤明的君王啊,
你的伤痛使我心疼,
但你不必为此忧伤。

"我在娘家时父母教会了口功,
刀伤和箭伤我都能疗理,
只要让我含着受伤的小指睡上几夜,
你的伤痛几天就会痊愈。"

国王每天晚上都在小王后房里睡觉,
南洁西把血淋淋的小指头含在嘴里,
三天后伤口就愈合结痂,
真是多亏小王后的精心护理。

善良的国王衷心感谢小王后说:
"南洁西呀,我心爱的娇妻,
是你解除了我身上的痛苦,
使我的伤口没有感染成疾。

"爱妻啊,要怎么感谢你呢,
你记住我的话吧,
如果你生下的儿子长大成人,
我就让他来把王位承袭。"

第五章 勐沓达腊塔 Chapter 5 The Kingdom of Dadalata

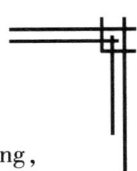

Hearing it, the youngest queen at once comforted the king,
"My wise king,
My heart aches for your pain,
But please don't get worried about it.

"When I was a child, my parents taught me oral curing skills.
I can treat both knife and arrow injuries.
Just let me mouth your injured finger for a few nights,
And it will be healed in a few days."

Every night the king slept in the little queen's room.
Nan Jiexi put his bloody little finger in her mouth.
Thanks to the careful attendance of the little queen.
Three days later, the wound was healed and scabby.

The kind king thanked the little queen heartily,
"Nan Jiexi, my beloved wife,
You relieved me of my pain,
Keeping my wound free from infection.

"My dear wife, how can I thank you?
Now remember my words:
If someday you give birth to a son,
I'll let him inherit the throne when he grows up."

小王后听了不知怎么感激,
合掌向夫王谢了又拜、拜了又谢,
衷心感谢国王的恩典,
并把这个秘密藏在心底。

二、求子

一天召沓达腊塔到森林去打猎,
想猎取马鹿和麂子,
他带着武将苏念达和沙腊梯,
背着弓塔弩走进了深山老林。

他们越过高山、穿过深箐,
来到莽莽苍苍的伊麻板森林,
他们恍惚见一只黄绒绒的麂子,
正在山下河边饮水。

国王举起神弓瞄准麂子射出一箭,
忽然河边传来了凄惨的哭喊声,
他们惊惶不安跑向河岸,
只见身穿袈裟的帕拉西在血泊中呻吟。

啊！原来是帕拉西到河边汲水,
召沓达腊塔把他误认为麂子射中,
国王俯身把他抱在怀里,
亲切地询问他的伤情:

第五章 勐沓达腊塔 Chapter 5 The Kingdom of Dadalata

Hearing his words, the little queen was truly grateful.
She bowed to him with folded palms again and again
To give her thanks for this great grace.
And she kept the secret deep in her heart.

Ⅱ Praying for a Son

One day, Zhao Dadalata went hunting in the forest,
He wanted to prey red deer and muntjac.
His generals Sunianda and Shalati followed him,
Carrying the crossbow and arrows into the deep mountain forest.

Having climbed over high mountains and waded through deep waters,
They finally reached the thick primitive forest of Yimaban.
They saw dimly a yellow muntjac,
Drinking by the river at the foot of the hill.

Raising his bow, the king shot an arrow at the muntjack.
Suddenly they heard a sad cry from the riverside.
They ran to the river bank in panic,
Only to see Palaxi in monk robe moaning in the blood.

Oh! It was Palaxi who went to the riverside to draw water.
And Zhao Dadalata mistook him for a muntjac and shot.
Bending over and holding Palaxi in his arms,
The king amiably asked about his wounds,

"福星高照的帕拉西啊,
你的伤势怎么样?
怪我有眼不识贵体,
用利箭伤害了你。"

遭受重伤的帕拉西啊,
胸口激烈地起伏,
他强忍着浑身剧烈的疼痛,
艰难地发出微弱的声音:

"三位高贵的猎人啊,
我是在森林修行的人,
我和你们无冤无仇,
你们为何这样残忍?

"人们射杀大象,
是需要它的一对牙齿,
人们射杀虎豹,
是需要它们的骨肉和毛皮。

"我身卑体贱不值分文,
你们为何把我射杀,
我从来没有得罪过你们,
你们竟如此丧尽良心!

"看来我是活不成了,
死神在叫我离开人世,
射杀我的人也会得到报应,
天神一定会惩罚他不得好死。"

第五章 勐沓达腊塔 Chapter 5 The Kingdom of Dadalata

"Much-blessed Palaxi,
What's the condition of your wound?
I was to blame for not having seen it were you,
And having hurt you with my sharp arrows."

Palaxi had been badly injured,
And his chest fluctuated violently.
Enduring severe pain all over his body,
He said in difficulty with a weak voice,

"Three noble hunters,
I am just a man practicing Buddhism in the forest.
I have done nothing wrong to you.
Why are you so cruel to hurt me?

"People shoot an elephant
For the pair of its tusks.
People shoot tigers and leopards
For their flesh, bones and fur.

"My body is worth nothing.
Why did you shoot me?
I have never offended you.
You are so heartless!

"It seems that I will not survive.
God of death is calling me to leave the world.
The man who shot me will pay their price,
And heavenly god will punish him with a terrible death."

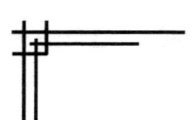

兰噶西贺 The Ten-Headed King of Langa

一阵不安涌上国王心头，
帕拉西的诅咒使他全身颤抖，
他怀着十分内疚的心情，
用谦卑的声音开了口：

"我是沓达腊塔的国王，
今天打猎来到森林，
我们把你误认为麂子射击，
只恨我们的眼睛没有看清。

"我是无心做了错事，
我要忏悔我的罪孽，
我们一定把你的箭伤医好，
恳请你以仁慈的胸襟把我宽容。"

国王勇于承认过错的美好品德，
深深感动了受伤的帕拉西，
他收回了刚才的诅咒，
紧紧拉着国王的手说：

"善良的国王陛下啊，
现在我的创伤已疼遍全身，
你们赶快把我抬回巴朗，
不然我会死在这荒山野林。"

国王一行抬着帕拉西回至巴朗，
采来治疗箭伤的草药给他敷上，
每天像奴仆一样尽心地护理换药，
不几天就治好了帕拉西的箭伤。

第五章　勐沓达腊塔　Chapter 5　The Kingdom of Dadalata

An uneasiness surged into the king's heart,
For Palaxi's curse made him shudder.
With a great sense of guilt,
He opened his mouth and spoke humbly,

"I am the King of Dadalata.
Today I came to the forest to hunt.
We mistook you for a muntjack,
We hated ourselves for not having seen clearly.

"I have done the wrong unintentionally,
And I am confessing to you my sins.
We will make sure to cure your arrow wounds,
And we plead you to forgive us with magnanimity."

The wounded Palaxi was touched deeply
By the king's courage to admit his own mistake.
And he took back his curse.
Holding the king's hand tightly, he said,

"My kind-hearted King,
Now the pains are all over my body.
Take me back to Balang as soon as you can,
Or I'll die in the wilderness."

The king and his party carried Palaxi back to Balang,
And they gathered herbs to treat his arrow wounds.
Every day, they took care of him like his servants,
And Palaxi's arrow wound was cured in a few days.

帕拉西很感激国王的精心护理，
他问国王有什么事需要帮忙，
召沓达腊塔急忙下拜，
请求帕拉西恩赐个孩子。

"尊敬的帕拉西啊，
我孤孤独独无儿无女，
祈求高贵的帕拉西开恩指点，
怎么才能生育金笋般的孩子。"

帕拉西和蔼地对国王说：
"我了解你求子的心情，
为了解除你的孤独与忧闷，
我赐给你两个香蕉带回宫去。

"这金子一样黄的香蕉，
沁人肺腑、芳香扑鼻，
你让王后吃进肚里，
就会生育金笋般的孩子。"

国王感激不尽地合掌叩首，
收下香蕉放进筒帕①。
他告别帕拉西，
三个人高高兴兴往回走。

---

① 筒帕：傣族男女自织的背在身上的彩色挎包。

第五章 勐沓达腊塔　Chapter 5　The Kingdom of Dadalata

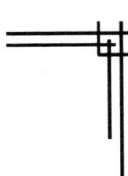

Palaxi was grateful to the king for his attentive care.
He asked the king what he could do for him.
Zhao Dadalata bowed down immediately,
And asked Palaxi to bless him with a child.

"Dear and respected Palaxi,
I still have no child in this world.
Pray to your honorable Palaxi for some advice,
How can I have children like golden bamboo shoots?"

Palaxi said kindly to the king,
"I understand your desire for a child.
To relieve your loneliness and depression,
I give you two bananas to take back to the palace.

"The bananas have the color of gold,
They are refreshing and fragrant.
Give them to your queens to eat,
They will have babies like golden bamboo shoots."

The king bowed with folded palms and endless gratitude.
He took the bananas and put them in his Tongpa①
After saying goodbye to Palaxi.
They three were on their way back home happily.

---

① Tongpa: a kind of hand-made colorful satchel of the Dai people.

途中国王摸着筒帕里的香蕉发愁：
"我有三个不能厚此薄彼的王后，
帕拉西只给了我两个香蕉，
不给哪个王后吃都没有理由。"

国王征询苏念达和沙腊梯的意见说：
"你们给我出个计谋，
我的三个王后要分吃两个香蕉，
怎样分配才不致引起烦忧？"

"依我们心想要公平合理分配，
最好是一个香蕉给大王后，
另外一个香蕉撇为两半，
一半给二王后，一半给三王后。"

国王嘴里夸赞这个主意，
可他心里还是在犯愁：
"三王后一向对我很好，
不给她一个香蕉她会很不好受。

"给她一个又不合大王后的心，
只给大王后和三王后吃，
二王后吃不到也会不高兴，
这件事真使我伤透了脑筋。

第五章 勐沓达腊塔　Chapter 5 The Kingdom of Dadalata

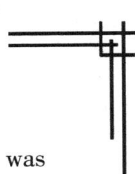

On halfway, the king felt the banana in his Tongpa and was worried,

"I have three queens and I could not favor one while mistreat others.

Respected Palaxi gave me only two bananas,

There is no reason for denying any one of them the banana."

The king consulted Sunianda and Shalati,

"You had better figure it out,

How I can distribute the two bananas

Among my three queens without recurring any trouble?"

"To make it a fair and reasonable distribution,

We'd better give a banana to the first queen,

And the other banana is cut into halves,

One half to the second queen and one to the third."

The king said that it was a good idea,

But he was still troubled in his heart,

"The little queen is always very kind to me.

She would feel bad if I would not give her one banana.

"If I give the third queen one, the first queen will not be happy.

Then if I give the two bananas to the first and third queen,

The second one would be unhappy since she has nothing to eat.

It was really a dilemma that gave me a great headache.

"两个香蕉三个人吃怎能均分,
要做到三个王后都满意怎么可能,
只好给大王后和三王后一人一个,
任随她们怎么分吃都行。"

三、朗玛降生

召沓达腊塔回到宫廷,
换下打猎服装来到内宫,
请来了三个王后坐定,
把打猎求子的事说给她们听。

国王一边与王后亲密地交谈,
一边把香蕉递了过去,
一个给了温顺的大王后南苏甘嫡,
一个给了美丽的小王后南洁西。

两位王后见香蕉只有两个,
二王后南苏米达没有份,
她们怕二王后心中难过,
一人撇了一半放在她手心。

三位王后一齐吃下香蕉,
感到周身舒畅甜蜜,
不久个个都怀了孕,
她们为有后嗣欢天喜地。

第五章 勐查达腊塔 Chapter 5 The Kingdom of Dadalata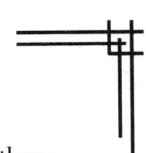

"How can two bananas be equally divided among three persons?

And how can it be possible to satisfy all three queens?
Maybe I just give the first and third queen each one,
And they can decide how to divide and eat them."

III The Birth of Langma

Zhao Dadalata was now back to the palace.
After changing his hunting clothes, he came to the inner palace.
Three queens were invited to sit down with him,
And he told them about hunting and getting blessed for children.

While talking to the queens intimately,
The king handed the bananas to the queens.
One to the gentle Queen Nan Sugandi,
And the other to the beautiful Queen Nan Jiexi.

The two queens saw there were only two bananas,
And no share for the Queen Nan Sumida,
They were afraid she would feel sad in her heart,
Then each of them shared with her half of their banana.

The three queens ate the bananas together,
And they felt a sensuous delight through their body.
Very soon each one of them was pregnant,
And they rejoiced in having their heirs to come.

三位王后得到宫女的精心护理,
护理的宫女一天要轮换几次,
天冷了给她们加衣服,
天热了给她们扇扇子。

三位王后怀孕十个月,
先后都生了金笋般的儿子,
召沓达腊塔几天来更加和气,
大臣们都来向他贺喜。

先分娩的是大王后南苏甘嫡,
生下的王子像闪闪发光的宝石,
身上均匀分布着三十二种颜色,
比天上的彩虹还要绚丽。

王子打扮起来就像一只金孔雀,
给宫廷增添了无限乐趣,
他的美丽又如十五的月亮,
谁见了都会啧啧称赞不已。

十几个奶妈轮流喂奶,
宫女们随时抱在怀里,
每天给他洗两次澡,
每天为他赕一次佛。

第五章 勐沓达腊塔 Chapter 5 The Kingdom of Dadalata

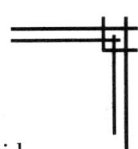

The three queens were carefully nursed by the palace maids,
Who had to rotate several times a day.
When it's cold, they served them with more clothes,
When it's hot, they fanned to cool them.

After being pregnant for ten months,
The three queens gave birth to sons like golden bamboo shoots.
Zhao Dadalata was more friendly than ever in those days.
The ministers came to congratulate him for the birth of his sons.

The first to give birth was the Queen Nan Sugandi,
Who delivered a prince like a sparkling gem.
His body was covered evenly by thirty-two colors,
which was more gorgeous than the rainbow in the sky.

The Prince was dressed up like a golden peacock,
And he brought infinite pleasure to the court.
He was as handsome as the full moon of the fifteenth,
Whoever saw him would be amazed at his beauty.

More than a dozen nannies took turns to feed him,
And the maids always held him in their arms.
They bathed him twice a day;
They worshiped Buddha everyday praying for him.

漂亮的王子长到满月,
洁净的身子像珍珠,
请来智慧老人帕麻纳,
为他取一个高尚的名字。

王子的属相不同凡俗,
王子的生辰正逢吉时,
王子将有崇高的名声和威望,
帕麻纳给他取名召朗玛。

二王后生的是双胞胎,
帕麻纳推算孩子的前程,
一个取名腊嘎纳,
一个取名沙达鲁嘎。

小王后南洁西生的儿子,
像熔化的金子一样光彩,
红润的脸庞像开放的荷花,
帕麻纳给他取名帕腊达。

召沓达腊塔有了四个王子,
就像大地上升起了四颗明星,
四个王子是国王的骄傲,
四个王子的出世提高了王国的声誉。

四个王子好像四棵大树,
四个王子犹如四头大象,
四个王子如同四根挺立的中柱,
支撑着王国威严的宫廷。

第五章 勐沓达腊塔 Chapter 5 The Kingdom of Dadalata

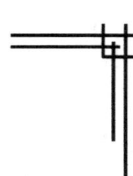

When the handsome prince was one month old,
He has a body as pure as a pearl.
The wise old man Pamana was invited
To give the prince a noble name.

The prince had an extraordinary zodiac.
And he was born at an auspicious time.
The prince would have a high reputation and prestige,
Therefore Pamana gave him the name of Zhao Langma.

The Second Queen gave birth to twins.
After divining their futures, Pamana named them.
One was called Lagana.
The other is called Shadaluga.

Another son was delivered by the little Queen of Nan Jiexi.
He was as bright as molten gold;
His ruddy face was like a blooming lotus flower,
And Pamana named him Palada.

So Zhao Dadalata had four princes,
Who were Like four stars rising from the earth.
The four princes were the pride of the king,
And their birth enhanced the reputation of kingdom.

The four princes were like four big trees;
The four princes were like four strong elephants;
The four princes were like four upright pillars,
which supported the magnificent court of the kingdom.

四个王子降生的喜讯被大风吹向远方,
前来祝贺的人像蝴蝶纷纷飞进宫殿,
前来送礼的使者络绎不绝,
王宫像赶摆一样热闹非凡。

四个王子在国王的膝前,
沐浴着父王母后的洪恩,
四个王子在国王的金伞下,
享受着父王母后的福荫。

四个王子一天天长大成人,
勐沓达腊塔的声望与日俱增,
一百零一勐都来朝拜上贡,
百姓们生活得安康又欢欣。

四、制服大乌鸦

在莽莽的伊麻板森林,
有个修行的帕拉西,
他孤身一人住在巴朗房里,
每天晚上盘腿打坐修身养性。

一年一月飞快地闪过,
帕拉西将要成佛,
每天在他居住的巴朗房里,
都供着菠萝、香瓜和野果……

第五章 勐沓达腊塔 Chapter 5 The Kingdom of Dadalata

　　The news of the four princes was spread everywhere by wind,
And the congratulatory people flocked into the palace like butterflies.
Messengers coming to give gifts were like an endless stream,
And the royal palace was hustling and bustling as a market fair.

　　The four princes grew at the king's knees,
Bathed in the grace of their father king, and mother queens.
The four princes were under the king's golden umbrella,
Enjoying the blessing shade of their dear father and mothers.

　　As the four princes grew up day by day,
The Kingdom of Dadalata gained increasing reputation.
One hundred and one nations came to pay tribute,
And its people lived in peace, health and joy.

Ⅳ　Taming Ravens

　　In the thick primitive forest of Yimaban,
There was a Buddhism-practising Palaxi.
He lived alone in his Balang. Every night,
He would sit with leg crossed practising meditation.

　　Time flew by months and years,
And Palaxi was about to become a Buddha.
Every day in the Balang where he lived,
There were offerings of pineapples, melons and wild fruits.

有一群体大如马的乌鸦，
觅食来到伊麻板森林，
凶恶的乌鸦"呱呱"叫着，
趁帕拉西外出，飞进屋里吃供品。

馋嘴的乌鸦在屋里乱啄乱抓，
成千的乌鸦在屋里出出进进，
每次都把巴朗践踏得乱七八糟，
每次都把供品啄吃得干干净净。

巴朗房遍地是乌鸦的毛和屎，
仁慈的帕拉西也生了气，
他诅咒嘴馋可恶的黑老鸹，
决定寻一个有本事的人来将它们驱赶。

天神昭示他召朗玛有此本事，
他便驾着祥云来到勐沓达腊塔，
进到王宫向召沓达腊塔请求，
让召朗玛去协助他赶走乌鸦。

召沓达腊塔听后有些为难，
他不想让眼珠般的朗玛离开身边，
"福气高照的帕拉西呀，
请原谅我不能让朗玛随你前去。

"我儿子年纪还小武艺不高，
恐难赶得走那些凶恶的乌鸦，
还是让我跟你去吧，
我保证把它们赶跑。"

第五章 勐杳达腊塔 Chapter 5 The Kingdom of Dadalata

A group of horse-sized crows,
They came to the forest of Yimaban for food.
The vicious crows croaked all the time. When Palaxi was out,
They would fly into the house to eat his offerings.

The gluttonous crows pecked everywhere;
Thousands of them went in and out of the house.
Every time they disturbed the Balang into a mess,
And every time they pecked and ate up the offerings.

The Balang house was full of raven's fur and shit,
And the benevolent Palaxi became really angry.
He cursed the old wicked and greedy crows,
Deciding to find a capable man to drive them away.

The heavenly god revealed to him Zhao Langma was the one,
So he flew to the Kingdom of Dadalata on colorful clouds.
He went to the palace to ask for the favor from Zhao Dadalata
To let Zhao Langma to help him drive away the crows.

Hearing this, Zhao Dadalata was in a dilemma,
He did not want his most dear Longma to leave him.
"Much-blessed Palaxi, please forgive me
I could not let Langma go with you.

"My son is too young to be a capable warrior,
I'm afraid he can't drive away those vicious crows.
Please let me go with you.
I promise I would drive all of them away."

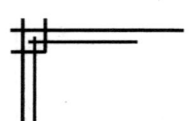

兰噶西贺 The Ten-Headed King of Langa

帕拉西怏怏不乐地走了,
一边走一边不高兴地摇头:
"既然你不愿意让召朗玛去,
我也不愿意你同我走。"

召沓达腊塔转念一想:
"帕拉西有困难应该相帮,
正如自己遇到不幸的事情,
大臣百姓也都为我操心奔忙。

"他找上门来求我帮助,
我竟一口回绝太不应当,
得罪了有福气的帕拉西,
往后会不会给儿子带来祸殃?"

他急忙命令侍从追回帕拉西,
乞请帕拉西把召朗玛带去,
他把宝贵的儿子叫来吩咐,
召朗玛高兴地立即做好准备。

戴上金光闪闪的王冠,
挎上威力无敌的弓塔弩,
带上三支锋利的宝箭,
神采奕奕来到帕拉西面前。

帕拉西马上转忧为喜,
带着召朗玛回到伊麻板森林,
他交代只能用箭声把乌鸦吓跑,
千万不要伤害它们的生命。

第五章 勐沓达腊塔　Chapter 5　The Kingdom of Dadalata

Palaxi walked away in a low mood,
Shaking his head unhappily as he walked.
"Since you don't want Zhao Langma to go,
I don't want you to go with me either."

Zhao Dadalata thought to himself afterward,
"I should help Palaxi when he is in trouble,
Just as my ministers and people do me the favors
When I encounter misfortunes.

"He came to my door asking for help,
It was too wrong for me to refuse him.
Will the offence against the blessed Palaxi
Bring disasters to my sons in the future?"

He urgently ordered his attendants to call Palaxi back,
He pleaded Palaxi to take Zhao Langma with him.
He sent for his precious son telling him to get ready,
Zhao Langma made the preparation immediately and happily.

Putting on a golden crown,
With the invincible crossbow on his back
And also three sharp arrows,
Zhao Langma came to Palaxi energetically.

The sad Palaxi at once became happy,
He took Zhao Langma with him and returned to the forest.
He asked him just to scare the crows away
By the sound of arrows and never to hurt their lives.

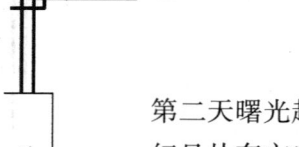

第二天曙光赶走了黑夜,
红日从东方冉冉升起,
帕拉西留下召朗玛一人看屋,
腾云驾雾向远方飞去。

乌鸦看见帕拉西出门就蜂拥飞来,
麇集在巴朗里外乱啄乱扒,
它们"呱呱"叫个不停,
没有发现躲着的召朗玛。

召朗玛拉动弓弦搭上箭,
射向遮天蔽日的鸦群,
箭声像千钧霹雳震撼大地,
吓得乌鸦纷纷逃遁。

箭声震得伊麻板山摇欲沉,
群鸦昏头涨脑飞向蓝天白云,
神箭像长着锐利的眼睛,
盯住鸦群旋转不停。

乌鸦在云层无处藏身,
丧魂落魄地钻进森林,
它们在林间拼命逃窜,
神箭也紧追不舍穿梭飞行。

惊惶的乌鸦眼见无法逃生,
只得飞下来"呱呱"地哀求饶命,
"有福气的高贵的召啊,
请动动你的恻隐之心。

第五章 勐沓达腊塔 Chapter 5 The Kingdom of Dadalata

The next day when the dawn drove away the night,
And the red sun rose steadily from the east,
Palaxi left Zhao Langma alone to guard the house
While he flew away by mist and clouds.

When the crows saw Palaxi go out,
They flocked to the house and pecked inside and outside.
They kept croaking all the time,
And did not notice the hidden Zhao Langma.

Zhao Langma drew his bow and got his arrows ready,
Then he shot them at the crows covering the sun and the sky.
The sound of arrows shook the earth like a thunderbolt,
The crows were so frightened that they began to flee.

The sound of arrows shook the mountain of Yimaban to sink,
And the crows grew dizzy and flew to the blue sky and white clouds.
The arrows were like having sharp eyes,
They kept following and swirling around the crows.

The crow could not hide in the clouds of the sky,
Losing their minds they went back into the forest.
They fled desperately in the woods,
But the arrows kept flying after them.

The frightened crows saw there would be no way to escape,
They could not do anything but fly down and beg for mercy.
"Blessed and noble Zhao,
Please have mercy and show us your compassion.

"千错万错只怪我们的嘴馋,
从今以后我们不敢再犯,
请你饶恕我们收回神箭,
我们将来一定报答你的恩典。"

召朗玛见乌鸦忏悔认错,
随即把神箭收回保存,
规劝它们别再侵扰别人,
同时赦免了它们的罪行。

众乌鸦感激不尽,
感谢他的宽宏和怜悯,
它们一齐扇开双翅向召朗玛下拜,
然后成群地飞回它们居住的森林。

黄昏时帕拉西从天空降临,
召朗玛把降服乌鸦的经过说给他听,
帕拉西连连夸赞召朗玛,
让他留下来传授给他技艺。

召朗玛在帕拉西身边虔诚修行,
学到了渊博的知识和高超的本领,
他在森林一住就是三年整,
成为一个精通武艺的年轻人。

第五章 勐沓达腊塔 Chapter 5 The Kingdom of Dadalata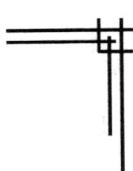

"It's all our faults to be so greedy.
We dare not do it again from now on.
Please forgive us and take back your magic arrows.
We are sure to repay you for your grace in the future."

When Zhao Langma saw the crows repent and confess their sins,
He immediately took back the arrows and kept them well.
He told them not to disturb others any more,
And he pardoned the crimes they had committed.

The crows were truly grateful
For his generosity and compassion.
Flapping their wings they bowed to Zhao Langma,
Then they flew back to the forest where they lived.

At dusk, Palaxi came down from the sky.
Zhao Langma told him the story of having the crows surrender.
Palaxi praised him again and again, and then,
He asked him to stay so he could teach him his skills.

Zhao Langma practiced what Palaxi taught devotedly.
He acquired profound knowledge and superb skills.
After living in the forest for three years,
He became a young man expert in martial arts.

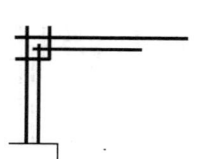

第六章 择婿

一、南西拉重生

伊麻板的纳里本花树当年被火烧化,
春天来临它又破土发芽,
被火化的南西拉也死而复活,
在纳里本花树里长大。

花树慢慢舒展手臂似的枝丫,
花树慢慢睁开亮晶晶的眼睛,
花树的树干越长越像姑娘的身躯,
纯洁的南西拉得到重生。

纳里本花树越长越健美,
忽然变成了漂亮的南西拉,
守候的山神地鬼见神女重现,
立即把她抓住报告召捧玛加。

第六章 择婿 Chapter 6 Choosing a Son-in-law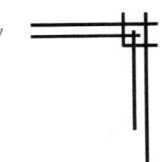

Chapter 6　Choosing a Son-in-law

I　The Rebirth of Nan Xila

The tree of Naliben in Yimaban had been burned into ashes.
But it sprouted again when the spring came.
The cremated Nan Xila also resurrected from death,
And she grew up in the flower tree of Naliben.

The flower tree slowly stretched its arms-like branches,
And the flower tree slowly opened its shining eyes.
Its trunk grew more like the body of a girl,
And Nan Xila with a pure heart came to life again.

The Naliben tree grew more healthy and beautiful.
Suddenly, it transformed into the pretty Nan Xila.
The god of mountain and the ghost of earth saw the goddess reappear,
They caught her immediately and reported it to Zhao Pengmajia.

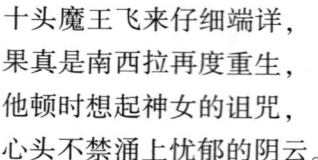

十头魔王飞来仔细端详,
果真是南西拉再度重生,
他顿时想起神女的诅咒,
心头不禁涌上忧郁的阴云。

"她诅咒要让我得到报应,
通过报应来毁灭我的一生,
我绝不能让她的诅咒实现,
得赶快结束她的生命。"

召捧玛加就和老臣西纳告商量,
西纳告认为这样做万万不行,说:
"尊贵的国王啊,
我们不能随便定罪杀人。

"对待普天下懦弱的妇女,
不能用刀箭伤害她们的生命,
对待珍珠般尊贵的神女,
处死她更失掉了道德的准绳。

"比较合乎道德的办法啊,
最好是让她睡在金棺材里,
放到江水中任它随波逐流,
要是她没有福气就让江水淹死。"

心神不定的召捧玛加听了,
立即命令赶做金粉涂的棺材,
十头魔王的命令谁敢不听,
金棺材很快就做好抬来。

第六章 择婿 Chapter 6 Choosing a Son-in-law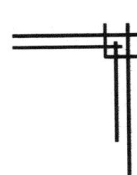

The ten-headed demon king flew to have a close look,
And it was true that Nan Xila came to life again.
The curse of the goddess occurred to him suddenly,
And his heart was shrouded with gloomy clouds.

"She had cursed me to pay for what I have done,
My life will be ruined by the retribution.
I must by no means let her curse come true,
So I should end her life as quickly as I could.

Zhao Pengmajia consulted it with his senior Minister Xinagao,
Who told the king it was the last thing that they should do.
"Your Majestic King,
We can't convict and kill people arbitrarily.

"As to the cowardly women of the whole world,
We should not hurt their lives with knives and arrows;
As to the goddess as noble as a pearl,
To execute her means the loss of the moral principles.

"It would be more appropriate ethically
To let her sleep in a golden coffin,
Which would be put into the river and drift with the waves.
She would be drown to death if she was not blessed."

Hearing this, Zhao Pengmajia with a disturbed mind
Immediately ordered to have a gold-painted coffin made.
Who dare disobey the orders of the ten-headed demon king?
Very soon the gold coffin was finished and brought to him.

刚刚复活的南西拉又面临死亡,
她被装进棺材丢进波涛翻滚的大江,
棺材就像树叶一样顺水漂荡,
七天七夜后漂到勐甘纳嘎的国土上。

再说年迈的勐甘纳嘎国王,
品德比山泉还清亮,
心地比金子还纯净,
他在全勐百姓中享有崇高的威望。

善良的国王和王后啊,
身边无儿又无女,
夫妻到处祷告求神拜佛,
多么想膝下有个后继。

他按照帕拉西旨意在江边赶摆,
这天人来人往盛况空前,
有的在江边撒网捕鱼,
有的在江里赛龙舟划船。

人们突然发现江上漂来一口棺材,
闪闪发出耀眼的光彩,
老国王命令把棺材捞起,
里面安详地睡着一个小女孩。

第六章 择婿　Chapter 6 Choosing a Son-in-law

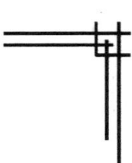

The newly-resurrected Nan Xila was facing death again.
She was put into the coffin and thrown into the rolling river.
The coffin drifted along the water like a leaf.
Seven days and nights later, it came to the Kingdom of Ganaga.

Now, let's us come to the aged King of Ganaga.
He had a character clearer than a mountain spring;
And he has a heart purer than gold.
He enjoyed high prestige among all his people.

The benevolent king and queen,
They have no children by their side.
The husband and wife went everywhere praying to Buddha,
How they wished to have a successor by their sides.

Following the advice of Palaxi, the king came to the fair by the river.
It was unprecedentedly grandiose with people coming and going.
Some were spreading their nets to catch fish at the riverside;
Some other were having a race of dragon boats on the river.

Suddenly people saw a coffin floating on the river,
It was sparkling and glittering brilliantly.
The old king ordered to have the coffin pulled ashore.
And they found a little girl sleeping peacefully in it.

摸摸心口小女孩并没有死,
只是紧紧闭着眼睛酣睡,
她的容貌就像下凡的仙女,
犹如一颗明珠放在金盒里。

国王和王后看见高兴万分,
轻轻把她抱起来吻了又吻,
收她做自己的女儿,
给孩子以父王母后的温存。

时间如行云流水过去,
转瞬公主已经十六岁,
她像湖水里的睡莲,
迎着雨露阳光越开越美。

光彩夺目的南西拉啊,
就像彩绸搭在栏杆上,
白天皮肤犹如彩虹,
夜晚皮肤宛似月亮。

丰润皎洁的南西拉,
头发不梳也像青苔一样光滑,
她不打扮也像花朵一样鲜艳,
哪个小伙子见了都眼花缭乱。

第六章 择婿 Chapter 6 Choosing a Son-in-law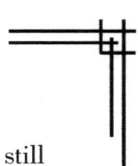

Someone feeling the heartbeat of the girl found her still alive,
She was just in a sound sleep with her eyes closed.
She was so beautiful as a fairy who came down to the earth.
And she was also like a pearl lying in a golden box.

The king and queen were overjoyed to see her.
They gently picked her up and kissed her again and again.
They adopted her as their daughter,
And gave her all the love of a father and a mother.

Time flew like floating clouds and flowing streams.
In a blink of eyes, the princess was sixteen years old.
Like a water lily in the lake, embracing the sunshine, rain and dew,
She was growing and blooming more and more beautiful.

Oh, Glorious Nan Xila,
Like colorful silk on the railings,
Her skin in the day was like a rainbow,
And at night it was like the moon.

Fair-and-soft-skinned Nan Xila,
Her hair was as smooth as moss even without combing,
And she was as bright as flowers even without dressing up.
Every young man would be dazzled when he saw her.

青春焕发的南西拉，
生就黄蜂般的苗条细腰，
长成孔雀般的柔软身材，
哪个小伙子见了都神魂颠倒。

南西拉的眼睛，
宛如两颗闪光明亮的黑色珍珠，
南西拉的嘴唇，
就像两片红彤彤的花瓣不厚不薄。

在南西拉的天姿国色面前，
阳光会失去光彩，
灯光会显得暗淡，
小伙子会呆痴痴忘记走开。

有福气的国王和王后啊，
疼爱自己的女儿就像自己的眼珠，
看到女儿已经长大成人，
特意盖了一幢漂亮的塔楼让她居住。

国王还怕女儿寂寞孤独，
把三个弟弟的三个女儿接来与她同住，
三个侄女像三朵鲜花，
终日陪伴着美丽的南西拉。

第六章 择婿 Chapter 6 Choosing a Son-in-law

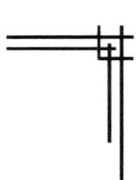

Young and energetic Nan Xila,
She had a waist as slim as that of a wasp,
And she had a figure as soft as that of a peacock.
Every young man was fascinated when he saw her.

The eyes of Nan Xila,
They are like two bright black pearls;
The lips of Nan Xila,
They are like two red petals neither thick nor thin.

Compared with the beauty of Nan Xila,
The sunshine lost its luster
And its lights seemed dim.
A young man would be bewitched by her forgetting to leave.

The blessed king and queen,
They loved their daughter like their own eyes.
When they saw their grown-up daughter,
They specially had a beautiful tower built for her to live in.

The king was afraid his daughter would feel lonely,
So he invited the three daughters of his three brothers to live with her.
The three nieces are like three flowers,
Accompanying the beautiful Nan Xila all day long.

南西拉的三个妹妹啊，
一个叫南娟达，
一个叫南吉达，
一个叫南谢玛。

她们长得像浪花一样闪光，
她们像小蜂一样热情，
她们像蝴蝶一样小心，
终日陪伴着高贵的南西拉。

四个公主和睦相处，
就像四个亲姐妹，
就像月亮和星星不分离，
就像连在一起的四颗珍珠。

二、求婚

南西拉美丽得像金孔雀，
她的美名四方传扬，
大陆上远近各勐不用说，
隔海的各勐王子也慕名向往。

是狮子才进得了虎穴，
是金山才留得住凤凰，
远近一百零一勐的王子啊，
想当狮子和凤凰。

第六章 择婿 Chapter 6 Choosing a Son-in-law

The three sisters of Nan Xila,
One is named Nan Juanda,
One is named Nan Jida
One is named Nan Xiema.

They grew as bright as waves;
They were as passionate as wasps;
They were as careful as butterflies.
All day long they accompanied the noble Nan Xila.

The four princesses got along well with each other,
They are like four sisters of one family.
They could not be separated as the moon and stars;
They were as close as four pearls threaded together.

II Marriage Proposal

Nan Xila was as beautiful as a golden peacock.
Her reputation had been spread to every corner of the world,
To the neighboring countries and the island across the sea,
Princes of each country yearned for her favor.

Only lion dares to break into the tiger's den,
And only the golden mountain can keep the phoenix.
The one hundred and one princes near and far,
They wanted to be the lion and the golden phoenix.

一百零一勐的王子啊,
用大象驮着珍贵的礼品,
骑着骏马和大象赶来,
向美丽的南西拉求婚。

一百零一勐的王子啊,
头戴塔形金帽,
身穿金瓣镶边的衣裳,
金片银片闪闪发光。

一百零一勐的王子啊,
个个腰间带着长刀,
人人肩上挎着弓箭,
显得威武、英俊和自豪。

一百零一勐的王子啊,
从四面八方纷纷驾临,
像一百零一只金凤凰飞来,
给勐甘纳嘎增添了光彩。

一百零一勐的王子啊,
在王宫前面的广场安顿好,
搭起一百零一个花毯帐篷,
帐篷里荡漾着欢乐的歌声。

一百零一双眼睛啊,
紧紧盯着王宫进出的大臣,
一百零一颗心啊,
思恋着南西拉跳个不停。

第六章 择婿　Chapter 6 Choosing a Son-in-law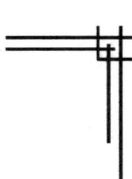

The one hundred and one princes,
With precious gifts loaded on the back of elephants,
Riding horses or elephants,
They came to propose to the beautiful Nan Xila.

The one hundred and one princes,
Wearing their golden tower-shaped caps,
Dressed in their gold-trimmed clothes,
They were shining like gold and silver.

The one hundred and one princes,
With long knives at their waists
And bows and arrows on their shoulders,
They looked mighty, handsome and confident.

The one hundred and one princes,
Coming from all directions,
Like one hundred and one golden phoenixes,
They added splendor to the Kingdom of Gannaga.

The one hundred and one princes,
They settled on the square in front of the palace.
One hundred and one tapestry tents were set up,
Which were filled with happy songs.

Their one hundred and one pairs of eyes
Followed the ministers coming in and out of the palace.
Their one hundred and one hearts
Throbbed excitedly all the time for missing Nan Xila.

各勐王子准备聘礼忙得不可开交，
看到别勐的聘礼比自己的珍贵，
他们又派人回去拿，
一心要使自己的聘礼比别人的更多更美。

勐甘纳嘎天天像赶摆一样，
从早到晚都很热闹，
各勐求婚的人本来就很多，
看热闹的人更是如海如潮。

大臣头人的姑娘花枝招展，
穿来挤去招蜂惹蝶，
可王子们哪有心思去搭理，
他们心目中只有南西拉一个美人儿。

在一个吉祥灿烂的黎明，
各勐王子像湖水般涌进宫廷，
送来的聘礼一个比一个贵重，
呈上一封比一封友好甜蜜的书信。

各勐都想和勐甘纳嘎联姻，
各勐王子都想和公主拴线，
这么多王子应该许给谁？
忧愁代替了国王的高兴。

第六章 择婿 Chapter 6 Choosing a Son-in-law

The princes busied themselves preparing the bride price.
When seeing the gifts of others were more precious than theirs,
They would send someone back home to get more,
For they are determined to offer the most precious bride price.

The Kingdom of Ganaga was now like a market fair.
It was busy and boisterous from morning till night.
There had already been a lot of people who came to propose,
And more people came like waves to watch the great scene.

The daughters of head minister dressed themselves up,
Loitering among the throngs to attract bees and butterflies.
But the princes had no time or mood flirting with them.
The only girl who occupied their mind was the beautiful Nan Xila.

On an auspicious and brilliant dawn,
The princes of all nations poured into the court like tides.
Their bride prices were getting more and more precious;
Their love letters were full of friendly and sweet words.

Every kingdom wanted to be allied to Ganaga by marriage.
Every prince desired to be tied to the Princess of Nan Xila.
Proposals from so many princes, which one should be accepted?
Such a dilemma turned the king's joy into sorrow.

205

金笋般的女儿只有一个，
不能像笋子可以切成一百零一节，
一百零一勐都很强大，
处理不当就会结下冤家。

国王急得左右为难，
心头就像一团无头的乱麻，
王子们得不到满意的回答，
就要在勐甘纳嘎长期住下。

三、比武

为了避免引起纷争，
不与各勐的关系恶化，
国王只得求救于叭英，
请天神下凡来排难解纷。

叭英得知国王的祷告，
夜晚悄悄来到宫殿，
赠给国王一把神圣的弓阿沙尖，
还有三支宝箭和赠言。

"请告诉各勐的王子，
谁能拉动弓阿沙尖射出宝箭，
谁就是有福气的人，
他与公主就有缘分。

第六章 择婿　Chapter 6 Choosing a Son-in-law

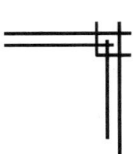

There was only one golden-bamboo-shoot-like daughter,

Who couldn't be cut into one hundred and one pieces as bamboo.

One hundred and one kingdoms were all mighty and powerful,

Improper handling of this matter will turn them into enemies.

The king got so upset by the dilemma

That his mind was like a messed knot.

If the princes could not get a satisfactory answer,

They would stay in the Kingdom of Ganaga for a long time.

III　Martial Arts Match

In order to avoid the possible disputes

And the deterioration of the relations with other kingdoms,

The king had no other way but to seek help from Baying,

Pleading the god to come down to the earth to solve the difficulty.

Having heard the prayers of the king,

Baying quietly came to the palace at night.

He gave the king a sacred bow of Ashajian,

And three precious arrows as well as his advice.

"Inform the princes of each nation:

Whoever can draw the bow of Ashajian

And shoot the arrows will be the blessed one.

He is destined to marry the Princess of Nan Xila.

207

"要是弓阿沙尖都拉不动,
还想娶公主南西拉,
那就是痴心妄想,
正如水中捞月一样。"

第二天清晨国王下了命令:
"迅速搭起一座高台,
我要进行比武择婿,
看看哪个王子最有本事。"

王宫前迅速搭起了高台,
台上放着弓阿沙尖和宝箭,
国王向各勐的来宾,
宣布了比武择婿的诺言。

"不论大勐小勐的王子,
不分贵贱和高低,
谁能拉动神弓射出宝箭,
我就招聘他为女婿。"

来自远近各勐的王子,
对国王比武择婿议论纷纷,
有的喜欢得像小雀跳,
认为这样才显得出高超的本领。

第六章 择婿 Chapter 6 Choosing a Son-in-law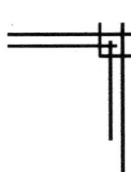

"Not being able to draw the bow of Ashajian
But still wanting to marry the Princess of Nan Xila,
This is just a wishful thinking,
Like fishing for the moon in the water."

The next morning the king gave an order,
"Set up a platform immediately,
I want to select my son-in-law through martial arts match,
Through which we will know which prince is the most skillful."

In front of the palace, a high platform was quickly erected,
On the platform were the bows of Ashajian and arrows.
The King addressed to his guests from each nation, announcing
The choice of his son-in-law through martial arts match.

"All the princes, whether he be from big or small nation,
Whether he be rich or poor, from noble class or lower class,
Whoever can pull the bow and shoot the arrow,
I will take him as my son-in-law."

Princes from each nation far or near had different voices
On the king's selection of son-in-law through martial arts match.
Some were so cheerful that they jumped up and down like birds,
Thinking it was truly a touchstone to select a man with superb skills.

209

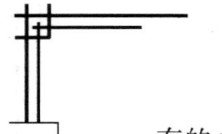

有的心中急得像火烧,
因为自己的胆子不大武艺不高,
有的灰心又丧气,
娶不到南西拉如何是好。

国王还为公主筑了一座楼房,
好让南西拉在窗口窥望,
看各勐的王子张弓射箭,
看哪个王子本领高强。

比武大会在锣鼓声中开始,
燃着炽烈爱情的各勐王子,
一个个争先恐后前去拉弓,
担心南西拉这朵鲜花被人摘去。

召捧玛加也冒充王子前来求婚,
今天喊声最高挤得最凶,
他傲然跃前走出人群,
跨上高台动手去拿弓。

他的力气抵得过十八头大象,
他的武艺超群出众,
但又硬又重的弓阿沙尖啊,
十八头大象的力气也拿不动。

第六章 择婿　Chapter 6 Choosing a Son-in-law

Some of them were so upset as they were sitting on fire,
Because they were neither brave nor skillful in martial arts.
Some others got thwarted and frustrated, thinking about
What they could do if they could not marry the Princess of Nan Xila.

The king also had a tower built for the princess
So that she could peep through the window at the match.
She could see how the princes draw the bow and shoot the arrows,
And she would know which prince to be the one with super skills.

The match began with the clamors of gongs and drums.
The princes, who were burning with passionate love
Rushed forward to draw the bow one by one for fear
That the flower of Nan Xila would be plucked by someone else.

Zhao Pengmajia also posed as a prince to propose.
He cried the loudest and pushed and shoved most fiercely.
He leaped arrogantly out of the crowd
And stepped onto the platform to get the bow.

He had the strength as much as that of eighteen elephants,
And no one was his match in the skills of martial arts.
But the stiff bow of Ashajian was so heavy that
Even a man with eighteen elephants' strength could not hold it up.

211

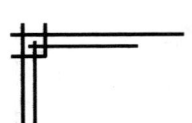
兰嘎西贺 The Ten-Headed King of Langa

他运足力气大吼一声，
神弓被提起刚刚离地，
忽然腰酸背痛手软无力，
提起的弓阿沙尖又落下去。

他休息一会恢复了力气，
第二次又去把弓阿沙尖提起，
刚刚举到胸膛正欲拉弦，
手脚瘫软力气又用完。

他慌忙放下弓阿沙尖，
像老牛一样喘着粗气，
满身大汗淋淋，
十个头挣得面红耳赤。

各勐王子相继上台比武，
有的挣得脸红脖子粗，
有的挣得瞪眼流鼻涕，
有的挣得摇头又咧嘴。

一个个都在神弓面前出丑，
徒劳地使尽吃奶的力气，
好像力大无穷的样子，
却没有一个能把弓阿沙尖提起。

第六章 择婿 Chapter 6 Choosing a Son-in-law

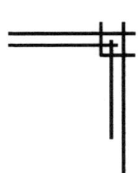

He gathered all his strength up and with a huge roar,
The bow was lifted just off the ground.
But all at once he felt his back ached and his hands weak,
And the raised bow of Ashajian fell off to the floor.

He restored his strength after a rest,
And for the second time he tried to lift the bow of Ashajian.
Just when he lifted it to his chest and was about to pull a string,
He felt exhausted with weak and limp arms and legs.

Hurriedly he lowered the bow of Ashajian down,
Panting like an old ox and
Drenched in sweat,
His ten heads turned scarlet out of the struggles.

All the princes came onto the platform in succession to have a try,
Some of them struggled with faces turning scarlet and necks thicker.
Some with their eyes popped out and with runny noses,
Some with their heads shaking and mouths twisted.

Every one made himself a fool in front of the magic bow.
They appeared to have infinite strength,
And they strained all their nerves, but only in vain.
None of them could even lift the bow of Ashajian.

王子们个个长吁短叹，
自愧与公主没有缘分，
不能与公主同床共枕，
真是死了也不甘心。

没有哪个王子提得起神弓，
更不用说拉弓射出宝箭，
有的怪国王条件太苛刻，
有的劝国王另定条件。

召捧玛加见大家都不如他，
便大言不惭地站出来开言：
"所有来这里求婚的王子，
没有哪个拿得动弓拉得开弦。

"唯有我虽然拉不开弦，
还把弓提起到胸前，
各勐王子中我最有本领，
在场的人都已看见。

"公主应该嫁给我，
国王同意给我当然更好，
不同意公主也是我的，
我要把她带回国去。"

王子们听了此番胡言乱语，
一个个心中都不服气，
一个个敢怒而不敢言，
都在看国王怎么处置。

第六章 择婿 Chapter 6 Choosing a Son-in-law

The princes sighed and groaned,
Ashamed for the loss of chance to marry the princess.
Not being able to share one bed with the princess of Nan Xila,
They would die with a regretful and unwilling heart.

No prince could lift the divine bow,
Let alone draw it and shoot an arrow.
Some blamed the king for his harsh terms,
And some advised him to set up other requirements.

Seeing that everybody was inferior to him,
Zhao Pengmajia stood up and said without shame,
"None of the princes who have come here to propose
Could draw the bow and pull up the string."

"Although I failed to pull the string,
I at least lifted the bow to my chest.
So I was the most powerful among the princes,
All the people present have seen it."

"The princess should marry me.
It would be better for the king to approve the marriage.
If he doesn't, I will still have the princess.
I will take her with me back to my country."

Hearing him talking such nonsense,
All the princes felt resentful in their heart.
But no one dared to speak out their grievance.
They all waited and saw how the king would handle this.

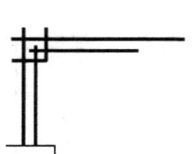

四、定亲

这天帕拉西带着朗玛来到勐甘纳嘎,
只见宫前广场上人声喧嚷,
帕拉西进王宫见了老国王,
国王忙把比武择婿的纠纷对他言讲。

帕拉西沉思一会儿后说:
"尊贵的国王啊,你可曾认真考虑,
假如一个穷苦孩子能拉弓射箭,
你愿不愿意降低门第?"

勐甘纳嘎国王马上回答说:
"我已说过不管贵贱高低,
只要能拉弓射箭就能娶我女儿,
我说话算数决不改变主意。"

第六章 择婿 Chapter 6 Choosing a Son-in-law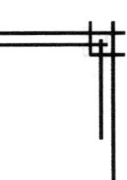

Ⅳ Engagement

Just on this day, Palaxi took Langma to the Kingdom of Ganaga.

They saw the boisterous throngs on the square in front of the palace.

Palaxi went to the palace to pay a visit to the old king.

The king could not wait to tell him about the dilemma he was in.

After a while of contemplation, Palaxi said,

"Your Majestic King, have you ever seriously considered this,

If a poor young man could draw the bow and shoot the arrows,

Would you lower your requirement for his social status?"

The King of Ganaga answered immediately,

"I have said no matter how high or low class he is from, the one

Who can draw the bow and shoot the arrows will marry my daughter.

My words count and I will never change my mind."

帕拉西听了十分喜悦地说：
"我带来了一个年轻的卡约①，
我想让他试一试，
看他有没有这份福气。"

召朗玛拨开拥挤的人群，
神态自若地向高台走去，
王子们见召朗玛小小年纪，
说出了讽刺挖苦的言语：

"一个帕拉西的奴仆，
自己也太不知趣，
不在深山老林吃野果，
竟想到坝子里来吃糯米。"

"这小子也不看看这是什么地方，
纵然拉动弓弦射出宝箭，
高贵的公主南西拉啊，
他穷小子怎能高攀得上？"

公主南西拉在楼房窥望，
见召朗玛威风凛凛气宇轩昂，
美丽得像十五的月亮，
她纯洁的心灵暗自思量：

---

① 卡约：对到佛寺修行未成佛爷以前的青年的称呼。

第六章 择婿　Chapter 6 Choosing a Son-in-law

Hearing this, Palaxi said with great joy,
"I brought with me a young Kayue①
I want him to have a try
And see if he has the good fortune."

Zhao Langma cut his way out from the crowd,
And he stepped onto the high platform with ease and composure.
When the princes saw Zhao Langma was so young,
They uttered such sarcastic remarks,

"He was just a servant of Palaxi,
He should be more sensible of his own status.
Instead of eating wild fruits in the deep mountain forest,
He dared to dream of eating glutinous rice in the village.

"The kid should open his eyes and see where he is.
Even if he could pull the bow string and shoot the arrows,
He really thinks a poor guy like him deserves
The noble princess of Nan Xila?"

Princess Nan Xila was peeping through in her room.
Seeing Zhao Langma so mighty and majestic,
As handsome as the full moon on the fifteenth day of a month,
In her pure heart she thought to herself,

---

① Kayue: the name of a young man who went to a Buddhist temple to practice before he became a Buddhist master.

"这样漂亮的小伙子,
正是我理想的丈夫,
就是不参加比武,
我也愿意永远和他在一起。"

摘下发髻上的金花、取出金线蜡条,
忐忑的心啊怦怦直跳,
炽热的情丝啊腾腾燃烧,
南西拉默默地对苍天祷告:

"众位天神啊,
请你们助他一臂之力,
让他拉动神弓射出宝箭,
就像女人纺线那样轻易。"

召朗玛上了高台站在弓前,
双手举到头顶默默向天神祷念:
"假使我和公主真的有缘分,
请天神保佑我比武成功。"

在命运高贵的召朗玛手里,
沉甸甸的神弓就像竹竿一样轻,
硬邦邦的弓弦就像烘过的篾片一样柔软,
他轻轻拉开神弓"嗖嗖嗖"射出三箭。

第六章 择婿 Chapter 6 Choosing a Son-in-law

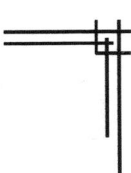

"Such a handsome young man,
He is exactly my ideal husband.
Even if he doesn't take part in the match,
I would like to be with him forever."

Taking the golden flowers off her hair,
Taking out the candle with golden thread,
She felt her heart throbbing wildly and excitedly.
With passionate love, Nan Xila prayed silently to the heaven,

"Your mighty gods of heaven,
Please give him a hand and power
So that he can draw the bow and shoot the arrows
As easily as a woman spins and weaves."

Standing in front of the bow on the high platform,
Zhao Langma raised his hands above his head and prayed,
"If I am really destined to be tied with the princess, Mighty gods,
Please bless me with a success in the martial arts match."

In the hands of noble Zhao Langma,
The heavy bow was as light as a bamboo pole.
The stiff bowstrings were as soft as thin bamboo strips.
He gently pulled open the bow and shoots three arrows.

第一箭射向高高的苍穹,
神箭穿云破雾直上九重,
箭声响彻甘纳嘎全勐,
全勐人的耳朵几乎震聋。

第二箭射向辽阔的森林,
莽莽丛林刮起怒涛狂风,
箭声吓得野兽跑出窝,
箭声吓得鸟雀齐飞上天空。

第三箭射向烟雾弥漫的海洋,
平静的海洋掀起万丈波浪,
箭声传遍勐埃森王国,
吓得水神喊爹又叫娘。

三声箭响震得十头魔王不寒而栗,
一百零一勐的王子们呆若木鸡,
南西拉像一朵含苞待放的荷花,
片片红晕在她白净的脸上泛起。

第六章 择婿　Chapter 6 Choosing a Son-in-law

The first one was shot into the high sky,

The magic arrow pierced the clouds and flew to the highest heaven.

The sound of the arrow rang through the kingdom of Ganaga,

Almost deafening the ears of all the people on land.

The second one was shot to the vast forest,

It was like raging waves and wind that swept over the wild jungle.

The sound of the arrow scared the beasts out of their dens.

And frightened the birds to flock into the sky.

The third one was shot to the smoky and foggy sea,

Waves as high as several miles were raised on the calm sea.

The sound of the arrows spread throughout the kingdom of Aisen.

The God of the sea was terrified to cry for his father and mother.

The sound of three arrows shook ten-headed demon shivering,

And one hundred and one princes dumbstruck like wooden chickens,

While Nan Xila was like a budding lotus flower,

With her white face flushing scarlet.

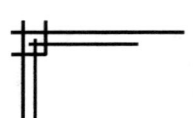

国王脸色难看心中不悦：
"怎么南西拉这样没有福气，
竟与乘骑大象的王子没有缘分，
却委身给帕拉西的一个奴仆。"

帕拉西立即上前向国王说出真情：
"拉动弓阿沙尖，
射出宝箭的小朗玛啊，
他是勐沓达腊塔的王孙。"

国王听了十分欢喜，
急忙叫召朗玛过来仔细打量：
"勐沓达腊塔的王子啊，
这真是千里姻缘牵一丝。

"南西拉这只年轻的孔雀啊，
需要鲜艳的金花银花衬托，
你这朵王室的鲜花栽在我们勐，
给勐甘纳嘎增添了福气。

"金花银花开在我女儿的寝宫，
定会焕发出沁人心脾的芳香，
祝愿你们这对幸福的金孔雀，
在蔚蓝色的天空展翅翱翔。"

第六章 择婿　Chapter 6 Choosing a Son-in-law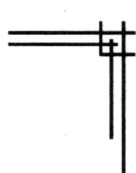

The king was unhappy with a long face.
"Why my dear Nan Xila has no blessing?
Not being destined to be with the prince riding an elephant,
Instead, she has to condescend herself to marry a servant of Palaxi."

At this moment Palaxi went up to tell the king the truth.
"The young Langma,
Who drew the bow of Ashajian and shot the magic arrows,
He is the grandson of the King of Dadalata."

The king was overjoyed to hear that.
He immediately summoned Langma to have a close look.
"The Prince of the kingdom of Dadalata,
He is really a fate match across a thousand miles."

"The young peacock of Nan Xila,
Can only be matched with bright flowers of gold and silver.
You, a royal flower now rooted in our land,
Will definitely bring good fortune to our nation of Ganaga."

"Flowers of gold and silver bloom in my daughter's room,
They will set forth refreshing fragrance.
I give my best wishes to you, a pair of happy golden peacocks,
Together you will spread your wings and soar into blue sky."

225

国王高兴地立即向全勐臣民宣布，
同意王子召朗玛为南西拉的佳婿，
他为王子和公主滴下圣洁的水，
准备三个月后举行盛大的婚礼。

第六章 择婿 Chapter 6 Choosing a Son-in-law

At once, the king announced happily to all his subjects

He was happy to have Prince of Langma as the husband of Nan Xila.

He dripped holy water onto the prince and princess.

They began to prepare for a grand wedding coming in three months.

第七章 婚礼

一、国王的吩咐

勐甘纳嘎沉浸在欢乐之中,
辉煌的宫殿挂满彩色旗幡,
宫殿的柱子重新刷上金粉,
宫殿的墙画上了新的图案。

隆重的婚礼不久就要举行,
召朗玛和南西拉即将拴线,
尽管距婚期还有三个月,
三个月啊国王只把它看成三天。

所有的东西都得事先准备,
所有的礼仪都得仔细考虑,
国王督促臣僚加紧备办,
场面的豪华壮观要超过登基典礼。

第七章 婚礼　Chapter 7 Wedding Ceremony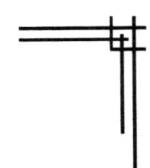

Chapter 7　Wedding Ceremony

I　The King's Orders

The kingdom of Ganaga was immersed in great joy,
The splendid palace was decorated with colorful banners and flags;
The pillar of the palace were repainted with golden powder;
The walls of the palace were furnished with paintings of new designs.

The grand wedding was soon to be held,
Zhao Langma and Nan Xila would be tied by marriage.
Although the wedding would come in three months,
The king thought three months as short as three days.

Everything had to be prepared beforehand,
And all the etiquette should be carefully considered.
The king urged his officials to work efficiently to make sure
The wedding would be grander than the enthronement ceremony.

为了勐沓达腊塔的荣誉，
为了尊重王室的父母和兄弟，
为了自己和公主的利益，
召朗玛向岳父提出：

"我与公主结婚是终身大事，
儿女婚事需征得父母的同意，
我还有三个和睦相处的弟弟，
也要请他们前来参加婚礼。"

国王听了欣然同意：
"我一定派官员专程去边境迎接，
我也有三个弟弟住在各自的领地，
也要邀请他们前来参加婚礼。"

召朗玛让弓塔弩发挥神奇的威力，
将写好的四封书信绑在箭翎上，
分别射向四个遥远的地方——
三封射给南西拉的叔父，一封射给父王。

召沓达腊塔接到儿子的喜讯，
立即命大臣做好参加婚礼的准备，
"我要亲自点数各勐的贺喜队伍，
贺喜队伍要雄壮威武。

"行进的队伍分成三十二路，
三十二路都要敲锣打鼓，
队列前要高举红杆黄布的旗幡，
士兵要穿虎皮衣服。"

第七章 婚礼 Chapter 7 Wedding Ceremony

For the honor of the kingdom of Dadalata,
For the respect to the royal parents and brothers,
For the well-beings of himself and the princess,
Zhao Langma proposed to his father-in-law,

"It's a once-in-a-life event for me to marry the princess,
I have to ask my parents for their consent of the marriage.
I also have three brothers to whom I am very close,
And I would like to invite them to attend the wedding."

When the king heard this, he readily agreed,
"I will send officials to the border to greet them.
I also have three brothers living in their own territories,
And I will invite them to the wedding too."

Zhao Langma exerted the magical power of his crossbow,
He attached the four letters to the heads of the arrows,
Which would be shot to four distant places,
Three to Nan Xila's three uncles and one to his father king.

At receiving the good news from his son, the King of Dadalata
Ordered the ministers to prepare for attending the wedding.
"I will check the congratulatory groups in person,
And they should look grand and magnificent.

"There should be thirty-two groups in the marching procession,
Each group should play gongs and drums while marching.
Yellow flags hung on red poles should be held high leading the queue,
And all the soldiers should wear uniform made of tiger skin."

231

兰噶西贺 The Ten-Headed King of Langa

"要赶快修一条通往森林的大路，
路宽八丈，路面铺上粗沙细石，
要选派胆大艺高的武士，
驱虎杀豹在莽莽森林开路。

"要准备一支威武的象队，
牙镀黄金，身披银片，
头安玻璃镜，尾挂珍珠链，
让最大的臣僚骑着公象走在前。

"一队骏马配上金鞍和银镫，
武官们骑上威风凛凛，
一对彩车载运珍贵的礼品，
上面坐着押送金银珠宝的大小头人。

"选好吉日良辰就启程，
出发的礼炮要装足火药，
要像打雷一样声威远震，
让全勐的人都听得清。

第七章 婚礼 Chapter 7 Wedding Ceremony

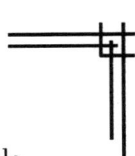

"We need to build a road to the forest as soon as possible.

It should be sixteen meters wide paved with sand and pebbles.

Brave warriors are to be selected to drive tigers and kill leopards

And carve a way out in the thick primitive forest.

"A team of mighty elephants should also be prepared,

Their tusks should be gilded and their body covered with silver sheets,

Decorate their heads with glass mirror and tail with threads of pearls.

The highest rank of official on a male elephant would lead the team.

"The horses should be equipped with gold saddles and silver stirrups,

The military officers riding on them shall appear mightily handsome.

Precious presents will be loaded onto a couple of colorful carts,

With the chiefs of big or small tribes safeguarding the treasures.

"Select the right day and time to set off on the journey.

The salute-guns should be filled with powerful powder.

They will make sound as loud and mighty as thunders,

So that all the people over the nation can hear them clearly.

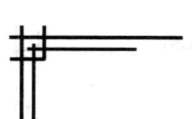

"沿途各站要搭棚设摊,
摆出最好的陈酒,
做出最美的菜肴,
让队伍吃饱喝足。

"到海里捕来鱿鱼和大虾,
从山上牵来肥牛和壮羊,
牛肉羊肉要架起火来烤黄,
鱼汤肉汤要熬得鲜美芳香。

"剁生①凉拌要放足作料,
米线米干要泡上鸡汤,
刮净牛皮猪皮做成油炸泡皮,
大家吃了精力旺盛。

"勐沓达腊塔出产的有名瓜果——香蕉、荔枝、香瓜、芒果和菠萝,
要摆满道路两旁,
让队伍吃了好解渴。

---

① 剁生:傣族用生猪肉、生鱼肉加作料做的一种菜。

第七章 婚礼 Chapter 7 Wedding Ceremony

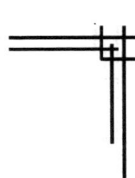

"Shelters and stalls should be set up along the road,
Present the best old wine,
Offer the most delicious dishes
So that all the groups have enough to eat and drink.

"Go to the sea to catch squids and shrimps,
Go to the mountains to get fat cow and sheep;
Beef and mutton are set on fire to roast brown,
The soup of fish and meat are stewed delicious.

"Enough ingredients should be put in the Duosheng①;
Rice curd and rice noodle should be soaked in chicken soup;
Scrape the skins of cattle and pigs to make fried foamed skins,
Everyone will be full of energy after eating the delicious food.

"The famous fruits produced in the Kingdom of Dadalata bananas, leeches, cantaloupes, mangoes and pineapples,
Should be placed on both sides of the road.
They will quench the thirst of the teams and the groups.

---

① Duosheng:a kind of cold appetizer with pork and fish chopped into small pieces and other ingredients mixed together.

"召朗玛回来时全国的人都要来欢迎,
会唱歌的赞哈,会跳舞的艺人,
还有会拉吹的乐师,
要一起进行精彩的表演。

"迎亲的人们要梳妆打扮,
妇女们要戴上金耳环,
小伙子要穿上华丽的衣裳,
姑娘们要头戴鲜花手打花伞。

"规模要比赶摆还热闹,
费用全由宫廷来承担,
这次迎亲一定要办好,
谁不尽职我要重重惩办。"

为了祝贺召朗玛成亲,
忙坏了大臣头人,
为了接回新媳妇南西垭,
惊动了全勐百姓。

按照召沓达腊塔的旨意,
臣僚们很快准备就绪,
象队车马集结待命,
贺喜的队伍即将启程。

第七章 婚礼 Chapter 7 Wedding Ceremony

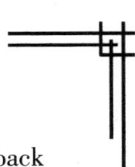

"All my people should come to welcome Langma back home,
All those who can sing and all those artists who can dance,
And the musicians who can play musical instruments,
They should perform together to give us a wonderful show.

"Those who go to escort the bride should be dressed up;
Women should wear their gold earrings;
Young men should wear their gorgeous clothes,
And girls should wear flowers and hold colorful umbrellas.

"The ceremony should be more lively and exciting than the fair,
And all the expenses will be covered by the court.
We must do the job of escorting the bride home wonderfully,
Those who fail to do their duty will be punished severely."

To prepare for the wedding ceremony of Zhao Langma,
The ministers of the court and tribe chiefs were awfully busy;
To escort the new wife Nan Xila to the kingdom of Dadalata,
People all over the nation were mobilized up.

Following the orders of Zhao Dadalata,
The ministers and officials got everything ready promptly.
The groups of elephants and horses were assembled and await orders.
The congratulatory teams would start on the journey.

人群像大海沸腾，
礼炮隆隆响了三声，
国王和三个王子登上象座，
召沓达腊塔下达了出发的命令。

行走步伐似千万爆竹炸响，
行进人流像江水奔泻不停，
欢声笑语洒满了大地，
人们唱着跳着走进森林。

二、婚礼

森林里闪射着道道霞光，
山箐里回荡着清脆的铃声，
欢乐的队伍晓行夜宿一个月，
到达了勐甘纳嘎国境。

按照世代相传的规矩，
国王派特使前往王宫呈交书信，
勐甘纳嘎国王立即下令，
准备迎接远道而来的国宾。

第七章 婚礼 Chapter 7 Wedding Ceremony

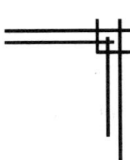

The crowds were boisterous and excited as surging sea.
After the salute guns were fired three times,
The king and the three princes boarded on the elephants.
Then the king gave the order to set out.

The steps of the procession sounded like tons of firecrackers set off;
The procession rushed forward like rolling water of huge river;
Happy laughter and cheerful voices were heard all the way;
Singing and dancing joyfully, they entered the forest.

II The Wedding Ceremony

The morning sunshine glittered in the forest,
Crisp bells were echoed in the mountains;
After a month of walking at day and rest at night,
The happy procession reached the frontier of the Kingdom of Ganaga.

Abiding by the conventions passed on from generation to generation,
The King sent envoys to the palace to submit letters.
Getting the letter, the king of Ganaga immediately gave orders
To get ready to welcome the distinguished guests from afar.

兰嘎西贺 The Ten-Headed King of Langa

神采焕发的召朗玛骑上大象，
偕同官员前往边境迎接父王，
他虔诚地向父王问候，
又向弟弟和侍臣们合掌。

勐甘纳嘎的大臣上前合十，
向勐沓达腊塔国王下拜，
献上花盘和蜡条，
欢迎贵宾不辞劳苦来到了勐甘纳嘎。

勐甘纳嘎百姓倾城出动，
男女老少聚集在王宫广场，
手中的花伞恰似千万朵彩云，
彩云下浮动着张张欢笑的脸庞。

欢迎的人群敲响铓锣，
大小象脚鼓擂得响彻云霄，
人们欢乐地呼喊着"水！水！水！"
簇拥着姻亲国王前往宫殿。

第七章 婚礼 Chapter 7 Wedding Ceremony

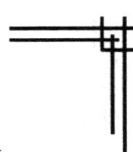

In high spirits, Zhao Langma mounted onto the elephant

And went to the frontier with officials to meet his father.

He greeted his father the king piously

And saluted his younger brothers and courtiers with folded palms.

Coming forward and saluting with folded palms,

The ministers of Ganaga bowed down to the King of Dadalata,

And they offered him flowers and wax sticks to welcome

The distinguished guests who took pains to come to Ganaga from afar.

The people of Ganaga poured out into the city.

Men, women and children gathered on the palace square.

The colorful umbrellas in their hands were like colorful clouds;

Under the colorful clouds were millions of smiling faces.

The welcoming crowds were beating their gongs;

And the sound of the elephant-foot-like drums resounded to the sky;

People cheerfully shouted "Water! Water! Water!"

They escorted the two royal families tied by marriage to the palace.

勐甘纳嘎国王的三个弟弟也及时赶到,
兄弟四人带着王族在殿前欢迎,
两国国王见面互相合掌,
手拉手肩并肩步入辉煌的宫廷。

两国国王并排坐在神圣的宝座上,
四位王子分别坐在宝座两旁,
两国王族在一起亲密交谈,
两国王族欢聚在一堂。

满堂共颂两国深厚的友谊,
满堂共祝两国结成了姻亲,
召沓达腊塔送上丰厚的聘礼,
勐甘纳嘎国王也回赠珍贵的礼品。

官员们纷纷前来朝拜,
宝石般的南西拉领着三个妹妹——南娟达、南吉达和南谢玛,
上殿来拜见两位父王。

四姊妹像四朵含苞欲放的荷花,
皮肤白里透红像有露水滴下,
身体比糯米粑粑还柔软,
一个个娉婷、温和、文雅。

第七章 婚礼 Chapter 7 Wedding Ceremony

The three brothers of the King Ganaga arrived in time.
The whole royal families greeted the guests in front of the palace.
The two kings met and saluted each other with folded palms.
They walked side by side into the splendid court.

The two kings sat next to each other on the sacred throne,
And the four princes sat on either side of them.
The royal families of the two countries had close conversations,
And they did have a happy gathering at the court.

All the people celebrated the friendship between the two countries;
All of them congratulated the two countries bound by marriage;
The King of Dadalata presented a generous bride price,
And the King of Ganaga gave precious gifts in return.

Officials in succession came forward to salute,
The jewel-like Nan Xila led her three young sisters
Nan Juanda, Nan Jida and Nan Xiema,
To the court to meet her two father-kings.

The four sisters were like four budding lotus flowers.
Their skins were white and red like dew drops,
And their bodies were softer than glutinous rice cake.
They were slender, gentle and in graceful manner.

四姊妹像睡莲一样娇艳美丽,
召沓达腊塔越看越欢喜,
他高兴地向亲家提出,
要联姻就干脆四个王子娶四个公主。

勐甘纳嘎国王询问三个弟弟,
他们都欣然同意这桩婚事,
愿意将女儿嫁给召朗玛弟兄,
建立起两国亲上加亲的情谊。

召沓达腊塔感激不尽,
用最美的语言把谢意说出:
"感谢你们为两国搭起牢固的金桥,
感谢你们为两国筑起宽广的大路。

"你们的女儿既然是我的儿媳,
我会把她们当亲生女儿一样爱护,
我的四个儿子就是你们的儿子,
他们会赤胆忠心保护你们免受凌辱。

"让两国像两只沙宝罕航行在海上,
让两国臣民像一条条江河汇入汪洋,
尊敬的亲家国王啊,
婚礼由你主持定会增添荣光。"

第七章 婚礼 Chapter 7 Wedding Ceremony

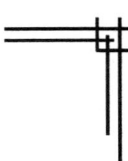

The four sisters were as beautiful as water lilies.
The more Zhao Dadalata looked, the more he liked them.
Happily, he put forward his idea to the King of Ganaga,
Maybe the other three princes could marry the other three princesses.

King of Ganaga asked his three brothers of their idea.
They all readily agreed on the proposed marriage.
They would marry their daughters to the brothers of Zhao Langma,
And establish a closer friendship between the two countries.

The king of Dadalata was truly thankful.
He expressed his gratitude with the most beautiful words,
"Thank you for building a golden bridge between our two countries,
Thank you for building broad roads linking our two nations."

"Since your daughters are my daughters-in-law,
I will love them as my own daughters;
And my four sons are your sons now.
They will be loyal to you protecting you from humiliation.

" Let the two countries be like two boats of treasure sailing on the sea,
Let the subjects of our countries unite like rivers merging into the sea.
Your majestic King of Ganaga, the father of my daughters-in-law,
Wedding presided over by you will bring us endless glory."

245

勐甘纳嘎国王非常激动，
在一个吉祥如意的日子，
为四对王子和公主，
举行了盛大的结婚典礼。

召朗玛和南西拉，腊嘎纳和南娟达，
帕腊达和南谢玛，沙达鲁嘎和南吉达，
四对比翼齐飞的凤凰，
一起接受人们撒下的祝福的米花。

公公为媳妇拴线，
祝愿新婚夫妇白头到老，
岳父岳母为女婿拴线，
祝愿新婚夫妇快乐幸福。

礼炮为婚礼添彩，
锣鼓为婚礼奏乐，
四对新人隆重而热闹的婚礼啊，
在灯火辉煌的王宫举行了七天七夜。

回国的日子到了，
召沓达腊塔偕同四个儿子，
来到王宫向四个亲家告别，
离别的时刻啊，难分难舍。

第七章 婚礼 Chapter 7 Wedding Ceremony

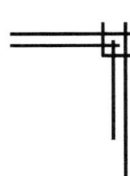

The King of Ganaga was also very excited.
On an auspicious and happy day,
A grand wedding ceremony was held
For the four couples of princes and princesses.

Zhao Langma and Nan Xila, Lagana and Nan Juanda,
Palada and Nan Xiema, Shadaluga and Nan Jida,
The four couple of phoenixes together accepted
Sprinkled rice from their people as their blessing.

The father of the bridegroom tied a thread for his daughter-in-law,
Wishing the newlyweds to stay together for their whole life,
The father and mother of the bride tied a thread for his son-in-law.
Wishing the newlyweds a long-lasting happy life.

Salute-guns were fired to cheer for the weddings,
Gongs and drums were played for the ceremonies.
The grand and lively weddings for the four couples
Last seven days and seven nights in the splendid palace.

Now It was time to go back home.
The King of Dadalata together with his four sons
Came to the palace to say goodbye to the four families by marriage.
All the families couldn't bear to part from each other.

老国王向女婿女儿祝福:
"让吉祥的星辰照着你们回去,
祝你们一路上平安顺利,
望我们两国保持永久的情谊。

"勐沓达腊塔的王子啊,
勐甘纳嘎的金孔雀,
你们一定要相亲相爱,
形影不离共担忧乐。"

四姊妹跟随自己的丈夫,
穿过坝子渐渐远去,
父母站在高高的城楼上,
直望到他们消失在丛山密林深处。

三、嫉妒

一百零一个王子比武失败,
一个个垂头丧气各怀鬼胎,
有的不服气耿耿于怀,
有的懊悔白白跑来。

力大无比的召捧玛加,
输给了年轻的召朗玛,
美人儿投入别人的怀抱,
气得他心肝碎裂肺爆炸。

第七章 婚礼 Chapter 7 Wedding Ceremony

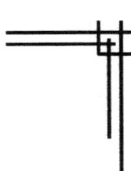

The old king blessed his sons-in-law and daughters,
"Let the auspicious stars shine on your way back home.
I wish you a peaceful and safe journey,
And our two countries will maintain lasting friendship.

"Princes of the kingdom of Dadalata,
The Golden Peacocks of our Ganaga,
You must love each other sharing your worries and joys.
You should accompany one another like shadows."

Following their husbands, the four sisters
Left home and gradually walked out of sight.
Standing on the tall tower, their parents' eyes followed them,
Till they disappeared into the depths of the mountains and forests.

III Jealousy

One hundred and one princes failed in the martial arts match.
They all got frustrated and had thoughts of their own.
Some of them were dissatisfied and resentful;
Some other regretted their efforts were wasted in vain.

Zhao Pengmajia, the herculean ten-headed demon King,
Was so exasperated that his heart and liver seemed to burst.
Since he was defeated by young Zhao Langma,
Now the beauty of Nan Xila was in the arms of the prince.

召捧玛加挥拳扇动他的人马说：
"我们不能蒙受这样的耻辱，
我们勐兰嘎光荣的声誉，
岂能容许召朗玛来玷污。

"召朗玛只能拉弓射箭，
他有什么了不起，
我的本领比他高强，
走，跟我一起杀上前去。"

他带来的求婚队伍一哄而起，
扬鞭跃马向召朗玛追击，
召朗玛听见后面人喊马叫，
顷刻间一群抢婚者蜂拥而至。

召朗玛从容向南西拉告别，
让父母和兄弟们一旁暂避，
他掉转马头质问杀气腾腾的来者：
"你们追赶我为了何事？"

召捧玛加挺身向前，
气势汹汹地回答：
"我是名扬天下的勐兰嘎国王，
你可知道我召捧玛加的名字？

第七章 婚礼 Chapter 7 Wedding Ceremony

Waving his fists, Zhao Pengmajia instigated his followers,
"We should not bear such humiliation,
The glorious reputation of our Langa
Should never be tarnished by Zhao Langma.

"Zhao Langma only knows archery.
What's great about him?
I have more skills than him.
Go and kill them with me."

His men were stirred up and rushed into mass action,
Riding on their horses they ran after Zhao Langma.
Zhao Langma heard men shouting and horses neighing from behind,
And then a crowd of bride robbers rushed to his sight.

Zhao Langma calmly bid farewell to Nan Xila.
He asked his parents and brothers to stay away from the trouble.
He turned his horse around and questioned the murderous comers,
"For what you are chasing me like this?"

Zhao Pengmajia stepped forward,
And he answered fiercely,
"I am the King of Langa known to the world.
Have you heard of my name Zhao Pengmajia?

"我像五月的野火一样凶猛①,
我像明亮的钢刀一样锋利,
召朗玛呀,难道你吃了虎胆,
竟敢抢走我心爱的美人儿。

"召朗玛呀,你要识时务,
给我留下美丽的南西拉,
不然你就要死在我的刀下,
让你们的尸体在森林里腐烂。"

召朗玛听了勃然大怒,
昂首挺胸逼近召捧玛加说:
"你就像一个疯子,
信口开河说瞎话。

"你也不睁眼看看我是何人,
我劝你还是不要来挑衅,
口出狂言威吓不了谁,
你想较量一下我一定奉陪。"

话未说完召捧玛加挥棍打来,
召朗玛迅速抽刀迎上把它砍断,
召捧玛加又举起镖枪掷了过来,
也被召朗玛一刀砍成两截。

---

① 西双版纳五月天气炎热,天旱无雨,最易发生野火烧山,其势猛烈。

第七章 婚礼 Chapter 7 Wedding Ceremony

"I am as fierce as the wildfire in May①
I am as sharp as a shining steel knife.
Have you eaten the gall of a tiger, Zhao Langma?
How dare you stole my beloved beauty."

"Zhao Langma, know better the situation you are in,
Leave me the beautiful Nan Xila.
Otherwise you will die under my knife.
And your body will rot in the forest."

Zhao Langma got furious at his words.
Holding his head high, he approached Zhao Pengmajia saying,
"You are like a madman
Talking nonsense through your hat.

"Why not open your eyes wide and see who I am.
You'd better not provoke me.
You can't intimidate anyone by speaking out loud.
I am here if you want to have a fight."

Before he finished his words, Zhao Pengmajia attacked with a stick,
Zhao Langma drew his knife and cut the stick into two halves.
Zhao Pengmajia again raised and threw his dart toward him,
The dart was also broken into two pieces by Zhao Langma's knife.

---

① During May, it is really hot in Xishuangbanna when there is no rain. With the dry weather, wild fire could be really fierce.

兰嘎西贺 The Ten-Headed King of Langa

召捧玛加默念咒语口吐烈火，
熊熊烈火烧着了森林，
火焰团团围住召朗玛，
但烧不着他的一根头发。

召朗玛也默默念起咒语，
天空马上降下倾盆大雨，
很快将烈火浇熄，
召朗玛的衣服一点都未湿。

召捧玛加又念起咒语，
一阵狂风吹开云雨，
他抱起大象般的石块飞上天，
照准召朗玛头顶砸下。

召捧玛加得意洋洋夸口：
"召朗玛啊，这次你输了吧，
快把南西拉交给我，
不然你马上就死在石下。"

召朗玛毫不惊慌巍然屹立，
嘴里喃喃地念着咒语，
巨石竟碎散成满天的鲜花，
纷纷落进召朗玛的筒帕。

第七章 婚礼 Chapter 7 Wedding Ceremony

Chanting incantation in his heart, Zhao Pengmajia spat out fire.

The raging flames set the forest on fire

And surrounded Zhao Langma completely.

But not even a single hair of Zhao Langma was burned.

Zhao Langma also chanted incantation in his heart,

Immediately heavy rain poured from the sky,

The raging fire was extinguished,

But Zhao Langma's clothes remained dry.

Zhao Pengmajia cast another spell in his heart.

Here came a gale of wind blowing the rain and clouds away.

Picking up a rock as huge as an elephant he flew up to the sky.

Aiming at the head of Zhao Langma, he dropped the stone.

Zhao Pengmajia boasted elatedly,

"Zhao Langma, you are doomed to lose this time.

Give Nan Xila to me hurriedly,

Otherwise you will die under the stone in a minute."

Zhao Langma stood calmly without any panic,

And he began to mutter magic words.

Then the huge rock was exploded into a sea of flowers,

Which dropped off into Zhao Langma's tongpa.

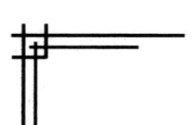

召捧玛加更加煞气,
施展出最后一招来对付,
他站在云端举起弓赛宰,
一边拉弓搭箭一边大骂道:

"愚蠢的召朗玛呀,
你还敢跟我作对吗?
你若怕死要求饶命,
你就给我乖乖跪下。

"你若不听从我的话,
你的命就要丧在我的箭下,
我手里拿的是弓赛宰,
它的威力有弓塔弩的十倍大。"

召朗玛听了感到不妙,
连忙向叭捧祈祷,
"请天神助我一臂之力,
让神箭都变成香蕉。"

恼羞成怒的召捧玛加用弓赛宰射箭,
神箭像流星般向召朗玛飞来,
连射四箭都围着召朗玛旋转落地,
变成金黄的香蕉给他解渴充饥。

第七章 婚礼 Chapter 7 Wedding Ceremony

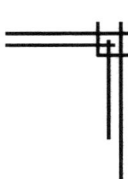

Zhao Pengmajia got more furious.
He decided to use his last card to deal with Zhao Langma
Standing in the clouds and raising his bow of Saizai,
Putting the arrow in position, he shouted his abuse,

"Stupid Zhao Langma,
How dare you fight against me?
Afraid of death? Then kneel down
And beg me to spare your life.

"If you don't obey me,
Your life will be taken away by my arrow.
In my hand is the most powerful Bow of Saizai,
Which is ten times mightier than your crossbow."

Zhao Langma felt uneasy hearing this.
He immediately prayed to the god of Bapeng,
"Heavenly God, Please do me a favor,
And turn the arrow into a banana."

The exasperate Zhao Pengmajia shot arrows with his Bow of Saizhai,
And the magic arrows flew toward Zhao Langma like shooting stars.
The arrows revolved around Zhao Langma and fell onto the ground,
Turning into bananas to quench his thirst and appease his hunger.

257

召捧玛加非常震惊,
浑身解数都已用完,
未伤着召朗玛头发一根,
慌忙驾起飞车带着兵马逃命。

召朗玛收兵并清点人马,
向着自己的祖国继续进发,
长途跋涉整整走了一个月,
才回到故土勐沓达腊塔。

屋里的织布机停止歌唱,
寨边的木碓也不再响,
举国上下的百姓捧着礼物,
迎接召朗玛娶亲回到了家乡。

第七章 婚礼 Chapter 7 Wedding Ceremony

Zhao Pengmajia got shocked and terrified,
Since he had already used up his tricks.
But not a single hair of Zhao Langma got hurt.
Jumping onto his flying cart, he led his men to run for life.

Zhao Langma gathered all his men and their horses,
They continued the journey back to their motherland.
It took them a whole month
To return to their motherland of Dadalata.

The looms inside houses stopped singing;
The wooden husking pestle of the village also stopped squeaking.
Holding their presents, people all over the nation came out
To welcome Zhao Langma and his bride back to his homeland.

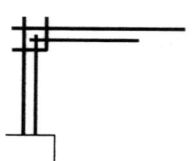

第八章 让位

一、果嘎腊国王的葬礼

勐果嘎腊国王身患重病后死亡,
王子苏万纳给远嫁的妹妹报丧,
噩耗很快送到勐沓达腊塔,
小王后哭得死去活来痛断肝肠。

南洁西找来儿子帕腊达,
把外公不幸逝世的消息告诉他,
为了哀悼敬爱的父王,
要儿子陪同她一起去勐果嘎腊。

母子征得老国王的同意,
在侍臣和卫兵护送下匆匆启程,
他们默默地穿过阴暗潮湿的森林,
一个月才赶到勐果嘎腊都城。

第八章 让位 Chapter 8 Abdication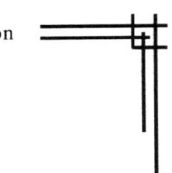

Chapter 8 Abdication

I The Funeral of the King of Guogala

The King of Guogala died of a serious disease.
The prince Suwanna reported it to his sister who married afar.
The sad news soon spread to the kingdom of Dadalata,
The youngest queen cried herself almost to death.

Nan Jiexi sent for her son Palada,
And told him the news of his grandfather's death.
She asked him to go with her to the Kingdom of Guogala
In mourning for her dear father-king.

After getting the permission from the old king,
Nan Jiexi and her son escorted by safeguards set on the journey.
Silently they passed through the damp and dark forest.
It took them one month to arrive in the capital of Guogala.

苏万纳得知妹妹前来奔丧,
率领臣僚和百姓出城迎接,
兄妹相见分外悲伤,
一起走进父王灵堂。

南洁西一见棺材就扑上去恸哭,
帕腊达呜咽着向外公灵柩磕头,
陪同的人一一向老国王默哀,
灵堂里充满着一片肃穆和哀愁。

南洁西捶胸顿足眼泪哭干,
才悲伤地领着儿子来拜见母后,
母女婆孙相见又痛哭一场,
外婆见外孙长大成人略减烦忧。

苏万纳为父王筹备隆重的葬礼,
在棺材上涂上金粉画上图案,
灵柩上面支放着塔形的帕纱①
帕纱上插着红红绿绿的神幡。

---

① 帕纱:竹扎纸糊的冥楼。

第八章 让位 Chapter 8 Abdication

Suwanna was informed of his sister's arrival for the funeral,
And he led his officials and people out of the city to greet her.
When seeing each other, the brother and sister got more mournful.
Together they went into the mourning hall set up for their father.

Seeing the coffin, Nan Jiexi threw herself onto it and cried sadly;
Palada also kowtowed toward his grandfather's coffin while weeping.
The accompanying people also mourned for the old king,
And the hall was filled with solemnity and sorrow.

Nan Jiexi beat her chest and cried her eyes out.
Then sorrowfully she took her son to visit her mother.
Meeting each other, they three again shed their tears.
At the sight of her grown-up grandson, the grandma felt less worried.

Suwanna prepared a grand and solemn funeral for his father the king.
The coffin had been gilded and painted with various patterns.
On the coffin sat a tower-shaped bamboo Pasha① for the old king.
And red and green divine banners were stuck in the bamboo tower.

---

① Pasha: a figurine of tower made of bamboo which is for the deceased to live in the underworld.

在一个吉利的日子举行安葬仪式,
灵柩被轻轻移上象车拉向坟地,
臣民百姓尾随灵车缓缓而行,
送葬的人一个个痛哭失声。

老国王遗体在烈火中升了天,
送葬的人都泪湿衣襟,
滚滚泪水几乎把大火浇熄,
人们守着直到遗体烧成灰烬。

苏万纳继承父亲的王位,
在万民欢呼声中登了基,
他像自己仁慈的父王一样,
励精图治把宽阔的王国治理。

过去了一个月以后,
南洁西留下儿子帕腊达,
辞别哥哥苏万纳和慈祥的母后,
带领护卫先回勐沓达腊塔。

二、挑拨

勐沓达腊塔国王已是半百年纪,
为了国家和百姓的利益,
他按照民族古老的传统规矩,
决定让召朗玛把王位承袭。

第八章 让位　Chapter 8　Abdication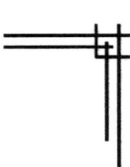

A funeral ceremony was held on an auspicious day.
The coffin was gently lifted and transported to the graveyard.
Following the hearse, the officials and subjects walked slowly.
The mourners wept bitterly until they lost their voice.

The body of the old king rose into the sky in the fire.
The mourners were all drenched with tears,
And their tears almost extinguished the fire.
People stayed until the remains was burned to ashes.

Suwanna succeeded to his father's throne,
And he was enthroned in the cheers of millions of people.
Like his benevolent father the King,
He made every effort to govern the huge kingdom.

A month had passed since the funeral,
Nan Jiexi said good-bye to her brother and her benevolent mother.
Leaving her son Palada behind and escorted by her guard,
Nan Jiexi went back to the Kingdom of Dadalata.

II　Discord Sown

The King of Dadalata was already half a century old.
For the benefit of the country and well-being of his people,
He decided to follow the ancient convention of his nation,
And let Zhao Langma succeed to his throne.

金笋般的大王子召朗玛啊,
有着聪明睿智的头脑,
有着善良谦逊的情操,
他是勐沓达腊塔王国的骄傲。

国王召集了大臣和头人,
庄严地宣告了召朗玛嗣位的决定,
国王的决定得到赞同和欢呼,
他又对可爱的儿子谆谆嘱咐:

"我年迈力衰已经精力不足,
需要解除繁重的宫廷政务,
我要把王位传给你,
自己到森林去修身养性。

"你将是一国臣民之首,
对百姓一定要仁慈宽厚,
国王对百姓公正廉洁,
他们才会热爱自己的君主。

"对你的三位母后啊,
要平等敬奉不分彼此,
对你的三个弟弟啊,
要像吃一个奶头的一样相处。

第八章 让位 Chapter 8 Abdication

Zhao Langma, the golden bamboo shoot-like prince,
He is wise and intelligent;
He is kind and modest;
And he is the pride of the kingdom of Dadalata.

The king summoned ministers and chieftains together,
Solemnly he declared his decision to enthrone Zhao Langma.
The king's decision was agreed and cheered.
And he instructed his beloved son earnestly and tirelessly,

"I am now too old and weak to run the country,
And I want to be freed from the heavy duty of governance.
I decide to pass on the throne to you,
And I will go to the forest to cultivate my mind."

"You will be the head of this country responsible for your subjects.
You must be benevolent and magnanimous to your people.
The king should be just and honest to everyone in his country,
Only then will the people love their monarch.

"As to the three queens,
You should treat them equally with respect and piety.
And to your three brothers,
You should love each other as you were fed by the same breast.

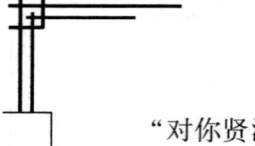

"对你贤淑的妻子啊,
要温存体贴,
对你的三个弟媳啊,
要一视同仁使她们不受委屈。

"你要汲取丰富的知识,
增强治国的本领,
你要把这些话牢记心上,
才能使我们国家繁荣富强。"

老国王倾吐了对儿子的期望,
又请来摩呼拉问卦占卜,
选定二月十五为良辰吉日,
黎明时举行盛大的登基典礼。

为了欢庆召朗玛继承王位,
国王下旨全勐举行大摆,
百姓纷纷涌进城来,
都城欢乐的人群如潮似海。

就在召朗玛登基大典的前夕,
南洁西奔丧完毕趱返回来,
她见城乡一派节日景象,
心中不免引起了疑猜。

第八章 让位 Chapter 8 Abdication

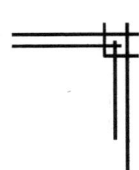

"To your kind and virtuous wife,

You should be gentle and considerate;

To your three sisters-in-law,

You should treat them equally making sure they won't feel wronged.

"You need to acquire more knowledge

To improve your ability to govern the country.

Keep all these words in your mind,

Only by this can we make our country prosperous and powerful."

After pouring out his expectation for his son,

The old king summoned Mohula, the divination officials to divine.

February fifteenth was chosen as the auspicious day,

And a grand enthronement was to be held at dawn.

In order to celebrate the succession of Zhao Langma to the throne,

The king ordered to put on grand shows and fairs.

The common people poured into the city,

In the capital were the happy crowds like tides and waves.

Just on the eve of Zhao Langma's inauguration ceremony

Nan Jiexi returned from her father's funeral.

When she saw a festival scene in urban and rural areas,

Naturally, suspicion was aroused in her heart.

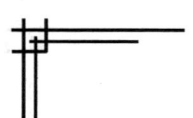

南洁西叫卫队停止前进,
派宫女达西前去探听,
勐沓达腊塔这样的欢乐,
究竟有什么大喜之事欢庆。

众多的人对达西说:
"明天是我们勐最神圣的日子,
尊贵的召朗玛要继承王位,
全勐臣民都来赶摆祝福。"

宫女达西回来报告了消息,
南洁西听了感到惊异,
她的脸色骤然变白,
一桩桩往事不断出现在脑际:

"当年国王援助叭英打仗伤了小手指,
经我精心护理很快痊愈,
国王曾许诺如果我生了儿子,
长大了就让他把王位承继。

"如今国王不履行诺言,
竟自食言将我欺骗,
趁我出国奔丧不在宫廷,
将王位传给召朗玛令人不平。"

第八章 让位 Chapter 8 Abdication

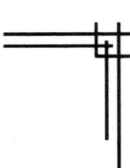

Nan Jiexi asked the guard to stop their procession,
And she sent her maid Daxi to find out the reason
For such joys and happiness in the kingdom of Dadalata.
What event on earth was there to be celebrated for?

Many people said to Daxi,
"Tomorrow is the most sacred day of our country.
The noble Zhao Langma will succeed to the throne.
People all over the country will come and give their best wishes."

The maid Daxi came back to report the news.
Nan Jiexi was astounded to hear it.
Her face suddenly turned white,
And the past events flashed in her mind,

"That year the king got his finger injured for helping Baying in fight,
It was out of my careful nursing that he soon recovered.
The King had promised me that if I gave a birth to a son,
He would succeed to the throne when he is grown up.

"Now the king broke his promise.
He ate his words and fooled me.
It is unfair that he took the advantage of my leaving
For the funeral to pass on the throne to Zhao Langma."

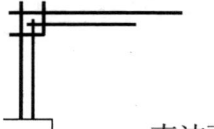

南洁西越思越想越生气,
爱搬弄是非的达西乘机插言:
"亲爱的王后啊,
国王过去曾向你许过心愿。

"你趁国王晚上来睡觉时,
要他履行过去的诺言,
并要他令召朗玛离宫出走,
限他十二年在外边漫游。"

南洁西听此言觉得有理,
带着满腹怨气回到了内殿卧室,
老国王见王后伤心啜泣,
便说出了轻言细语:

"我亲爱的王后啊,
是什么使你这样的悲凄,
是不是我对你照护不周,
是不是有人得罪了你?

"如我有错你别闷在肚里,
如我有过也要等以后再议,
今天可是个大喜的日子,
我们不该郁郁不乐悲悲戚戚。"

第八章 让位 Chapter 8 Abdication

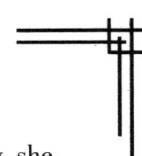

The more Nan Jiexi thought about it, the more angry she became.

Daxi, who was a gossip, took the opportunity to interfere,

"Your majestic Queen,

The king has made promise to you.

When the king comes to your bed tonight,

you should remind him to keep his promise.

Ask him to order Zhao Langma to leave the palace

And stay in the wilderness for twelve years."

Nan Jiexi thought the maid's words made sense.

Holding grudge in her heart, she returned to her inner chamber.

When the old king saw the queen sobbing sadly,

He asked her in a most soft voice,

"My dear queen,

What made you so sad?

Is it because I didn't take good care of you?

Or is there anyone who has offended you?

"If I have done something wrong, don't keep it to yourself.

But please wait until another day for me to right my wrong.

Today is a big day for us to celebrate.

It's no good for us to be gloomy and depressed."

南洁西微微转过头来,
向国王倾泻出怨气:
"我是什么亲爱的王后,
你少来些甜言蜜语。

"你是真心实意爱我吗?
你心里哪还有我的位置,
你说过的话还算不算数?
乘骑大象的国王还讲不讲信义?"

国王觉得南洁西说得突兀,
一时发了愣,半天才说出话:
"哪一天哪一时哪个地方,
我说出口的话变了卦?"

南洁西冷冷一笑:
"我高贵的国王呀,
你是人老昏庸,
还是假装糊涂?

"当年你上天援助叭英打仗,
左手小指头受了刀伤,
是我精心护理才得痊愈,
你可还记得你当时对我怎么讲?

第八章 让位 Chapter 8 Abdication

Tilting her head to the king,
Nan Jiexi vented her resentment,
"What dear queen I am?
Spare your sweet talk."

"Do you really love me?
Do you still have me in your heart?
Do your words still count?
Are you the king riding an elephant true to your words?"

Stunned at Nan Jiexi's abrupt words,
The king didn't speak until a while later,
"At what time what day and where
I changed my mind about what I said?"

Nan Jiexi responded with a sneer,
"My noble king,
Are you really too old to remember things?
Or you just pretended to be so forgetful?

"That year when you went to the heaven to help Baying in fight,
You got your left little finger seriously injured.
It was only out of my careful nursing that you finally recovered.
Do you still remember what you had said to me at that time?

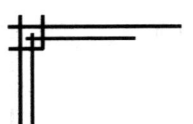

兰嘎西贺 The Ten-Headed King of Langa

"现在帕腊达已长大成人,
他的英俊和威望天下传闻,
你不应该毁约食言,
你应当把王位让他继承。

"你让召朗玛到森林去修行,
十二年不准他回王宫团聚,
当芬芳的芒果花开过十二次,
王位再转让给你的长子。"

走错了路可以返回重走,
说过的话就没法往回收,
面对南洁西提出的要求,
国王没有抵赖和反驳的理由。

国王一阵昏晕周身颤抖,
嘴巴像堵住了一块石头,
他心头有难言的痛苦啊,
紧紧拉着南洁西的手说:

"南洁西呀,我的爱妻,
你的话真使我难受,
我一向真心实意爱你,
当时那样说是一时偏激。

第八章 让位 Chapter 8 Abdication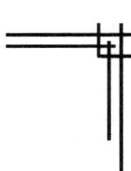

"Now our son Palada has grown up,
His brilliance and reputation are known to the world.
You shouldn't eat your words and break the promise.
It is him that you should choose to ascend the throne.

"Let Zhao Langma go to the forest to practice Buddhism.
He can't come back to the palace for family reunion in twelves years.
Only when the fragrant mango trees bloom for twelve times,
The throne can be transferred to him——your first son."

If you walk the wrong way, you can return and make another choice.
But you can not take back what you have said.
Challenged by Nan Jiexi's demands,
The king could not find anything to deny or refute.

The King fainted with his body trembling terribly.
As a rock was stuffed in his mouth,
Unspeakable pains were stuck in his heart.
Holding Nan Jiexi's hands tightly, he said,

"Nan Jiexi, my beloved wife,
Your words hurt me much.
I have always loved you with all my heart.
I said those words that year in an extreme condition.

"王位自古都是长子承袭,
召朗玛当国王是众望所归,
他敬你胜过对他的亲生母亲,
你不应该对此愤愤不平。

"召朗玛对弟兄情长谊深,
弟弟们对长兄都很尊敬,
你企图为亲生的儿子争王位,
帕腊达决没这个奢念和贪心。

"我们为人处世不能有偏心,
偏心会使亲人造成不幸,
你其他的所有要求都好办,
唯独这个企求不能应允。"

南洁西听了越发激愤,
站起来气冲冲越说越伤心,
"你自己违背自己的诺言,
你撒谎,你骗人!

"我一直把你的话当作金子,
原来我是多么的幼稚轻信,
既然你不答应我也没法,
这可是你自己损坏自己的名声。

"你还教育我要诚恳老实,
而你自己却不守信义,
如果你将王位交给召朗玛,
我就吃下毒药离开你。"

第八章 让位 Chapter 8 Abdication

"For all ages, it is the first son who ascends to the throne.
Zhao Langma to be the King is expected and cheered by all.
He respects you more than he does to his own mother.
You should not remain resentful for his enthronement.

"Zhao Langma has deep affection for his brothers.
The young brothers are also respectful to him.
You attempt to get the throne for your own son,
But Palada himself is by no means so greedy.

"We should be impartial when interacting with people.
Partiality will incur misfortune among our families and relatives.
I can meet all your other requirements,
But for this one, I am resolved to refuse."

Nan Jiexi got more indignant at hearing this.
She stood up angrily and talked more sadly,
"You broke your own promise,
And you lied, you are a liar.

"I have always taken your words as gold,
Now I know how naive and credulous I was.
I can't do anything if you won't keep your promise.
But remember you are ruining your own reputation.

"You preach to me to be honest,
But you yourself are not true to your words.
If you let Zhao Langma ascend to the throne,
I will take poison and leave you forever."

这一说吓得国王周身战栗，
就像毒蛇咬伤无药医治，
就像嘴含槟榔石灰咬破舌头①
就像烈火烧身疼痛不止。

三、召朗玛的决心

东方露出了晨曦，
金鼓已响过三次，
登基典礼都安排就绪，
大臣们个个在宫殿上侍立。

久等不见老国王上殿，
大臣苏门纳到寝宫去请，
只见国王忧郁呆坐，
好半天才开口长叹一声：

"有谁知道我心中的苦楚，
我内心如毒蛇噬咬苦痛万分，
我本要把王位传给大王子，
三王后竟从中作梗。

---

① 傣族习惯，用槟榔加上石灰在嘴里嚼，保护牙齿。石灰味辣，如舌头被咬破，极痛苦。

第八章 让位 Chapter 8 Abdication

Hearing this, the king was in a fit of uncontrollable shudder,
As if he was incurable out of a bite by a poisonous snake.
Or he had to chew betel nut and lime with an injured tongue.①
More as if he was on a raging fire and suffering endless pain.

Ⅲ Zhao Langma's Resolution

The morning sunlight appeared in the east,
And the golden drum had been struck three times.
Everything was ready for the enthronement ceremony,
And the ministers and officials stood in the court side by side.

Having waited for a long time for the old king,
The minister Sumenna went to his bedroom to enquire,
Only to find the old king sitting there sadly.
He didn't make any sound but a long sigh after quite a while,

"Nobody understands what distress I am suffering.
As if I had been bitten by a venomous snake and I am so painful.
I had thought to let the first Prince succeed to the throne,
But now the third queen stood in the way giving me great trouble.

---

① It was the Dai custom to chew betel nut and lime to protect their teeth. Lime is pungent and it would be terribly pain if the tongue got injured with lime in the mouth.

"你赶快把召朗玛找来,
我要当面和他商量,
王位究竟传授给谁,
需要听听他的主张。"

召朗玛应召前来拜见父王,
见父王面带愁容、王后怒气冲冲,
他走近前轻言细语地问:
"有什么不幸的事把双亲折磨?

"是不是嫌我们勐版图小,
父王还想把疆域开拓?
是不是父王身体不适,
还是有什么灾祸在我们勐降落?

"是不是不肖儿有什么不是,
才给父王母后带来了不睦,
纵使我有千条罪万条过,
恳求父王母后宽容饶恕。

"就是下地狱我也不怕,
儿愿替父王母后分担忧愁。"
南洁西瞅瞅国王不开腔,
忍不住自己首先开口:

第八章 让位　Chapter 8 Abdication

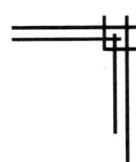

"Hurry up and call Zhao Langma to come here,
I want to have a discussion with him face-to-face.
To whom should I pass on the throne?
I need to know what's in his mind."

Zhao Langma came as summoned to visit his father.
Seeing his father wearing a sad face and the queen in her anger,
He approached forward and asked them in a most soft voice,
"Is there any misfortune afflicting you two, my parents?

"Is it because you think our kingdom is not big enough
So that Father wants to expand our territory?
Or is it because Father doesn't feel very well,
Or some disaster will happen to our country?

"Or is it because I have done something wrong
That brought the discord between you two my parents.
Even if I have made thousands of mistakes and sins,
I still want to beg for your forgiveness.

"I am not afraid of going to the hell,
As long as I can take some share of your worries."
Seeing the king would not open his mouth,
Nan Jiexi could not wait but speak herself first,

"大王子啊,你父王身体无恙,
我们勐也风调雨顺百姓安康,
我对你将实话明讲,
他正在为传王位的事忧伤。

"只为你们弟兄出世前他有言在先,
曾许诺我生的儿子继位为王,
现在我要他履行诺言,
他又反悔要找你商量。"

像金鹿一样善良的召朗玛,
听了这番话无限惆怅,
他思考怎样兑现父王的诺言,
让三王后的心上不致留下创伤。

他听到臣民对自己的赞扬,
仿佛压上石头一样内心惶惶,
他了解纯洁正直的弟弟帕腊达,
论才干和品德完全可以当国王。

召朗玛不愿看到和睦的四兄弟,
在宫廷闹出同根相煎的纠纷,
他没有丝毫愤愤和半点哀怨,
他心地坦然态度十分安详。

第八章 让位 Chapter 8 Abdication

"Our first Prince, your father is safe and sound;
Our country enjoys favorable weather, our people living a happy life.
Here I will tell you the truth,
He is troubled by the succession of the throne.

"He had words before you four brothers were born,
Promising that the son out of my womb would be the King.
Now I ask him to keep his words,
But he regretted for his promise and wanted to consult you."

Zhao Langma, as kind as a gold deer,
Hearing this, he was filled with endless melancholy.
He thought it over how to help Father keep his promise,
And make sure the third queen wouldn't be traumatized.

When he heard the praise of him by the officials and the people,
He felt so uneasy as if a rock was pressed on his heart.
He understood his younger brother Palada of purity and integrity,
Who had enough capability and virtues to be the King.

Zhao Langma didn't expect the discord among their four brothers,
Fearing that could incur the tragedy of fights among families.
Having thought it out, he felt calm and peaceful
Without any indignation, resentment or sadness in his heart.

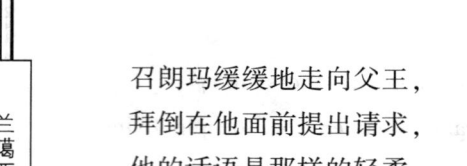

召朗玛缓缓地走向父王,
拜倒在他面前提出请求,
他的话语是那样的轻柔,
宛如平坦的林间悠悠的溪流。

"父王啊,既然过去你已经许诺,
就应该遵守自己说过的话,
我心甘情愿不要王位,
请父王将王位传给弟弟帕腊达。

"他的干练和品德能管理好王国,
他的智慧和善良能处理好纠纷,
他的为人和胸襟能获得臣民爱戴,
他的沉着和勇敢能抵御强敌入侵。

"请父王母后答应我的请求,
允许我离开你们走出宫廷,
儿过去受帕拉西的多年教诲,
深感不足还应再出门学习本领。

"儿要一个人到森林中去修行,
陪伴帕拉西十二个冬春,
儿的话毫无半点虚情假意,
十二年以后儿再跨进宫门。"

第八章 让位 Chapter 8 Abdication

Zhao Langma went to his father slowly,
And he knelt down in front of him and made his request.
He spoke with a gentle voice,
And his words were like quiet stream flowing on a flat plain.

"My dear father the king, since you have made your promise,
You should be true to your words.
I will give up the throne with a willing heart.
Father, please pass on the throne to Palada my youngest brother.

"He has enough ability and morality to govern the country;
He is kind and wise enough to handle all kinds of disputes;
His integrity and generosity will earn him the respect of our people.
He is calm and brave to resist the invasion of powerful enemies.

"Your majestic King and Queen,
Please grant me the permission to leave you and the palace,
Although I have been taught by Palaxi for many years,
I still feel insufficient and need to leave home to improve myself.

"I want to go to the forest alone for practising Buddhism
Accompanying Palaxi for twelve springs and winters.
I said this from the bottom my heart,
And I won't come back to the palace until twelve years later."

像宁静湖面突然卷起狂风，
像万里晴空突然飞来乌云，
儿子的话使父王战栗，
老国王低垂的头猛然抬起。

"像金子铸成的儿子啊，
你不能再到深山老林去，
你已经向帕拉西学过本领，
沓达腊塔王国正等待你来治理。

"禽类啊，唯有凤凰配当百鸟王，
兽类啊，唯有狮子配当林中王，
一个国王有几个王子啊，
长子继承王位理所应当。

"你是长子不在我的跟前，
做父王的我怎能安心，
除非我的心脏停止跳动，
我不能让你到森林去修行。"

"父王是一勐之主说话重千斤，
儿是遵循你的诺言才离开宫廷，
父王既然已向母后许了愿，
就一定要兑现才能取信于民。

第八章　让位　Chapter 8　Abdication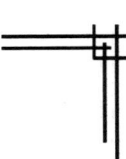

As a gale swept over the surface of a peaceful lake,
Or a clear blue sky was suddenly covered by dark clouds,
The father shuddered at his son Zhao Langma's words.
Then the king raised his drooped head abruptly.

"My dear son, you have a golden heart.
You can not go back to the deep mountain forest.
You have already learned much from Palaxi,
And our Kingdom of Dadalata needs your governance.

"Among birds, only phoenix can be the king,
Among beasts, only lion deserves to be the king of forest.
A king can have many princes,
But only the first-born son has the right to ascend to the throne.

"You are my first son, if you are not by my side,
How can I be free from worries?
Unless my heart stops beating,
I won't let you to go to the forest for practising Buddhism."

"Father, as the king of our nation, your words carry much weight.
I won't leave palace if not for keeping your promise.
Since Father has given your words to the queen,
You have to make it true to earn the trust of your people."

国王见儿子出走的意志坚定,
顿觉周身无力头脑阵阵昏晕,
他望着儿子热泪盈眶,
他哆嗦着拉住儿子的手泣不成声。

这件事很快在臣僚百姓中传开,
就像在平静的湖水里投下石块,
人们纷纷议论谁该执掌宫廷大印,
召朗玛受到全勐臣民的拥戴。

"我们的召朗玛胸怀坦荡,
我们的召朗玛本领高强,
我们的召朗玛又是老国王长子,
应该由他来当我们的新国王。"

四、南西拉的忠贞

荷花啊,在默默流泪,
风儿啊,在低声哀泣,
恩爱夫妻很快就要分离了,
召朗玛思索着怎样和妻子话别。

召朗玛心情沉重地缓步回到内宫,
南西拉满怀喜悦出来迎接,
召朗玛为王她满心高兴,
但却见丈夫双眉紧锁不欢愉。

第八章 让位 Chapter 8 Abdication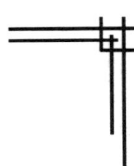

The king witnessed his son's resolution to leave,
All at a sudden, he felt completely weak and dizzy.
Looking at his son and holding his hands,
He sobbed so hard that he could not get a single word out.

The news was spread quickly among the officials and people,
And it was like a rock thrown into a peaceful lake.
People had heated discussion on who should get the court seal,
And all of them agreed that Zhao Langma was the right person.

"Our Zhao Langma has a big heart and open mind.
Our Zhao Langma has great ability and many skills.
Our Zhao Langma is the first-born son of our old king,
He is sure to be the new king of our great kingdom."

Ⅳ The Loyalty of Nan Xila

Lotus was weeping in silence;
Wind was sobbing in low voice.
The loving couple will soon be separated.
Zhao Langma was wondering how to say goodbye to his wife.

Zhao Langma slowly returned to the inner palace with a heavy heart,
And Nan Xila came out to greet him with joy.
She was happy that he would be the king,
But then she found her husband's sad face with a frown.

平时他们犹如一对斑鸠难舍难分，
世上没有谁比他们更缱绻贴心，
还没等南西拉启齿问候，
召朗玛就开口倾诉衷情：

"亲爱的南西拉啊，
痛苦折磨着我的心灵，
我的心啊像已破碎，
我的身啊像失魄落魂。

"我就要和你分别了，
我恰似一只孤船要远出航行，
在烟波浩渺的大海里，
不知要漂浮到哪里留停？

"我要到深山老林中去修行，
要在外生活十二个冬春，
你不要因我出走悲伤难过，
不要用泪水送别远行的亲人。"

南西拉感到异常的突然，
就像五雷轰击脑门心，
南西拉感到十分的惊讶，
问丈夫是否在说疯话。

第八章 让位　Chapter 8　Abdication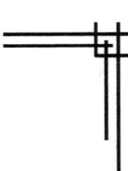

They were always like a pair of inseparable doves.
No couple in the world were more intimate than them.
Before Nan Xila had the chance to greet him,
Zhao Langma started first to pour out his feelings,

"My dearest Nan Xila,
My mind is being tormented;
My heart is almost broken;
I have been battered out of my senses.

"I have to depart from you,
I will travel far as a lonely boat sailing out.
On the vast and misty ocean,
Where can I stop for a rest?

"I am going to the deep mountain forest to practise Buddhism.
There I will live alone for twelve springs and winters.
Don't be sad for my departure;
Don't bid farewell to your loved one with tears."

Nan Xila felt so abrupt and shocked,
As if she was struck by five thunders.
In great surprise, Nan Xila asked her husband
If he lost his mind and was talking crazy.

召朗玛啊却对妻子娓娓话别:
"王位要由弟弟帕腊达继承,
我与你生离不一定是死别,
十二年后我再回王室团聚。

"你对年老的父王和三个母后,
要像亲生女儿一样孝敬,
要在他们心上播下欢乐的种子,
不要招惹他们生气烦心。

"你还要和弟妹们和睦相处,
要使几个妯娌相敬相亲,
你对宫女也要像亲姐妹,
和和气气,平等待人。

"弟弟帕腊达继承了王位,
你不要羡慕也不要嫉妒,
要像女仆一样效忠贤明的君主,
又像姐姐那样尽到嫂嫂的责任。

"你要循规蹈矩奉命唯谨,
你在宫中如感到寂寞孤零,
想回到娘家侍奉年老的双亲,
我也没有疑义任你择定。

第八章 让位 Chapter 8 Abdication

Zhao Langma said goodbye to his wife gently,
"My younger brother Palada will be enthroned.
We will be parted but not for ever.
Twelves years later, I will come back and we will reunion.

"To our old father the king and the three queens,
You should be pious and respectful as their own daughter.
You should sow the seed of happiness in their hearts.
Never provoke them to get angry or upset.

"You should also live in peace with our younger brothers and sisters.
And try your best to make sisters-in-law respect and love each other.
Treat maids as they were your own sisters.
Treat people around you kindly and equally.

"My younger brother Palada will ascend to the throne.
Don't ever be envious or jealous of him.
You should serve him as a servant to her wise monarch;
Be conscientious of your duty as his sister-in-law.

"Follow our traditions and do as your duties command.
If you feel lonely in our palace,
And want to go back to your home to serve your old parents,
I won't have any doubt but let you yourself make the decision.

兰嘎西贺 The Ten-Headed King of Langa

"我就要离开你了,
走向那茂密的原始森林,
从此后苍翠的树木和我做伴,
从此后葱郁的花草陪我修行。"

南西拉聆听着丈夫的叮嘱,
泪珠像廊檐水点点浸湿衣襟,
辛酸的哽咽撕裂着召朗玛的肺腑,
低沉的话语震撼着召朗玛的心。

"像宝石一样晶亮的夫君啊,
你为何声声说着离别的话?
我俩相亲相爱亲密无间,
你为何要摒弃你眷恋着的妻子?

"我们俩已经结婚多年,
你的妻子一直对你忠贞如一,
让我们一辈子永远在一起,
就是死也要一同去死。

"难道你忘了我父王的教诲,
要我为你分担欢乐和烦忧,
要我们相敬如宾休戚与共,
要我们永不分离形影相随。

第八章 让位 Chapter 8 Abdication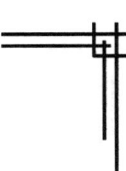

"Now I have to say goodbye to you,
I will walk into the thick primitive forest;
Verdant trees will be my companies;
Lush flowers and grass will be with me practising Buddhism."

Nan Xila listened to her husband's repeated advice,
Her tears like raindrops along the eaves drenched her clothes.
Her bitter weeping tore Zhao Langma's heart apart.
And her words in low voice touched his heart.

"My dear husband, you are as bright as a precious stone.
Why you kept saying these departing words?
We love each other and we are so intimate,
Why you abandon your beloved wife?

"We have been married for so many years.
You know your wife has always been faithful to you.
Let us live together for our whole life,
Let us be with each other till our death.

"Have you forgotten the teachings of my father the king?
I should share with you the joys and the sorrows;
We should love and respect each other in times of good and bad;
And we should be inseparable like shadows of one another.

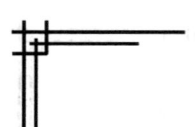

"恩爱的斑鸠永远不分离,
就是狂风暴雨来袭击,
两只斑鸠也要依偎在一起,
你丢下我一人生活多么孤寂。

"你是我亲爱的丈夫,
我是你随身的影子,
你走到天涯海角我都跟随你,
你赴汤蹈火我也要跟着你去。

"你的心地像日月星辰那样光明,
你不愿为王,决心出走我无异议,
请让我跟随到荒林去侍候你,
让我尽到妻子对丈夫的职责。

"比水重的是山上的石头,
比石头重的是夫妻的情义,
义重如山的恩爱夫妻啊,
千钧霹雳也不能轰裂。

"如果你因为不再爱我而离开,
你不想让我随你去,
那我宁愿结束我短暂的生命,
让你无牵无挂四处游荡。"

第八章 让位 Chapter 8 Abdication

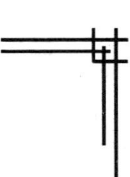

"The doves in love stay together forever.
Even when they are attacked by storms,
They will snuggle against each other.
How lonely my life will be if you leave me.

"You are my dear husband,
And I am your shadow,
I will follow you to the ends of the earth.
I will follow you through fires and waters.

"Your heart is as bright as the sun, the moon and the stars.
I have no objection to your resolution to give up the throne and leave.
But please let me follow you to the wilderness to serve you.
Let me do my duty as a wife to her husband.

"What is heavier than water is the rocks on the mountains;
What is heavier than rocks is the love between husband and wife.
The affectionate husband and wife with love are as firm as a hill,
Even the most terrible thunders can not tear them apart.

"If you leave because you don't love me any more,
And you don't want me to follow you,
Then I would rather end my short life,
And you can wander around free from any care."

南西拉痛苦地边诉边泣,
召朗玛用好言好语劝慰:
"我亲爱的妻子啊,
我从未编造谎言欺骗过你。

"我对你没半点厌烦心思,
我并未生枝生叶要抛弃你,
我俩情投意合相亲相爱,
我们的爱情天下无与伦比。

"我美丽的娇妻啊,
我对你没半点虚情假意,
如果我存有丝毫的异心,
上苍可察觉,神灵来惩治。

"我不忍心让你同去,
只因为山路陡峭崎岖,
只因为森林虎狼出没,
只因为原野丛生荆棘。

"我担心你随我到荒林去,
饥寒的生活折磨你,
吸血的蚊虻叮咬你,
凶猛的野兽伤害你。

第八章 让位　Chapter 8　Abdication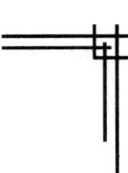

Nan Xila sobbed bitterly as she poured out her heart.
Zhao Langma comforted her with most gentle words,
"My dear beloved wife,
I have never made up lies to deceive you.

"My beloved wife, how could I have been bored with you?
I am leaving you not because I have other branches or leaves.
We are kindred spirits loving each other so much;
There is unparalleled love to ours in the world.

"My beautiful wife,
I am always true to you without any affectation,
If I am not faithful to you in any way,
The heaven will detect it and let me be punished.

"I can't bear the idea of your going with me,
Since the mountain road is rough and steep,
In the forest tigers and wolves haunt;
And thorns and thistles grow rampantly in the wilderness.

"I am afraid if you follow me to the wilderness,
You will be tortured by hunger and bitter cold.
Blood-sucking mosquitoes will bite you,
And the fierce beasts will attack and hurt you.

"白天只能找野果来充饥,
夜晚只能在草地上栖息,
日晒只能在树荫下乘凉,
雨来只能在大树旁躲避。

"这些说不尽的艰辛苦楚,
你怎么能忍受得住,
你这么娇嫩的身躯,
怎么受得了风雨侵袭。

"想到这些我心烦意乱,
请你听我的忠言规劝,
你还是安住在宫廷之中,
打消跟随我去莽林的意念。

"十二年的时间说来不算短,
不然你就回勐甘纳嘎去,
在那里耐心地等待我,
十二年后我俩再见面。"

召朗玛历数出走的艰难困苦,
坚贞的南西拉听了毫不介意,
她祈求的脸上挂满泪珠,
任召朗玛如何抚慰也无法止住。

第八章 让位 Chapter 8 Abdication

"During the day only wild fruits can be found to meet your stomach,

At night you can take a rest on nothing else but the grass on the land.

You can only be cooled by the shades of trees when it's too hot.

And there are only trees that can be your shelter from the rains.

"How you, my dear love, can endure
All these unspeakable hardships?
How your delicate body can withstand
All the attacks of heavy rain and wind?

"I got so upset and troubled whenever I thought of this.
Please listen to me and follow my advice,
You'd better still stay in the palace.
Dismiss the idea of following me to the forests.

"Twelve years is not a short period of time,
Maybe you can go back to the kingdom of Gannaga.
Wait for me there patiently,
We'll meet again in twelve years."

Zhao Langma enumerated all the hardships on the road,
But faithful Nan Xila did not mind those at all.
Her pleading face was covered with unstoppable tears,
No matter how hard Zhao Langma tried to comfort her.

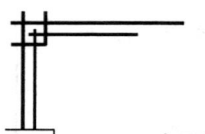

南西拉激动地诉说：
"金叶子般的哥哥呀，
我知道你爱我胜于真金，
你知道我爱你白璧无瑕。

"如果你不嫌弃我这个妻子，
就答应我随你一道出走，
让我俩一同去欢度自由的生活，
让我俩一同去经历命运的坎坷。

"没有不配彩旗的车子，
车子没有彩旗就不美丽，
没有离开丈夫的妻子，
妻子离开丈夫就会遭凌辱。

"人们围园栽种果树，
结果时不会不摘采，
妻子保持的贞节，
难道你甘愿遭人破坏。

"你就像喜爱花卉的蜜蜂，
我犹如你吮吸过的花蕊，
鲜花多么需要蜜蜂的抚慰，
你怎么能听凭花儿遭雨淋风吹。

"你说的丛林里那些艰辛苦楚，
比起我俩的爱情又算得了什么，
只要有你伴随在我的身边，
就是再艰苦心里也舒服。

第八章 让位　Chapter 8 Abdication

Nan Xila said to Zhao Langma excitedly,
"My gold-leave-like big brother,
I know you love me more than real gold,
And you know I love you more than pure jade.

"If you don't intend to abandon me your wife,
Please let me go with you to the forest.
Let us live a happy and free life together;
Let us go through the hardships together.

"There is no cart that isn't decorated with banners.
A cart without colorful banners is not pretty.
There is no wife that lives away from her husband.
A wife living alone will be insulted by others.

"An orchard is kept to plant fruit trees.
When they bear fruits, gardeners will harvest them.
Your wife keeps her chasteness.
Can you bear it will be defiled by somebody else?

"You are like a bee who loves flowers.
I am like a flower that you have sucked.
A flower needs a bee's touch and comfort.
How can you leave the flower destroyed by rain and wind?

"The hardships in the jungle are nothing
Compared to the sweetness of our love.
As long as you are by my side,
I feel comfortable in spite of the hardships.

"只要和你在一起,
就是野果充饥也醇美,
就是树叶垫着睡也安逸,
就是虎狼成群也胆粗。

"就像麂子离不开草地,
南西拉怎能离得开丈夫,
就是你一辈子住在森林里,
我都永远愉快地跟随你。"

有这样一个矢志忠贞的妻子,
召朗玛感到无限的幸福,
妻子的话如同火塘暖和着他的心,
他感激地把爱妻紧紧搂在怀里。

"亲爱的南西拉啊,
你的话是多么的熨帖,
你珍重夫妻情义决心随我出走,
我还有什么话来阻挡你。

"你的一片忠贞使我十分感动,
你真诚的要求我同意,
我要把你当作一颗珍珠,
永远藏在随身的筒帕里。"

南西拉听到丈夫表示同意,
破涕为笑,转悲为喜,
她按照召朗玛的嘱咐,
迅速做好远行的准备。

第八章 让位 Chapter 8 Abdication

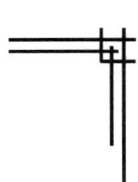

"As long as we are together,
It's good to have wild fruits to fill my stomach;
It's cosy to sleep on the stacks of leaves;
And I will be brave enough to face tigers and wolves.

"Just as muntjac can not live without grass,
How can Nan Xila live without her husband?
Even if you will live in the forest for the rest of your life,
I will follow you happily, wherever and forever."

Having such a steadfastly faithful wife,
Zhao Langma felt a surge of indefinite happiness.
His wife's words warmed his heart like a stove,
And appreciatively he held his wife tightly in his arms.

"My dear Nan Xila,
It's so considerate of you to say this to me.
You treasure our love and resolve to leave with me.
I can't say anything more to stop you.

"Your faithfulness touches me deeply,
And I approve of your sincere request.
I will treat you as the most precious pearl,
I will hide you in my Tongpa that follows me forever."

When Nan Xila heard her husband's consent,
Her tears turned to smiles, sadness to happiness.
She did everything as Zhao Langma instructed
To promptly get ready for the long journey.

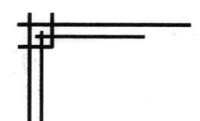

兰嘎西贺 The Ten-Headed King of Langa

召朗玛临行向腊嘎纳告别，
把出走的原因详细告诉二弟，
腊嘎纳敬佩哥哥心胸宽广，
腊嘎纳称颂嫂嫂品德高尚。

腊嘎纳的心啊像烈火在燃烧，
他请求和哥哥一同远走高飞，
召朗玛费尽口舌多方劝阻，
腊嘎纳仍然执意尾随。

腊嘎纳担心哥哥嫂嫂的安危，
他要手持弓箭把他们保卫，
他要忠心耿耿服侍哥哥嫂嫂，
凭借他的勇气和智慧。

忠厚善良的腊嘎纳啊，
要尽到做弟弟的责任，
他的情谊比海洋还深沉，
召朗玛只得答应他一道远行。

第八章 让位　Chapter 8 Abdication

Before leaving, Zhao Langma said goodbye to Lagana,
And he explained in details about his departure.
Lagana admired his older brother's magnanimity,
And he praised his sister-in-law for her noble character.

The heart of Lagana was burning like fire,
And he asked to fly away with his brother.
Zhao Langma tried hard to dissuade him from the idea,
But Lagana was still determined to follow him.

Lagana was concerned about his brother and sister-in-law.
He wanted to protect them with his bow and arrows.
He wanted to serve his oldest brother and sister-in-law
With his loyalty, his courage and his wisdom.

The sincere and kind Lagana,
He wanted to fulfil his duty as a younger brother,
And his love was deeper than the ocean.
Zhao Langma could not refuse but let him to go with him.

第九章 出走

一、去森林修行

黎明时人们还未睡醒,
宫廷是那样的寂静,
召朗玛带上宝刀、飞鞋和弓箭,
与妻子和弟弟悄悄从后门离开宫廷。

他们匆匆走得急促,
出城穿坝又进入了雾瘴弥漫的森林,
不料他们的行动被一个侍臣看见了,
他急忙跑进宫向国王禀报。

国王急令沙腊梯前去追赶,
沙腊梯立即骑马奔向森林,
从早晨直追到太阳落山,
才追上了召朗玛他们三人。

"尊贵的两位王子和公主啊,
我带来的国王的旨意胜过黄金,
要你们三位快返回王宫,
免得他们终日为你们担心。"

第九章 出走 Chapter 9 Exodus

Chapter 9 Exodus

I To Practice Buddhism in the Forest

At dawn, everyone was still in their dreams.
The court was really quiet. Zhao Langma,
Taking his magic knife, flying shoes and bow with arrows,
Left quietly through the back gate with his wife and younger brother.

They went along their way hurriedly,
Out of the city, across the plain and into the foggy forest.
Unexpectedly, they were seen by a courtier,
Who rushed into the palace to report to the King.

The king ordered Shalati to go and run after them.
Shalati jumped onto a horse and galloped to the forest.
He ran after them from morning till sunset,
Finally he caught up with the three of them.

"Distinguished two princes and princess,
The order from the King that I brought is heavier than gold.
He asks you three to return to the palace,
Lest they worry about you all day long."

英俊的召朗玛回答说:
"谢谢你了,沙腊梯,
请回去禀告父王和母后,
我们既已出走就不回头。

"前面的旅途还很遥远,
我们还要翻山越岭赶路程,
要到森林的帕拉西那儿去修行,
学好了经典和本领再回宫廷。"

沙腊梯说尽好话劝阻,
三朵鲜花听不进一星半点,
他们来到撒腊树腊江边,
夜幕降临还各自坚持己见。

四人在茂密的树林里休息,
困倦的流浪者安睡在树叶床上,
夜里林间吹拂的山风,
飒飒声响催他们进入梦乡。

当沙腊梯正睡得香甜,
召朗玛他们又悄悄启程,
待到太阳从山头升起,
三朵鲜花已经翻越了几座山岭。

第九章 出走 Chapter 9 Exodus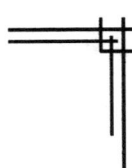

The handsome Zhao Langma answered,
"Thank you very much, Shalati.
Please tell my father the king and mother the queen
There is no turning back the moment we started our journey.

"We have a very long way to go,
Climbing over mountains to the forest.
We will practice Buddhism with Palaxi learning classics
And we will come back home after we have acquired all skills."

Shalati tried hard to talk them out of their idea,
But the three fresh flowers turned a deaf ear to his words.
Till they came to the river of Salashula at dusk,
Both sides still insisted on their own views.

The four of them took a rest in the dense woods,
And like tired travelers they slept on the bed of leaves.
The wind from mountain swept through the woods at night,
The rustling sound accompanied them into their dreams.

When Shalati was still in sound sleep,
Zhao Langma they three started out secretly.
Till the sun rose from the top of mountain,
The three fresh flowers have already climbed over several hills.

古木参天的森林幽深茂密，
箐沟和溪流清澈见底，
良辰美景他们无心欣赏，
绮丽风光提不起他们的兴趣。

三朵鲜花在一条澄澈的河边休息，
只见一群群游鱼在水中嬉戏，
腊嘎纳从林间摘来甜果，
递给哥哥嫂嫂解渴充饥。

三朵鲜花穿行在阴森的丛林，
只有树上的鸟雀和他们伴行，
寻伴的黄鹂在箐间孤声啼叫，
阵阵啼声是那样的哀怨悲切。

可怜娇贵的南西拉啊，
树枝挂乱了她的头发，
荆棘钩破了她的衣裳，
白嫩的脚杆划出了斑斑血迹。

南西拉从小没有走过山路，
痛苦折磨着她孱弱的身躯，
她忍不住疼痛暗中饮泣，
召朗玛听了犹如心肝穿刺。

第九章 出走 Chapter 9 Exodus

The forest was deep and serene with old and tall trees.
The streams were so clear that you could see into the bottom.
But they were not in the mood appreciating the pretty scenery,
Or not in the spirit enjoying themselves on this beautiful day.

The three fresh flowers took a break by a clear river.
They saw swarms of fish having a frolic in the water.
Lagana gathered melons and fruits from the woods,
And he handed them to his brother and sister-in-law to eat.

The three fresh flowers walking through the dark woods,
Only birds in the trees accompanied them on the way.
A golden oriole in search of companions warbled at night.
His warbling sounded so forlorn and sorrowful.

The poor delicate Nan Xila,
Her hair got tangled by the branches of trees;
Her clothes were torn out by the thistle and thorns;
And her tender legs were scratched strips of bloodstains.

Since childhood, Nan Xila had never walked on a mountain path.
Her frail body was tortured by all kinds of sores and pains.
She could not help but weep quietly. Hearing her weeping,
Zhao Langma felt as if his heart were stabbed and pierced.

他搀扶着她好言相慰：
"亲爱的南西拉呀，
你如当初听我的劝告，
现在也不会受此苦楚。

"今天看到你受这样的煎熬，
就像撕破我的五脏六腑，
如今既已从王宫出来，
就不要惧怕旅途的险阻。"

温柔的南西拉非常体贴丈夫，
强颜作笑忍住了泣哭说：
"那是太阳晒得汗水淌，
不是妹妹滴落的泪珠。

"夫君啊，只要跟你在一起，
含辛茹苦心里也舒服，
还要感谢弟弟腊嘎纳，
多亏他一路上把我们照顾。"

三朵鲜花走走停停，
昼行夜宿趱行了一个月，
终于来到了巴腊米底森林，
蹒跚地走进修行者的茅屋。

三朵鲜花上前合掌致意：
"好心肠的帕拉西啊，
我们三人向你问好，
你在森林日子过得可幸福？"

第九章 出走 Chapter 9 Exodus

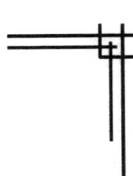

He helped her by her arm and comforted her,
"My dear Nan Xila,
If you had taken my advice,
You wouldn't have to suffer all these.

"Seeing what you have suffered today,
I felt so painful as if my body were torn apart.
Since we have already been out of the palace,
Don't be afraid of the hardships on the journey."

The gentle Nan Xila was considerate to her husband.
She tried hard to stop weeping and put on a smile, saying,
"That was not the tears that I shed,
But the drops of sweat under the hot sun.

"My dear husband, as long as we are together,
I feel good even facing all sorts of hardship.
What's more, I should give thanks to Lagana, our brother,
For his taking care of us all the way."

The three fresh flowers journeyed on and off.
After a month of travelling at day time and rest at night,
They finally got to the forest of Balamidi,
And they staggered into the thatched cottage of hermits.

The three fresh flowers came forward with folded palms,
"Our kind-hearted Palaxi,
Please accept our greeting.
Are you living a happy life in the forest?"

317

福星高照的帕拉西答道：
"感谢你们三人的问候，
我在这里隐居修行多年，
生活无忧无虑深居简出。

"你们三人长得堂堂正正，
一个个像王族的子孙，
你们从什么地方来，
是不是有心来修行？"

召朗玛说明了心愿和来意，
又谦和地叙述了出走的经过，
年老的帕拉西听了十分高兴，
欣然收下他们做他的徒弟。

帕拉西摆出新鲜瓜果，
盛情款待三个王室的子孙，
从此他们虔诚地念经拜佛，
陪伴帕拉西修行苦度时日。

二、国王之死

太阳已经照亮了山峦，
成群的鸟儿欢跳鸣啭，
沉睡的沙腊梯从睡梦中醒来，
三朵鲜花已不在身边。

第九章 出走 Chapter 9 Exodus

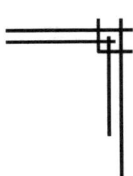

The much-blessed Palaxi responded,
"Thank you three for your greeting.
I have been living in seclusion here for many years,
Having little contact with the world, I am living a carefree life.

"You three have majestic bearings,
Looking like descendants of royal families.
Where are you from?
Do you come here for practising Buddhism?"

Zhao Langma told him their plan and wishes,
And also their experience of the journey.
The old Palaxi was very glad to hear these,
And accepted them happily as his disciples.

Palaxi got out fresh melons and fruits
To entertain the three royal descendants.
Ever since then devoutly chanting sutra and worshiping Buddha,
They accompanied Palaxi and lived a simple and hard life.

II   The Death of the King

The sunlight brightened the mountains,
And flocks of birds chirped in the woods.
Shalati was woken up from his dream
Only to find the three fresh flowers had disappeared.

他睡眼惺忪四处寻觅,
急得像热锅上的蚂蚁,
跑疼了脚板,喊哑了嗓子,
也不见三朵鲜花的踪迹。

沙腊梯只好回宫禀报真情,
老国王悲痛得一阵昏迷,
众臣僚和王后连忙急救,
他醒来又呼唤出走的儿子和儿媳。

老国王只要一闭上眼睛,
就好像召朗玛站在面前,
睁开眼睛又什么也不见,
不几天就在梦呓中闭眼长眠。

失掉丈夫的三个王后,
跪在国王身边放声恸哭,
她们哭得趴下又直起,
泪水像山泉潺湲落地。

宫女们跟着王后伤心掉泪,
大臣头人也都低首抽泣,
宫廷里一片悲戚,
哀号声宛如八月山野的蝉鸣。

第九章 出走 Chapter 9 Exodus

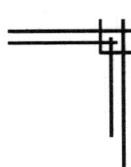

He searched around for them with sleepy eyes,
And he was as worried as ants on a hot pan.
He has got his feet sore and voice lost,
But still he could not find any trace of the three fresh flowers.

Shalati could not do anything but to go back to the palace to report it.

Hearing it, the old king was in such a grief that he went into coma.

With the help from his officials and queens, he came back to life.

Then he called his sons and daughter-in-law again and again.

Whenever the old king closed his eyes,
He felt Zhao Langma standing in front of him.
But when he opened his eyes, he didn't find anything.
Only a few days later, in dreams he closed his eyes forever.

The three queens lost their husband,
And they knelt down by the side of the king and cried.
They cried so hard that they collapsed onto the ground,
Their tears ran down like waterfall from the top of the mountain.

The maid shed their sorrowful tears by the side of the queens.

The officials and tribe chiefs sobbed with their lowered heads.

The palace was filled with infinite grief,
The wails were like the cries of cicadas in the wilderness in August.

小王子沙达鲁嘎强忍住悲痛,
召集全勐的大臣头人议事,
三个哥哥都不在王宫里,
只有他出面为父王准备丧仪。

官员们忙碌着积极筹备,
制作了形似宫殿的帕纱,
镶嵌的金珠银粒闪闪发光,
又用金条银片镶成国王遗像。

油漆棺材涂上金粉,
灵堂昼夜灯火通明,
祭奠的人群络绎不绝,
大臣和头人们轮流守灵。

武官苏念达和沙腊梯坐上战车,
奉命去接三王子帕腊达,
他们马不停蹄日夜赶路,
一个多月才到达金色的勐果嘎腊。

他们见了三王子帕腊达,
聪明的沙腊梯上前报禀:
"奉国王旨意前来接你回去,
请王子即刻启程。"

第九章 出走 Chapter 9 Exodus

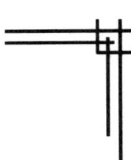

The youngest prince Shadaluga held back his sorrow,
And summoned the officials and chieftains together for consultation.
None of his three old brothers was in the palace,
So he was the only one to prepare for the funeral of his father.

The official hurried to get the funeral ready.
A miniature palace-like bamboo house was made,
The golden and silver grains that decorated it sparkling.
They framed the picture of the king with golden and silver strips.

The coffin was gilded with gold powder.
The mourning hall was lighted day and night;
The mourning people came in like endless stream;
And the ministers and chieftains kept the wake in turn.

The general Sunianda and Shalati rode on a chariot,
Following the order to get Palada the third prince back.
They traveled day and night without a break for a month,
And finally they arrived at the golden kingdom of Guogala.

When they met the third prince Palada,
The cleaver Shalati went forward to report,
"We are under the king's order to get you back.
Your majestic, please set out on the journey right now."

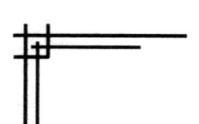

兰噶西贺 The Ten-Headed King of Langa

帕腊达辞别了外婆和舅父，
坐上战车立即上路，
他们驱车踏进祖国的边境，
边境的森林异常的阴沉。

他们看不见花开，听不到鸟叫，
偶闻猴子发出一声声心寒的哀鸣，
老周鸟和乌鸦凄厉地叫着掠过头顶，
有的环绕战车飞个不停。

帕腊达见此情景心中惴惴不安，
用疑虑的口吻询问两个侍臣：
"这是什么样的征兆？
是不是我们勐发生不幸？"

苏念达和沙腊梯极力掩藏内心的痛苦，
不愿在旅途中对王子吐露真情，
"放心吧，这不是什么不祥的预兆，
猴鸣鸟飞是对你的问候和欢迎。"

帕腊达听了两个侍臣的话，
一直没有消除心中的疑雾愁云，
他归心似箭命令驱车狂奔，
一个月后终于回到了自己的都城。

第九章 出走 Chapter 9 Exodus

After bidding farewell to his grandmother and uncle,
Palada jumped onto the chariot and started the journey.
When they stepped on the frontier of their motherland,
The forest seemed exceptionally gloomy and sombre.

They didn't see blooming flowers or hear birds chirping.
Occasionally they heard the sorrowful wails of monkeys.
The black crows flew over their heads cracking mournfully,
Some of them even circling around their chariot.

At the sight of the scene, Palada felt uneasy in his heart.
He questioned the two officials doubtfully,
"What kind of omen is this?
Any misfortune befell our country?"

Sunianda and shalati struggled to hide their inner pains,
Unwilling to tell prince Palada the truth during the journey.
"Take it easy, this is not any ominous omen.
Monkey and birds came to greet and welcome you back home."

The words of the two courtiers still could not disperse
The doubtful clouds haunted in the heart of Palada.
He was so anxious to be home that he ordered to travel at full gallop.
A month later, they finally returned to their home city.

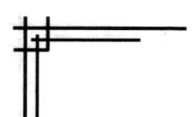

百姓们见帕腊达驱车归来,
蜂拥着纷纷向王子朝拜,
可是他们一个个愁容满面,
有的噙着眼泪向他进言:

"我们尊敬的正直的王子啊,
你的父王已闭上双眼离开人间,
现在全勐臣民正为他筹办国葬,
你快进王宫前往灵堂祭奠。"

帕腊达听后惊得发愣,
转过头来问两位侍臣:
"苏念达、沙腊梯呀,
他们说的事是假还是真?"

满脸忧愁的沙腊梯痛苦地回答:
"他们说的是真情。"
帕腊达有些愠怒地质问:
"那在旅途中你们为什么不露风声?"

苏念达、沙腊梯泪水滚滚,
"请王子体谅我俩的良苦用心,
一路上没把真情向你透露,
是担心你知道后悲极伤身。"

第九章 出走 Chapter 9 Exodus

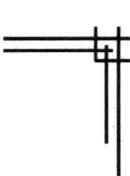

When people saw Palada galloping back,
They flocked to greet and bow to him.
But everyone of them wore a sorrowful face,
And some of them went up to tell him in tears,

"Our respectable and righteous prince,
Your father has closed his eyes and left the world.
Now all his officials and subject are preparing a state funeral for him.
Hurry up to the mourning hall in the palace for the memorial service."

Palada got totally stunned at the news.
Turning his head, he asked the two courtiers,
"Sunianda and Shalati,
What they said is true or false?"

The sorrowful-faced Shalati responded painfully,
"What they said is true."
Palada questioned him angrily,
"Then why you didn't mention even one word about it?"

Sunianda and Shalati answered in rolling tears,
" Your highness, please understand we lied with good intentions.
We didn't tell you the truth on the way back home
In case that you would be struck down by great grief."

帕腊达理解了他们的心意,
没再责怪就急忙奔进灵堂,
他虽然没有放声啼哭,
可泪水已遮住了视线。

宫女达西闻讯前来拜见,
按照南洁西的吩咐向王子进言:
"王子啊,你们母子前去奔丧之时,
老国王就已决定让位给他的长子。

"你母亲回来要求他履行前约,
让你来把王位承嗣,
大王子知情后毅然出走,
为的是让你父王实践诺言。

"老国王一气之下驾崩归天,
由你继承王位是理所当然,
你哥哥召朗玛自愿让位给你,
你就心安理得地把国家掌管。"

帕腊达听了悲痛已极,
他的心啊犹如万箭穿刺,
他大声叱责宫女达西,
不准她多嘴多舌再胡说下去。

第九章 出走　Chapter 9　Exodus

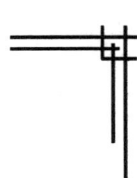

Palada understood that they meant well,
He rushed into the mourning hall without blaming them.
Although he didn't cry out,
Tears filled and covered over his eyes.

The maid Daxi got the news and came to greet him.
As ordered by Nan Jiexi, she said to the prince,
"Your prince, when you and your mother left for the funeral,
The old king had decided to pass on the throne to his first-born son.

"When your mother came back and asked him to keep his promise
That you should be the successor to the throne.
When the prince Zhao Langma got to know this,
He left home resolutely so that your father could be true to his words.

"The old king got so sad and angry that he demised in a few days.
It is natural for you to ascend to the throne.
You older brother voluntarily gave the throne to you,
And you can govern the country with a clear conscience."

Palada was in extreme grief at hearing this,
As if his heart had been pierced by thousands of arrows.
He chided the maid Daxi in a loud voice
Asking her to stop talking nonsense like this.

善良纯洁的沙达鲁嘎来看望哥哥，
兄弟俩商量为父王举行隆重奠祭，
为了老国王的灵魂能够升天，
全勐上下要祭赕一个月。

到了庄严洁净的日子，
全勐臣民将灵柩送进了森林，
有福气的老人点着了柴薪，
老国王的尸体在大火中化成灰烬。

三位王后哭着向丈夫告别，
哀伤的眼泪像雨点洒淋，
千万人的哭声和眼泪啊，
像要把大地和森林侵吞。

三天后收拢骨灰装进陶罐，
又把陶罐安放在陵墓中，
请佛爷念佛诵经，
超度老国王的灵魂升天庭。

三、拒绝回宫

一个勐不能没有主宰的国王，
帕腊达兄弟为哥嫂的出走十分伤心，
正直的帕腊达不愿坐国王的宝座，
他特意去和三位母后商量。

第九章 出走 Chapter 9 Exodus

The pure and kind Shadaluga came to visit his older brother.
They discussed to hold a grand memorial ceremony for their father.
For the soul of the old king to ascend to heaven,
The whole nation should offer sacrifice for a whole month.

When the solemn and clean day came,
The officials and subjects carried the coffin into the forest.
The blessed old people set the firewood on fire,
The corpse of the old king was cremated into ashes.

Three queens cried goodbye to their husband,
Their sorrowful tears fell off like rain drops.
The weeping and tears of tens of millions of people
Seemed to swallow the forest and the earth.

Three days later the ashes were gathered in a pottery pot,
Which was then placed safe in the mausoleum.
Monks were invited to chant Buddhist sutra
So as to save the soul of the old king ascending to heaven.

III Refusal to Go Back to the Palace

It is impossible for a country not to have a governing King.
Feeling very sad for the departure of his brothers and sister-in-law,
The upright Palada didn't want to sit on the throne of the king.
So he went specially to consult with the three queens.

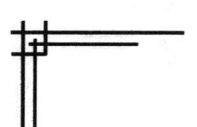

"尊敬的母后啊,
按照传统理应由大哥召朗玛继位,
生身的母亲啊,
你不该把父王过去的诺言当作把柄。

"你端出父王的诺言大哥哪能不谦让,
他出走完全是为了维护父王的威望,
大哥是一位品行高尚本领高强的人,
我们应请他回来主持全勐的朝政。"

兄弟俩和母后们商议决定,
立即带领人马去把召朗玛三人找寻,
他们在深山老林里找了一个多月,
终于在一簇树丛中找到了他们三人。

三人用树枝树叶搭了一间草屋,
火塘边一堆堆树疙瘩,
屋角摆放着野菜野果,
这一切显示着修行者的淡泊生涯。

第九章 出走 Chapter 9 Exodus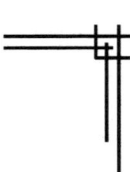

"Your Majesty queens, according to our tradition,
My oldest brother Zhao Langma should be the king.
My dear mother,
You should not have used the words of Father as a hostage.

"You used Father's promise as a pretext, my brother had no choice.
He left home just to defend our father's reputation.
Our big brother is man of integrity and capability.
We should plead him to come back and be the ruler of the country."

After discussing with the queens, the two brothers made the decision.
Leading the troops, they set off to look for Zhao Langma them three.
They searched for them for a month in the deep mountain forest.
And finally they found them three among a groove of trees.

They had built a cottage with tree branches and leaves.
By the fireplace were stacks of dead tree roots as firewood.
At the corner of the house were placed wild vegetables and fruits.
All these were evidence of the simple life of Buddhism practitioner.

兄弟母子别后重逢悲喜交加，
大王后说出像糯米饭柔软的话：
"三个心爱的儿啊，
你们为什么要远离自己的爹妈？

"全勐百姓都为失掉你们而伤心，
妈妈想念你们都想出了病，
现在你们的父王已寿终正寝，
召朗玛是长子理应回去把王位继承。"

三王后南洁西愧疚地说：
"我不该听信谗言和调唆，
不该让嫉妒占据我的心，
只有你们返回宫廷我的罪责才会减轻。"

宛似宝像般的召朗玛三人，
听到父王逝世的消息泪流不止，
知道了母后和弟弟的来意，
召朗玛强忍住悲痛安慰母后南洁西：

第九章 出走　Chapter 9 Exodus

When they met each other, the brothers, the mothers and the sons,

They felt a mixture of sadness and happiness.

The first queen said in a voice as soft as the cooked glutinous rice,

"My children, why you separated yourselves from your parents?"

"The people all over the country were sad for the loss of you;

I, your mother, got sick out of missing you so much.

Now your father the king had passed away.

You as the first son should go back and succeed to the throne."

The youngest queen Nan Jiexi said guiltily,

"I should not have been so credulous of slander and instigation,

Nor should I have let jealousy occupy my heart.

My guilt can only be alleviated by your return to the palace."

Zhao Langma they three, as precious as dignified as statues of Buddha,

Could not hold back their tears at the news of their father's death.

When he got to know the intention of his mother queens and brothers,

Langma suppressed his sorrow and comforted the queen of Nan Jiexi,

"金叶般的南洁西母后啊,
你让父王履行诺言合乎情理,
儿子丝毫没有埋怨之意,
请你不要为这件事烦恼折磨自己。

"既然父王盟誓有言在先,
做儿子的就应该遵奉先辈的诺言,
我离开宫廷到森林里修行,
绝不是对母后和弟弟有什么怨恨。

"到森林修行是我今生的心愿,
我要在磨难中把自己锤炼,
人的一生总要碰到曲折和痛苦,
就是上苍叭英也难免。

"我已将心愿向叭英盟誓,
发过的誓言不能违逆,
现在修行的日子才开始,
我们要在古老的森林度过十二年。"

心胸宽阔的召朗玛,
从案台上拿下父王恩赐的一双神鞋,
一只送给三弟帕腊达,
一只送给四弟沙达鲁嘎。

第九章 出走 Chapter 9 Exodus

"Your Majesty, Golden-leaf-like queen of Nan Jiexi,
It is reasonable for you to ask Father to keep his promise,
And I as your son didn't hold any grudge against it.
Please, don't upset and torture yourself for this issue.

"Since Father the king made his promise beforehand,
As his son I should observe his words.
I left the palace to the forest for practising Buddhism,
By no means for bearing a grudge against brother or mother queen.

"To practice Buddhism in forests is my long-cherished wish.
I want to temper myself in all kinds of hardships.
It is unavoidable, even for the heavenly-god Baying,
To experience twists and turns, setbacks and pains on the road of life.

"I have made my oath to Baying the heavenly god.
I can not act against the oath that I have made.
It is just the very beginning of my life of practising Buddhism,
And we will live in the primitive forest for twelve years."

The broad-minded Zhao Langma,
Getting his pair of flying shoes down from the table,
He gave one of the shoes to his younger brother Palada;
And the other one to Shadaluga, the youngest brother.

"父王恩赐的这双神鞋,
你们要倍加珍重爱护,
要把它放在父王的宝座上,
像孝敬父王那样顶礼膜拜。

"这双金底银板的神鞋,
是天神赏给父王的宝贝,
它能为全勐消灾免祸,
它能为全勐驱邪除恶。

"忠诚的帕腊达弟弟啊,
你们还是回去吧,
你要潜心把国家治理,
为全勐黎民百姓造福。"

恳求的眼泪动摇不了召朗玛的决心,
他们只得郁郁不悦地返回宫廷,
正直的帕腊达也不愿继承王位,
他也离开宫廷步哥哥们的后尘。

哥哥们一个个出走去修行,
宫廷里剩下纯洁无邪的沙达鲁嘎,
他忍受着亲骨肉分离的痛苦,
代行王权治理着勐沓达腊塔。

第九章 出走　Chapter 9 Exodus

"The flying shoes were bestowed by our father,
You should be exceptionally careful to protect them.
Put them on the throne of our father the King,
And worship them as you do to our father.

"The magic shoes with soles made of gold and silver,
They were treasures given by heavenly god to our father.
They can protect our people from disasters and calamities;
They can drive away evils and eradicate demons for the nation.

"My faithful brother, Palada,
Go back to the palace our home.
Devote yourself to governing the country,
And bring benefit to the populace of our nation."

The pleading tears failed to waver the resolution of Zhao Langma.

They had to return to the palace in depression.

The upright Palada was unwilling to ascend to the throne too,

And he followed the steps of his older brothers and left the palace.

The three older brothers departed for practising Buddhism one by one,

Only the pure Shadaluga was left in the palace.

Enduring the pains of separation from his blood-and-flesh brothers,

He acted on behalf of his eldest brother to govern the kingdom.

第十章　勐基沙

一、宝角①牛诞生

在古老茂密的原始森林里，
在广阔丰饶的勐基沙原野，
出现了一头凶猛的公牛，
它把五千头母牛当成自己的妻妾。

牛王是一头金角水牛，
尖利的金角有七索②长，
粗壮的身子有三③高，
它的力气胜过四条公象。

它为了把母牛占为己有，
不许五千头母牛与别的公牛接近，
它仗恃自己剽悍力气大，
蛮横地独占了整个牛群。

----

① 宝角：宝是珍贵，角指牛角，后指拥有珍贵牛角的公牛。
② 索：傣族长度单位，一小臂长为一索。
③ 三：两臂平伸展开的距离为"一"。

第十章 勐基沙 Chapter 10 The Kingdom of Jisha

Chapter 10 The Kingdom of Jisha

I The Birth of Baojio① Bull

In the ancient and dense primitive forest
Of the vast and prosperous Kingdom of Jisha
A fierce and greedy bull appeared in the wilderness.
It made five thousands of cows his wives and concubines.

The bull king had a pair of golden horns,
Which were as long as seven Suo②.
With a body as tall as three③,
It was stronger than four male elephants.

To occupy the five thousand cows as its own alone,
It didn't allow any bull to approach them.
Resorting to its exceptional strength and fierce,
Peremptorily, it had the whole flocks of cow to his own.

---

① Baojiao: Bao means treasure, Jiao means horn, hereafter, Bull of precious horns is used.
② Suo: measurement unit for length, as long as one's arm.
③ San: three. "one" is used a measurement unit for length, is about 2 meters.

兰嘎西贺 The Ten-Headed King of Langa

五千头母牛困守在它身旁,
忍受着它的欺侮凌辱,
为了避免有公牛和它争霸,
它的手段十分残酷毒辣。

每天有一百条母牛怀孕,
每天有一百条母牛产子,
如果生下的小牛是母的,
牛王就让它长大成自己的小妾。

要是生下的小牛是公的,
牛王就残忍地把它杀害,
它用尖利的金角把它戳死,
它用沉重的双蹄把它踩成泥。

可怜一个个无辜的小牯子,
刚刚坠地就丧失生的权利,
被它戳死踩烂的牯子啊,
成千上万无法算计。

一头白宝石般的母牛怀孕了,
它整天为胎儿的命运焦虑,
每天噙着汪汪的眼泪,
只敢把忧伤藏在心底。

"但愿我肚里的胎儿是牝牛,
免得一出世就被它父亲害死,
我怎忍心看到刚落地的孩子,
转眼间变成了碎肉烂泥。"

第十章 勐基沙 Chapter 10 The Kingdom of Jisha

The five thousand cows were imprisoned by its side,
Suffering its bullying and humiliation.
To avoid the other bulls to compete with it,
It used all kinds of cruel and evil means.

Every day one hundred cows would be pregnant,
Every day one hundred cows would deliver.
If the cow gave birth to a heifer,
The bull king would keep it and later turn it to his wife.

If a bull-calf was delivered,
The bull king would kill it brutally.
It used his sharp golden horns to pierce through the calf;
It used his heavy hooves to stamp it into mud of meat.

Poor those innocent bull-calves,
They were deprived of the right of life
the moment they came to the world.
Uncountable calves were killed by its horns or its hooves.

One day a pure-jade-like cow got pregnant.
She worried about the fate of her baby all day long
With tears filled with her bright eyes.
And she had to hide her sadness deep in her heart.

"I wish that the baby in my womb would be a heifer,
Lest it be killed by its own father the moment it was delivered.
How could I bear seeing my newly-born baby
Turn into mud of pieced meat in a blink of eyes."

想来想去只有偷偷离开牛群，
逃进偏僻的伊麻板森林，
行到远离牛王三千约的地方，
在一个隐蔽的岩洞里藏身。

不久，它艰难地分娩了，
一个可爱的牤子平安降生，
一生下来就吃青草嫩叶，
四脚落地便能翻山越岭。

它周身皮毛像棉花那样洁白，
那双初生的宝角啊，
如同刚长齐的象牙一般纯净，
就像太阳下闪闪发光的白金。

温暖多雨的伊麻板森林，
青草比田坝的秧苗还鲜嫩，
泉水比三月的蜂蜜还香甜，
把宝角牛喂养得膘壮腰圆。

时间转眼过去了三年，
三岁的宝角牛膘厚体健，
巍巍身高足有三，
矫健的四脚腾飞如闪电。

第十章 勐基沙 Chapter 10 The Kingdom of Jisha

She thought it over and at last she secretly left the cattle,
Escaping to the remote forest of Yimaban.
Walking to a place so far away from the sight of the bull king,
She found a hidden cave to conceal herself.

Not long before, she laboriously delivered a baby.
A cute bull-calf came to the world safely.
The moment it was born, it began to eat grass;
When its feet landed on the ground, it could run over the mountains.

It had fur as white as cotton,
And the newly-grown horns
As pure and precious as the tusks of elephants.
They were sparkling like silver under the sun.

The forest of Yimaban, warm and rich in rain,
Its grass was more tender than the rice sidling in the village;
Its springs and streams were sweeter than honey in March.
They fed the bull-calf of precious horns round and robust.

In a blink of eyes three years had passed,
The three-year-old bull of precious horns was thick and strong,
It had a body as tall as six meters.
It could run as fast as lightening with four vigorous legs.

刚懂事的宝角牛询问妈妈：
"为什么从来没见过阿爸？
为什么住在这人迹罕见的深山老林，
没有兄弟姊妹来和我们做伴玩耍？"

母亲还未回答就眼泪汪汪：
"三年来妈妈不敢对你明讲实情，
只因为你年幼无知，
不应该过早使你心灵有创伤。

"今天你已成长壮大，
看来已明白事理听得懂话，
妈妈就把根由细说给你，
你要把它牢牢记在心上。

"你父亲是世间罕见的狠毒牛王，
它有比批哈竜瘟神更可怕的心肠，
五千头母牛是它的妻妾，
供它蹂躏、供它役使。

"它是一头欲壑难填的老公牛，
私欲驱使他不认亲生儿子，
生下小母牛它留下做妻妾，
生下小牯子就把它戳死踩成烂泥。

第十章 勐基沙 Chapter 10 The Kingdom of Jisha

When treasure-horned calf got to know the world,
He asked his mother, "why have I never seen my Daddy?
Why should we live in this remote and ancient mountain forest
Having no brothers or sisters to play with?"

Before she could answer, tears came to the mother,
"For three years, I dare not tell you the truth.
Since you were still an innocent baby,
I don't want you to be traumatized in your early childhood.

"But now you are grown up,
It seems that you are sensible and understand my words.
Let Mother tell you the story in details,
You must firmly keep it in your mind.

"Your father was a bull king whose wickedness was rare in the world.
He had a heart eviler than that of Pihalong, the god of plague.
He took five thousand of cows as his wives.
They were like slaves for him to abuse.

"He was an old bull with insatiable desire.
Selfishness drove him not to acknowledge his own sons.
He kept the delivered heifer to be his wife,
And ruthlessly pierced and stamped the newly-born bullocks to death.

347

"我躲进这深山老林的岩洞里,
为的是保存你的宝贵生命,
孤苦伶仃生下你,
提心吊胆度过了三年光阴。"

角粗颈壮的宝角牛听了,
不由得怒火充满心间,
它要去和父王说理,
为众多死去的兄弟们申冤。

它摆动闪光的宝角,
仰起头对伤心的母亲说道:
"我对一切都清楚明了,
请带我去制止父王的凶暴。"

耳灵目明的母亲急忙劝告:
"你这个想法为时太早,
你年轻体单力还薄,
怎抵得住它那犀利的双角?

"你要是有决心除暴安良,
可试一试洞外那块高大坚硬的岩石,
你若能一角把它挑成细沙碎末,
说明你已具备了防身的本事。"

宝角牛听了心中欢喜,
按照妈妈的吩咐跃跃欲试,
它说一声"请看儿的宝角吧!"
便风驰电掣般朝洞外岩石冲去。

第十章 勐基沙 Chapter 10 The Kingdom of Jisha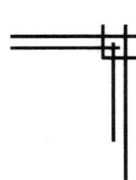

"I hid in this cave in the ancient mountain forest
To protect your precious life.
I was here alone and gave birth to you.
For three years I had my heart in my mouth."

At hearing this, the strong Bull of precious horns
Was simmering with rage,
It wanted to go and argue with his father
And find the justice for his dead brothers.

Shaking its shining precious horns,
It looked up to his sad mother and said,
"Everything is clear to me now,
Please take me to stop the brutality of my father."

The wise mother immediately advised him,
"It is too early for you to have such an idea.
You are still too young to be strong enough.
How could you resist its two sharp horns?

"If you are determined to get rid of the evil for the good,
You can try the huge solid rock outside the cave.
If you can smash it into fine sands with one attack of your horns,
That means you are capable of protecting yourself."

"You can't defend yourself without keen eyesight and agile legs,
You will be poked to death by your father.
Then it is too late for me your mother to regret.
My dear kid, it is still not the time for you to go.

霎时伊麻板撼天动地,
坚硬的岩石被撞得粉碎,
森林上空扬起阵阵灰尘,
伊麻板大地撒满细沙碎石。

宝角牛转过身来问妈妈:
"儿的力气可以把一块磐石摧垮,
本领是不是比父王的还大,
阿妈呀, 带儿去找牛群吧!"

"孩子啊! 你虽有一身大力气,
但你还没有敏锐的眼力,
如果我现在带你回去,
你还是可能被你父亲置于死地。

"你的父亲朝右冲来,
用金角能挑断你的四腿,
你的父亲从左攻击,
用金角能插进你的心肺。

"你眼不疾腿不快没法防备,
就会被你父亲一下戳死,
那时妈妈后悔也来不及,
孩子啊! 你现在还不能去。

第十章　勐基沙　Chapter 10　The Kingdom of Jisha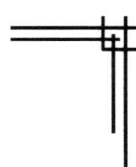

The bull of precious horns was glad to hear that.
It could not wait to have a try as its mother said.
With words of "Have a good look at my precious horns",
It rushed out of the cave as quickly as a flash.

In a blink the forest of Yimaban was shaking and trembling,
The hard rock was bumped into pieces,
The dust flew into the sky over the forest,
Then Yimaban was covered by sands and pulverized stones.

The Bull of precious horns turned to its mother,
"I am strong enough to destroy a huge hard rock.
Am I more capable than my father?
Mom, take me to the cattle."

"My kid, although you have great strength,
You have not got keen eyesight.
If I take you to him now,
You probably will be killed by your father.

"If your father charges toward you from the right,
It can break your four legs with its golden horns.
If it charges toward you from the left,
Its golden horns will pierce your heart.

"有心报仇,十年不为迟,
你要勤学苦练真本事,
练出高超的武艺,
练出敏锐的眼力。"

儿子对母亲言听计从,
天天在林中磨角练眼力,
整整练了九个月,
三座高山被它磨成平地。

宝角磨炼得比神象牙还锋利,
眼力练得像闪电一般迅疾,
这时白宝石母牛要试试它的本领,
把要求和条件告诉儿子。

"河岸上长有一棵橄榄树,
树上结着千万个橄榄果,
你要用头撞击橄榄树,
把树上的果子全部震落。

"随即用你灵巧的双角,
把果子——顶进大河里,
不让一个滚落下地,
你这才有胜过你父亲的眼力。"

儿子一听满心欢喜,
甩动宝角向河边走去,
对准粗大的橄榄树干,
腾空而起迅猛撞击。

第十章 勐基沙 Chapter 10 The Kingdom of Jisha

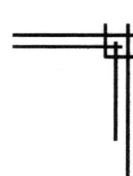

"It is never too late to take a revenge.
You should work hard to learn real skills.
Till you are expert in martial arts;
Till you have keen eyesight."

The son followed the mother's advice, and every day
It rubbed his horns and exercise his eyes in the forest.
For nine whole months it worked hard on these
Till three mountains had been ground flat by it.

Its precious horns had been rubbed sharper than tusks of elephant;
Its eyes could move as fast as flashes.
The pure-gem-like cow still wanted to test its son's capability,
And she asked him to meet the following requirements.

"At the bank of the river stood an olive tree,
Which bore tens of thousands of fruits.
You go and bump into the olive tree
To shake off all its fruits.

"And then use your dexterous horns,
To bump each of the fruits into the river.
If none of them fell off to the ground,
You then have better eyesight than your father."

The son was glad to hear that.
It swung its tail and went toward the riverside.
Aiming at the bulky trunk of the olive tree,
It rose high into the sky and rushed to bump it.

353

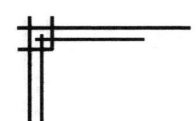

兰嘎西贺 The Ten-Headed King of Langa

橄榄果落下像倾盆大雨,
要一粒粒顶进河里谈何容易,
但目光敏锐、动作迅疾的宝角牛,
到底还是创造了惊人的奇迹。

四面八方落下的果子,
三万三千粒圆圆的果子,
被它的双角——顶进河里,
没有一粒掉落在地。

这时宝角牛又向母亲提出,
要同凶残的父王比比高低:
"告诉儿下山的路吧,
告诉儿父亲的样子。"

母亲惊喜儿子有了高强的本领,
带着儿子离开伊麻板,
来到广阔的勐基沙平原草坝,
牛王和牛群就在前面居住。

心明眼亮的母亲停下脚步,
对儿子——细心嘱咐:
"这儿离牛群已经不远,
你先从脚印上辨认你的生父。

"平地上那些最大最深的脚印,
就是你父亲的脚印,
这时候你不要暴露来意,
你要与它的脚印比比分寸。

第十章 勐基沙 Chapter 10 The Kingdom of Jisha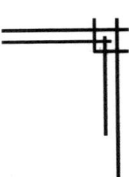

The fruits of olive fell off like pour of rain.
It was never easy to hit each of them into the river.
But thanks to its keen eyesight and agility
The Bull of precious horns created a marvellous wonder.

The fruits fell off in all directions.
Altogether there were thirty-three thousand of them.
The bull hit all of them into the river with its horns,
And none of them fell onto the ground.

Then the Bull of precious horns asked its mother again
To let it have a duel with its brutal father,
"Tell me the way to go down the mountain,
And tell me what my father looks like?"

The mother was surprised to see her son's super skills.
So she took it to leave the forest of Yimaban.
They came to the vast grassland on the plain of Jisha.
The bull king and the cattle were living just ahead.

The clever mother stopped her step,
And carefully she told her son again and again,
"It is not far from the cattle now,
You should first identify the footprint of your father.

"The hugest and deepest footprints on the ground,
They were left by your father.
You should not expose yourself,
but compare your footprints with his first.

"要是你的脚印比它的更深更大,
说明你的力气一定胜过了它,
如果你的脚印同它的一般深大,
说明你们的力气不相上下。

"假若你的脚印比它的浅小,
儿啊,你就会被它轻易打垮,
你就不要去找牛群,
要立刻返回森林来找妈妈。"

宝角牛辞别母亲警惕地走向平坝,
只见平地上脚印密密麻麻,
它发现有一路脚印格外深大,
量了一量足有十拃。

宝角牛料定是父亲的脚印,
但这脚印装不下它的蹄甲,
它便信心百倍地往前走,
高昂着头寻找牛群中的恶霸。

二、老牛王的惨败

在靠近森林的坝子边缘,
宝角牛走进了熙熙攘攘的牛群,
它沿着草地上深大的脚印寻找,
锐利的目光看到了金角闪亮的父亲。

第十章 勐基沙 Chapter 10 The Kingdom of Jisha

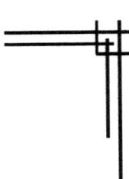

"If yours are larger and deeper than his,
That means you are stronger than him.
But if yours are as large and deep as his,
That means you are an equal to him in strength.

"If yours are smaller and shallower than his,
My dear son, you will be easily defeated by him.
Don't go to look for the cattle,
But turn to the forest to find Mother."

Saying goodbye to its mother, the young bull went toward the plain.

It saw thickly-dotted footprints on the ground,

Among them was there a trail of exceptionally huge and deep ones.

It measured it and found it was at least one and half meters long.

The Bull of precious horns was sure those were his father's.

But they were not as big and deep as its owns.

Therefore it walked forward with great confidence.

Keeping its head high, it looked for the evil tyrant among the cattle.

II   The Total Defeat of the Old Bull King

On the edge of the plain neighboring the forest,
The Bull of precious horns walked into the crowded cattle.
It traced along the huge footprints on the grassland,
And its sharp eyes saw its father with sparkling golden horns.

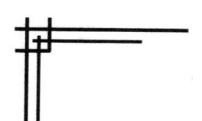

傲慢的牛王向来目中无人，
突然发现在自己横行的天下，
竟会冒出一条威武公牛的身影，
心中不禁大吃一惊。

它甩动着明晃晃的一双金角，
两眼发红，鼻孔喷着怒气，
它气势汹汹朝宝角牛冲来，
奔跑的蹄声震动着宽阔的草地。

牛王像一座大山压过来，
就像天将崩溃地要裂开，
宝角牛不惊不慌沉住气，
待父亲冲到跟前急忙下拜。

"我是你的亲生儿子，
今天见面是平生第一次，
你怎忍心挥动金色的双角，
无情地把亲骨肉置于死地。

"允许儿子生活在父亲身边，
让公牛母牛都有生的权利，
我一定全心全意辅佐您，
把牛群管理得勃勃有生机。"

第十章 勐基沙 Chapter 10 The Kingdom of Jisha

The arrogant bull king always turned his nose up into the air.
Suddenly it was so surprised to find
That a mighty young bull intruding
Into its own world which it ran like a tyrant.

It slung his two bright golden horns,
With red eyes and nostrils spurting his anger,
Overbearingly, it rushed to the Bull of precious horns.
Its running hooves shook the vast grassland.

The bull king threw itself onto the young bull like a mountain,
It seemed that even the sky would be torn apart by such great strength.
The Bull of precious horns was not panic at all,
Calmly it knelt down when its father dashed to the front of it.

"I am your own son,
This is our first meeting.
How could you bear swinging your golden horns
And killing your own blood and flesh ruthlessly?

"Please allow your son to live by your side.
And let heifer and bullock all have the right of life.
I will certainly to help you with all my heart
Run the cattle to make it more prolific and prosperous."

凶残成性的牛王哪里听得进去，
胸中像有几堆大火烧起，
两眼圆瞪，脖子挺直，
扬着金角冲向自己的儿子。

宝角牛一边防卫一边退避，
牛王毫不放松步步逼近，
宝角牛断定残暴的父亲难以劝转，
只有同它拼个我活你死。

宝角牛不再向后退让，
挥动宝角抵住父亲的金角，
暴怒的父子开始交锋，
角锋相对，势不两立。

两头牛憋足了怒气，
它们的力气不相上下，
父子俩展开了激烈的角斗，
角碰角迸发出吓人的火花。

宝角和金角相撞，
犹如闪电在空中交叉，
撞击的巨大声响，
就像霹雳在云间爆炸。

第十章 勐基沙 Chapter 10 The Kingdom of Jisha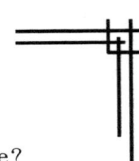

How could the brutal bull king listen to words like these?
It felt the burning fire in its chest.
With widely-opened eyes and stiff neck,
It raised his horns and rushed to his own son.

The Bull of precious horns retreated to defend itself.
The bull king didn't slack off but pressed on step by step.
The young bull concluded it's impossible to change its father's mind.
It had no choice but to fight against him till one of them would die.

Th young bull didn't draw back any more.
It threw its horns against the golden horns of his father.
The raging father and son started a real fight,
Horns against horns, they fought like two enemies.

The two bulls were burst with rage;
Being equals in strength,
The father and the son had a fight of life and death,
Their horns clashing and setting off terrifying sparks.

The golden horns collided with the precious horns,
They were like lightening intersecting in the air.
The huge sounds of their crashing
Were like thunderbolts exploding in the clouds.

它们从平地打到森林，
又从森林斗到高山，
大树被撞倒，石头被踩碎，
青青的草地变成了一片泥潭。

斗了一天不分胜负，
双方身上的创伤像蜂窝，
鲜血染红了身躯，
皮上的牛毛犹如火烧过。

直打到太阳落下山，
夜幕开始笼罩大地，
天漆黑看不清对方的身子，
两头公牛的打斗才宣告停止。

好好睡一觉养精蓄锐，
各自去找地方休息，
不获胜利岂肯罢休，
等待天明再决胜负。

金角牛王睡在橄榄树下，
困乏无力，气喘吁吁，
宝角小牛睡在宋贝树①下，

---

① 宋贝树：傣族人民认为是最有威力的树，能驱鬼魔。传说宝角牛由于宋贝树上的水滴在头上而增添了气力，使它能战胜金角牛。现在傣族人民还用宋贝树上滴下的水洗头，象征吉祥。

第十章 勐基沙 Chapter 10 The Kingdom of Jisha

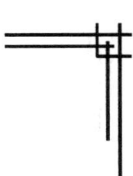

They kept fighting, moving from the plain to the forest,
And then from the forest to the mountain.
The huge trees were crashed and stones stamped into pieces;
The green grassland was turned into a patch of marsh.

They fought for a whole day but no one could win.
The injures on their body were like the hives.
Blood drenched their bodies,
And their fur looked like burned by fire.

They fought till the sun disappeared behind the hills;
The earth was enveloped in a curtain of darkness.
It was so dark that they could not see each other.
The two bulls had to stop their fight.

They needed a good sleep to refresh themselves.
So both of them went to find a place for a rest.
They waited for the morning to come and they would fight again.
They would never stop unless the battle was won.

The golden-horn bull king slept under an olive tree.
Exhausted and breathless;
The young Bull of precious horns slept under the Songbei tree①,

---

① Songbei Tree: the Dai people regard it as the most powerful tree, which can drive off ghost and devils. It is said that the the Bull of precious horns recovered its strength thanks to the dew drops from the Songbei tree and so it won over the golden-horned bull. Now the Dai people still use the dew drops from Songbei tree to wash their hair for good luck.

恢复精力，倍增斗志。

太阳从东方冉冉升起，
牛群开始把青草啃吃，
两头公牛就像两块磁石，
从很远的距离向对方冲去。

脖颈挽住脖颈摔打，
牛角顶着牛角对峙，
四只眼睛放射出血样的红光，
两张嘴巴喷着泡沫和热气。

小公牛愈战愈勇猛，
锋利的宝角犹如飞剑，
连续不断的快速攻击，
宛如划破云层的闪电。

老公牛的气力渐渐不支，
四只大脚已经站立不稳，
只觉得头昏眼花浑身发抖，
一失足掉进了一个水坑。

小公牛趁势低头冲刺，
一支角击中牛王的大腿，
牛王猛一下翻身站起来，
两个牛头又紧紧相对。

第十章 勐基沙 Chapter 10 The Kingdom of Jisha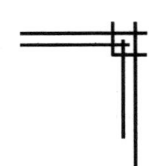

Refreshed and energetic with raised fighting spirit.

The sun gradually rose from the east,
And the cattle started to graze on the grassland.
Like two magnetic stones,
The two bulls rushed to each other from a distance.

They wrestled with neck against neck;
They fought with horns against horns.
Two pairs of eyes radiated blood-like light,
Two mouths spurted foams and hot breath.

As the battle progressed, the young bull's courage mounted.
Its sharp precious horns were like flying swords.
They attacked in such a fast speed
That they were like lightening piercing through the clouds.

The old bull gradually lost its strength,
His four huge feet could not stand firm on the ground.
It felt dizzy and trembled violently,
All of a sudden he slipped and fell into a puddle.

The young bull took the chance to rush forward with lowered head,
One of its horns hit into one leg of the bull king.
The bull king turned its body over and stood up,
And again they butted against each other.

父子俩在土包上顶撞，
头对头相持了七天，
七天七夜过去了，
牛王终于筋疲力尽四脚朝天。

宝角牛一跃跳上前去，
一脚紧紧踩住牛王的脖子，
挥动宝角左挑右戳，
牛王再也没有还手之力。

牛王的双眼，
被儿子的宝角挑瞎了，
牛王的肚皮，
被儿子的宝角戳通了。

宝角牛在它脖子上又戳又踩，
牛王再也抬不起头来，
它伸长舌头断了气，
再也不能为非作歹。

三、宝角牛之死

宝角牛杀死了残暴的父王，
又把牛王的大权执掌，
但它比父亲更作恶多端，
还给人类带来无穷的祸殃。

第十章 勐基沙 Chapter 10 The Kingdom of Jisha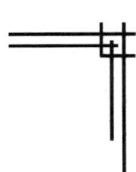

The father and the son fought on a hillock.
They kept butting for seven days.
Seven days and seven night passed, finally,
The bull king was so exhausted that he lay flat on the ground.

The Bull of precious horns jumped forward,
Stepped onto the neck of the bull king,
And swung his horns left and right, poking and thrusting;
The bull king did not have any strength to fight back.

The pair of eyes of the bull king
Were poked blind by its son's precious horns;
The belly of the bull king
Was pierced through by its son's sharp horns.

The young bull stood on his neck, trampling and stamping,
The bull king could not raise his head any more.
With its tongue stuck out he breathed his last breath.
Never could he again do evils or commit crimes.

Ⅲ The Death of the Bull of Precious Horns

After the Bull of precious horns killed his ferocious father,
He took his place and got in charge of the cattle.
But he turned out to be more diabolic than his father,
And brought endless disasters to human kind.

虽然它不对母牛们虐待，
虽然它不把小公牛踩死，
但它破坏果树和庄稼，
但它摧毁房舍和村寨。

它带领着几千条大牛，
骄横地驰骋在平坝和森林，
山头被它们推平，
大地被践踏得灰尘滚滚。

森林树木一片片被撞倒，
庄稼果园一块块被踏平，
所有的江河堤坝，
被它用宝角一道道摧垮。

宝角牛自以为天下无敌，
世界上数自己最有本领，
它那对锋利的宝角，
不辨善良丑恶一概挑衅。

它越来越自不量力，
到处闯祸，四面树敌，
常常口出狂言高声辱骂，
帝娃拉①也不放在眼里。

---

① 帝娃拉：女天神，保护村寨、森林的神，地位低于叭英。

第十章 勐基沙 Chapter 10 The Kingdom of Jisha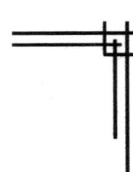

He would not trample the bullocks to death,
Nor did he abuse or maltreat the cows.
But he ruined fruit trees and crops in the field,
And he destroyed houses and villages.

Leading thousands of huge bulls,
He domineeringly galloped across the plains and forests.
The hills had been flattened by them,
And their trampling turned earth into waves of dust.

Large pieces of woods and trees were crashed down;
Patches of crop fields and orchard were trampled flat;
All the banks of the rivers and lakes,
One by one were destroyed by its precious horns.

The Bull of precious horns thought itself invincible
And the most capable in the whole world.
With its pair of precious horns,
It provoked and defied everything, be it good or bad.

It became more and more arrogant and overweening,
Making troubles and enemies everywhere.
It always boasted itself and threw its abuses loudly around.
It even didn't show any respect to Diwala①, the goddess of the forest.

---

① Diwala: The goddess protecting village and forest, who is inferior to Baying.

附近的老百姓纷纷逃亡，
帝娃拉被它赶出森林，
无论神灵和黎民百姓，
一个个莫不义愤填膺。

"桀骜不驯的宝角牛啊，
不要被胜利把头脑冲昏，
天下比你本领高强的还有，
劝你莫再霸道横行。

"不信你就去和猴王较量较量，
在善良的猴王面前你会感到害羞，
在威武的猴王面前你会显得渺小，
同勇敢的猴王作战你会浑身发抖。"

宝角牛听了心肺几乎要气炸，
认为帝娃拉他们有意耻笑它，
它暴怒地呐喊："小猴王在哪里？
我撒泡尿也能把它淹死。"

帝娃拉笑着告诉它：
"你们就住在它的国家，
你们就受着它的管辖，
怎么连自己的国王也不认识啦！

第十章 勐基沙　Chapter 10　The Kingdom of Jisha

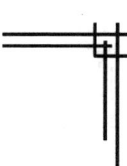

Local people had to escape from their homeland,
Diwala was driven out of the forest by it.
Both the gods and the common people
Were burning with indignation.

"Defiant and unruly Bull of precious horns,
Don't be blinded by your victory.
There are many in the world who are more capable than you.
Listen to our advice and don't be so overbearing or run wildly.

"Go and challenge the kind monkey King if you don't believe us.
You will feel shameful of yourself in the face of him.
You will be thwarted by its majesty and might.
Fighting with the brave monkey King will make you trembling."

Hearing this, the bull felt his heart and lung bursting.
He thought Diwala and others were deliberately mocking at him.
In violent rage he shouted, "Where is the small monkey King?
Even a piss of mine could get him drowned to death."

Diwala laughed and told him,
"You are living in his kingdom,
And you are under his ruling,
How could you not even know your own king?

兰嘎西贺 The Ten-Headed King of Langa

"管辖你的国王叫巴力莫,
它是叭龙统治着勐基沙,
它居住在大海的北岸,
这条河的上游就是它的家。"

被激怒的宝角牛心头火起,
暴跳如雷昂首扬蹄,
它从下游一口气奔到上游,
冲进勐基沙繁华的都城里。

凶暴的宝角牛冲撞猴群,
不少猴子在它的角蹄下丧生,
勐基沙惨遭蹂躏,
猴子们吓得四散逃遁。

宝角牛洋洋得意破口叫骂:
"你们谁的本事最大,
就来和我较量一番,
不然我宝角牛可不客气啦!

第十章 勐基沙 Chapter 10 The Kingdom of Jisha

"The king that rules over you is named Balimo.

He is the highest tribe chief ruling the kingdom of Jisha.

He lives on the northern side of the sea.

The upper reaches of this river is where his home is located."

Burning rage rose in the heart of the provoked Bull of precious horns.

Jumping up and down in violent indignation and holding its head up,

It galloped from the lower reaches to the upper ones at one breath.

And it rushed into the prosperous capital of the kingdom of Jisha.

The ferocious Bull of precious horns crashed into flocks of monkeys,

And many monkeys died under its horns and hooves.

The capital city of Jisha was brutally and ruthlessly trampled on.

Monkeys were scared to run for their lives in four directions.

The Bull of precious horns burst into abuses elatedly,

"Who is the most powerful one among you?

Come and fight with me!

Otherwise, Just wait to see what I can do to you!"

373

"小猴王你躲在哪里?
为什么如此装聋作哑,
你再不立刻出来见我,
我就要踏平勐基沙。"

巴力莫听到这些狂言恶语,
气得从宝座上纵身跳下,
它手握宝刀飞上天空,
对宝角牛嬉笑怒骂:

"我早就要制伏你这条作恶的公牛了,
想不到你今天亲自送上门来,
是命运注定我们要相会,
我要叫你尝尝我的厉害。"

心比石头还坚硬的巴力莫,
犹如一阵飓风冲向大地,
它挥舞宝刀向宝角牛砍去,
宝角牛见刀来立刻躲避。

巴力莫转身又飞上天去,
一个筋斗又翻身下来,
宝刀像闪电迅猛剁砍,
宝角如利剑左右挡开。

第十章 勐基沙 Chapter 10 The Kingdom of Jisha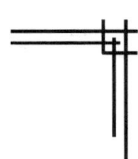

"Where are you hiding? You little monkey King.
Why you play deaf and dumb like this.
If you don't come out to see me immediately,
I will trample the Kingdom of Jisha flat."

When Balimo heard such crazy and vicious talks,
He got so angry that he jumped down from his throne.
Holding his precious sword, he flew into the sky,
He chided the Bull of precious horns angrily,

"I have long ago thought to subdue you, the evil bull,
And I didn't expect that you threw yourself into the net today.
We are doomed to meet each other,
And I will teach you a hard lesson."

Balimo, with a will stronger than a hard rock,
He dived toward the earth like a hurricane.
Swinging his magic sword toward the Bull of precious horns,
Who ducked and dodged immediately at the sight of it.

Balimo turned his back and flew into the sky,
With a somersault he charged toward the bull again.
He swung and jabbed his magic sword as fast as flashes.
The bull warded off the attacks with his horns as sharp as swords.

宝刀和宝角撞得火星四溅,
没有伤着宝角牛半点皮毛,
巴力莫立即改变主意,
变强攻硬砍为声东击西。

它机动灵活左右躲闪,
围着牛王旋转不已,
把笨重的牛王弄得晕头转向,
瞅准一刀砍向它的脖子。

鲜血染红了发光的宝角,
顺着牛王的颈项流淌,
巴力莫飞快抓住了牛的双角,
终于掀翻了骄横跋扈的牛王。

巴力莫立即挥刀猛砍,
眼看牛王就要断气,
不料它突然挣起,
一甩头把猴王摔倒在地。

第十章 勐基沙 Chapter 10 The Kingdom of Jisha

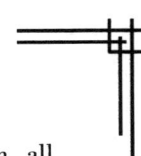

The sword bumped into horns setting off sparks in all direction.

But the bull, even its fur, didn't get hurt at all.

Balimo immediately changed his tact,

Shifting the forcing battle into diversionary tactics.

It agilely ducked and dodged from left to the right,

Swirling around the bull king nonstop.

When the awkward bull king got dizzy and disoriented,

He gave a fatal chop to the neck of the bull.

The spurting blood tainted the glittering precious horns red,

And it ran down along the neck of the bull king.

Balimo rapidly took hold of both horns of the bull,

And finally he overturned the arrogant and overweening bull king.

Balimo again swung his sword and chopped the bull again and again.

It seemed that the bull king would die in any minute.

But unexpectedly, it suddenly struggled to stand up.

It swung his head and had the monkey king fall off to the ground.

牛王趁势冲到猴王跟前,
用一角把猴王的尾巴挑断,
鲜血染红了它的臀部,
从此猴子永远留下这个标志①。

宝角牛不敢再恋战,
迅速逃进一个宽大的岩洞里,
巴力莫带领群猴尾追而至,
在岩洞口布下重兵严密监视。

巴力莫把弟弟嘎林叫来,
将它的决战计划详细交代:
"你带领官兵紧紧把守洞口,
我深入洞内与牛王搏斗。

"你在洞口要注意观察,
如果是紫红色的血从洞内流出,
那就是宝角牛被我杀死,
你们就为我战胜牛王而尽情欢呼。

---

① 傣族传说,现在猴子尾巴短,屁股红,即源于此。

第十章 勐基沙　Chapter 10　The Kingdom of Jisha

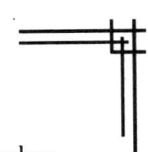

The bull king took the chance and rushed to the monkey king,

And it used his horns and got the tail of the monkey king broken.

The fresh blood stained his bottoms red. That's why

Ever since then monkeys have short tails and red rear ends①.

The Bull of precious horns dare not continue the fight,

Rapidly, it escaped to and hid in a big cave.

Balimo, leading flocks of monkeys, ran after him till the cave.

And he ordered the moneys to station there and keep a close look.

Balimo sent for his younger brother Galin,

And told him in details his plan of the battle.

"You take the troops to guard the mouth of the cave

While I go into the cave to fight against the bull.

"You should observe carefully at the gate of the cave,

If purplish red blood runs out of the cave,

That means the bull has been killed by me.

Then you can cheer for my victory over the bull King.

---

① In the legend of the Dai, that is why monkey has short tail and red rear ends.

"要是流出来的血是淡红色的,
说明我已被牛王的宝角戳死,
你们就赶快搬来石块,
紧紧把岩洞口堵死。

"用的石块要有老象那么大,
堵的洞口要严严实实,
不让恶牛再出来伤人,
让它与我在洞中一同死去。"

猴王说完提着宝刀冲进岩洞,
警惕地在岩洞中搜索前进,
越往里走越黑暗,
走了很远也不见宝角牛的踪影。

巴力莫紧握宝刀左右挥动,
直到把二百米深的岩洞走完,
忽然宝刀击中宝角火光一闪,
它才发现牛王倒在泉水旁边。

宝角牛见猴王追到跟前,
睁大血红的双眼跃起迎战,
黑暗中两个王又厮杀起来,
双方都负伤累累血迹斑斑。

第十章 勐基沙 Chapter 10 The Kingdom of Jisha

"If the blood running out of the cave is pinkish red,
That means I have been jabbed to death by the horns of the bull.
Then you hurry up to get huge rocks
And block up the mouth of the cave tightly.

"The rocks should be as big as an elephant,
And seal the cave with the rocks seamlessly
So that the evil bull will die with me in the cave,
And it could never come out of the cave to hurt people."

Finishing his words, he rushed into the cave with his magic sword,
And vigilantly he groped forward in the cave.
The further he went, the darker the cave was.
He went for long but still did not see any trace of the bull King.

Balimo held his magic sword tight and swung it left and right,
When he got to the end of the four-hundred-meter long cave,
Suddenly the magic sword struck the horns sending off sparks,
Then he saw the bull king lying by the side of a stream.

When the bull saw the monkey king in front of it,
It jumped up to meet the fight with bloodshot eyes.
In the dark the two kings went on with their battle,
And both of them got wounded and were bleeding.

猴王趁牛王四脚失足滑倒之机,
抡起宝刀砍断牛王的喉管,
宝角牛伸开四脚倒在地上,
就像中了圈套的野兔不能动弹。

巴力莫在它身上又补了几刀,
把牛王粗壮的脖子砍断,
紫红的血浆涌如喷泉,
不可一世的牛王从此完蛋。

紫红的牛血同泉水一起流淌,
流出洞口的血色已经冲淡,
淡红的血水啊,不祥的兆头,
这个打击使嘎林肝裂肠断。

嘎林唯恐牛王出洞为害,
命令猴子们立刻搬来石块,
层层叠叠严严密密,
把洞口死死堵起来。

第十章 勐基沙 Chapter 10 The Kingdom of Jisha

When the bull slipped off to the ground, the monkey took the chance,

He brandished his sword and cut broken the throat of the bull.

The Bull of precious horns fell to the ground with stretched feet,

Like a trapped rabbit it could not move any more.

Balimo did not stop but chopped him again and again.
The stalk neck of the bull king was chopped broken,
And its purplish red blood gushed out like water of fountain.
That was the last day of the overbearing bull King.

The purplish red blood ran out of the cave along with the stream.

Reaching the mouth of the cave, the blood had been diluted into pink.

Pinkish blood! It was an ominous sign.

At the sight of it, Galin fell into extreme grief with a broken heart.

For fear that the bull king would come out to do evils,
Galin ordered the monkeys to get the rocks.
Layers of rocks were moved to the mouth of the cave,
And blocked the cave tightly and seamlessly.

嘎林向着洞口跪倒在地，
向死去的哥哥哀悼致意，
嘎林痛哭失声昏厥几次，
猴子们也为猴王的死而悲泣。

嘎林在哀痛中离开了岩洞，
率领哥哥的官兵回到都城，
勐基沙不能没有国王，
哥哥死了理当弟弟来继承。

诚实勇敢的嘎林当上国王，
举国上下欢呼雀跃，
它把大牛训练来耕地，
猴子国的百姓安居乐业。

四、嘎林的冤仇

话说巴力莫战胜了宝角牛，
自己也身负重伤筋疲力尽，
它昏昏沉沉倒在血泊中，
不知过了多少时间才苏醒。

第十章 勐基沙 Chapter 10 The Kingdom of Jisha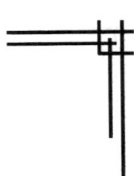

Galin knelt down toward the cave,
Mourning for his dead brother.
He cried himself into coma several times;
The other monkeys also wept for the death of their king.

In agony and sorrow, Galin left the cave.
He led the troops of his brother's back to the capital.
The kingdom of Jisha could not function without a king.
Since the older brother had died, naturally Galin should be the king.

The honest and brave Galin became the king,
And the whole country cheered for it.
It trained the bulls to plough the fields
And the people of the kingdom lived a peaceful and happy life.

Ⅳ   Grievance of Galin

Now let's go back to Balimo. After winning over the bull,
He himself also got seriously wounded and exhausted.
In a coma he fell off to the pool of blood.
He didn't come back to life until long time later.

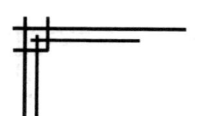

兰噶西贺 The Ten-Headed King of Langa

它用宝刀砍下宝角扛在肩上，
准备向百姓报喜，牛王已被它杀戮，
奇怪的是走到头也不见一线光明，
也听不见猴子们胜利的欢呼。

原来洞口已被石头堵严，
巴力莫顿时怒火冲天：
"嘎林阴谋篡位想把我闷死在山洞里面，
他真是野心勃勃，无法无天。"

巴力莫竭尽全力也挖不开洞口，
就拿起七索长的宝角来凿石，
宝角具有无比的威力，
坚硬的岩石立即纷纷落地。

巴力莫怀着满腔怨恨回到宫廷，
破口大骂弟弟和大臣，
嘎林见哥哥生还惊喜交集，
忙向它解释堵塞洞口的原因。

第十章 勐基沙 Chapter 10 The Kingdom of Jisha

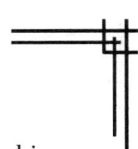

He chopped the horns off the bull and carried them on his shoulder

To report the good news to his people the bull king had been killed.

But he felt it strange there wasn't a thread of light even at the exit;

And he didn't hear monkeys' cheers for the victory outside the cave.

Figuring it out that the exit had been blocked up by the rocks,

Balimo all at a sudden became furious and thought to himself,

"Plotting to supplant me, Galin would get me smothered in the cave.

He was burning with ambition and committed such an unruly crime."

Balimo made all his efforts to dig the exit through but in vain.

Then he took the seven-Suo-long precious horns to cut the stone.

The precious horns had infinite power,

And immediately the hard rocks broke into pieces.

Balimo came back to the palace with a heart of resentment,

And he showered abuses on his brother and officials.

Galin was so happy to see his elder brother still alive

And he hurried to explain why they had blocked the exit of the cave.

巴力莫根本听不进，
指着弟弟的鼻子高声诅咒：
"明明是紫红色的牛血流成小河，
你却有意堵死洞口。

"为了篡夺我的王位，
你竟对亲哥哥下毒手，
你的滔天大罪绝不能宽恕，
你已变成了我的寇仇。

"凤凰窝里竟藏着怪鹰，
隔着肚皮你藏着贼心，
今天不把你杀死，
解除不了我心中的仇恨。"

臣僚和百姓苦苦哀告求情，
请求巴力莫别错怪了好人：
"嘎林是你忠实的弟弟，
它勇敢、正直又单纯。

"它的一举一动我们最清楚，
洞里流出的是淡红的血水，
我们以为你已遭到不幸，
才搬来大石头把洞口堵紧。

"别让乌云遮住了视线，
别让污泥把清水搅浑，
嘎林是清白无辜的好人，
是非善恶请国王分清。

第十章 勐基沙 Chapter 10 The Kingdom of Jisha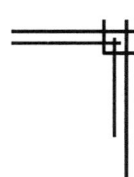

Balimo turned a deaf ear to his explanation,
And pointing at his brother's nose, he cursed loudly,
"Obviously it was the purplish red blood that ran like a river,
You still intentionally had the exit blocked up.

"In order to usurp my throne,
You had the nerve to kill your own brother.
You can't be forgiven for committing such a crime.
Now you are my sworn enemy rather than my brother.

"Who can expect a weird vulture in the nest of phoenix?
Who can look through your belly and detect your evil heart?
I could never relieve the hatred from my heart
Unless I kill you by my hands today."

His officials and people pled for leniency on Galin's behalf.
They begged him not to wrong a good person,
"Garlin is your brother who is faithful to you,
He is brave, honest and has a pure heart.

"We were clear about whatever he had done.
It was pinkish red blood that ran out of the cave,
And we thought that misfortune had befallen you.
So we moved the rocks over to block up the exit of the cave.

"Don't let dark clouds obscure your vision.
Don't let the sludge get the clear water muddy.
Galin is innocent and kind. Your majestic King,
Please distinguish between right and wrong.

"你平安地回来了,
你仍然是全勐的首领,
嘎林做你的好助手,
勐基沙仍然繁荣昌盛。"

猜忌和怨恨咬烂了巴力莫的心,
它的暴怒像大火燃烧森林,
它拔出宝剑挥舞着痛骂臣民,
骂声犹如八月的雷鸣。

"你们是一个竹筒里的臭虫,
你们的心肠像扭在一起的老鸹藤,
我决不允许任何人反抗我的意志,
我怎能让毒蛇留在我的宫廷。

"就算我留下嘎林的狗命,
也不准勐基沙出现它的身影,
要活命就只有一条路,
嘎林,你快收拾东西启程。

"只是你的妻子必须留下来,
让她做我的仆人,
天天沏茶倒水侍候我,
作为你赎罪的替身。"

嘎林内心无比痛苦,
满腹冤屈无处申诉,
它不忍心无辜的臣民受连累,
它不愿挑起兄弟间的杀戮。

第十章 勐基沙 Chapter 10 The Kingdom of Jisha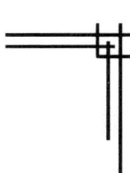

"Now that you have been back safe and sound,
You are still the leader of our kingdom.
Galin will serve you as an assistant,
Our nation will be as prosperous and peaceful as usual."

Suspicions and resentment had eaten Balimo's heart.
His flaming rage was like fire that could burn the forest.
He took out and brandished his magic sword,
While his cursing was as loud as the thunderbolts of August.

"You are like bugs in a bamboo tube.
Your hearts were as distorted as the twisted crow vines.
I could never tolerate anyone who dares not to obey me.
How could I keep a poisonous serpent in my court?

"Even if I could spare Galin's fucking life,
He mustn't appear again within the territory of Jisha.
There is only one way to keep your life, Galin.
Go and pack up your things to get out of my way.

"And you must leave your wife behind.
She will be my servant maid.
From now on, she will serve me in my daily life,
To make atonement in your place."

Galin felt infinite pains in his heart.
There was nowhere for him to pour out his grievance.
He could not bear getting the innocent officials and people implicated,
Nor did he expect to stir up the fight between brothers.

像有万支利箭穿入心胸，
它也不当众呻吟一声，
它悲痛欲绝与爱妻告别，
含冤忍恨离开宫廷。

嘎林忍受着奇耻大辱，
只身在异国的森林里徘徊，
无依无靠的生活啊，
孤苦伶仃，无限悲哀。

嘎林循着野象的足迹，
孤独地在森林里流浪，
它走了一个多月，
来到了伊麻板地方。

这里有一棵枝叶繁茂的大青树，
嘎林爬到树上去休息，
它的眼睛里装满了泪水，
脑海里不断闪现故乡的山水和爱妻……

第十章 勐基沙　Chapter 10　The Kingdom of Jisha

He felt so painful as thousands of arrows piercing his heart,
But he did not heave a groan in front of others.
Grief-stricken, he bid farewell to his beloved wife.
And he left the court with grievance and resentment.

Enduring unspeakable disgrace and humiliation,
Galin wandered in the forest of a foreign country.
Like a helpless orphan who had no one to turn to,
He lived a miserable life with endless sorrow.

Galin trailed along the footprints of elephants,
And roamed in the forest alone.
He kept walking for more than a month
Till he reached the place of Yimaban.

There was a lush and verdant tree of Daqing.
Galin climbed onto it to take a rest.
His eyes were filled with tears,
His motherland and wife kept flashing in his mind...

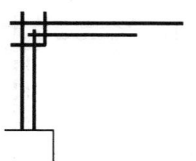

第十一章　遭难

一、林间

恩爱宝石般的召朗玛领着妻子和弟弟，
居住在静谧的伊麻板森林里，
抛开了人世间的烦扰和情欲，
虔诚地修身，和帕拉西在一起。

他们向博学的帕拉西学得才能，
他们向高贵的帕拉西学得武艺，
无边的森林雨了又晴，晴了又雨，
漫长的岁月像流水般悄悄逝去。

一天，三个人要到森林里漫游，
辞别了慈祥的帕拉西，
离开了简陋的巴朗屋，
向幽深、古老的森林走去。

第十一章 遭难 Chapter 11 Sufferings

Chapter 11　Sufferings

I　In the Woods

The precious-gem-like Zhao Langma led his wife and brothers,
And they lived in the tranquil forest of Yimaban.
Free from the troubles and desire of the earthly world,
They followed Palaxi to practice Buddhism devotedly.

They learn skills from the erudite Palaxi,
And the noble Palaxi taught them martial arts too.
With the changing weather from rain to sunshine and sunshine to rain,
Long years elapsed like running water in the endless forest.

One day, the three of them thought to wander in the woods,
After saying goodbye to the benign Palaxi,
They left the simple and crude house of Balang,
And walked into the dark, quiet and ancient forest.

兰嘎西贺 The Ten-Headed King of Langa

他们像三只飞翔的鹦鹉，
三只翩跹起舞的蝴蝶，
又像三只嬉戏的金鹿，
在伊麻板的草地上漫步。

处处盛开着色彩缤纷的鲜花，
蜜蜂嗡嗡，鸟儿喳喳，
绚烂的花木散发出浓郁的芳香，
森林草地犹如一幅彩色的图画。

三人分享着百花的清香，
尽情欣赏着美丽的景色，
他们像蜜蜂似的团结友爱，
犹如小鸟一样自由快乐。

召朗玛左面是善良忠实的弟弟，
右边是美丽温顺的妻子，
他们像两颗明亮的珍珠，
深深嵌镶在他的心坎里。

召朗玛摘来一束清馨的鲜花——
浓郁的梭腊枇，奇异的阿糯扎，
鲜艳的洛沾比，芳香的缅桂花，
献给温柔的妻子南西拉。

第十一章 遭难 Chapter 11 Sufferings

Like three flying parrots,
Also like three dancing butterflies,
Or three frolic golden deer,
They roamed on the grassland of Yimaban.

Colorful flowers were blooming everywhere,
The bees droning and the birds chirping,
Brilliant flowers and trees emanated strong fragrance.
The grassland in the forest was like a colorful picture.

The three of them enjoyed the fragrance of all kinds of flowers,
And they appreciated the beautiful scenery to their heart's consent.
They worked together and helped each other like bees,
And they were as free and happy as little birds.

On the left side of Zhao Langma was his kind and loyal brother,
On his right side was his beautiful and meek wife.
They were like two bright pearls,
Which were embedded deep into his heart.

Zhao Langma plucked a bundle of fresh flowers,
The strong-flavored flowers of loquat, the exotic Anuozha,
The bright Luozhanbi and the fragrant magnolia,
And he presented the flowers to his wife Nan Xila.

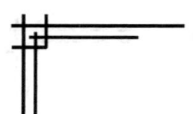

兰噶西贺 The Ten-Headed King of Langa

南西拉编成一个花环戴在发髻上，
引来成群的蜂蝶在头上飞翔，
阳光照亮南西拉红润的脸庞，
她比香艳娇嫩的花朵还漂亮。

山中的溪涧轻轻流淌，
声音像马铃子一样清脆，
他们一起在河中沐浴，
啜饮清凉甘甜的泉水。

树枝上挂满成熟的果子，
成千只鸟儿在枝头啄食，
南西拉呆呆地看着——
问丈夫这些树叫什么名字。

"左边枝叶茂盛的那棵，
人们给它取的名字叫宗补，
叶片明亮细叶下垂的那棵，
是百鸟的乐园波沙来罕果树。

"右边高大挺拔直指蓝天的那棵，
它叫梅妞——千里香艳，
它是百鸟餐前餐后的宫殿，
所有的雀儿都喜欢栖息在上面。"

第十一章 遭难 Chapter 11 Sufferings

Nan Xila wreathed the flowers into a garland and put it on her head,

Which attracted warms of bees and butterflies flying over their heads.

The sunlight brightened Nan Xila's rosy cheeks,

She was more beautiful than those fragrant and tender flowers.

Streams flowed along slowly and gently in the mountains,

Their tinkling sound was like ringing bells of horses.

They bathed in the streams together,

And drank the cool and sweet spring water.

Rape fruits were hung on the trees,

Thousands of birds pecking the fruits on the branches.

Nan Xila fixed her eyes on the trees,

And asked her husband their names.

"The tree with lush branches and leaves on the left,

People named it Zongbu.

That one with bright and slim leaves,

It was fruit tree of Boshalaihan, the paradise of birds.

"On the right, the tall and straight one towering into the blue sky,

Its name was Meiniu, its fragrance wafting hundreds miles away.

It was the palace for birds to stay before or after meals.

All the birds enjoyed perching on it."

他们愉快地穿行在高山、峡谷、草地,
饿了分享着各种酸甜的果实,
欢笑声在林间时起时伏,
他们的生活啊,无忧无虑。

黑夜来临他们在大树下投宿,
柔软的树叶就是床铺和枕头,
当灿烂的朝晖透进密林,
他们又迎着晨曦向前走。

二、南西拉被劫

波涛汹涌的海边森林里,
住着黑心肠的妖婆妲里哈达,
它的哥哥是勐兰嘎国王叭兰巴,
它的侄孙是十头王捧玛加。

妲里哈达身边有两个儿子,
大的叫谢达,小的叫独腊沙,
它们都栖身在勐兰嘎宫殿,
像奴仆一样效忠国王捧玛加。

野心勃勃的妲里哈达,
一心想把一片森林独霸,
以便饱吃珍禽异兽和甜美的果子,
随心所欲管辖一片天下。

第十一章 遭难 Chapter 11 Sufferings

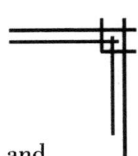

They happily travelled through mountains, valleys and grassland,
When hungry they shared all kinds of sweet or sour fruits.
Their laughter flew up and down in the woods.
They were living such a carefree and happy life.

When nights drew in, they slept under a big tree
With soft leaves as their beds and pillows.
When the morning sunlight pierced into the dense forest,
Facing the morning sun they walked on and on.

II Nan Xila Was Robbed Away

In the forest by the side of the waving sea,
Lived an evil witch called Dalihada.
Her elder brother was Ba Lanba, the king of Langa.
The ten-headed king Pengmajia was her grandniece.

Dalihada had two sons by her side.
The elder was called Xieda, and the younger was Dulasha.
Both of them lived in the palace of the kingdom of Langa,
Serving the king Pengmajia as his servants.

Dalihada was rather ambitious.
She longed to have the forest to her own so that she could eat
The rare birds and animal or sweet fruits as much as she wanted.
And she could rule the place and do whatever she desired to.

它领着儿子去见捧玛加,
母子三个拜倒在宝座之下,
妲里哈达提出一个请求,
话语说得低声下气又狡猾。

"像天王一样的侄孙啊,
海洋的四周都是你的天下,
请你到彼岸幽静的伊麻板,
划一片森林给我们母子管辖。"

有威望的十头王捧玛加,
爽快地答应了它们的要求,
急忙乘上甫萨乐低神车飞翔,
母子三个紧紧跟随身后。

捧玛加和母子三个越过海洋飞向北方,
一直来到大洋彼岸的伊麻板,
捧玛加指着一片阴暗的森林说:
"这片森林就交给你们掌管。

"里面的飞禽走兽,野菜瓜果,
你们可以随心所欲享受,
有人路过这片丛林草地,
你们可以把他当作美餐。"

第十一章 遭难 Chapter 11 Sufferings

She, together with her two son, came to visit Pengmajia,
The three of them knelt down under the front of his throne.
Dalihada put forward one request,
And in a servile and sly way, she said,

"My dear grandniece, you were as majestic as a heavenly god.
The surrounding areas of the sea belong to you.
Could you come to the quiet Yimaban on the other side of the sea
And designate a patch of forest for me and my two sons to rule?"

The notorious ten-headed king Pengmajia
Readily granted their request.
He jumped onto his magic flying cart of Pushaledi,
Followed closely by Dalihada and her two sons.

The four of them flew over the sea to the north,
And arrived at Yimaban on the other side of the sea.
Pointing to a patch of dark forest, Pengmajia said,
"This patch of forest is to be under your ruling.

"The flying birds and walking beasts, the vegetables and fruits,
You can eat whatever you want to your hearts' content.
If someone passes through the woods or the grassland,
You can also have him as your meals."

403

捧玛加封了领地就飞回勐兰嘎，
妲里哈达天天提着大刀堵守山道，
吞吃了不少马鹿、麂子和猪羊，
杀死了不少大象、野牛和虎豹。

南西拉、腊嘎纳伴着召朗玛，
正向这一片荒山野林走来，
他们谈笑嬉戏绕过一棵大青树，
一抬头撞见了这三个黑毛妖怪。

妲里哈达见到他们喜得眉飞色舞，
张牙舞爪向他们扑来，
"哈哈，我们的餐桌还缺少人肉，
今天苍天赐福送来三份好菜。"

神威的召朗玛大声吆喝：
"你这个黑毛绿眼的妖怪，
竟敢开口就要吃人，
不许你在森林里为非作歹。"

妲里哈达狞笑着口出狂言：
"这片森林归我们掌管，
任何人来到此地都休想活命，
你们自投罗网，是上门的肴馔。"

第十一章 遭难 Chapter 11 Sufferings

After granting the land to Dalihada, Pengmajia flew back to Langa.

Since then, Dalihada took her sword to block the path every day.

She swallowed down countless deer, muntjac, hogs and goats;

And she killed numerous elephants, wild bulls, tigers and leopards.

Zhao Langma, together with Nan Xila and Lagana,
They three were walking toward the forest.
Talking and laughing they bypassed an evergreen tree,
And at no time they saw the three black-furred monsters.

At the sight of them three, Dalihada beamed with great joy.
She threw herself to them ferociously,
"Haw haw! We had never got human meat on our dinner table,
Now heavenly god blessed us with three pieces of delicious dish."

The mighty Zhao Langma yelled at her angrily,
"You, the black-furred and green-eyed monster,
How dare you boast eating human meat?
I won't allow you to act so wildly and unruly in the forest."

Laughing malignantly Dalihada boasted,
"This patch of forest was under our ruling,
No one would expect to walk out of here alive.
You threw yourself into the net to be our delicious dish."

说完三个妖怪挥刀砍来,
召朗玛拉动神弓射出一箭,
狡猾的妖怪迅速躲避,
利箭也被它砍落在地。

腊嘎纳乘机一箭射向谢达,
谢达立刻中箭倒下地,
召朗玛拉弓向独腊沙射去,
独腊沙应声断了气。

妲里哈达大惊失色,
夺路逃出伊麻板,
心惊胆战窜回勐兰嘎宫殿,
向十头王捧玛加叫苦连天:

"三个恶人闯进我们的领地,
我带着儿子前去阻拦,
他们射出无情的毒箭,
你的两个表叔死得好凄惨。

"我心如刀绞悲痛万分,
你一定要替我报仇把冤申。"
妲里哈达见捧玛加默不作声,
又想出办法叫他动心。

"三个人里有一个天仙般的美女,
她的身子像金子一样纯净,
皮肤白皙透出红润,
眼睛明亮宛如星星。

第十一章 遭难 Chapter 11 Sufferings

Then the three monsters brandished their swords toward them.

Zhao Langma drew his bow and shot an arrow,
The cunning monsters rapidly dodged from it,
And the sharp arrow was also cut off by them.

Lagana took the chance to shoot an arrow at Xieda,
Who got hit and fell onto the ground.
Zhao Langma then targeted at Dulasha,
Who died at the sound of the shot arrow.

Dalihada turned pale with fright.
She ran wildly out of the forest of Yimaban.
Trembling with fear, she fled back to the palace of Langa.
And she complained to the ten-headed king Pengmajia.

"Three evil doers intruded into our territory,
And I took my sons to stop them.
I didn't expect they shot us with poisonous arrows,
And your two uncles died a miserable death.

"I was so painful as if a knife was twisted in my heart.
You must take a revenge for us."
Seeing that Pengmajia kept silent,
Dalihada figured out a way to convince him.

"Among them three was there a fairy beauty.
She has a body as pure as gold,
Her skin is fair and rosy;
And her eyes are as bright as stars.

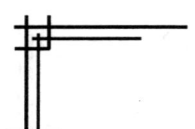

兰嘎西贺 The Ten-Headed King of Langa

"勐兰嘎所有的美女都比不上她,
丰姿艳丽天下难寻,
就是铁石心肠的男人,
见了她也不会不动心。

"她应该做勐兰嘎的王后,
现在却漂泊在深山老林,
只有你配做她的丈夫啊,
她身边的男人该在刀下丧生。"

好色的捧玛加听了这一席话,
心荡神移,难以平静,
恨不得马上把美女抢来,
搂抱在怀中同床共枕。

但是他思前想后一阵战栗,
对妲里哈达说出自己的顾虑:
"你说的这个美女定是南西拉,
她陪伴着召朗玛流浪在森林里。

"她的美貌确是天下第一,
为了娶她我已经做过尝试,
举不起神弓我丢尽了脸,
小朗玛却碰上了好运气。

"为了抢南西拉我同朗玛较量过,
他武艺高强曾让我碰壁,
我看朗玛身上有很大的神威,
绝不是人间的凡夫俗子。

第十一章 遭难 Chapter 11 Sufferings

All the beautiful girls in Langa are nothing to her,
She is an incomparable beauty in the world.
Even a man with a heart as hard as rock
Will be attracted and enchanted by her.

"She should be the queen of the kingdom of Langa.
But now she is wandering in the deep mountain forest.
Only you deserve to be her husband,
The man by her side should die under your sword."

Hearing this, the lustful Pengmajia felt his mind disturbed.
The desire was so strong that he could not subdue it.
He wish he could immediately rob the beauty to his side,
And hold her in his arms and they would share one bed.

But he shuddered at a second thought,
And he told Dalihada his misgivings and worries,
"The beauty you mentioned must be Nan Xila.
She is accompanying Zhao Langma wandering in the forest.

"It's true that her beauty is incomparable in the world,
And I have made attempts to marry her.
I lost my face for not having raised the magic bow,
But the young Zhao Langma had a very good luck.

"To get Nan Xila I had battles with Zhao Langma.
I was defeated since he was superb in martial arts.
What I can see is Zhao Langma has magic power.
He is by no means of a common mortal.

"朗玛这个人我已经熟悉，
另一个男子可能是他的弟弟，
同朗玛作对可不能鲁莽从事，
要抢南西拉啊，谈何容易。"

姐里哈达不甘心儿子白死，
又向捧玛加献出一条毒计：
"好孙儿呀，你不必犹豫，
姑奶奶自有办法让你达到目的。

"不是让你硬拼硬打强行抢夺，
动脑筋施妙计美人就可以到手，
我变成一只漂亮的宝角金鹿，
在他们面前出没引诱。

"美人见了必然十分喜爱，
定会叫丈夫追扑这只野兽，
你只要躲在茂密的树丛中等候，
朗玛一离开，你抱起南西拉就飞走。

"你把她深藏进森严的宫殿，
谁知道美丽的公主是你偷走，
召朗玛只当妻子喂进老虎口，
最后南西拉必定成为你的王后。"

第十一章 遭难 Chapter 11 Sufferings

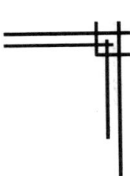

"I know Langma very well,
And the other man could be his younger brother.
We can't act rashly to fight against Langma.
And it is surely not easy to rob Nan Xila away from him."

Dalihada was still resentful with the death of her sons,
So she put forward another evil plan,
"My good grandniece! Don't hesitate.
I have a good idea to help you reach your end.

"You don't need to rob her by force.
Use your brain and you will get the beauty.
I will turn myself into a golden deer with precious horns,
And I will appear before them to tempt the beauty.

"The beauty is sure to be fond of golden deer.
So she will ask her husband to prey it for her.
You just need to hide and wait in the dense woods,
And snatch Nan Xila the moment Langma runs after the deer.

"Hide her in your heavily-guarded palace, no one would know
That it was you who robbed the beautiful princess away.
Zhao Langma would think his wife has been eaten by a tiger.
And in the end, Nan Xila is sure to be your queen."

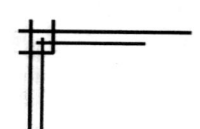

一番话说得捧玛加心荡神浮,
为了弄到罕见的美人他不怕断头,
他赞赏姑奶奶的锦囊妙计,
催促着妲里哈达赶快带他走。

他们来到幽深的伊麻板,
找到了召朗玛三人休息的地方,
捧玛加躲藏在密林深处,
紧紧盯住美丽的南西拉不放。

妲里哈达变成一只乖顺的金鹿,
身上的颜色像金子一样纯黄,
它从南西拉面前悠闲地走过,
森林被它照得闪闪发光。

南西拉看得头晕目眩,
惊喜地抓住召朗玛的手说:
"这么漂亮的宝角金鹿,
我长这么大从未见过。

"它是多么机灵可爱呀!
请你把它生擒活捉给我,
以后你和弟弟外出寻找食物,
让它陪伴我解除寂寞。"

召朗玛心中有几分疑惑:
"这只金鹿长相十分特殊,
在阴暗神秘的森林里不怕人,
会不会是变了形的妖魔?"

第十一章 遭难 Chapter 11 Sufferings

These words stirred up Pengmajia's mind and roused his desire.
To get the rare beauty he had no fear of death any more.
Praising and approving of his grandaunt's clever plan,
He urged Dalihada to lead him to the forest.

They arrived at the deep and quiet forest of Yimaban,
And found the place where Zhao Langma the three rested.
Pengmajia hid himself in the recess of the dark woods,
Fixing his eyes on the beautiful Nan Xila.

Dalihada transformed herself into a meek yellow deer.
The color of its body is as golden as the pure gold.
It wandered leisurely in front of Nan Xila.
The woods were brightened by its appearance.

Nan Xila was enchanted by it into a fit of dizziness.
Excitedly, she grabbed Zhao Langma's hands and said,
"Look, such a beautiful golden dear with precious horns,
I have never seen one like this ever before.

"How agile and how cute it is!
Please catch it alive for me.
Later when you and your brother go out for food,
It can accompany me to relieve my loneliness."

Zhao Langma had doubts in his heart,
"This golden deer has a very special look.
It is not afraid of people in this dark and mysterious forest.
Couldn't it be some sort of transformed evil spirit?"

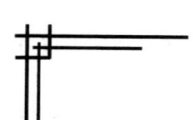

兰噶西贺 The Ten-Headed King of Langa

着了迷的南西拉十分执拗，
不以为然地连连恳求：
"谁不知你神威广大，
妖魔怎么敢来戏弄挑逗。"

南西拉被金鹿的魅力引诱，
召朗玛经不住爱妻的再三请求，
他只好答应去追捕金鹿，
临走前对弟弟一再叮嘱：

"这地方有许多毒蛇猛虎，
千万不要离开你嫂嫂一步，
凶兽好提防，假象易迷惑，
你可不能大意疏忽。"

召朗玛说罢去追逐金鹿，
金鹿时隐时现、若即若离，
眼看就要追上它了，
它却又窜进深谷里。

第十一章 遭难 Chapter 11 Sufferings

The enchanted Nan Xila insisted on it.
Not taking her husband's words seriously, she pled,
"Everybody knows you are omnipotent.
How dare the evil spirit play games with you?"

Nan Xila was totally tempted by the charm of the golden deer.
Zhao Langma could not resist his beloved wife's repeated pleading,
Finally he had to promise to hunt for the golden deer.
Before leaving he instructed his younger brother again and again,

"There are lots of poisonous snakes and fierce tigers,
Never be one step away from your sister-in-law.
It is easy to keep animals away, but also to be fooled by guise.
You couldn't be more careful."

Finishing his words, Zhao Langma went to hunt for the golden deer,
Which appeared in and out of his sight, keeping at one arm's distance.
On one second it seemed so closed to get caught,
The next minute it fled to the deep valley.

415

召朗玛抓住最好的时机,
对准金鹿一箭射去,
只见金鹿应声扑倒在地,
召朗玛心中好不欢喜。

他急速向负伤的金鹿扑去,
伸出手要把它按倒在地,
不料它却突然一跃而起,
一瘸一拐向前逃去。

召朗玛盯着金鹿紧追,
金鹿忽然腾空飞起,
他急忙射出闪电般的利箭,
金鹿被射穿脖子落下地。

随着金鹿的尸体落地,
一团烟雾卷向空中,
妲里哈达现出了原形,
模仿着召朗玛的声音。

"好弟弟腊嘎纳,快来帮我一下,
金鹿已被我的利箭射中,
可是我的右脚被竹签刺破,
鲜血直流,疼痛难忍。"

这呼救声凄凉悲切,
句句似是召朗玛的呼唤,
南西拉听了心如刀绞,
催促弟弟赶快前去察看。

第十一章 遭难 Chapter 11 Sufferings

Zhao Langma took the best opportunity
To aim and shoot at the golden deer.
With just shot, the golden deer fell off to the ground.
Zhao Langma felt delighted in his heart.

He rapidly threw himself to the injured golden deer,
Stretching his arm to press it onto the ground.
Unexpectedly, it jumped to its feet
And then limped forward.

Zhao Langma kept running after it.
Suddenly the golden deer jumped into the air.
Zhao Langma hurried to shoot his flashing arrow.
The golden deer got shot at its neck and fell onto the ground.

When the golden deer landed on the ground,
A wisp of smoke spiraled into the air.
Dalihada appeared in her usual form,
And she imitated Zhao Langma's voice.

"My dear brother, Lagana, come to help me.
The golden deer has been shot by me,
But my right foot was pricked by bamboo slips,
It is bleeding and got me so much hurt."

The cry for help sounded so miserable,
Each word seemed like Zhao Langma's call.
Nan Xila felt her heart was being cut out at hearing this,
And she urged their younger brother to go and have a look.

腊嘎纳感到疑惑和为难：
"哥哥刚才嘱咐再三，
要我千万不要离开你，
绝对保证你的平安。

"嫂嫂不要过分担忧，
我看哥哥不会如此胆怯地呼喊。"
南西拉担心召朗玛的安全，
责怪弟弟犹豫不前。

"你哥哥一个人没有伙伴，
他的处境肯定十分困难，
我听出是他在远处声声呼唤，
快去吧，我这里没有什么危险。"

腊嘎纳经不住嫂嫂一再敦促，
只好去帮助远处的哥哥，
他用箭在嫂嫂周围画了一个圆圈，
祈求土地之神把嫂嫂保护。

"土地之神啊，请多加照顾，
嫂嫂啊，你千万要牢牢记住，
不管发生什么事情，
你都不能走出这个圆圈一步。"

腊嘎纳飞一般穿过密林，
循着声音寻找哥哥召朗玛，
躲在暗处的十头王捧玛加，
趁机扑向圈中的南西拉。

第十一章 遭难 Chapter 11 Sufferings

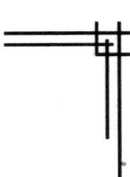

Lagana felt confused and caught in a dilemma,
"Brother told me just now again and again
That I should never leave you alone
To make sure of your safety.

"Sister-in-law, please don't be over worried.
My brother would never cry for help in such a timid way."
Nan Xila got so anxious about the safety of Zhao Langma
That she blamed their brother for his hesitation.

"Your brother is alone without an accompany,
And he must be in a very difficult situation.
I could hear his cries for help in the distance.
Hurry up, I am here without any threat of danger."

Lagana could not resist his sister-in-law's urge,
And he had no other choice but to go and help his brother.
He drew a circle with his arrow around his sister-in-law
To pray that the god of the earth could protect her.

"God of the earth, Please take care of my sister-in-law.
Sister-in-law, Please do remember
By no means you shall step out of the circle
No matter whatever happens."

Lagana ran through the woods as fast as he could.
Following the cries, he looked for his brother Zhao Langma.
Then the ten-headed king Pengmajia who had hidden in the dark
Took the chance to throw himself to Nan Xila in the circle.

土地之神紧紧吸住南西拉，
捧玛加使尽力气也拉不动她，
南西拉的身子重如万座大山，
双脚好像有根须深深插进地下。①

忠实的腊嘎纳来到哥哥身边，
召朗玛见了大吃一惊：
"弟弟呀，你怎么也来了，
让你嫂嫂一个人留在森林。"

"哥哥呀，听到你的声声呼唤，
我只得请土地神保护嫂嫂的安全，
我在她周围画了一个圆圈，
只要她不动谁也靠拢不了她的身边。"

不祥的预兆使召朗玛焦躁不安，
他愤愤地责怪弟弟腊嘎纳：
"土地神不会说话，
你怎能请他守护南西拉。

---

① 还有一种传说为捧玛加冒充帕拉西托钵化缘，南西拉拿着供品走出圈外，被捧玛加掳走。

第十一章 遭难 Chapter 11 Sufferings

The god of the earth held Nan Xila tightly,

No matter how hard Pengmajia tried, he failed to pull her out.

Nan Xila seemed as heavy as thousands of mountains,

And her feet were deep-seated into the earth like tree roots.①

The faithful Lagana found his brother and came to him.

Zhao Langma was so surprised to see him,

"Brother, How come you were here

And left your sister-in-law alone in the woods?"

"Brother, we heard your cries for help

And I had to ask the god of the earth to protect sister-in-law.

I had drawn a circle around her,

Nobody can get close to her as long as she remains still."

The ominous premonition made Zhao Langma uneasy and restless,

And he blamed his brother Lagana angrily,

"The god of the earth could not speak,

How could you ask him to protect Nan Xila?

---

① Another legend says that Pengmajia pretended to be a Palaxi taking a bowl with him to beg for alms, and Nan Xila went out of the circle to give him some offerings. Then Pengmajia robbed her away.

421

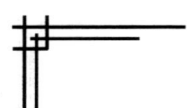

"刚才我追的是一个女妖,
它狡猾地变成那只金鹿,
我用利箭把它射死,
你看它已原形毕露。

"刚才我并没有向你呼救,
看来我们中了女妖的奸计,
快,我们赶快回去,
你的嫂嫂必定危在旦夕。"

召朗玛越说越生气,
说着说着用脚猛跺大地,
土地神受到侮辱非常震怒,
干脆放弃对南西拉的保护。

捧玛加看见保护的圆圈消失,
粗鲁地一下把南西拉抱住,
他心潮激荡,目光淫秽,
犹如饥饿的豺狼捕到了久追的猎物。

南西拉不顾捧玛加的威吓,
在他怀中拼命挣扎,
捧玛加把她放进甫萨乐低神车,
腾云驾雾飞向勐兰嘎。

第十一章 遭难 Chapter 11 Sufferings

"What I ran after just now turned out to be an evil spirit,
She slyly transformed herself into that golden deer,
Which I had shot to death.
Look, it had returned to its usual form.

"I had not called for your help.
It seemed that we had fallen into evil spirit's trap.
Hurry up, let's go back,
Your sister-in-law must be in great danger."

The more Zhao Langma said, the angrier he got,
While shouting, he even stamped heavily on the ground.
The god of the earth felt insulted and angry about it.
So he was unwilling to protect Nan Xila any more.

The protective circle then disappeared. At the sight of it,
Pengmajia snatched Nan Xila into his arms rudely.
He was like a hungry wolf that had got his long-desired prey
With obscene looks in his eyes and erotic feelings surging in his heart.

Regardless of the intimidation of Pengmajia,
Nan Xila struggled violently in his arms.
Pengmajia put her into his flying cart of Pushaledi,
And flew back to the kingdom of Langa on clouds.

兰嘎西贺 The Ten-Headed King of Langa

南西拉在空中放声哭喊，
声声悲戚向召朗玛呼唤求救：
"亲爱的丈夫召朗玛啊，
你的妻子已被十头魔王抢走。

"现在他抓住我在天上飞行，
他的神车犹如风一样快，
不知道越过多少重大山，
眼看已经临近碧波大海。

"不知他要把我劫向哪里，
也许要带我到魔鬼的地方，
威武的召朗玛，英勇的弟弟，
你们快来拯救我脱离魔掌。"

南西拉哭得声音嘶哑，
眼泪犹如雨点飘洒，
捧玛加挟持着南西拉，
匆匆飞向岛国勐兰嘎。

乌鸦看见捧玛加的抢劫行径，
它们想起召朗玛的恩情：
"十头王抢的是召朗玛的妻子，
我们决不能让他的阴谋得逞。

第十一章 遭难 Chapter 11 Sufferings

Nan Xila cried out loud in the sky,
Mournfully she cried to Zhao Langma for help,
"My beloved husband Zhao Langma,
Your wife had been robbed away by the ten-headed demon king.

"Now he took me flying in the sky,
His magic cart ran as fast as the wind.
I don't know how many mountains we have flown over,
Now we are approaching the waving sea.

"I don't know where he would take me,
Maybe to the place where demons live.
My mighty Zhao Langma, my heroic younger brother,
Hurry up to save me out of the demon's clutches."

Nan Xila cried till she almost lost her voice.
Her tears drifted down like raindrops.
Pengmajia took Nan Xila by force with him
To fly hurriedly to the island kingdom of Langa.

The crows saw Pengmajia's robbery.
They thought of Zhao Langma's kindness to them,
"The one the ten-headed king robbed was Zhao Langma's wife,
We could never let him have his way.

"以前我们糟蹋了帕拉西的圣地,
召朗玛却没有伤害我们的生命,
我们曾经发过誓言,
以后一定报答召朗玛的恩情。

"如今召朗玛的妻子遭到不幸,
我们怎能袖手旁观不闻不问?"
千万只乌鸦奋勇地飞上天空,
抓十头王的头脸、啄他的眼睛。

捧玛加慌忙抽出宝刀迎战,
向扑上来的乌鸦乱杀乱砍,
乌鸦的头脚和翅膀纷纷碎断,
鲜血染红了云彩,血雨洒向人间。

乌鸦的碎尸挂满林间,
捧玛加战胜了鸦群继续向前,
南西拉遥见大树上有个影子,
就竭尽全力对它呼喊:

"过路的大哥请听着,
请你告诉森林里的召朗玛,
南西拉已被十头王抢走,
要他快快来搭救我。"

第十一章 遭难 Chapter 11 Sufferings

"We had once destroyed the sacred place of Palaxi,
But Zhao Langma didn't take our life or hurt us.
We had made our promise
To repay Zhanglangma's kindness.

"Now Zhao Langma's wife is in danger,
How could we just be onlookers doing nothing?"
Millions of crows bravely flew into the sky
And they pecked Pengmajia's heads, faces and eyes.

Pengmajia hurriedly drew out his magic sword
And brandished and thrust it at the crows wildly.
The heads, feet and wings of many crows were cut off,
And their blood tainted the clouds and fell onto the earth like rains.

The pieces of crows' corpses were hung over the trees in the forest.
Pengmajia defeated the flocks of crows and went on his way.
Nan Xila saw a shadow on a huge tree in the distance,
And she exerted all her efforts to cry to him,

"The brother who passes by, please listen to me.
Tell Zhao Langma who lives in the forest
That Nan Xila was robbed away by the ten-headed king.
Tell him to come and save me as soon as possible."

兰嘎西贺 The Ten-Headed King of Langa

这个影子是猴子嘎林,
遭受冤屈的它正在树上闷不作声,
听到凄厉的哭声凌空而过,
它的心中产生巨大的同情。

捧玛加劫持南西拉回到勐兰嘎,
花言巧语想诱惑南西拉,
他胡说召朗玛已死在森林,
气得南西拉圆睁双目将他痛骂:

"你这十头魔王胆大包天,
竟敢抢劫别人的妻子,
就算天上的雷公不劈你,
召朗玛也定会百倍惩罚你。

"赶快把我送回去,
不然你的十个脑袋,
就要像熟透的果子,
一个个从身上掉落下来。"

坚贞不屈的南西拉,
周身燃烧着仇恨的烈火,
十头王无法和她接近,
只能呆呆地睁着淫秽的眼睛。

第十一章 遭难 Chapter 11 Sufferings

The shadow was Galin, the monkey,
Who had suffered wrongs and now rested on the tree quietly.
Hearing the miserable cries floating in the air,
He felt great compassion aroused in its heart.

Pengmajia kidnapped Nan Xila back to the kingdom of Langa.
He tried to tempt Nan Xila with his sweet talks.
And he lied that Zhao Langma had been dead in the jungle.
Nan Xila got furious and rebuked him harshly with wide-opened eyes,

"You, the outrageous ten-headed demon king,
How dare you robbed the wife of someone else.
Even if the god of thunderbolt won't split you,
Zhao Langma is sure to punish you much more harshly.

"Send me back immediately,
Otherwise your ten heads
Will fall off your body one by one
Like ripen fruits."

The faithful and unyielding Nan Xila,
Her whole body set off the flaming fire of hatred.
The ten-headed king could not get close to her,
And he just blankly stared at her with obscene eyes.

429

捧玛加把她关进御花园，
囚禁在一个幽静的塔楼里，
塔楼十分雄伟高达九层，
上上下下把守着许多士兵。

十头王又四面增派兵马，
严密卫戍着辽阔的勐兰嘎，
为了防备有人抢救南西拉，
勐兰嘎牢固得像个不漏水的铁桶。

三、召朗玛寻妻

召朗玛兄弟心急如焚赶回原处，
果然看不到鲜花般的南西拉，
兄弟俩悲伤地到处搜寻，
犹如两匹在森林里乱窜的野马。

兄弟俩眼泪汪汪悲痛万分，
两个王子像两棵雨淋的金笋，
"南西拉，你在哪里？
请回答我们一声。"

他们以为她去采花摘果，
可找遍每个花丛不见她的身影，
他们以为她到山溪中洗澡，
可踏遍溪流也不见她的脚印。

第十一章 遭难 Chapter 11 Sufferings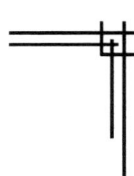

Pengmajia confined her in a quiet tower
Which was in his imperial garden.
The majestic tower was high with nine storeys,
And many soldiers guarded on each floor.

The ten-headed king sent more soldiers to the frontiers
So as to watch closely over the vast kingdom of Langa
In case someone would come and rescue Nan Xila.
Langa was wholly guarded like an iron barrel that never leaks.

Ⅲ Zhao Langma's Search for His Wife

Zhao Langma and his brother worriedly hurried back to their place.

As expected, they didn't find the flower-like Nan Xila.
They two then searched for her everywhere
Like two wild horses which ran wildly in the woods.

The two brothers were full of grief and tears,
And they were like two gold bamboo shoots in rain.
"Nan Xila, Where are you?
Just answer us, please."

They thought she had gone out to pluck flowers and fruits.
So they searched in every clump of flowers but didn't find her.
They thought she had gone to take a bath in the mountain spring,
And they searched each spring but didn't see any of her footprints.

兰嘎西贺 The Ten-Headed King of Langa

他们站到高山云巅瞭望，
他们钻进密林深处找寻，
走遍了莽原、峡谷、山岭，
亲爱的南西拉无踪无影。

召朗玛望着苍天喊南西拉，
白云默默飘过不回答，
腊嘎纳望着远山喊嫂嫂，
群山回荡着他的喊话。

树上的哈光鸟声声哀叫，
似乎在呼唤着失去的伴侣，
枝头的黄鹂鸟上下跳跃，
好像在等待着伴侣回巢。

山风吹来阵阵寒气，
树叶纷纷飘落草地，
召朗玛兄弟满腹悲愁走了一天，
忘了喝水，忘了吃东西。

林中飘来缅桂花的香味，
召朗玛仿佛闻到了妻子的气息，
树上钟情鸟互相理顺羽毛，
召朗玛似乎看见了南西拉的影子。

第十一章 遭难 Chapter 11 Sufferings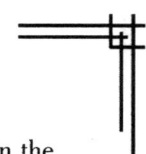

They look into the distance on the top of the mountains in the clouds;

They went deep into the dense forest to search for her.

They had scouted everywhere—the plains, the valleys and mountains,

But they had not got any trace of their dear Nan Xila.

Zhao Langma looked up to the sky and called for Nan Xila.

The clouds floated by silently with no answer;

Lagana looked far into the mountains calling for his sister-in-law.

His shouts echoed among the ranges of mountains.

The Birds of Haguang whimpered sadly in the trees

As if they were calling their lost partners;

The orioles were jumping up and down on the branches,

As if they were waiting for their mates to come back to their nests.

The chill came with the wind from the mountain,

And leaves fell off onto the grassland.

Zhao Langma and his brother walked in grief for a whole day

And they forgot to drink or eat.

In the woods wafted the fragrance of magnolia,

And Zhao Langma seemed to have smelt his wife's scent.

On the trees beloved birds were preening for each other,

And Zhao Langma seemed to have seen Nan Xila's shadow.

召朗玛捧起一掬泉水，
朝着日落的西方下跪，
"亲爱的南西拉呀，
都是我疏忽大意造成的罪。

"从此口渴不能给你送水，
天寒不能给你盖被，
亲爱的妹妹啊，
现在你究竟在哪里安睡？"

他们不觉又回到帕拉西的住处，
向帕拉西打听南西拉的去向：
"她是先回到这里来了，
还是离开森林返回家乡？"

帕拉西说他也没见着南西拉，
心中疑惑，要寻找答案，
他取下木板写下古拉①，
翻开经书仔细卜卦。

---

① 古拉：数学一类的经文。

第十一章 遭难 Chapter 11 Sufferings

Zhao Langma cupped his fingers and got water from a spring,
And he knelt down facing the sunset in the west,
"My dear Nan Xila,
It's I who made such a mistake out of carelessness.

"From now on I can not get water for you when you are thirsty,
Nor can I tuck the quilt for you at night when it's getting cold.
My dear wife and sister,
Where on earth are you falling asleep right now?"

Then they found they were again at the place of Palaxi,
And they asked Palaxi about the whereabouts of Nan Xila,
"Has she been back here before?
Or she has left the forest for homeland?"

Palaxi told them that he had not seen Nan Xila either.
With doubts, he decided to look for the truth.
He got down the board and wrote Gula① on it
And he opened the scripture book to divine carefully.

---

① Gula: a kind of divination with numbers.

帕拉西占卜发现了乌鸦,
它们在死亡中哀叫挣扎,
一齐呼唤着召朗玛,
声声咒骂着捧玛加。

帕拉西告诉召朗玛:
"你那美丽的粉团花,
已被贪得无厌的捧玛加掠走,
装进飞车劫到了勐兰嘎。"

召朗玛伤心得说不出一句话,
就像嘴里含着槟榔,
舌头被石灰咬伤,
虽知道疼痛,却不能张口讲。

他半天才抑制住悲愤哽咽说道:
"不把南西拉找回来,
我就是至死的那一天,
也不会闭上饮恨的双眼。

"帕拉西,请告诉我,
勐兰嘎在海洋的哪一边?
怎样走才能到达那里?
如何才能同南西拉重新见面?"

第十一章 遭难 Chapter 11 Sufferings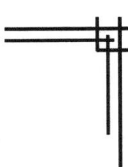

Palaxi saw the crows in his divination
Struggling and whining in the coming death.
They all called for Zhao Langma
And cursed Pengmajia again and again.

Palaxi told Zhao Langma,
"Your beautiful flower-like wife
Has been robbed away by ravenous Pengmajia.
He had taken her back to the kingdom of Langa in his flying cart."

Zhao Langma got so sorrowful that he could not say a single word.
It was as if he kept betel nut in his mouth
While his tongue had been hurt by lime.
He felt great pain but could not open his mouth to speak.

For a long while he held back his sorrowful weeping and said,
"Unless I get my Nan Xila back,
I would never close my eyes full of grievances
Even till the day of my last breath.

"Palaxi, please tell me,
On which side of the sea is the Kingdom of Langa?
How can I get there?
How can I meet Nan Xila again?"

知识渊博的帕拉西说:
"金团银团般的兄弟俩啊,
我为了传授佛经曾经周游天下,
也到过神圣的勐兰嘎。

"勐兰嘎岛离这里太遥远,
路程不能用目测来计算,
中间隔着波涛汹涌的大海,
三千约的深度,三千约的海面。

"去勐兰嘎的路途也很艰难,
有决心的人总可以走到,
出了森林条条道路通大海,
野象常常到海边洗澡。

"大象走过的地方踏出一条路,
你们顺着象踏出的路往前走,
途中的羊肠岔道很多,
要仔细分辨才不会走错。

"左边的岔道通向勐腊达,
那里居住着众多的人家,
平坝宽阔、富饶,
那个勐啊,热闹又繁华。

"一条路通往勐龙奉纳嘎腊,
那是象类生长繁殖的国度,
灰象、白象、棕象数不胜数,
大人小孩都骑着大象走路。

第十一章 遭难 Chapter 11 Sufferings

The erudite Palaxi responded,
"Your brothers of gold and silver,
I have travelled around the world to teach Buddhist sutra,
So I have also been to the sacred kingdom of Langa.

"The island of Langa is too far away from here
To be measured by how far human beings can see.
And it is also separated from us by a wavy ocean
Which is thousands of Yue wide and deep.

"The journey to the kingdom of Langa is really difficult,
But the determined ones can still get to it.
Out of the forest are roads to the ocean,
And wild elephants often go to bathe in the sea.

"There is a path that elephant have traveled through,
Along which you should walk straight.
On the way are there many small forks,
You have to be very careful so that you won't get lost.

"The bypass on the left leads to the kingdom of Lada,
That was a country where many people live.
The plain there was vast and prosperous,
And the country was full of life and bustling activity.

"One bypass leads to the kingdom of Longfengnagala.
That was the country where all kinds of elephants lived.
Grey, white and brown elephants were numerous,
And grown-ups and children all rode on elephants.

兰嘎西贺 The Ten-Headed King of Langa

"右边的岔道通向勐嘎拉，
嘎拉人皮肤雪白眼睛蓝绿，
那里的人们很会做生意，
多少金银财宝落到他们手里。

"一条大路通向猴子国勐基沙，
猴子们管辖着高山、森林和平坝，
它们的国家临近大海，
从那里跨海就能到达勐兰嘎。

"十头王强悍凶暴神通广大，
没有智慧和力量救不回南西拉，
你们牢记我说的话，
勇敢地去战斗吧。"

朗玛兄弟感谢帕拉西的指点，
按照帕拉西指点的方向出发，
在穿越莽莽林海时，
见到一堆堆伤亡的乌鸦。

有的双脚摔断躺在地上，
有的缺少翅膀在树下挣扎，
有的气息奄奄流着鲜血，
有的呱呱惨叫在树上倒挂。

第十一章 遭难 Chapter 11 Sufferings

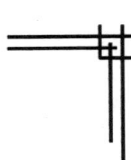

"The bypass on the right leads to the kingdom of Gala.
The people in Gala have fair skin and blue or green eyes.
They were very good at doing business,
And lots of gold, silver and treasures fell into their hands.

"The main road leads to Jisha, the kingdom of monkeys.
These monkeys were ruling the mountains, forests and plains.
Their country was very close to the sea,
And from there you can cross the sea to the kingdom of Langa.

"The ten-headed king was fierce and brutal with magic power.
You could only rescue Nan Xila back with wisdom and strength.
Keep my words in your mind,
Go and fight bravely and wisely."

Langma and his brother thanked Palaxi for his help,
And they set out as Palaxi had instructed them.
While they were walking through the thick woods,
They saw stacks of injured and dead crows.

Some of them had got broken legs lying on the ground;
Some had lost their wings and were struggling under the trees;
Some were still bleeding at their last gasp;
And more were hung upside down on the tree whining miserably.

441

听到乌鸦的哀啼，
兄弟俩心如针扎，
渺无人烟的深山老林，
为什么死伤这么多乌鸦？

召朗玛走到树下，
询问挂在枝头的乌鸦：
"什么人这样残酷，
对你们乱砍乱杀？"

"逞凶作恶的捧玛加，
偷偷劫走了你的南西拉，
他挟着南西拉在天上飞行，
我们义愤填膺岂肯饶他。

"忘不了昔日你的救命恩情，
我们相约飞上去同十头王冲杀，
可是我们没有他的本领大，
英勇地死伤在他的屠刀之下。

"英明、善良的召朗玛呀，
请你救救这些可怜的乌鸦，
用灵丹仙法使它们还原复活，
你的大恩大德一定报答。"

第十一章 遭难 Chapter 11 Sufferings

At hearing the sorrowful moaning of the crows,
The two brothers felt as being pierced by needles.
This mountain forest was so remote that few people came,
And why so many crows were injured and killed?

Zhao Langma approached and stood under the tree,
And he asked the crows which were hung on the branches,
"Who were those brutal people
That slaughtered so many of you?"

"Pengmajia, the brutal evil-doer,
He secretly robbed your Nan Xila away,
And hijacked her flying in the sky.
We got so indignant that there was no way for us to spare him.

"We didn't forget the favor you had done to save us,
So we flew up into the air to fight against the ten-headed king.
But we were not as powerful as he was,
And many of us died heroically under his slaughtering sword.

"You wise and kind Zhao Langma,
Please save these poor crows,
Use panacea to get them back to life.
Your holy grace will surely be repaid."

召朗玛听了十分感动，
马上拯救舍己为人的乌鸦，
怎样使飞禽走兽起死回生，
帕拉西曾给他传授过神法。

他对死伤的乌鸦吹气洒水，
霎时遭难的乌鸦又有了生命，
它们呱呱地感谢又飞向高空，
森林里只剩下召朗玛兄弟二人。

第十一章 遭难 Chapter 11 Sufferings

Zhao Langma was moved by what he had heard and immediately

He tried to save the crows who had sacrificed themselves for others.

How to bring the dead flying birds and walking beasts into life?

Palaxi had taught him the magic.

He breathed to and sprinkled water over the injured or dead crows.

Suddenly the demised crows came back to life.

They cracked their thanks to him and flew to the air,

And now only Zhao Langma and his brother were left in the forest.

第十二章　结盟

一、患难之交

召朗玛兄弟沿着象踏出的路前进，
跨过深谷、翻过高山，
又在茫茫的森林里穿行，
来到了猴国勐基沙的边沿。

痛苦折磨着他们的身心，
热汗浸湿了他们的单衣，
长途跋涉累得腰腿酸软，
他们倒在一棵大青树下休息。

召朗玛疲倦地嘱咐弟弟：
"我感到周身酸软无力，
让哥哥先睡一会儿，
待我醒过来再替换你。"

第十二章 结盟 Chapter 12 Alliance Formed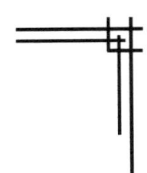

Chapter 12　Alliance Formed

Ⅰ　Friends in Need

After walking along the road trodden by elephants,
And through the valleys and over the mountains,
Zhang Langma and his brother continued on through the dense forest.
Finally they arrived at the border of Jisha, the Kingdom of monkeys.

Pains were torturing their bodies and hearts.
Their garments were drenched in sweats.
The long trek got their backs and legs aching.
They fell onto the ground under an evergreen tree to take a rest.

Zhao Langma told his brother tiredly,
"I had ache all over my body.
Let me sleep for a while,
And you can have a rest when I wake up."

447

召朗玛枕着弟弟的身体，
躺在腊嘎纳的身旁，
不一会就呼呼入睡，
均匀的鼾声飘向四方。

生活在森林中的饥饿的蚊蝇，
嗡嗡叫着纷纷向他们飞来，
拼命叮咬召朗玛身上的血，
腊嘎纳轻轻把蚊蝇赶开。

忠厚的弟弟腊嘎纳，
脱下衣服盖住哥哥的手脚，
蚊蝇都飞到腊嘎纳的身上，
它们在光赤的脊背上叮咬。

腊嘎纳的背上麋集着蚊蝇，
他忍住疼痛一动不动，
既不吭声也不拍打，
因为他怕惊醒哥哥的好梦。

却说猴子嘎林正坐在这棵树上，
它看见兄弟俩如此亲密，
弟弟对哥哥这样真诚，
不禁联想起自己的悲惨遭遇。

第十二章 结盟 Chapter 12 Alliance Formed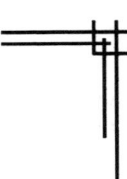

Lying by the side of Lagana,
Zhao Langma rested on him.
He fell into sound sleep in a minute,
And his even snores wafted around.

The hungry mosquitoes and bugs living in the forest
Swarmed to attack them.
They sucked as hard as possible the blood of Zhao Langma,
Lagana drove away the mosquitoes gently.

The loyal brother Lagana took off his own clothes
To cover his brother's hands and feet.
The mosquitoes flew to Lagana,
And bit on his bare back.

On the back of Lagana assembled lots of mosquitoes.
He endured the itching pain and kept still.
He didn't make any sound or clapped the mosquitoes on his back
For fear that his brother would be woken up from his dreams.

At this moment, Galin, the monkey was sitting on the tree.
He had seen the two brothers so close to each other,
And the younger brother so loyal to the elder one,
He could not help but to think of his own miserable sufferings.

"我也有一个亲生哥哥,
却是那样蛮横不讲理,
诬害我企图篡夺它的王位,
赶我出家门,霸占我妻子。"

想到这里嘎林一阵辛酸,
泪珠儿扑簌簌往下滴,
泪水滴在召朗玛的脸上,
惊动了树下的两兄弟。

召朗玛醒来询问弟弟:
"是不是你又在哭泣,
或是天上正在下雨,
我的脸上是泪珠还是水滴?"

兄弟俩抬头仔细看,
看见树上蹲着一只大猴子,
顿时心中十分生气,
误以为猴子对他们无礼。

召朗玛大声吼道:
"你这傲慢该死的东西,
竟敢洒水在我们身上,
把我们轻视为一片叶子。

"你今天定逃不出我们的弓箭,
我们要让你死在这里。"
嘎林急得像热锅上的蚂蚁,
慌忙跳下树来好言解释:

第十二章 结盟 Chapter 12 Alliance Formed

"I also have a brother of my own,
But he was so overweening and unreasonable.
He wronged me accusing me of attempting to take his throne,
And drove me out of my home and took my wife."

Thinking of this, Galin felt a fit of bitterness.
His tears swished down from his cheeks.
And they dropped onto the face of Zhao Langma,
Which disturbed the two brothers under the tree.

Zhao Langma woke up and asked his brother,
"It was you who were crying?
Or was it raining?
On my face are tears or raindrops?"

The two brothers looked up carefully,
And found a big monkey crouching in the tree.
They got very angry at the thought
that the monkey did something rude.

Zhao Langma yelled at it loudly,
"You, so arrogant and rude,
How dare you pissed on us
Looking down upon us as a piece of leave.

"You can't certainly escape our bow and arrows,
And today we want you to die here."
Galin got so worried like an ant on a hot pot,
And he hurried to jump down from the tree to explain,

"两位英明的召啊,
我没有一点侮辱你们之意,
因为见到你们兄弟俩异常亲密,
我想起了自己的身世。

"对比之下使我忍不住哭泣,
落在你们身上的是我伤心的泪水,
悲愤像重石压着我的心,
请饶恕我这苦命的嘎林。"

嘎林讲述了自己苦难的经历,
又关切地询问善良的弟兄:
"看你们脸孔上布满愁云,
是不是心中也有难言的苦痛?"

兄弟俩听了顿时消了气,
深深同情嘎林的悲惨遭遇,
召朗玛也叙述了自己的不幸,
然后细心地询问猴子:

"可恶的十头王把南西拉抢走,
你是否看见他飞过这里?"
"十头王驾着飞车挟持你的妻子,
正是飞过这片林地。

第十二章 结盟 Chapter 12 Alliance Formed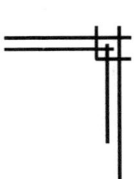

"You two wise Zhaos,
I didn't have any intention to insult you at all.
Seeing you two brothers so close to each other,
I could not help thinking of my own life.

"The comparison between you and us brought me sad tears.
What had dropped down onto you were my tears of sadness.
Grief and anger were like heavy rocks on my heart.
Please forgive me, your miserable Galin."

Then Galin told them the sufferings he had gone through,
And he showed his great concerns to the kind brothers,
"Look at the gloomy clouds on your faces,
Do you also have unspeakable agonies in your heart?"

At his words, the two brothers' anger disappeared into thin air.
They were sympathetic with the miserable experience of Galin,
And Zhao Langma also recounted his own misfortune.
Then he asked the Monkey carefully,

"The damned ten-headed king has robbed Nan Xila away.
Have you ever seen him flying over here?"
"Yes, the ten-headed king hijacked your wife in his flying cart,
And they flew over exactly this patch of wood."

453

"他这不义的抢劫行为,
我在树上看得十分清晰,
南西拉在捧玛加怀中拼命挣扎,
声声呼唤着你的名字。"

召朗玛听了犹如刀割心肺,
难言的悲痛使他流出眼泪,
他感谢嘎林告诉真情,
又请求嘎林相助一臂之力。

"嘎林啊,我们的命运相同,
让我们结下终身的友谊,
若你能帮我救出南西拉,
我会一辈子感激你。"

嘎林听了连忙合十下拜:
"我愿意和你结成终身的盟友,
但是我的哥哥巴力莫为非作歹,
望你先帮助我把它从宝座上踢下来。

"只有你的神弓利箭,
才能战胜十恶不赦的巴力莫,
只有我当上了勐基沙猴王,
才有打败捧玛加的力量。"

第十二章 结盟 Chapter 12 Alliance Formed

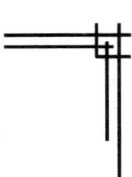

"I saw clearly on the tree
His evil act of robbery.
Nan Xila struggled hard in the arms of Pengmajia,
And she cried out loud for your name."

Hearing this, Zhao Langma felt as his heart was cut into pieces.
Unspeakable grief brought out his tears.
He expressed his thanks to Galin for his help,
And then asked if Galin could give them a hand.

"Galin, we have the same fate,
Let form our life-long friendship.
If you could help me rescue Nan Xila out,
I will be grateful to you for the rest of my life."

Hearing his words, Galin hurried to kneel down with folded palms,
"Sure, I would like to be your life-long friend.
But you know my older brother Balimo now is an evil doer,
I wish you could help me kick him off his throne first.

"Only with your magic bow and sharp arrows
Can we have the victory over the atrocious Balimo.
Only when I am the king of Jisha,
Can we have enough power to defeat Pengmajia."

召朗玛和腊嘎纳觉得有道理，
满口答应首先实现它的要求，
他们立下坚如磐石的盟誓，
结成了同生死共患难的朋友。

嘎林忧心忡忡地说道：
"巴力莫本领高强有力气，
皮厚腰粗，身体魁梧，
对付它可是不容易。"

召朗玛说："就算它大如天柱山，
也顶不住我无坚不摧的宝箭，
让我试射宝箭给你看看，
再厉害的敌人也休想生还。"

说罢拉开宝弓射出一箭，
声如霹雳，威震大地，
"嗖嗖"地穿透了七棵大树，
飞箭又回到召朗玛手里。

嘎林目瞪口呆又惊又喜，
对战胜邪恶不再怀疑，
召朗玛增加了患难兄弟，
犹如猛虎下山添了双翼。

第十二章 结盟 Chapter 12 Alliance Formed

Zhao Langma and Lagana thought his words sensible,
So they promised to meet his request first.
They swore an oath of alliance as steadfast as a rock,
And they became friends going through ups and downs together.

Galin said to the brothers in great depression,
"Balimo is enormously strong with super skills.
He has thick hide and is tall and sturdy,
It is not easy to deal with him."

Zhao Langma said, "Even if he was as huge as a mountain,
He could not resist my magic arrows which can destroy everything.
Let me show you how powerful my magic arrows are.
When I shoot one, even more powerful enemies could never survive."

Finishing his words, he drew his bow and shot an arrow.
Like thunderbolt, the sound of it shook the earth.
The arrow pierced through seven huge trees
And it flew back to the hand of Zhao Langma.

Galin got dumbstruck and at the same time surprisingly happy.
He didn't have any doubt about the victory over the evil.
Zhao Langma now had got another brother whom he could depend on,
He felt like a mighty tiger coming down the mountain with wings.

二、嘎林继位

嘎林领着朗玛兄弟越岭穿林,
来到了勐基沙首府城下,
它面临大海背靠森林,
这就是蜚声于世的猴国勐基沙。

国王巴力莫手下有不少兵马,
儿子旺果,大将阿努曼,
聪明的占卜官是摩米,
勇敢的将领有腊塔和阿哈。

召朗玛提出一个作战方法,
由嘎林一个人前去叫骂,
把巴力莫单身引出宫殿,
召朗玛躲在林中把它射杀。

眼睛里燃烧着仇恨火焰的嘎林,
纵身跳到勐基沙上空,
把对巴力莫的冤仇尽情发泄,
怒骂声比火烧茅草还猛烈。

"昏庸无耻的巴力莫听着,
今天嘎林要来给你算账,
要和你比个高低输赢,
今天定要叫你死在我手上。"

第十二章 结盟 Chapter 12 Alliance Formed

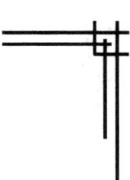

II Galin's Ascendance to Throne

Galin led Langma brothers across the mountains and woods,
And they arrived at the foot of the city wall of the capital of Jisha.
The capital faced the sea and backed against the forests,
And here is the kingdom of monkeys, Jisha known to the world.

The king Balimo had many troops and soldiers,
And his son Wangguo, his general Anuman,
And Momi, the intelligent official of divination,
As well as other brave officials such as Lata and Aha.

Zhao Langma put forward one strategy of the battle.
Galin alone would go and shout his curses,
So that Balimo himself would be drawn out of the palace.
Then Zhao Langma hiding in the woods would shoot him to death.

With burning hatred in the eyes,
Galin jumped into the air over the palace of Jisha.
He burst out his grievance and resentment toward Balimo.
His angry abuses were more violent than flaming hey.

"Fatuous and shameless Balimo, you listen carefully,
Now Galin came to settle all our accounts.
Come and let's have a duet
And you are doomed to die at my hands today."

凶狠暴躁的巴力莫，
哪能忍得住这番嘲骂，
头身手脚热得像火燎，
心肝肺腑几乎要爆炸。

它一头冲出宫廷的大门，
气势汹汹飞到白云底下，
两兄弟见面犹如仇敌相逢，
迫不及待立刻扭住厮打。

你咬我的身，我抓你的头，
又叫又骂，拳脚交加，
一下嘎林骑着巴力莫，
忽而巴力莫又把嘎林踩在脚下。

它们打得乌云翻滚，
它们打得天昏地暗，
兄弟俩像旋风扭成一团，
召朗玛、腊嘎纳望得眼花缭乱。

忽见嘎林手软脚瘫无力气，
是巴力莫卡住它的脖子，
被重重踢了几脚后跌落下地，
直条条躺在树丛里喘息。

第十二章 结盟 Chapter 12 Alliance Formed

The fierce and hot-tempered Balimo,
How could he bear such abuses and curses.
He felt as if his whole body was on fire,
And his heart and lung would explode.

He rushed out of the gate of the palace,
And flew fiercely to the white clouds.
The two brothers met as two enemies,
And they could not wait to grapple each other for a fight.

One bit the body of the other and the other grabbed one's head.
Shouting and cursing, they fought with both their hands and feet.
For one second, Galin rode on Balimo,
But for another second, Balimo stepped on Galin.

They fought till black clouds rolled about,
Till the sky got murky and the earth dark.
The two brothers wriggled together like whirlwind,
Zhao Langma and Lagana watched them and got dazed.

Suddenly Galin felt out of breath with weak hands and feet.
It was because Balimo had strangled his neck.
And he was kicked heavily and dropped off onto the ground.
Lying flat on the grass in the woods, he could not get his breath.

巴力莫站在云端哈哈笑,
得意扬扬飞回宫廷,
嘎林挣扎起来无比气愤,
对召朗玛兄弟发泄不平:

"原来你兄弟俩欺骗我,
哄我去同巴力莫交锋,
你们不遵守信誓来援助,
反而袖手旁观、按兵不动。"

两个王子连忙对它解释道:
"不是我们践踏诺言,
纵然有天大的本领也无法施展,
几次拉弓成月都放不成箭。

"你们俩都是白猴子,
毛发同色,嘴脸一个样子,
在空中辨不出哥和弟,
我们怕宝箭失误伤害了你。

"患难与共的嘎林你别着急,
许下的诺言我们绝不违背,
现在好好休息一晚,
养足力气明天再战。"

第十二章 结盟 Chapter 12 Alliance Formed

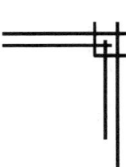

Standing on the top of the clouds, Balimo laughed,
And elatedly he flew back to his court.
Struggling to his feet with indignation,
Galin vented his anger on Zhao Langma and his brother,

"You two had taken me in,
Coaxing me to fight against Balimo.
You did not come to help me as you promised,
Instead, you stayed put and just looked on."

The two princes hurried to explain to Galin,
"We would not and didn't break our promise.
We had tried many times to shoot at him,
But no matter how skillful we are, we had to give it up.

"Since you two are both white monkeys,
You look exactly the same with hair of same color.
Not being able to distinguish you from your brother,
We were afraid my magic arrows could hurt you by mistake.

"Don't worry, we are brothers going through foul and fair together.
We would never break the promise that we have made.
Tonight, let's take a good rest,
And we will be refreshed and energetic for tomorrow's fight."

第二天腊嘎纳从树上摘来野果，
三个坐在一起咬嚼，
用野果填饱了肚子，
用泉水解除了干渴。

召朗玛嚼烂甘涩的槟榔，
用鲜红的槟榔水染在嘎林头上，
嘎林的头恰似一个红果，
与它哥哥的头完全两样。①

嘎林纵身跃上宫廷上空，
叫骂声比昨天的更响，
骂声传进巴力莫的耳朵，
仿佛有人撒尿在它头上。

"这家伙昨天才一败涂地，
今天又来挑衅，不自量力，
看来得把它除掉才解恨，
免得它以后再来闹事。"

巴力莫暴跳如雷又气又急，
像兀鹰扑去立刻把嘎林抱住，

———————

① 还有一种说法是用槟榔水染红它的脸和屁股，因此现在猴子的脸和屁股都是红的。

第十二章 结盟 Chapter 12 Alliance Formed

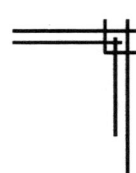

The next day, Lagana plucked some wild fruits
And the three of them sat together eating.
They filled their stomachs with the fruits
And they quenched their thirst with sweet spring.

Zhao Langma chewed some sweet and unripe betel nut,
And he dyed Galin's hair with the juice of the betel nuts.
Now Galin's head looked very much like a red fruit,
Which is totally different from his brother's.①

Galin jumped high into the air over the palace,
And he cursed and called for a fight more loudly than the day before.
His curses spread into Balimo's ears,
He felt as if he had been pissed on his head.

"It was only yesterday that he was beaten badly,
How dare he came and provoked me like this today.
It seemed I had to get rid of him once for all,
In case he would come back and make troubles again."

Balimo stamped about in a frenzy,
Then he flew to Galin like a vulture and seized him in his arms.

---

① Another saying is that both his head and bottoms have been dyed red by the juice of betel nuts. That explains why now monkeys have red faces and bottoms.

两人激烈地扭在一起厮杀,
打得难分难解不分胜负。

嘎林忽然施展了脱身计,
甩脱巴力莫掉头向森林跑去,
巴力莫以为嘎林害怕了,
紧紧追赶不让它喘息。

它刚抓住嘎林的脖子,
就被嘎林翻身踢了一脚,
巴力莫滚了几滚,
站在那里喘粗气。

躲在树上的召朗玛,
看清了发红的标记,
辨明了哥哥和弟弟,
把致命的利箭向巴力莫射去。

巴力莫脸腮中了神箭,
一个跟头摔到树林里,
它疼痛难忍不断呻吟,
挣扎着高声怒斥:

"我两兄弟是冤家对头,
在天空中互相斗殴,
是谁躲在森林里射来暗箭?
我与你有什么不解的冤仇?"

第十二章 结盟 Chapter 12 Alliance Formed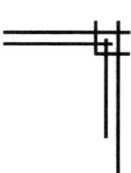

They two grappled together and fought fiercely,
And no one could get an upper hand.

Suddenly, Galin got himself out of the grip of Balimo,
And he turned around to run toward the forest.
Balimo took it for granted that Galin lost his guts
And he chased him giving him no moment to take a breath.

The moment he caught Galin's neck,
He was kicked hard by Galin,
Which sent him rolling away on the ground.
Then panting heavily he got to his feet.

Zhao Langma was hidden on the tree,
And he could see clearly who was who now
Because of the red hair he made for Galin.
And he shot a fatal arrow at Balimo.

Balimo got shot at his cheek by the magic arrow,
And he fell onto the ground in the woods.
He was so much hurt that he could not help but keep moaning,
Still he struggled to his feet and cursed angrily,

"We two brothers were enemies
And we fought against each other in the air.
Who are you hiding in the woods to shoot me behind my back?
Is there any rancour between you and me?"

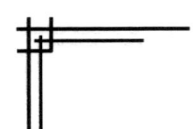

召朗玛和腊嘎纳走过去，
对猴王巴力莫坦率开口，
把事情的经过对它说明，
承认神箭出自他俩之手。

"我们同情嘎林的遭遇，
欣然接受它的请求，
我们立下了坚定的盟誓，
互相帮助消灭双方的仇寇。"

巴力莫听了这个回答，
气得全身战栗眼冒金花，
恨得五脏六腑火辣辣，
怒视着大声质问召朗玛：

"我与你俩没有什么仇恨，
我们兄弟的事你们凭什么过问，
为什么要偏心袒护嘎林，
伤害一个素不相识的好人？"

召朗玛义正词严痛加驳斥：
"天下的丑恶我都仇恨，
邪恶的行为哪能容忍，
世上的好坏我们分得清。

"嘎林忠实地执行你的命令，
你却反口诬陷把骨肉当成仇敌，
嘎林无辜受到冤屈，
你不给一点申辩的余地。

第十二章 结盟 Chapter 12 Alliance Formed

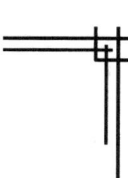

Zhao Langma and Lagana went toward him,
And they spoke to the monkey king frankly
Explaining all that had happened.
They admitted that it was they who shot him.

"Out of our sympathy with Galin for his suffering,
We readily agreed to help him under his request.
And we had given our solemn oath,
Helping each other to get rid of our enemies."

Hearing their explanation, Balimo was so angry
that he shuddered with a dizzy head.
Feeling the fire of indignation swirling in his body,
Balimo stared at Zhao Langma and questioned him,

"I didn't have any rancour with you.
Why you interfered between me and my brother?
Why you favored and sided with Galin
And hurt a kind man whom you have never known?"

Zhao Langma refuted him justly and severely,
"I hate all the dirty things in the world
And can not bear to see the evil-doings.
And we can tell the right from wrong.

"Galin faithfully did what you had ordered him to do.
But you framed him up turning your own blood and flesh into enemy.
Innocent Galin was so wronged by you,
And you even didn't give him any chance to explain.

"我的妻子南西拉遭了灾难,
万恶的十头王把她抢去,
嘎林的悲惨遭遇和我相同,
共同的命运使我们团结对敌。

"它赞助我去讨伐捧玛加,
夺回我被劫走的妻子,
我们答应帮它惩治你,
今天我才一箭把你置于死地。"

巴力莫听了浑身发抖,
慌忙伏地向召朗玛磕头:
"请你发善心积美德饶我活命,
为我拔出神箭医好伤口。

"只要我能脱离死难的苦海,
一定报答你的大恩大义,
我也愿为你去讨伐十头王,
夺回南西拉让你们夫妻团聚。"

召朗玛见它有所忏悔,
宽容地从它身上拔出箭头,
箭毒已渗透它的全身,
他告诉猴王已无法挽救。

第十二章 结盟 Chapter 12 Alliance Formed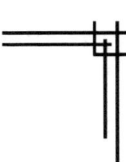

"A disaster also happened to my dear wife Nan Xila,
Who was robbed away by the evil ten-headed King.
Galin's suffering was very much like mine,
So we were united together by our shared fate.

"Galin will assist me in fighting against the ten-headed king,
And getting back my wife who had been snatched away from me.
And we had given him our promise to punish you.
That's why I shot at you with my arrow which would take your life."

Balimo shuddered violently at hearing this.
He knelt down and kowtowed to Zhao Langma,
"Please be kind and virtuous to leave me alive,
And pull out the magic arrow and get my wound healed.

"As long as I can stay out of the bitter sea of death,
I am sure to repay your great kindness.
I will go with you to fight against the ten-headed king
And get your wife back and you two will reunion."

Zhao Langma saw his repentance,
And leniently he took the arrow out of him. But unfortunately,
The poison on the arrow head has penetrated his body.
He had to tell the monkey king there was nothing he could do.

兰嘎西贺　The Ten-Headed King of Langa

巴力莫听了哑口无言，
知道死神已饶不过自己，
它用微微发颤的声音，
要求召朗玛答应它一件事。

"高贵的召啊，
我今生有一个好儿子，
它能征善战、英勇无敌，
旺果就是它的名字。

"倘若弟弟嘎林做了大王，
请把旺果留在它的身旁，
用它做侍从辅助嘎林，
让儿子替我还清罪账。"

召朗玛一口答应它最后的要求，
巴力莫脸上露出一丝笑意，
这位至死才悔悟的暴君，
默默地闭上眼睛死去。

嘎林跪下向兄长告别，
把它安葬在勐基沙森林里，
然后带着召朗玛两兄弟，
离开森林向宫殿走去。

所有生活在勐基沙的猴子，
纷纷前来祝福诚实的嘎林，
所有的武官大臣，
纷纷前来朝拜召朗玛兄弟二人。

第十二章 结盟 Chapter 12 Alliance Formed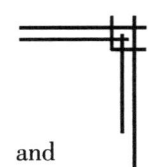

Hearing Zhao Langma's words, Balimo got dumb and speechless.

He knew that the God of death wouldn't forget him.

With a trembling voice,

Balimo asked Zhao Langma to promise him one thing.

"Your Majestic Zhao,

I am blessed with a very good son,

Who is a skilled warrior, very brave in battles.

Wangguo is his name.

"If someday my brother Galin becomes the king,

Please keep Wangguo at his side.

My son will serve and help Galin,

And repay the debts that I owed to him."

Zhao Langma immediately agreed on his last request.

A weak smile appeared on Balimo's face.

The tyrant, who didn't repent until his death,

Slowly closed his eyes and passed away.

Galin knelt down to say goodbye to his elder brother,

And he buried him in the forest of Kingdom of Jisha.

Then leading Zhao Langma and his brother

He left the forest and headed for the palace.

All the monkeys in the Kingdom of Jisha

Came to give their blessings to the honest Galin;

All the officials and generals of the court

Came to pay their respect to Zhao Langma and his brother.

它们簇拥在胜利者的身旁,
关切地询问他们的经历、生平,
召朗玛把苦难的遭遇细讲,
又谈到猴王的继承人嘎林。

"嘎林正直、善良,
蒙受屈辱,流放在森林,
今天巴力莫已经升天,
勐基沙的王位应让它来继承。

"旺果谙熟猴子国的法规,
应让它叔侄同心治理勐基沙,
我请求由它俩率领千军万马,
和我们一道去战胜邪恶的捧玛加。"

臣民们同意召朗玛的请求,
推举嘎林做了勐基沙大王,
推举旺果做它的辅国大臣,
立即调兵遣将准备跨海出征。

三、出征

摩米占卦选定出征的时辰,
嘎林集结部队加紧练兵,
士兵们成群结队来到都城,
黑压压一片犹如重雾浓云。

第十二章 结盟 Chapter 12 Alliance Formed

They centered around the winners,
Asking about their life experiences.
Zhao Langma gave them detailed accounts of his sufferings
And he also spoke of Galin, the successor of Monkey King.

"Galin is honest and kind,
but was wrongly humiliated and exiled to the woods.
Now that Balimo has passed away,
It is time for Galin to succeed to the throne.

"Wangguo is expert in the rules and regulations of your kingdom,
So he should help his uncle to govern the kingdom of Jisha.
Could I ask them to lead your powerful army
And go with us to win the victory over the evil Pengmajia?"

The officials and people agreed on the request of Zhao Langma,
And they elected Galin the king of the Kingdom of Jisha,
And Wangguo the prime minster of their country.
Immediately they got their army ready for the voyage to war.

Ⅲ Military Expedition

After Momi divined the right time to set out for the expedition,
Galin gathered his armies to get them trained.
Groups after groups of soldiers swarmed to the capital city
Hovering around like dark and heavy clouds.

475

列队的有白猴、红猴和灰猴,
它们都是勇将健卒,个个威风凛凛,
有的拿着长矛大刀,
有的扛着弓弩梭镖。

听说就要跨海出征,
个个欢喜得手舞足蹈,
有的耍刀弄箭显示武艺,
有的一个筋斗跃上树梢。

出征的日子已经来临,
官兵们的誓言激动人心:
"穿洋过海我们是善游的鱼龙,
腾云驾雾我们赛过高飞的雄鹰。

"我们要像飓风一样,
劈波斩浪越过海洋,
我们要像雷电一样,
气势磅礴冲进勐兰嘎。

"捣毁十头王的宫殿,
征服作恶的捧玛加,
杀死勐兰嘎的魔王,
救出美丽的南西拉。"

第十二章 结盟 Chapter 12 Alliance Formed

Among the procession were white, red and gray monkeys,
All brave generals and soldiers with awe-inspiring appearance.
Some of them took spears and knives
And some others with bows and arrows.

Hearing they would be on a military expedition,
All of them joyfully swung their arms and stamp their feet.
Some played with knives and bows to show off their battling skills,
Some others jumping high onto the tops of trees.

Now it's time to set out for the battle,
Generals and soldiers solemnly made their oaths,
"We will be like dragons to swim across the seas,
We will be like soaring eagles to fly on clouds.

"We are as powerful as hurricanes
To ride on the waves to cross the ocean;
We are as mighty as thunders and lightening
To dash into the Kingdom of Langa overwhelmingly.

"We will destroy the palace of ten-headed king.
And Pengmajia, the evil king of Langa
Will be caught and killed by us.
And we will rescue the beautiful Nan Xila."

出发的礼炮隆隆响起,
召朗玛兄弟走在前面,
嘎林带着猴将猴兵,
浩浩荡荡离开都城。

紧跟着嘎林的后边,
是侄儿旺果和它的兵马,
它们敲着清脆的铜锣,
雄赳赳迈着大步向前跨。

接着是神通广大的阿努曼,
它的精壮、威风的兵马,
手持大刀长矛身背弓箭,
神气十足步步紧跟着它。

接着是占卜能手摩米,
它率领的猴兵肩扛长矛,
士兵个个身材高大,
腰间挎着明晃晃的大刀。

最后是年轻的玛尼腊和阿哈武官,
还有胆大的腊塔、老练的嘎木达,
它们的兵马个个精神抖擞,
腾云快如飞,潜水像鱼虾。

第十二章 结盟 Chapter 12 Alliance Formed

The thunderous gun salutes announced the time to set out.
Zhao Langma and his brother marched at the very front,
Followed by Galin leading his generals and soldiers.
Mightily they marched out of the capital city.

The one who was closely following Galin
Was his niece Wangguo leading his soldiers.
Striking their resounding brass gongs,
They marched forward mightily and majestically.

Next was the powerful Anuman
And his strong and impressive troops.
Holding knives, spears and bows on their backs,
They followed him energetically step by step.

Next marched Momi, the one expert in divination.
The troops it led were soldiers with long spears.
All of them were tall and stout.
Some carried shining swords at their sides.

The last came young military officials Manila and Aha,
And also the bald Lata and sophisticated Gamuda.
Their troops were all energetic and vigorous.
They could fly in the clouds and dive into the seas.

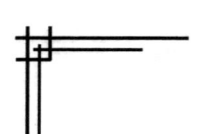

敲着铜锣和金鼓，
吹着银笛和唢呐，
高举着旗幡的八路队伍，
铺天盖地、密密麻麻。

林中的缅桂花随风飘散幽香，
一只只杜鹃鸟在树枝上歌唱，
鸟语花香召朗玛无意欣赏，
他的心啊，早已飞过海洋。

第十二章 结盟 Chapter 12 Alliance Formed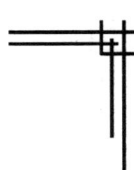

Striking the brass gong and golden drum,

Playing the silver flute and Suona,

The eight routes of troops marched with banners high in the air,

There were so many of them that they blotted the sky and the earth.

The fragrance of magnolia in the woods wafted with wind,

Groups of cuckoos were chirping on the branches.

But Zhao Langma was not in the mood appreciating all these,

His heart had already flown over the vast oceans.

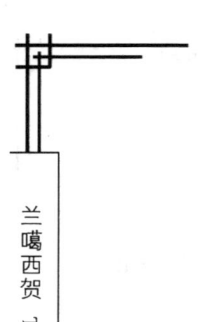

第十三章 阿努曼

一、风神之子

海洋上笼罩着朦胧的烟雾，
三千约的海面望不到边，
汹涌的波涛挡住了去路，
出征的大军在海岸徘徊不前。

召朗玛望着海洋久久地叹息，
焦急不安地把嘎林请来，
问它在千军万马之中，
有谁能飞过烟波浩渺的大海。

"现在我的妻子南西拉死活不知，
要派一个最有本事的人到兰嘎探清虚实，
如果她仍然忠实于丈夫，我们就挥戈前往，
如果她已变心，我们就不必动众兴师。"

第十三章 阿努曼 Chapter 13 Anuman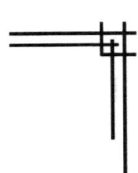

Chapter 13   Anuman

I   Son of God of Wind

The misty fog shrouded the surface of the sea,
The three-thousand-Yue-wide sea was boundless.
The surging waves blocked the way to the other side,
The army of expedition had to stop by the seaside.

Zhao Langma looked at the sea with deep sighs.
He became agitated and sent for Galin.
He needed to know among his thousands of soldiers
Who could fly over this vast expanse of misty ocean.

"Now I even don't know if my wife Nan Xila is still alive or not.

The most capable one should be sent to Langa to check it out.

If she is still loyal to me, we will go forward with all our weapons;

If she has changed her heart, then it won't be worth our endeavor."

嘎林立刻召集手下的武官，
问它们谁有本事飞过三千约海洋，
腊塔说："我只能纵身三十约，
再上去就全身没有力量。"

嘎木达说："我只能腾空四十约，
再高一些手脚就软弱无力。"
玛尼腊说："我可以在云层穿梭，
但超过五十约就要落下地。"

能卜善战的摩米表示：
"我可以腾云驾雾六十约，
再多一点就力气不济，
请留下我看守阵地。"

二猴王旺果站出来下拜：
"我只能飞达七十约的空间，
超过七十约就全身瘫软，
请原谅我飞不过宽阔的海面。"

猴王嘎林急忙表示歉意：
"我也只有侄子同样的本事，
越过七十约就会落进海里，
过海侦探我是无能为力。"

最后站出来英勇干练的阿努曼，
它的话语中含着难言的痛苦：
"现在我只能飞腾八十约，
也是心有余，力不足。"

第十三章 阿努曼 Chapter 13 Anuman

Galin gathered up all his generals instantly,
Asking who could fly over the three-thousand-Yue-wide sea.
Lata said, "I can only fly as far as thirty Yues,
The longer distance is beyond my limit."

Gamuda said, "I can jump as high as forty Yues.
My feet will be feeble if I jumped a little higher."
Manila said, "I can fly and walk among the clouds,
But I will fall to the ground if it is higher than fifty Yues."

Momi who was good at divination and fighting said,
"I can fly on clouds for sixty Yues,
And there is no way for me to do more than that.
Please let me stay here and keep on watch."

The junior monkey king Wangguo stepped out,
"I can only fly over a space of seventy Yues,
I won't be able to move if I am to fly a little further,
Please forgive me that I can't fly over the sea."

The monkey king Galin expressed his regrets,
"I am also only able to do what my niece can do.
I will fall down into the sea if I fly further than seventy Yues.
I am sorry that I am not able to fly across to check it out."

The last one to stand out was the Brave Anuman,
His words was full of unspoken sorrow,
"Currently I can only fly as far as eighty Yues,
Sorry that my capability falls short of my wishes."

召朗玛满面愁容喃喃自语：
"难道我们就找不出跨海的英雄？"
摩米上前举荐阿努曼，
向召朗玛说出了它的底细。

"阿努曼是风神叭汶纳之子①
一生下地就行走如风，
父亲把自己的本事传给它，
它从小就力大无穷。

"阿努曼从小任性爱发脾气，
它一动怒大地也要去掉一层皮，
谨慎的母亲怕它放荡不羁，
临终前曾把遗言留给儿子：

"'你在森林中觅找食物，
见到有个最红最亮的果子，
那是一种最热最烫的东西，
千万不要飞去摘取。

---

① 传说风神叭汶纳与南裴相爱，生下猴子阿努曼。阿努曼的身世原稿中有专门章节叙述，约六百行，其中有些情节较荒诞，有些游离。整理时根据内容需要移在此处叙述。

第十三章 阿努曼 Chapter 13 Anuman

Zhao Langma murmured to himself sadly,
"Isn't there a hero among us who can cross the sea?"
Momi stepped up and recommended Anuman.
He explained why Anuman could be the candidate.

"Anuman is the son of the god of Wind Bawenna.①
He started to walk like wind the moment he was born.
His father had passed on all his feats to him.
So Anuman was superbly strong since he was a boy.

"Anuman was a wilful kid with bad temper,
A layer of dust would be stripped from the ground once he got angry.
His prudent mom worried that he would have full swing in the future,
So she gave her son her last words before she passed away,

"'When you search for foods in the forest,
Maybe you will see a reddest and brightest fruit,
That's the most scorching thing in the world.
You mustn't pluck it, let alone eat it up.

---

① It was said that the god of wind Bawenna fell in love with Naipei and they had the monkey Son Anuman. In the original tale there was a whole chapter with six hundreds of lines about the life of Anuman. But some parts of the story was too ridiculous and digressive. Therefore. the story was reorganized with some parts deleted and some parts moved to this chapter.

"'那些酸甜苦涩的果子,
你都可以随便摘来充饥,
唯独那个最红最亮的果子,
绝不能有摘取它的尝试。'

"阿努曼记住母亲的嘱咐,
天上地下尝遍各种果实,
果汁滋润着它的身体,
小猴子长得聪明伶俐。

"十五年来它都遵循母亲的嘱咐,
但十五岁时阿努曼再也忍耐不住,
它变得天不怕地不怕雄心勃勃,
决心尝尝那个最红最亮的大果。

"一个寒冷的冬天的早晨,
太阳从东方徐徐上升,
好像贴在蓝蓝的天空,
犹如挂在高高的树顶。

"'我每天吃的是矮树上的酸果,
还不知道这天上果子的滋味,
它成熟得这样通红通红,
一定比麻宗补更要甜蜜。'

"阿努曼这样想着弯腰跃起,
径直向红太阳飞过去,
伸手就要摘这个硕大的果子,
太阳被抓了一下十分惊惧。

第十三章 阿努曼 Chapter 13 Anuman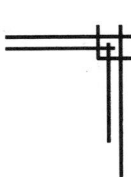

" ' All the other fruits, whether bitter or sour,
You can get and eat them for food.
Except that reddest and brightest fruit,
You can't even make a try to get it. '

"Anuman always kept his mother's words in mind.
He had tried all kinds of wild fruits all over the world.
With so much fruit juice nurturing his body,
The little monkey grew more and more clever and agile.

"For fifteen years Anuman had been following his mother's advice.
And then Anuman couldn't hold on to his promise anymore.
At the age to fifteen, he was ambitious and afraid of nothing.
He decided to have a taste of the reddest and brightest fruit.

"It was on one chilly winter morning.
The sun rose slowly from the east horizon.
The red sun set against the blue sky,
And it seemed hanging on the top of the tree.

" ' Each day I can only eat the sour fruits from the low trees.
I still don't know the taste of this fruit hanging in the sky.
It is ripe and red all over now.
It must taste sweeter than the fruit of Mazongbu. '

"While thinking, Anuman bent his back for a high jump,
Then he flew straight up to the red sun.
He reached out to snatch this huge fruit.
The sun was frightened at the scratch.

"太阳马上向叭英报告,
'天王呀,人间有个妖怪,
竟敢飞上天来抓我,
请求你对它给予惩处。'

"叭英听了勃然大怒,
立即使出闪光的宝斧,
劈伤了小猴子的腮巴骨,
阿努曼突然从天上跌落。

"阿努曼落地昏死过去,
风神叭汶纳十分焦急,
眼看儿子要失去生命,
连忙飞上天向叭英求情。

'它不是人间的妖怪,
它错把太阳当作果子摘取,
得罪了太阳应该惩治,
但请你宽恕它年幼无知。'

"叭英见阿努曼勇敢、诚实,
不仅宽恕了它无知的过失,
还治好了它的腮巴骨,
赐给它超人的本事。

"'让灾难和疾病永远远离你,
在波浪滔滔的大海上,
你可以快步行走如履平地,
站在激流中你就像坚硬的岩石。

第十三章 阿努曼 Chapter 13 Anuman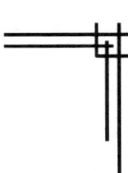

"The sun reported it to Baying immediately,
' Dear king of heaven, there is a monster in the world.
He has the guts to fly to the sky and scratch me,
Please punish this fearless monster severely.'

"Baying was furious at hearing this;
He took out his shining axe and slashed.
Anuman got hurt in his cheekbone,
Then he fell down from the sky suddenly.

"Anuman landed on the ground and passed out,
Bawenna, the god of wind, got upset at this.
Knowing that his son could lose his life very soon,
He flew to the heaven and begged Baying to spare his son's life.

' He was not a monster in the human world.
He happened to mistake the sun as a fruit to pluck.
He should be punished for his offence to the Sun,
But please forgive him for his innocence and ignorance.'

"Baying saw that Anuman was brave and honest,
He forgave him for his mistake out of ignorance.
He not only got the injury of his cheekbone cured,
But also bestowed Anuman with super capability.

"' May disaster and illness stay away from you
You will be able to walk on the wavy sea
As fast as you walk on the solid ground.
You can stand like a solid rock in violent currents.

兰嘎西贺 The Ten-Headed King of Langa

"'假如你落入熊熊的烈火之中,
你会像洗冷水澡一样舒适,
要是把你放进碓窝里,
也不能舂碎你的身体。

"'刀斧矛弩伤不了你一根毫毛,
你的本领会威力无穷。'
自此阿努曼精神抖擞地遨游太空,
一口气可飞出三千约的行程。

"阿努曼得到叭英的赏识,
练就了一身神通广大的本领,
它的脾气和性格还是没有改,
总喜欢戏弄嘲笑虔诚的人们。

"它经常追逐大佛爷戏耍,
往它们身上抛掷泥巴,
吓得佛爷们东奔西窜,
它又跳过去撕烂他们的黄袈裟。

"有一次众佛爷向帕拉西学经,
阿努曼把经书撕烂、蒲团乱扔,
惹得众佛爷哭笑不得,
对它的恶作剧莫不切齿痛恨。

第十三章 阿努曼 Chapter 13 Anuman

" ' If you by chance fall into burning flames,
You will feel cool as if you were bathing in cold water.
When you were put in the mortar and pounded upon
Your body would remain intact and you won't get hurt.

" ' No weapon could even hurt a single hair of you.
You will have feats which are super powerful.'
Ever since then Anuman could fly freely in the universe,
He could fly over three thousand Yues with one breath.

"Anuman was appreciated and favored by Baying.
Under his coach he became more powerful and capable.
While his naughty temperament remained the same,
He enjoyed himself in laughing at the devout people.

"He always chased and made fool of those Buddhist monks.
He cast mud onto them to make fun of them
The monks were scared and scattered all over the place.
Then he jumped and tore their yellow kasayas into pieces.

"One time the monks were learning Buddhist scripture from Palaxi,
Anuman shredded their books and threw their rush cushions around,
The monks were both amused and annoyed,
They got so tired of all his mischievous acts.

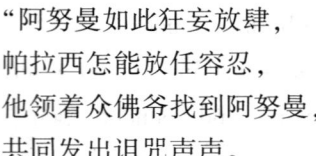

兰噶西贺 The Ten-Headed King of Langa

"阿努曼如此狂妄放肆,
帕拉西怎能放任容忍,
他领着众佛爷找到阿努曼,
共同发出诅咒声声。

"'阿努曼你这该死的白猴,
竟敢骄横无礼、戏弄神灵,
纵然你有天大的本领,
你的力气将逐渐丧尽。

"'你将永远让病魔缠身,
瘦得皮包骨头不成形,
你碰见大大小小的飞禽走兽,
都将胆怯得战战兢兢。'

"在帕拉西的诅咒声中,
阿努曼得了一场重病,
高烧不退、昏迷不醒,
身体变得瘦骨嶙峋。

"阿努曼大病以后手脚瘫软,
攀藤爬树都没有力气,
就像野牛折断了犄角,
犹如青龙脱落了牙齿。

"阿努曼到处寻药求医,
一个能起死回生的医生问它,
'你去过什么不该去的地方?
你干过什么不该干的坏事?'

第十三章 阿努曼 Chapter 13 Anuman

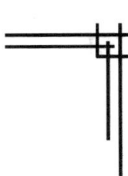

"Anuman became bolder and more naughty,
How could Palaxi let him do whatever he liked.
He led all the monks and found Anuman,
Together, they started to lay curses on him.

"'Anuman, you damned white monkey,
You are too rude and haughty to tease deities.
However powerful or capable you are now,
Your strength and skills will wear out with time.

"'You will be tortured by ailment for all your life;
You will be a bag of bones and shapelessly weak;
When you encounter the tiny animals or small birds,
You will be frightened and stay in panic.'

"Under the spells of the curses from Palaxi,
Anuman had got a serious disease.
High fevers brought him into a coma,
Then he became extremely thin and haggard.

"Anuman became almost paralyzed after the illness.
He was so weak that he couldn't even climb up a tree.
He was like a buffalo with broken horns,
Also like a dragon losing all his teeth.

"Anuman went to see doctors all over the world for help.
A doctor who could bring the dying back to life asked him,
'Have you ever been to some place that you shouldn't go?
Have you ever done anything that you are forbidden to do?'

"阿努曼承认耍弄欺负过大佛爷,
医生立即明白了其中的奥秘,说:
'阿努曼啊,如果是这样的话,
吃什么灵丹妙药都无济于事。'

"最后是一个摩米向它献计:
'你必须跟我去朝拜帕拉西,
虔诚地承认自己做了错事,
恳求他宽宏大量赦免你。'

"阿努曼由摩米带领,
走进森林前去朝拜帕拉西,
阿努曼忏悔得罪了众佛爷,
请求帕拉西宽恕自己的过失。

"帕拉西原谅它年幼无知。
但心里又暗暗思虑:
'如果让它的疾病全部消除。
它还可能捣乱调皮。'

"帕拉西请摩米作证说:
'现在我可以把它的罪过减轻,
但它要长时间地等待,
一时还不能恢复高飞的本领。

"'当阿努曼遇见一位王子时,
这位王子善良、开明,正直,
只要王子在它背上抚摸三下,
阿努曼就恢复风神之子的威力。'"

第十三章 阿努曼 Chapter 13 Anuman

"Anuman confessed that he had made fun of the monks.
Immediately, the doctor understood and told him the secret.
'Oh, Anuman, you were under the spell of those monks,
Even panacea or the magic drug would not work on you.'

"At last a Momi came up and made suggestions,
'You had better come with me to pay a visit to Palaxi.
You need to confess and repent on your wrongs honestly,
And beg him to have mercy on you and remove the spells.'

"Anuman was led by Momi to the forest,
They were to pay a visit to Palaxi.
Anuman repented on his offense to the monks,
And he asked Palaxi to forgive him for his sins.

"Palaxi forgave him for being young and ignorant,
But he had some deeper worry at the same time.
'If his illness was completely cleansed here and now,
He might be naughty and play planks again next time.'

"Palaxi asked Momi to be their witness,
'Now I can alleviate the punishment inflicted on him.
But he needs to wait for long patiently,
He won't recover his feat of flying high in short time.

"'Someday Anuman would meet a prince
Who is kind, broad-minded and righteous,
As long as the prince tap on his back for three times,
Anuman will regain his power as the son of the god of wind.'"

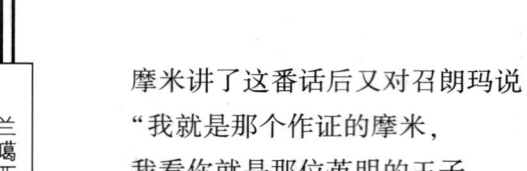

摩米讲了这番话后又对召朗玛说：
"我就是那个作证的摩米，
我看你就是那位英明的王子，
这一切是否应验请你试一试。"

大家把瘦弱的阿努曼叫来，
满怀希望簇拥着召朗玛，
年轻的王子心中充满同情，
在阿努曼背脊上抚摸了三下。

第一下，阿努曼的病好了一半，
仿佛觉得解除了身上缠绕的藤蔓，
第二下，阿努曼的病已痊愈，
它高兴得在地上乱滚乱翻。

召朗玛庄严地抚摸了第三下，
阿努曼顿时全身力气向上涌，
轻快敏捷如释重负，
一跃飞上三千约的高空。

阿努曼高兴得放声大叫：
"以后天上地下随我遨游，
我向威力无比的天神发誓，
不打垮十头王决不罢休。"

第十三章 阿努曼 Chapter 13 Anuman

After the story, Momi said to Zhao Langma again,
"I am that Momi who had been the witness.
I see you are the wise prince Palaxi talked about,
You can have a try to test if all this is true."

They called in Anuman who was thin and weak,
Everyone surrounded Zhao Langma in great hope.
The young prince was full of affection in his heart,
And he tapped Anuman on his back for three times.

After the first tap half of Anuman's illness was gone,
As if the vines clinging tightly around him were torn away;
After the second tap Anuman was fully recovered,
He was so happy that he kept jumping and rolling.

Zhao Langma patted him for a third time solemnly,
Anuman suddenly felt his energy surging inside him.
He felt agile again as if heavy burden had been lifted from him.
With one jump he flew to the sky as high as three thousand Yues.

Anuman shouted in excitement,
"I will be able to fly anywhere I want.
I swear to the invincible gods in heaven
That I will never give up till I defeat the ten-headed king."

它向召朗玛表示感激：
"请王子放心不必忧虑，
我会很快飞过茫茫的大海，
探明兰嘎岛的虚实。"

二、阿努曼出探

召朗玛立即写了一封信，
又拿出一只金手镯交给阿努曼，
"请你把这信物交给南西拉，
她见了信物就会心中明白。

"你告诉她我们即将越过大海，
要把她从魔鬼的手中拯救出来。"
阿努曼接受使命迅速告辞，
一纵身穿过了蓝天上的白云。

眨眼的工夫阿努曼飞进了兰嘎城，
只见高大的瓦屋像蜂房一层挨着一层，
屋檐垂挂着菩提叶般的金片，
风吹金片发出叮当的声音。

阿努曼变成一只灵巧的花虫①，
飞进金碧辉煌的宫殿，
它四处寻找被劫的南西拉，
宽阔的王宫被它找遍。

---

① 花虫：傣语称为缅乃，是一种会叮人的花虫，状似苍蝇。还有的传说是阿努曼是变为小猫或小蜂。

第十三章 阿努曼 Chapter 13 Anuman

He said to Zhao Langma in gratitude,
"Dear Prince, no need to worry any more.
I will fly over the vast sea very soon,
And I will spy on what's happening in Langa."

II Anuman Started His Journey

Zhao Langma wrote a letter immediately.
Then he took out a gold bracelet and handed it to Anuman.
"Please deliver the bracelet and letter to Nan Xila.
Once she sees them she would understand everything.

"Please tell her that we will cross the sea,
And we will save her out of the devil's hands."
Anuman accepted the mission and bade farewell,
Then he jumped through the white clouds in the sky.

Anuman flew into the city of Langa in a blink of eyes.
He saw the tall houses nestling with each other like beehives.
The decorated golden Boldhi tree leaves hang under the roof.
They swung and tinkled in gentle breeze.

Anuman turned himself into a flower beetle, ①
And he flew into the glamorous palace.
He searched Nan Xila all over the place,
He rummaged each corner carefully.

---

① Flower beetle: In the language of the Dai, it is called Miannai. It is a kind of flower beetle which looks like fly and sometimes bits people. It is also said that Anuman turned itself into a kitten or a bee.

看不见南西拉的身影，
听不到有关她的一点音讯，
只见脸抹脂粉的千百个宫女，
在宫里出出进进。

最后它飞上寝殿的梁檐，
看到十头王正在床上睡眠，
身边躺着几个半裸的美女，
淫秽的丑态叫人不堪入眼。

"纵然日出西方海枯见底，
南西拉也不会如此卑贱，
即使河水倒流高山崩裂，
南西拉也不会出卖贞洁。"

阿努曼认定里面没有南西拉，
一看时间已是半夜三更，
它就来到十头王的宝座上，
舒舒服服进入梦境。

公鸡的啼叫把它从梦中惊醒，
它清楚记得刚刚做了一个梦，
梦见它走进花园看见南西拉靠着花丛，
跑近一看却又无影无踪。

第十三章 阿努曼 Chapter 13 Anuman

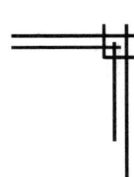

There was no sign of Nan Xila in the palace;
Not even one word about her could be heard.
He only saw thousands of servant maids,
They were filing in and out of the palace.

Finally he landed on the beam of the king's bedroom.
He saw the ten-headed king sleeping in the bed.
Lying right beside him were several half naked beauties,
Anuman felt the obscene scene intolerable to his eyes.

"Even if the sun rose from the west or the sea dried up,
Nan Xila will never debase herself like this.
Even if river flowed backward and the mountain cracked up
Nan Xila will never trade off her purity."

Anuman was sure Nan Xila wasn't in the room.
It was almost midnight by then,
So he took a rest on the throne of the king.
There he fell asleep and had a dream.

The croak of the rooster woke him up.
He remembered clearly that he had a dream.
In the dream he saw Nan Xila next to the flowers in the garden,
Once he came close, everything vanished into thin air suddenly.

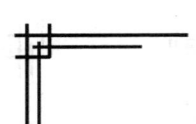

兰噶西贺 The Ten-Headed King of Langa

阿努曼立即飞进御花园里，
看见一座九层高的独柱塔楼，
发现一个妇女孤独地坐在里面，
外面有众多的卫兵把守。

美丽的人儿在悄悄流泪，
乌发垂肩形容憔悴，
一只鸟儿飞过她也会吃惊，
一片树叶落地她也会颤抖。

就像圆月被黑云遮蔽，
犹如莲花受风雨摧残，
但愁云掩盖不了美丽的面容，
她和召朗玛描绘的样子不差半分。

变作花虫的阿努曼，
爬在窗口暗暗思量：
"我要在这里观察南西拉，
看看她的心有没有变化。"

好色淫荡的捧玛加一觉醒来，
想把美丽的南西拉抱进胸怀，
可就像井边望月看得见摸不着，
几次尝试接近都遭到失败。

捧玛加把舞队叫进花园跳舞唱歌，
好让南西拉舒展忧愁的面容，
为了求得南西拉回心转意，
他出口的话句句像抹上蜂蜜。

第十三章 阿努曼 Chapter 13 Anuman

Anuman immediately flew into the royal garden
Where he saw a tower as high as nine stories.
In the tower he found a lady sitting alone,
Outside around the tower were plenty of guards.

That pretty lady was weeping silently.
Her haggard face was blocked by her dark hairs.
She could be startled by a bird flying by.
She would tremble when a leaf falling down.

Like the full moon blocked by dark clouds,
Like a lotus flower devastated by the storm,
She still had the beauty that couldn't be clouded by her sorrow.
She was exactly the same as Zhao Langma had described.

The beetle, the transformed Anuman,
Climbed onto the window and thought to itself,
"I will stay here to take a close look at Nan Xila,
Then I will know if she has changed her heart."

The lewd Pengmajia woke up in the morning.
He went close to Nan Xila trying to hold her in his arms.
But Nan Xila was like the moon's reflection in the well,
He attempted for several times but could not get her.

Pengmajia called in the dancing girls into the garden,
They danced and sang trying to drive away her sorrow.
Then making great efforts to win Nan Xila's heart,
Pengmajia persuaded her in his most sweet words.

"开在悬崖顶上美丽的花朵,
藏在眼眶里澄澈的珍珠,
七月的荷花没有你妩媚,
六月的缅桂比不上你馥郁。

"你身材这么窈窕多姿,
可惜脸上不见了笑窝,
我想你想得睡不着啊,
心头像被红红的火炭烧灼。

"你若答应我的要求,
我要立你为勐兰嘎的王后,
满宫嫔妃随你使唤,
我也甘愿为奴将你伺候。

"只要你答应我,
勐兰嘎的海洋、土地由你管,
勐兰嘎的宫殿由你安排,
勐兰嘎的财宝任你挥霍。

"只要你点头说一声同意,
你可以一辈子坐着吃躺着喝,
热了有人为你摇金扇,
冷了有人给你加被窝。

"你比星星还辉耀明亮啊,
不要让它白白地放出光彩,
把无能的流浪者召朗玛忘掉吧,
何苦为他把你自己折磨。

第十三章 阿努曼 Chapter 13 Anuman

"You are like the pretty flower blooming on top of the cliff;
Your pupils are like shining pearls hidden in your eyes.
You are more charming than the lotus flower in July;
You are more fragrant than the blooming magnolia in June.

"You are such a gentle and graceful lady,
It is a pity that there is no smile on your face.
I can't fall asleep because I miss you so much;
My passion is like burning charcoal scorching my heart.

"If you accept my proposal,
I will make you the queen of Langa.
All the maids in the palace will be at your service;
I myself will be happy to serve you as your slave.

"Once you agree to marry me,
The sea and land of Langa will be under your ruling.
You will be in charge of the palace of Langa,
And all the treasures of Langa are in your hand.

"Once you nod your head to say yes,
You will enjoy your remaining life leisurely doing nothing.
Someone will cool you with a golden fan when it's hot;
And someone will put more quilt for you on chilly nights.

"You are more shining than the stars in the sky,
Don't let your glamour fade away in vain.
Forget the loser and wanderer Zhao Langma,
Why torture yourself for the sake of him?

"召朗玛没有办法寻到你,
山高海深、路途遥远,
凶恶的野兽四处出没,
听说他已在途中丧命归天。

"就算召朗玛有天大的本事,
也越不过三千约的海洋,
就算他冒险来到勐兰嘎,
他也逃不出我铁一般的手掌。

"宝石没有我爱你的心纯洁,
太阳没有我爱你的心火热,
我对你一片深情、一片忠诚,
你怎忍心一再把我拒绝。

"跟我住进豪华的宫殿吧,
那里有柔软的象牙床铺,
让我们相亲相爱在一起,
让我那三个妻子做你的奴仆。"

捧玛加说着张开双臂扑过来,
南西拉像白兔躲避着秃鹰追捕,
她的眼睛射出愤怒的火花,
话音随着泪水滚滚流出。

"住手,可恶的十头魔,
你休想挨近我洁净的身躯,
铜窗铁门掩盖不住你尽人皆知的罪过,
甜言蜜语改变不了我对召朗玛的忠贞。

第十三章 阿努曼 Chapter 13 Anuman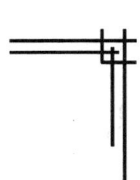

"There is no way that Zhao Langma would find you.
It is a too long journey over high mountains and deep seas.
Ferocious wild animals run about to hunt for food,
It is said that he has already been killed on his way here.

"However strong or capable Zhao Langma is,
He can never cross the three-thousand-Yue-wide sea.
Even if he ventured and reached the kingdom of Langa,
He could never survive my iron-like hands.

"My love for you is purer than precious gems;
My passion for you is hotter than the sun.
I give you all my heart together with the greatest loyalty,
How can you be so cruel to turn me down again and again.

"Come and live in the luxurious palace with me.
There are ivory beds covered with soft linens.
Let us stay together and love one another,
Let my three wives be your servants too."

Then Pengmaji opened his arms and charged to Nan Xila,
Nan Xila dodged and ducked like a rabbit chased by vulture.
Anger flared in her eyes;
Tears were falling down as she spoke up.

"Stop it, you damned ten-headed devil,
You can never come close to my pure body.
The iron door and bars on the window can't cover up your crimes;
Your sweet talk can never change my loyalty to Zhao Langma.

"你的心比老鸹还黑,
竟敢把善良的召朗玛贬辱,
你不过是路边一块古怪的石头,
他却是山上一棵参天的大青树。

"只要我还有一口气活着,
你就永远得不到我,
除了品德高尚的召朗玛,
在人间我不爱任何一个。

"我劝你还是丢掉邪恶的念头,
赶快把我送回伊麻板森林,
要是你执迷不悟,
你罪恶的宫殿将变成齑粉。

"如果你用强力玷污我,
众人将千年万年向你吐唾沫,
召朗玛的怒火你更抵挡不住,
他将重重惩罚你的罪过。

"召朗玛的本领和为人你也清楚,
他一定会越过大海来拯救我,
那时你的十个头颅啊,
会像熟透的果子一个个蒂落。

"可怜的是勐兰嘎无辜的百姓,
你的贪婪将连累着他们,
如果你不想断送大好的河山,
就该立即把我送回大海那边。"

第十三章 阿努曼 Chapter 13 Anuman

"Your heart is darker than the color of crow,
How dare you degrade and insult kind Zhao Langma?
You are only a bizarre rock on the roadside,
While he is a high evergreen tree on top of the mountain.

"As long as I am alive with one last breath,
You can never get my body.
Except the noble Zhao Langma,
I love no one else in this world.

"You'd better cast away your dirty thoughts,
And send me back to the forest of Yimaban.
If you remain impenitent and go on doing wrongs,
Your evil palace will be crumbled into pieces.

"If you insulted me with your brutal force,
You will be drown in spits and cursed for thousands of years.
You can never escape from the revenge from Zhao Langma,
He will surely punish you for what you have done on me.

"You know well about Zhao Langma and his courage,
He is sure to cross the sea and save me out.
By then your ten heads will be on the grounds
Like the ripe fruits falling off the tree one by one.

"I feel pity for the innocent people of Langa,
They were involved into this because of your greed.
If you don't want your kingdom to be totally destroyed,
You should send me back to the other side of sea right now."

十头王被骂得心惊胆战，
恼恨、沮丧、满脸羞惭，
他悻悻溜出南西拉的房间说：
"要不是她美貌迷人早就把她处斩。"

捧玛加给看守下了一道命令：
"现在我给她七天的期限，
如果回心转意依了我，
我才让她活在人间。

"要是她还恋着召朗玛，
你们就把她千刀万剐，
给我用浓烟熏、用烈火烤，
把她晒成一块块干巴。"

阿努曼把这一切看在眼里，
看得心中一阵阵欢喜，
它立即恢复原形走上前去，
向愁苦的南西拉合掌行礼。

"尊贵的南西拉，
我是召朗玛派来的阿努曼，
专门来侦察勐兰嘎的虚实，
特意见你一面。"

第十三章 阿努曼 Chapter 13 Anuman

The ten-headed king was shocked by her righteous remarks.

He became crestfallen with frustration and shame all over his face.

Resentfully he slipped out of Nan Xila's room murmuring to himself,

"She had already been dead several times if she was not so pretty."

Pengmajia ordered the guards before he left,
"I will give her the time limit of seven days.
There is no way for her to live in this world any more
Unless she changes her mind and surrenders to me.

"If she is still infatuated with Zhao Langma by then,
You just slice her into thousands of pieces.
And then smoke and roast them on fire
Till they burned into pieces of dry meat."

Anuman saw everything with his own eyes.
He was glad to see and hear what had happened.
Immediately he transformed back into his original shape,
And he approached and bowed to Nan Xila with his palms folded.

"You distinguished Nan Xila
I am Anuman sent here by Zhao Langma.
I come here to size up the situation in Langa,
And especially I got the order to meet you."

南西拉猛抬头异常惊愕，
企盼中又产生阵阵猜疑说：
"什么神仙鬼怪也休想欺骗我，
你定是十头王变成的猴子。"

阿努曼讲述了召朗玛的身世，
又拿出信件和金手镯交到她手里，
南西拉至此才深信不疑，
捧着丈夫的信物泪下如雨。

南西拉把信物放在头上敬了三次，
绝望的心灵再次泛起生机，
召朗玛的书信一字一句重如千金，
温柔诚挚的语言慰藉着她的心灵。

"比我的生命还珍贵的南西拉，
菩提树才发出嫩绿的幼芽，
就遭到无情的风霜吹打，
我们的爱情受到恶人的践踏。

"纯洁的宝石、明亮的珍珠，
被黑色的秃鹰偷偷叼劫，
光辉的天地刹那间黑暗昏沉，
我失去心中最珍贵的一切。

第十三章 阿努曼 Chapter 13 Anuman

Nan Xila raised her head and got astonished,
She was hopeful at the same time full of doubts.
"Even deities or ghosts can't fool me,
You must be the transformation of the ten-headed king."

Anuman retold her the story of Zhao Langma,
And he handed her the letter and gold bracelet.
Until then did Nan Xila have no shadow of doubt.
Holding the letter, she shed tears like pouring rain.

Nan Xila held the letter over her head and bowed three times,
Gleams of hope came back into her desperate heart.
Each word in the letter seemed to weigh one thousand kilo,
The gentle and sincere words in the letter comforted her greatly.

"My dear Nan Xila, you are more precious than my own life.
The moment new leaves sprouted on the bodhi tree,
They were devastated by relentlessly fateful frost.
Just like the new leaves, our love was tramped by a villain.

"You are my precious gem and bright pearl,
But you are snatched away by the black vulture.
All of a sudden the bright sky sunk into total darkness.
I lost the most precious thing cherished in my heart.

515

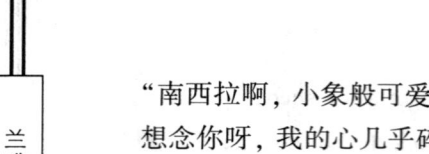

"南西拉啊,小象般可爱的妻子,
想念你呀,我的心几乎碎裂,
悲伤的泪水常常遮蔽我的眼睛,
犹如阵阵风雨覆盖林间的树叶。

"从你被劫走的那一天开始,
我和弟弟四处将你寻觅,
哪一条河我们没有涉过?
哪一座山没有我们的足迹?

"走遍了茫茫的森林,
片片树叶沾着我们的眼泪,
跨过了广阔的原野,
寸寸土地渗透我们的汗水。

"从遥远的伊麻板森林,
一直寻找到猴国勐基沙,
我们与猴王嘎林联盟誓师出发,
现在大军已进到海岸边驻扎。

"汪洋大海暂时挡住了去路,
我们派尊贵的阿努曼先去侦察,
它是无敌的白猴、忠实的使者,
你完全可以信赖它。

"营救你的大队人马,
不久就会浩浩荡荡开来,
而我想念你的心啊,
早已随着风云飞过大海。

第十三章 阿努曼 Chapter 13 Anuman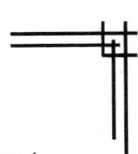

"Oh, Nan Xila, my wife, you are as cute as a cub elephant.
I missed you so much that I felt my heart almost broken.
My eyes are always covered with sorrowful tears,
Just like the leaves in the woods shrouded in the mist and rain.

"Ever since the day you were hijacked away from me,
My brother and I have been searching for you everywhere.
There is no river that we have not trekked through;
There is no mountain that we have not left our footprints on.

"When we walked through dense forests,
Each leaf was soaked with our tears;
When we rummaged over vast plains,
Each inch of land was drenched with our sweats.

"We started from the remote Yimaban forest,
Till we reached the monkey kingdom of Jisha.
We made alliance with the monkey king Galin,
Now the joint troops are stationed on the seaside.

"We are now temporarily blocked by the vast sea,
So we sent respected Anuman to scout the situation.
He is the invincible white monkey and a trustworthy envoy.
You can totally put your trust on him.

"The troops to save you out are ready,
They will soon start off in formidable array,
All my heart and mind is on you,
Now it has flown across the sea with the wind.

"荷花般的南西拉啊,
你要耐心等待不要过分悲戚,
眼泪啊,它比金粒还要珍贵,
流多了会损伤你的身体。

"眼皮像菩提树叶的妻子,
你的美貌会使捧玛加垂涎三尺,
但是我相信你的誓言,
它会使捧玛加随时碰壁。

"你是蓝天上一颗璀璨的星辰,
乌云不能使你的光辉熄灭,
你是海底一颗明亮的珍珠,
泥沙不能玷污你的纯洁。

"愿你如同象牙那么坚硬纯洁,
愿你好像完美的碧玉没有瑕疵,
我决不允许魔鬼玷污你,
我要尽快为你报仇雪耻。

"即使你被劫进铜铸的宫殿,
朗玛也一定要把它推倒,
即使你被囚禁在铁打的地牢,
朗玛也一定要把你找到。

"哪怕他们把你沉到大海深处,
哪怕他们把你藏到宇宙的顶端,
我也要背着宝刀和弓箭,
把你搭救回我的身边。

第十三章 阿努曼 Chapter 13 Anuman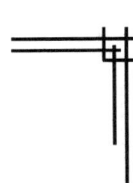

"Oh My dear lotus-flower-like Nan Xila,
You must wait patiently and don't sink in your sorrow.
Your tears are more precious than grains of gold,
And too many tears will do harm to your health.

"My wife, your eyelids are like the bodhi tree leaves,
Pengmajia always gloated over your beauty.
But I believe in your oath
Which will keep Pengmajia away from you.

"You are the most shining star in the blue sky,
Dark clouds can't obliterate your glamour;
You are the most brilliant pearl at the bottom of the sea,
Neither mud nor sand can contaminate your purity.

"May you be as pure and hard as ivory tusk;
May you be as fleckless as a perfect jade.
I would never allow the devil to get his hand on you,
And I will take revenge for the insults he did to you.

"Even if you were imprisoned in an copper fortress,
Your husband Langma is sure to topple it down;
Even if you were confined in an iron dungeon,
Langma will surely rush into it and get you out.

"No matter they sank you down to the bottom of the sea;
Or hid you somewhere on the top of the universe,
With my precious sword, bow and arrow on my back,
I will go and find you and get you back to my side.

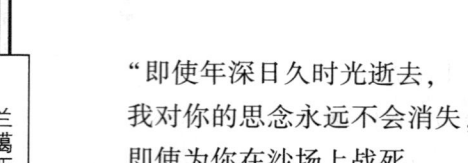

"即使年深日久时光逝去,
我对你的思念永远不会消失,
即使为你在沙场上战死,
我也心甘情愿在所不惜。

"就算灾难使我俩离别百年,
百年中我也时时将你怀念,
百年后我离开了人间,
我的灵魂也保持着对你的爱恋。

"为了迎接美丽的南西拉,
我要左手举着芳香的鲜花,
为了铲除缠绕你的毒蛇,
我要右手紧握锋利的宝刀。

"我要挥动犀利的宝刀,
去斩断恶魔的十个头颅,
我要编结绚丽的花环,
把心爱的南西拉紧紧环绕。"

南西拉读完召朗玛深情的书信,
晶莹的泪水遮住了眼睛,
像久旱的花朵吸到了雨露,
如云蔽的月亮重见了光明。

"感谢你呀,阿努曼,
我丈夫的勇敢的使者,
你给我带来了召朗玛赤诚的心,
你给我带来了新的生命。

第十三章 阿努曼 Chapter 13 Anuman

"No matter how long it will take and how old we are,
My love for you will never fade with time passing by.
Even if someday I shall die on the battlefield for you,
I would do it willingly without any hesitation or regret.

"Even if the disaster would keep us separated for a century,
I will be always missing you during the one hundred years.
Even when I have to leave this world after the hundred years,
My soul will still linger in my love for you.

"To welcome my beautiful Nan Xila,
I will hold fresh flowers in my left hand;
To eradicate the serpent clinging around you,
I will take a sharp sword in my right hand.

"I will brandish my sharp sword
To chop off the ten heads of the devil;
I will weave a beautiful wreath,
To crown my dear Nan Xila with it."

After reading the affectionate letter from Zhao Langma,
Nan Xila' eyes were flooded with crystal tears.
She seemed like a thirsty flower bathed in raindrops;
Also like a dark-cloud-covered moon seeing light again.

"Oh, Anuman, thank you so much.
You are a brave envoy of my husband.
You brought me the loyal heart of Zhao Langma;
You brought a new life to me indeed.

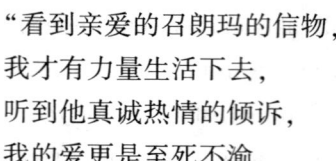

"看到亲爱的召朗玛的信物,
我才有力量生活下去,
听到他真诚热情的倾诉,
我的爱更是至死不渝。

"可是宽阔万约的大地,
被蔚蓝无边的海洋隔断,
召朗玛的大军怎能来到兰嘎?
看来我一时难以同丈夫见面。

"你勇敢机智本领高强,
只身能够跨过宽阔的海面,
而我是一个软弱无能的女子,
又怎能回到丈夫的身边?

"为了保证你胜利完成使命,
你快先离开这里,
把情况告诉召朗玛,
我等着他一举攻下允兰嘎。"

阿努曼对南西拉说道:
"你不要担心海洋辽阔,
只要你允许的话,
我可以背你穿云飞过。"

"普天下的女子,
没有哪个像我这般受苦受难。
普天下的女子,
没有哪个像我这样寂寞孤单。

第十三章 阿努曼 Chapter 13 Anuman

"Seeing the tokens from my dear Zhao Langma,
I have regained the strength to live on;
Reading his warm and passionate words
I know I will love him till the end of my life.

"But the distance between us is as wide as ten thousand Yues,
And it is separated by the endless sea.
How can Zhao Langma's troops make it to Langa?
It seems to take quite a while for me to see my husband again.

"You are brave, clever and capable,
And you can cross the vast sea alone.
But I am just a weak and helpless woman,
How can I get back to my husband?

"To make sure that your mission can be fulfilled,
You had better leave here as soon as possible.
You should inform Zhao Langma of the situation here,
And I am waiting for him to take down the city of Langa."

Anuman told Nan Xila,
"You don't need to worry about the vast sea
As long as you approve of my plan,
I can carry you on my back and fly over the sea."

"Of all the women in this world,
No one has suffered as much as I have.
Of all the women under the sky,
No one is as lonely as I am.

523

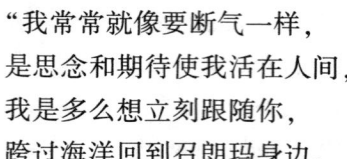

"我常常就像要断气一样,
是思念和期待使我活在人间,
我是多么想立刻跟随你,
跨过海洋回到召朗玛身边。

"可是不行呀,阿努曼,
为了忠实于我的丈夫,
在十头王把我抢劫到勐兰嘎之后,
我曾经向天神发过誓言:

"'除了我的丈夫召朗玛,
任何男人都不能贴近我的身子,
谁要是接触了我,
他就会减弱神威和力气。'

"你是男人我是女人,
我怎能让你背着我飞行?
人们看见了会耻笑,
天神知道了要严惩。

"我只有在此将你们盼望,
请你不要管我快回去报信,
叫召朗玛快快前来搭救我,
让我尽早脱离这苦海险境。"

南西拉说完泣不成声,
好半天才恢复了心情的平静,
她拔下七根黝黑的头发,
表示对召朗玛的绝对忠诚。

第十三章 阿努曼 Chapter 13 Anuman

"I always feel like a walking dead woman,
And it was love and hope that kept me alive.
How much I want to go with you now,
So that I can cross the sea to unite with my husband.

"But I can't go with you, Anuman.
I must remain faithful to my husband.
After the ten-headed King took me to Langa,
I have sworn to heavenly gods,

"'Except my husband Zhao Langma,
No man could ever draw close to my body.
Whoever gets physical contact with me,
His power and strength will be diminished.'

"You are a man while I am a woman.
How can I let you carry me on your back flying across the sea?
People who see this will sneer at us;
Heavenly gods who know about this will punish us severely.

"What I can do is stay here waiting for you.
Please leave me alone and hurry back to report this.
Tell Zhao Langma to come here immediately to save me
So that I can get out of bitter prison as early as possible."

Finishing this, Nan Xila choke with sobs.
It took a while for her to recover her calmness.
She plucked seven dark hairs from her head,
Which was a token of her absolute loyalty to Zhao Langma.

她取下脖子上的金项链，
表达自己爱情的坚贞，
这些贴身的物品，
托阿努曼带给召朗玛珍存。

三、火烧允兰嘎

御花园里的奇花异卉，
阿努曼把它用脚踩碎，
它告别南西拉正要起飞，
被守卫的士兵发现重重包围。

他们大叫大吼扑过来：
"你这白毛猴子还不赶快下跪，
今天你不投降就不得好死，
我们要把你剁成肉酱踩成泥灰。"

阿努曼顺手拔起椰子树迎战，
把围拢的士兵扫倒一大片，
支援的士兵又蜂拥上来，
阿努曼又把他们打得四脚朝天。

一个卫兵急忙跑去报告捧玛加：
"居于我们头上的无比神威的王，
有一只白猴单身闯进御花园，
把我们许多卫兵打死打伤。

第十三章 阿努曼 Chapter 13 Anuman

She took off her gold necklace from her neck
Which stood for her pure and everlasting love.
She entrusted Anuman with these personal objects,
Asking him to take them to her husband Zhao Langma.

Ⅲ The City of Langa on Fire

There were many exotic flowers in the royal garden.
Anuman tramped all of them under his feet.
After saying goodbye to Nan Xila, he was just about to take off,
Then he was spotted and surrounded tightly by the guards.

The guards rushed to Anuman shouting loudly,
"You, the white-haired monkey, kneel down now.
You will die a terrible death if you don't surrender.
You will be chopped and smashed into meat sauce."

Anuman uprooted a coconut tree to fight back.
The guards around him were swept down to the ground.
Swarms of backup sentries rushed up to him,
Anuman again got them fallen down on their back.

A guard rushed to report to Pengmajia,
"Our mighty king above our heads,
A white monkey broke into the royal garden alone,
And many of our guards had been injured or killed by him.

"它武艺高超、神通广大,
请赶快派大将去捉拿,
去晚了御花园会变成平地,
也难以保住塔楼里的南西拉。"

捧玛加听了怒火满腔,
气得十个头左右摇晃,
他命令儿子英达西达:
"你快带些兵去把猴子捉来。"

队伍像蚂蚁似的向花园驶去,
一齐射出雨点般密集的箭,
阿努曼拔起大青树来遮挡,
被英达西达的利箭射成两截。

发怒的阿努曼又拔起糖棕树,
犹如五月的山火气势猛烈,
被它扫倒的士兵堆满花园,
就像纷纷掉落地上的树叶。

英达西达吓得掉头逃走,
士兵跟着他就像受惊的马群,
他惊魂未定向捧玛加报信:
"大事不好,我的父亲。

第十三章 阿努曼 Chapter 13 Anuman

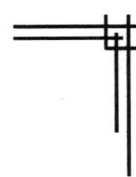

"He is expert in martial arts and super powerful,
Please send a general to catch and take him now.
Our royal garden will be leveled if it is delayed,
And it will be difficult to keep Nan Xila inside the tower."

Pengmajia became so furious at hearing this
That his ten heads were shaking from left to right.
He gave the order to his son Yingdaxida,
"Take some soldiers and bring the monkey to me."

Swarms of troops like ants marched to the garden.
They shot their arrows which flew like tense raindrops.
Anuman pulled up an evergreen tree as a shield,
Which was split into halves by Yingdaxida's sharp arrow.

The furious Anuman again uprooted a palm tree and swung it.
He was as fierce as the wild fire in May.
The body of the soldiers who had been hit stacked up in the garden,
They fell down like the leaves blown off the tree.

Yingdaxida was so scared that he turned his back to escape.
The soldiers like panicked horses followed him.
Still badly shaken, he reported to Pengmajia,
"My dear father, disaster is falling down upon us.

兰噶西贺 The Ten-Headed King of Langa

"我率领士兵去捉拿猴子，
不料他本领高超难以战胜，
它的力气抵得上千头大象，
美丽的御花园已被它踏平。"

傲慢无比的捧玛加怒火冲天，
像发疯的公象跳出宫殿大门，
他命令英达西达带领更多的士兵，
布下天罗地网把御花园围困。

阿努曼隐藏在高高的椰子树顶，
众兵丁四处寻找不见踪影，
他们以为阿努曼已经逃遁，
一齐赞颂十头王的威风。

"我们大王的十个头颅，
哪个见了不胆战心惊，
听说他要亲自带人来捉猴子，
小白猴吓得赶快逃遁。"

他们坐在椰子树下休息，
有的说笑，有的打盹，
顽皮的猴子在树上撒了一泡尿，
尿撒空中就像细雨纷纷。

英达西达感到很纳闷：
"不对，太阳当空天大晴，
是什么水这样腥臭难闻？
像雨点泼了我一脸一身。"

第十三章 阿努曼 Chapter 13 Anuman

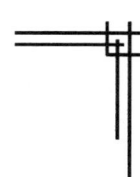

"I led the soldiers to catch the monkey.
I didn't expect he was too powerful to be defeated.
He is as strong as one thousand elephants,
Our beautiful garden has already been leveled by him."

The haughty Pengmajia felt a surge of great fury.
Like a mad elephant he jumped out of the palace.
He ordered Yingdaxida to take more soldiers with him.
They surrounded the royal garden tightly like a seamless net.

Anuman hid himself on the top of a coconut tree.
The soldiers searched everywhere but failed to find him.
They thought Anuman had already escaped out.
They began to flatter the ten-headed king on his power.

"Our mighty king has ten heads,
Everyone is scared to death seeing them.
Knowing that our king himself came after it,
The little white monkey has run for his life."

The sentries rested under the coconut tree,
Some were napping; some were laughing.
Naughty Anuman pissed down from the top of the tree.
The pee scattered in the air like drizzles.

Yingdaxida was puzzled with the drizzle,
"No, something is wrong since it's a sunny day.
What kind of water can smell so terribly stinking?
Like raindrops they sprayed all over my head and face."

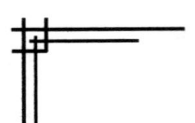

兰噶西贺 The Ten-Headed King of Langa

众兵丁抬头往上看,
只见白猴叉腰站在树顶,
他们慌忙拉弓射出密箭,
椰树被击成碎片糠粉。

椰树和阿努曼都没有了踪影,
只见一股浓烟直往上升,
"白猴已被我们射成肉酱,
就连它的毛也变成了灰尘。"

士兵们幸灾乐祸得意忘形,
还没笑完,烟尘散尽,
忽见在另一棵参天贝叶树梢,
白猴坐在叶柄上讥笑他们。

英达西达勃然大怒,
把三支神箭射向贝叶树,
神箭旋绕变成三条绳索,
把阿努曼的身子紧紧捆住。

力大无比的阿努曼用力一挣,
三根绳子断成碎条,
但是阿努曼用力过猛伤了元气,
霎时头昏眼花脚站不稳。

它从贝叶树上跌落下来,
士兵蜂拥而上把它捆紧,
阿努曼被押到宫廷,
仇恨满腔的捧玛加亲自审问。

第十三章 阿努曼 Chapter 13 Anuman

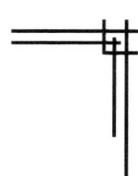

Soldiers lifted their head and looked up,
They saw the white monkey standing akimbo on the tree.
They hurried to raise their bows and shoot together,
The intense arrows smashed the coconut tree into pieces.

Anuman disappeared together with the coconut tree.
Only a whiff of dark fog rose to the air from the ground.
"The white monkey had been shot by us into a meat sauce,
Even his hair had been turned into dusts."

The soldiers were excited and elated to see the tragedy.
But the fog and dust disappeared while they were still laughing.
And suddenly they saw on top of a tall Beiye tree
The white money sitting on the branch jeering at them.

Yingdaxida was furious at the sight of it.
He let go of three arrows shooting at the Beiye tree.
The arrows revolved and turned into three ropes,
They clung to Anuman and bundled him up tightly.

Powerful Anuman struggled to get rid of the ropes,
Then the three ropes burst into pieces.
But Anuman struggled too hard that he used up his energy,
He felt dizzy and couldn't stand firm on the ground.

Anuman fell down from the top of the Beiye tree.
Soldiers swarmed up and bound him with rope.
He was dragged and escorted to the court.
The resentful Pengmajia himself interrogated him.

兰噶西贺 The Ten-Headed King of Langa

"你是什么地方的野物？
竟敢践踏我的御花园，
你来我的王宫干什么？
是谁派你钻进我的宫殿？"

"我破坏你的御花园，
是对你的一个小小的警告，
你要是还不悔悟继续作恶，
你还会戕害你的岛国。"

骄横的十头王怒不可遏，
下令结束阿努曼的生命：
"你们把它抬到城外的森林，
把它剁成肉酱方解我心头之恨。"

四十五个士兵抬着捆紧的白猴，
吵吵嚷嚷来到阴暗的森林，
他们举刀向白猴的腰杆砍去，
却只斩断了阿努曼身上的棕绳。

阿努曼忽地站起身，
抡起抬它的扁担横扫士兵，
只留下四条大汉，
其余士兵逃不脱死亡的厄运。

阿努曼又抱起手来，
命四个大汉把它捆紧，
四个大汉只得乖乖听令，
又把白猴抬回宫廷。

第十三章 阿努曼 Chapter 13 Anuman

"From which sordid corner are you from?
How dare you tramp on and destroy my garden?
For what did you come here in my country?
Who sent you to sneak into my palace?"

"I did destroy your royal garden purposely.
It was just a small warning to remind you.
If you still don't repent and go on doing evils,
Your will incur the devastation of your island kingdom."

The haughty ten-headed king became furious,
And he gave order to have Anuman executed,
"Carry him out of the town and into the forest,
Chop him up to meat sauce so that I can vent my hatred."

Forty five soldiers carried the bounded white monkey,
With great clamour they reached the dark forest.
Soldiers raised their swords and slashed at white monkey's waist,
But only the ropes around Anuman got broken.

Unscathed Anuman stood up suddenly,
He swung the stick that had been used to carry him,
Only four soldiers survived his sudden attack,
All the others couldn't escape from the god of death.

Anuman folded his arms and hands,
Ordering the four soldiers to bundle him tight again.
The four soldiers could do nothing but obey him,
And they carried him back to the palace again.

捧玛加见了气得咬牙切齿：
"你们把它放进石碓里，
一百个人轮流用力舂，
把这可恶的白猴舂成肉泥。"

众士兵高兴地舂着碓，
阿努曼觉得有人帮它捶背，
兵丁舂得精疲力竭大汗淋漓，
阿努曼在碓里闭着眼睛打瞌睡。

捧玛加见了又惊又气，
下令用烈火将它烧死，
阿努曼被丢进炉子关上盖，
一百个士兵拉动风箱鼓气。

炉子比太阳还红火，
士兵们热得汗流如雨，
打开炉盖不见白猴的骨灰，
却见它敞衣乘凉坐在风箱里。

炭火没有烧焦白猴一根毫毛，
士兵们个个惊愕，面面相觑：
"白猴的身子比黄牛还大，
竹筒粗的风箱口它怎么进得去？"

第十三章 阿努曼 Chapter 13 Anuman

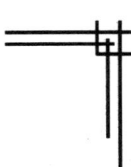

At the sight of them, Pengmajia gritted his teeth,
"Put him in a stone mortar,
Then one hundred soldiers take turns to pound.
Pound this damn white monkey into dirt of meat."

The soldiers pounded Anuman in the mortar happily;
For Anuman it was as if someone were massaging on his back.
The soldiers all got exhausted drenched in drips of sweat.
While Anuman closed his eyes and took a nap in the mortar.

Pengmajia was surprised and angry to see this.
Then he gave another order to burn him to death.
The soldiers tossed Anuman into a furnace and capped it,
The one hundred soldiers started to pump wind into it.

The furnace was redder and brighter than the sun now.
Soldiers got so hot that their sweats dripped down like rain.
Then they lifted the lid of the furnace to gather the bones and ashes,
Only to find him sitting in the wind box enjoying the cool air.

Not a single hair of the monkey was scorched by the fire!
The soldiers looked at and asked each other with astonishment,
"The white monkey is bigger than a bull,
How can he squeeze into the pump vent as slim as a bamboo?"

捧玛加颤抖的心更加疑虑：
"这个白猴神威太不同一般，
它可能是召朗玛派来的暗探，
我定要杀掉它以免后患。"

十头王向大臣和武官下达命令：
"快把白猴抬到偏僻的深沟，
用长长的土布把它从脚裹到头，
还要运去几十桶芝麻油。

"把芝麻油煮得沸腾滚烫，
泼在白猴身上，
渗透猴毛，再点起大火把土布烧着，
就算它有天大的本领也活不了。"

阿努曼听了暗暗好笑，
装着胆怯心悸发出哀叫：
"我的命系在尾巴上，
请你们只烧身子别让尾巴烧焦。"

十头王听了暗自高兴，
命令士兵从猴子尾巴烧起，
他以为这一招万无一失，
定把白猴置于死地。

士兵把白猴抬到偏僻的山洼，
阿努曼的身子变得越来越大，
长长的土布只够裹尾巴，
点燃了土布就像烧着一个火把。

第十三章 阿努曼　Chapter 13　Anuman

Pengmajia' heart was trembling with more puzzles,
"This white monkey is exceptionally powerful.
He might be the spy sent by Zhao Langma,
I must get him killed to avoid more trouble."

Pengmajia gave another order to his generals and ministers,
"Carry this white monkey to a remote ditch,
Wrap him from head to toe with the long cloth,
And also take dozen barrels of sesame oil with you.

"Heat the sesame oil till it boils,
Pour the boiling oil onto the white monkey
Get his hair soaked with oil and set fire on the cloth,
No matter what magic he has, he would never survive this."

Anuman sneered in his heart at Pengmajia's plan,
But he pretended to be scared and cried out with fear,
"All my life hangs on my tail,
Please burn only my body and get my tail spared."

The ten-headed king was glad to hear this.
He ordered the soldiers to set fire from the tail,
He thought this wouldn't fail under any circumstances,
And the white monkey was definitely to be killed.

The soldiers carried Anuman to a remote valley.
Anuman's body was becoming bigger and bigger.
The long cloth could only cover his tail,
Which looked like a torch when it was set on fire.

浸油的土布比蜡条还易燃，
比干季的野火烧得更快，
阿努曼突然大吼一声，
带着"火把"腾空飞起来。

阿努曼飞进允兰嘎到处乱窜，
穿过密密的房子又钻进宫殿，
窜到哪里尾巴把火种带到哪，
允兰嘎到处烈焰翻卷。

捧玛加惊慌失措手忙脚乱，
拿着弓赛宰跑出宫殿，
坐上飞车去到遥远的原始森林，
托帕拉西替他把神弓保管。

"好心的圣者帕拉西，
这是天神父亲恩赐给我的弓赛宰，
它能制敌死命有无穷的威力，
而我自己的生命就系在这把弓里。

"现在猴子阿努曼正在纵火行凶，
允兰嘎许多地方烈火熊熊，
烧毁这把弓箭我就失去生命啊，
只好请你保存日后我再来取回王宫。"

第十三章 阿努曼 Chapter 13 Anuman

The oil-drenched cloth was easier to be kindled than wax.
The fire expanded faster than the wild fire in dry season.
Suddenly Anuman burst out a loud cry,
Then he flew into the air with the burning "torch".

Anuman flew into the city of Langa and jumped all around,
He passed the dense houses and flew into the palace.
Wherever he went, the fire on his tail was like a kindling,
Bright flame roared and roamed all over the city of Langa.

Pengmajia was thrown into great panic and confusion.
He took up his bow of Saizai and ran out of the palace.
In his flying cart he flew to the remote primeval forest.
He went to Palaxi and asked him to keep the bow for him.

"Dear kind-hearted Saint Palaxi,
My father, the heavenly god, gave me the bow.
It has magic power to take the lives of any enemies.
And my own life is also dependent on this magic bow.

"Now the white monkey Anuman was making heinous crime,
Many places of the city of Langa was on fire because of him.
If this bow was destroyed by fire, I would also lose my life.
Please keep it for me and I will get it back to the palace later."

捧玛加带来一块竹片①,
上面刻着古怪的符号和文字,
一刀劈开各人拿一半在手里,
作为日后领取弓赛宰的证据。

阿努曼巧计放火烧着了允兰嘎,
迅速带着身上的火钻进海洋里,
身上的火苗淹灭了,
唯有尾巴还冒烟不熄。

阿努曼只好飞进森林求救,
帕拉西给它指出一个秘诀:
"海水不能把你尾巴的火苗淹熄,
只有你身上的水可以把它浇灭。"

聪明的阿努曼立即明白了,
撒了一泡尿把尾巴上的火浇熄,
它卸掉身上的负担无比欢喜,
轻快地向烟雾弥漫的海面飞去。

四、出探归来

捧玛加匆匆赶回都城,
看见到处是烟火、灰烬和瓦砾,

---

① 另一传说是用两根棍子,上刻一百道线纹,两人各持一棍,作为凭证。

第十三章 阿努曼 Chapter 13 Anuman

Pengmajia took out a slip of bamboo,
On which was inscribed strange signs and writing.①
He split the slip into two halves and gave one to Palaxi.
These would be the proof to get the bow back later.

Anuman tactically set the city of Langa on fire.
Then he dived into the sea with the fire burning on him.
The fire on his body was put out,
But smoke still belched from his tail.

Anuman could only fly to the forest to ask help.
Palaxi offered him a magic code,
"The fire on your tail can't be extinguished by sea water;
Only the water coming from your own body can do the trick."

Clever Anuman understood what he meant immediately.
He pissed on his own tail and the fire was put out.
He got happy for the burdens had been relieved from him.
Then briskly he flew back to the smoky and foggy sea.

Ⅳ   Return from Scouting

Pengmajia returned to his palace hurriedly.
He saw smoke, ashes and crumbles everywhere.

---

①　Another version of the story is that they were two sticks, on each of which were inscribed 100 lines. And they two each got one as proof in the future.

恨得十双大眼闪出血光,
立即派诡计多端的维亚干追击猴子。

维亚干腾云驾雾朝前赶,
落到白猴必须经过的海面,
他将身子变成一个绿色的小岛,
长出的瓜果芳香又鲜艳。

这样新鲜的瓜果谁不爱吃,
白猴见了更是会垂涎下地,
只等阿努曼把瓜果吃进肚子,
就把它压到深深的海底。

阿努曼飞到宽阔的海洋上空,
看见下面有个瓜熟果香的小岛,
它回想来时这里烟波浩渺,
怀疑是十头王暗害它设下的圈套。

阿努曼跃上一千约的高空,
又像老鹰似地俯冲下来,
用它的双脚猛蹬小岛,
把岸边的岩石踩塌了一大块。

第十三章 阿努曼 Chapter 13 Anuman

He was so resentful that his twenty eyes were emitting light of blood.

Then he ordered the crafty Weiyagan to pursue and attack the monkey.

Weiyagan flew into the clouds and hurried forward.
He landed on the sea where Anuman had to pass.
Then he turned himself into a small green island,
All the melons and fruits on it smelt and looked good.

Nobody could resist the delicious and fresh melons.
The sight of them would certainly make Anuman's mouth water.
As long as Anuman swallowed down the melons and fruits,
He will be plunged and sunk to the bottom of the deep sea.

Now Anuman was flying across the vast sea,
He spotted the small island full of ripe melons.
He recalled his last journey over the vast expanse of water,
He doubted that it was a trap set up by the ten-headed king.

Anuman flew into the ten-thousand-Yue-high sky,
Then he plunged down like an eagle.
With the great diving force he stamped the island,
One piece of rock was torn off from the island.

维亚干痛得大声惨叫，
见阿努曼不上他的圈套，
只能恢复原形跳离海面，
在空中还一阵阵心惊肉跳。

维亚干鼓足力气扑向阿努曼，
白猴一跃腾空一千多约，
然后像箭一般俯冲过去，
一把抓住维亚干扭打起来。

大力士维亚干忽地闪开，
把阿努曼甩出一千多约，
阿努曼落地又跳回来，
两个扭成一团难分难解。

他们从海洋打到岸上，
又从陆地打到空中，
就像两只扭打在一起的黄蜂，
分辨不出谁雌谁雄。

维亚干觉得显示力气的时候到了，
拔起一棵粗大的椰子树猛打过来，
神威的阿努曼也拔起丁香树，
把维亚干手中的椰子树打下大海。

第十三章 阿努曼 Chapter 13 Anuman

Weiyagan was hurt badly and cried out loud,
Seeing that Anuman didn't fall for his trick,
He transformed back to his own shape and jumped out of the sea,
His heart was still pounding wildly even after he was high in the sky.

Weiyagan gathered all his strength and rushed to Anuman.
Anuman lifted himself up one thousand Yues higher,
Then he dived down like a flying arrow,
He caught Weiyagan and they grappled with each other.

The powerful Weiyagan suddenly shook off Anuman,
And Anuman was bounced off one thousand Yues away.
Anuman landed on the sea then jumped back,
They wrestled so hard that it's difficult to get them apart.

They fought in the air above the sea then landed on the beach,
After a while they flew back into the air going on fighting.
They grappled each other like two wasps twined together,
Nobody could distinguish the one from the other.

Weiyagan thought it was time to show his great strength.
He uprooted a thick coconut tree and swung to Anuman.
Mighty Anuman also pulled up a clove tree to fight back,
The coconut tree in Weiyagan's hand was knocked off to the sea.

阿努曼冲过去抓住维亚干，
把他远远地摔下大海，
维亚干落到海面又飞起来，
两人本领相当不分胜败。

阿努曼心生一计，
抱起手对维亚干开了腔：
"我们都是能征善战的武将，
只是效忠的王各不一样。

"我们这样胡抓乱打，
犹如小孩子玩游戏，
打了半天不过瘾，
不疼不痒白费力气。

"现在我俩来比一比，
谁力气最大、最有本事，
每人拔起三棵糖棕树，
轮流敲打对方的头三次。

"谁的头骨最坚硬，
谁经得住大树敲打，
就算他的神威最高，
就算他的本领最大。

"如果谁被打死了，
就是他命该如此，
我现在就等着你，
你就从我先打起。"

第十三章 阿努曼 Chapter 13 Anuman

Anuman dashed to Weiyagan and grasped him,
And threw him far into the sea.
Weiyagan landed on the sea and flew up again.
They were equally matched and no one could win.

Anuman came up with a good idea.
He saluted Weiyagan with hands folded and raised,
"Both of us are generals who are good at fighting,
While we are just serving different kings loyally.

"We were scratching and wrestling with each other
Just as two little kids were playing games.
We fought so long but no one could win.
It was no fun at all but only wasted our energy.

"Let's have a match in another way
To see which of us is more strong and capable.
We each pull up three palm trees, with which
We take turns to knock the head of the other for three times.

"The one who has a tougher skull and
Who can stand the pounding by the big tree,
He will be counted as the more powerful one,
As well as the more capable one.

"If one is hit to death,
That's his doomed fate.
Now I am waiting for you here,
And you can start hitting on me."

549

维亚干听了十分高兴,
觉得白猴真比肥猪还蠢,
"叫我先动手是个好机会,
我可一棒就使白猴命归阴。"

维亚干拔起三棵糖棕树,
瞅准白猴的头顶打下来,
机灵的阿努曼一闪身飞到云天外,
维亚干第一次出手就失败。

维亚干第二次打来,
阿努曼一侧身钻进海里,
过一会儿又从水面冒出头,
呼唤维亚干再来最后一击。

维亚干急得像大火烧身,
使出吃奶力气砸向白猴的头顶,
只见水花飞溅波浪滚滚,
白猴又站在他面前完好无损。

阿努曼笑嘻嘻地对维亚干说:
"我已承受你的三次打击,
现在轮到你低头站在我面前,
让我举起大树来打你。"

第十三章 阿努曼 Chapter 13 Anuman

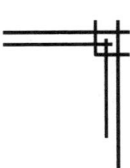

Weiyagan was excited to hear this,
Thinking the white monkey is stupider than a fat pig.
"He offered a good chance to me by asking me to start.
Just one blow would kill the white monkey instantly."

Weiyagan uprooted three palm trees,
He targeted them on the head of the monkey and hit onto it.
The agile Anuman dodged and flew into the air.
Weiyagan's first effort failed completely.

Weiyagan hit the white monkey for a second time.
Anuman ducked aside and dived into the sea.
After a while he swam out of the water,
And he asked Weiyagan to try his last luck.

Weiyagan was desperate as if he was on fire.
He gathered all his strength to hit at the top of Anuman's head.
Then it was seen that waves splashed and water sprayed all over,
While the white monkey stood in front of him safe and sound.

Anuman said to Weiyagan with a smile,
"I have already been hit by you for three times.
Now it is your turn to stand with head drooped in front of me,
And I will hold up my trees to hit them at you."

551

阿努曼拔起三棵糖棕树,
把三棵树紧紧扭在一起,
它向维亚干举起大树,
故意装着要打的样子。

狡猾的维亚干立即躲进地底,
阿努曼并没有打下去,
维亚干以为没事探出头来,
阿努曼瞅准了给他闪电般的一击。

维亚干的头骨被敲得粉碎,
脑浆和乌血四面溅飞,
杀死了拦路的鬼魅,
阿努曼高兴地继续返回。

到了召朗玛和腊嘎纳面前,
阿努曼把出探的结果禀告:
"尊贵的召朗玛,
阿努曼已去到勐兰嘎。

"我见到了天镜般明净的南西拉,
她孤独一人被关进高塔,
她坚贞不屈忠于你,
没有谁能挨近她。

第十三章 阿努曼 Chapter 13 Anuman

Anuman pulled up three palm trees,
And he twisted them together tightly.
Then he raised the trees and aimed at Weiyagan
Pretending to strike him with them.

Sly Weiyagan hid into the ground immediately
But Anuman didn't actually strike down.
When Weiyagan thought it was safe, he stuck his head out,
All at once Anuman hit him on the head with the speed of lightening.

Weiyagan's skull was smashed into pieces;
His blood flew all over together with his brain tissue.
After killing this monster who had blocked his way,
Anuman happily went on his journey back to his troops.

Anuman went forward to Zhao Langma and Lagana,
And he reported what he had seen in the kingdom of Langa.
"Your majestic Zhao Langma,
Anuman just returned from the kingdom of Langa.

"I have seen Nan Xila who is as pure as crystal mirror,
She alone is imprisoned in a high tower.
She remains loyal to you as always.
Nobody was able to get close to her.

"捧玛加对她苦苦追求,
说了多少比蜜还甜的好话,
又威胁利诱南西拉把你忘掉,
他愿把整个勐兰嘎交给她。

"善良、忠贞的南西拉,
声声把可恶的十头王痛骂,
甜言蜜语不听,
威胁利诱不怕。

"为了保持自己宝石般的纯洁,
她被劫后已向苍天发出誓言,
除了自己的丈夫召朗玛,
天下所有的男人都不能挨近她。

"贪淫好色的捧玛加,
不敢对她非礼动脚动手,
只能眼巴巴看着心里难受,
就是因为害怕南西拉的诅咒。

"你的信件她捧在胸前,
读了一遍又一遍,
眼泪像八月的雨点,
倾泻不尽对你深深的怀念。

"她拔下自己的七根头发,
表示和你的心紧紧相连,
她取下脖子上的金项链,
表示永远围绕在你的身边。

第十三章 阿努曼 Chapter 13 Anuman

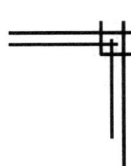

"Pengmajia has played every trick to pursue her,
Coaxing her with words sweeter than honey.
And he also seduced and threatened Nan Xila to forget you,
Saying he was willing to trade the whole kingdom for her love.

"The kind-hearted and faithful Nan Xila,
She has been cursing the vicious ten-headed king.
She wouldn't listen to his honeyed words,
She was not afraid of any threats or seductions.

"In order to keep her purity as that of precious gems,
She has made a vow to heaven after being hijacked,
That no other man in the world can draw near to her
Except her own husband Zhao Langma.

"The licentious and debauched Pengmajia,
He didn't have the nerve to take her by force.
He was afraid of the curse from Nan Xila,
So he could only look at her with fire in his heart.

"She held your letter with both hands,
And she read it again and again.
Her tears were like the raindrops of August,
Those were her pouring love for you.

"She plucked seven of her hairs,
Which meant her heart was always with yours;
She took off the gold necklace from her neck,
Which meant she would always be around you.

"我正要离开南西拉,
不料被卫兵发现捉住,
十头王下令把我烧死,
我将计就计烧着了宫殿和房屋。

"我本想把她背回来,
由于我是一个男子汉,
她不愿意损害我的神威,
声声催促我只身赶回。

"南西拉托我把这些信物交给你,
表示永不变心将你等待,
请迅速把大军开进勐兰嘎,
她盼你营救、准备迎接胜利到来。"

召朗玛接过项链和头发,
深情地亲吻了一下,
妻子的忠贞使他感到安慰,
南西拉的遭遇又使他伤心落泪。

他把妻子的头发放进衣袋,
把闪闪发光的项链贴在胸怀,
亲爱的妻子南西拉啊,
仿佛就在自己眼前接受抚爱。

他仿佛听见南西拉的声声呼唤,
他好像看见南西拉站着盼望救援,
迅速渡海和捧玛加决一死战,
在召朗玛心中已是刻不容缓。

第十三章 阿努曼 Chapter 13 Anuman

"Just when I was to leave Nan Xila,
Unexpectedly the sentries found and caught me.
The ten-headed king asked his soldiers to burn me to death.
I turned his trick to my own use and burned his palace and the city.

"I had thought to carry her on my back and return.
But since I am an adult man,
And she didn't want to hurt my power because of her curse.
So she just urged me to hurry back here alone.

"Nan Xila entrusted me to give these two items to you.
She said she would wait for you and never change her heart.
Please send the troops to the Kingdom of Langa immediately.
She is waiting for you to rescue her and to celebrate your victory."

Zhao Langma received the necklace and hairs,
He gave them an affectionate kiss.
His wife's loyalty relieved his anxiety,
While her sufferings made him cry in tears.

He put his wife's hairs into his pocket;
He put on her necklace and felt it on his chest.
Oh, it seemed that he could feel his dear wife Nan Xila
Standing in front of him and enjoying his caresses.

He seemed to hear Nan Xila's calling for his name;
He seemed to see Nen Xila standing there waiting for rescue.
He was determined to cross the sea and defeat Pengmajia.
That was the utmost important thing in his mind now.

第十四章 战前

一、架桥

猴子大军在海岸边安营扎寨,
等待漂洋过海的命令,
阿努曼送信侦察胜利而归,
召朗玛命令把大桥赶造起来。

猴兵猴将像蜜蜂倾巢出动,
海边热闹忙碌胜过赶摆,
它们从森林砍来大树小树,
它们从山上搬来大小石块。

有的深入海底建造桥墩,
有的在岸上来回运输奔忙不停,
歌声、笑声和呼唤声,
震撼着辽阔的海洋和森林。

满山遍野是猴子,
一座座大山被搬平,
有的在陆地上行走,
有的从空中飞行。

第十四章 战前 Chapter 14 Before The War

Chapter 14   Before The War

Ⅰ   Building the Bridge

The monkey armies camped by the seaside
Waiting for the order to cross the sea.
Anuman returned in triumph after delivering the letter and scouting,
Zhao Langma ordered to build up a bridge over the sea.

Monkey soldiers rushed out like bees out of the beehive.
The seaside seemed more boisterous than a marketplace.
Big tress were cut down and transported here from the forest;
Rocks and boulders were moved down from the hills nearby.

Some monkeys dived into the sea to set up the foundation;
Some transported materials back and forth on the land.
Songs, laughter and shouting were all over the beach,
They echoed resonantly over the vast sea and forest.

Monkeys were all over the mountains and valleys.
They leveled the mountains and moved the rocks.
Some monkeys walked on the land,
Some were flying in the sky.

一排高大的岩石墩，
整齐地屹立在海面上，
猴子大军艰辛劳动三个月，
巍巍大桥飞跨辽阔的海洋。

猴兵猴将们高兴万分，
谁知突然发生了不幸，
一个个桥墩全部塌陷，
大桥被汹涌的波涛冲毁。

召朗玛和嘎林，
指挥猴子再次建桥，
运来比大象还大的石头，
把桥墩垒得更加坚牢。

阿努曼一次抬来一百棵树，
嘎林王一次搬来一座大山，
眼看大桥就要通向勐兰嘎，
大海一阵震动，又把大桥摧垮。

温和的召朗玛也变得暴跳如雷，
挥动宝刀催促队伍重新搭架，
勐基沙的大小百姓完全出动，
人马更多，声势更浩大。

第十四章 战前 Chapter 14 Before The War

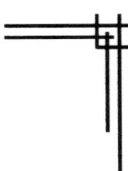

Piles of rock foundations were set up,
Which stood neatly out of the surface of the sea.
The monkey armies had worked hard for three months,
And now a mighty bridge spanned over the vast sea.

The monkey generals and soldiers were excited with their project.
But who could expect that disaster would befall without warning?
One by one the rock foundation of the bridge collapsed.
The bridge was suddenly destroyed by the surging waves.

Zhao Langma and Galin got together,
And they directed the monkeys to build another bridge.
Boulders bigger than elephant were transported again.
More solid foundations were set up one after another.

Anuman carried one hundred trees at a time;
The King Galin moved one mountain in one breath.
The bridge was soon reaching the kingdom of Langa,
But the billows tore it down once again.

Mild-tempered Zhao Langma now became furious.
He waved his sword and ordered the bridge to be rebuilt.
All people from the Kingdom of Jisha were mobilized,
With more people and horses, the scene was more grandiose.

天空、地面、海上、森林，
全是架桥的猴兵和人群，
白天黑夜又苦战了七个月，
架起的大桥又被怒吼的海浪掀平。

三次架桥三次都失败，
召朗玛冷静下来细细思考：
"是海底有什么怪物同我作对，
还是我的福分菲薄命运不好？"

他派阿努曼上天请叭英指点，
叭英说是海底有大螃蟹作怪，
它用大脚横扫海底，
架起的大桥就东倒西歪。

阿努曼立即返回地上，
用它的神眼向海洋深处探望，
果见一只斑壳大蟹在海底平躺，
倒塌的石块滚落在爪子两旁。

螃蟹的身子比山还大，
螃蟹的大脚有一百约长，
螃蟹在海底横行霸道，
不除掉它就休想架起桥梁。

第十四章 战前　Chapter 14 Before The War

In the sky, on the earth, over the sea and in the forest,
Everywhere were the people and monkeys busy with the bridge.
They worked hectically day and night for another seven months.
But the new bridge was torn down by the angry waves again.

All the three attempts to build a bridge ended with failure.
Now Zhao Langma calmed down and thought it over.
"Was there any monsters under the sea fighting against me?
Or is it because of my bad luck leading to the continuous failures?"

He sent Anuman to the heaven and ask advice from Baying.
Baying told him it was because of the crab monster under the sea.
When it swept his long legs cross the sea floor,
The bridge would tremble, shake and then crumble down.

Anuman immediately flew back to the land.
With his sharp eyes, he looked into the deep sea.
Indeed, a crab monster with colorful shell lying on the seabed.
The crumbled boulders was scattered all around its claws.

Its body was huger than a mountain;
Its legs were longer than one hundred Yues.
With the crab monster running wild on the floor,
The bridge could never be set up successfully.

563

阿努曼准备下海擒拿螃蟹，
特地把自己的尾巴伸长，
它叫大家拖住他的尾巴，
尾巴摆动就把它拉上岸。

阿努曼纵身跳进深深的海底，
紧紧抓住大螃蟹的双夹，
大家在岸上发现尾巴摇动，
立即把大蟹拉上沙滩准备宰杀。

慈善的召朗玛嘱咐大家：
"你们不要一气之下杀害它，
只要砍掉它的两只前夹，
它就没有本事把大桥摧垮。"

螃蟹被阿努曼扭断前夹，
扔到海里就气衰力竭一命呜呼，
召朗玛用一只前夹做了一面螃蟹大鼓，
频频鼓声催动士兵前进的脚步。

另一只前夹送给天上的叭英，
叭英也用它做了一面大鼓，
从此只要天上鼓声隆隆，
广袤的人间大地就大雨如注。①

---

① 还有一种说法，只要天上敲响螃蟹夹做的大鼓，人世间鸡群便扑翅应啼。

第十四章 战前 Chapter 14 Before The War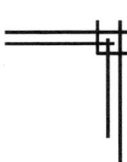

Anuman decided to dive into the sea to catch the crab.
He used his magic power to lengthen his tail.
And then he asked the monkeys to hold the tail tight.
When he wiggled his tail, they should drag him out of the water.

Now Anuman jumped and dived into the deep sea.
He grasped tightly the front claws of the crab.
When monkeys saw his tail wiggling, they pulled it together.
Now the crab was on the beach and they planned to kill it.

The kindly Zhao Langma said to them,
"Please don't kill it out of your anger.
Just chopped off its two front claws,
So that it can't destroy our bridge anymore."

Anuman tore off the front claws of the crab.
Then he tossed it back into the sea, which still died in a minute.
Zhao Langma made a drum with one claw of the crab.
The sound of the drum enhanced his soldiers' morale.

The other claw was sent to Baying,
And it was made into a drum too.
Ever since the drum was pounded in the heaven,
Heavy rain would fall down to the ground mysteriously.①

---

① Another version of this story is that as long as the drum made of crab craw is pounded, the rosters on the earth would crow while patting their wings.

召朗玛和嘎林下令再次造桥，
不屈不挠的精神终于结出硕果，
一道长虹跨越大海的碧波，
浩浩荡荡的队伍从桥上走过。

猴子大军吹响金笛、银笛，
敲响螃蟹大鼓和金筒银锣，
队伍在兰嘎岛岸边集结，
营房犹如天上落下的白云朵朵。

二、救活彼亚沙

黎明前的黑夜还笼罩着王宫，
捧玛加做了一个奇怪的梦，
海洋上飞来一只白毛老鹰，
盘旋在勐兰嘎宫殿的上空。

守卫宫殿的黑色老鹰，
和白鹰展开了激烈的搏斗，
黑鹰被撕断了翅膀，
鲜红的血水直往下流。

黑鹰重重跌落在地上，
惨死在兰嘎宫殿门口，
日出时十头王一觉惊醒过来，
宫殿里静悄悄什么事也没有。

第十四章 战前 Chapter 14 Before The War

Zhao Langma and Galin ordered to build another bridge.
Their indomitable spirits bore fruit at last.
The bridge like a rainbow spanned the sea.
The mighty armies walked through the bridge to the other side.

The monkey armies blew their flutes of gold and silver;
They pounded on the crab claw drum and brass gongs.
The troop gathered at the beach of Langa island;
Their camps looked like white clouds landing on the ground.

Ⅱ Biyasha Was Rescued

The palace was still covered in darkness before the dawn,
Pengmajia had a strange dream at that moment.
In his dream a white eagle emerged from the sea,
It hovered in the sky above the palace of the Kingdom of Langa.

A black eagle was safeguarding the palace.
It flew up and fought with the white eagle.
Then the wings of the black eagle got broken,
Red blood gushed out from the wound.

Then the black eagle fell down to the ground,
It died wretchedly at the gate of the palace.
The ten-headed king woke up from the nightmare at dawn,
But it was quiet in the palace and nothing had happened.

捧玛加心里忐忑不安，
不知这是个什么征兆的梦，
他急忙把弟弟彼亚沙叫来，
叫他占卜是吉还是凶。

知识渊博的彼亚沙，
轻轻翻开神灵的天书，
用神笔在木板上写画，
为哥哥的噩梦占卜。

暗淡的阴云呈现在方格里，
犹如窗户蒙上了黑纱，
彼亚沙知道这是不祥的预兆，
一场灾难就要降临勐兰嘎。

心地善良的弟弟彼亚沙，
向刚愎自用的捧玛加作了解答：
"海外的白鹰飞进勐兰嘎，
预示着陈兵边境的召朗玛的行动。

"你引来了一场不可避免的灾难，
你劫来了宝石般的南西拉，
南西拉的丈夫率领千军万马，
要来攻打我们的海岛国家。

第十四章 战前 Chapter 14 Before The War

Pengmajia felt agitated over the dream.
He want to know the interpretation of it.
He immediately called in his brother Biyasha,
Asking him to divine to see if it is good or bad.

The knowledgeable Biyasha,
He opened his sacred prophet book gently;
He wrote on a board with his sacred brush.
He read the signs and interpreted his brother's nightmare.

Dark cloud appeared in the square of his drawing.
As if a window was shrouded with a dark curtain.
Biyasha knew it was an ominous sign,
A disaster was to befall the Kingdom of Langa.

The kind-hearted Biyasha,
He explained to his haughty brother Pengmajia,
"The white eagle flew from overseas to the Kingdom of Langa,
It foretells the next move of Zhao Langma stationing on the border.

"You have invited an inevitable disaster,
Since you hijacked the jade-like Nan Xila.
Her husband is leading thousands of soldiers
On the way to attack our island kingdom.

"请哥哥原谅我冒昧直说,
守卫宫殿的黑毛老鹰,
代表着黄金般珍贵的大王,
正是你——无比威望的哥哥。

"我们的国家已经年迈力衰,
经不起战乱的折腾破坏,
如果我们再与他们作对,
将无法逃脱战争的失败。

"哥哥呀,你不能再被贪婪淫乱蒙住眼睛,
是聪明的人识时务,
时间虽然紧得像待发的弩箭,
但现在你还来得及改邪归正。

"趁早把南西拉送还给召朗玛,
求他宽恕你一时的过错,
只有哥哥你这样做了,
才能解除这场可怕的灾祸。"

无比傲慢固执的捧玛加,
听不进弟弟的诤谏和忠告,
他面红耳赤、怒火中烧,
犹如发疯的野牛狂吼乱叫。

"只问你一点小事,
你竟然这么喋喋不休,
你不是给我献计献策,
却这样一派胡言乱语。

第十四章 战前 Chapter 14 Before The War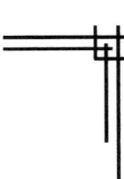

"Dear brother, please forgive me for my frankness,
The black eagle guarding the palace in your dream
Symbolized a king as precious as gold.
That was you—my mighty elder brother.

"Our kingdom has turned senile and fragile,
So it can't stand the devastation of another war.
If we continue to clash with them in a war
We are doomed to be defeated and lose all.

"My dear brother, please stop being blinded by your avarice.
A wise man knows to suit their actions to the times.
Time is clicking like an arrow on the bow.
But it is still not too late for you to rectify yourself.

"Please give Nan Xila back to Zhao Langma right away.
And beg him to forgive your impulsive mistake.
Only by doing as what I have said
Can this kingdom be spared from a terrible havoc."

The stubborn and haughty Pengmajia
Turned a deaf ear to brother's sincere advice.
He flared up with anger and flushed to his ears.
He was shouting and scowling like a mad buffalo.

"I only asked you to do such a small thing,
But you are blabbering on and on without stopping.
You are not trying to come up with the tactics,
You are just talking nonsense like this.

"你简直是在扰乱军心,
大敌当前你却妄自菲薄,
你是隐藏在勐兰嘎的毒蛇,
是隐藏在我身边的灾祸。

"你说出这么多不吉利的话,
你把我说得还不如蚂蚁,
简直是长敌人威风、灭我的志气,
我要把你这胆小鬼丢进海洋里。"

十头王越骂越气愤,
抓住彼亚沙脚踢拳打,
彼亚沙受伤的心啊,
卷缩得像晒枯的荷花。

正直的彼亚沙又慷慨陈词:
"杀了我也要把事情说个明白,
召朗玛并没有侵害过我们,
是你把他的妻子无理抢来。

"现在召朗玛的军队近在咫尺,
我们的国家危在旦夕,
召朗玛伸张正义有天神佑助,
你怎么能拿国家命运当儿戏?

"回想天神父亲曾对我们谆谆嘱咐,
森林里的白猴不能屠杀,
正直善良的王子不能欺侮,
我看召朗玛就是这个王子。"

第十四章 战前 Chapter 14 Before The War

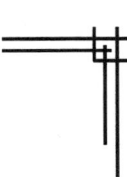

"You are trying to stir unrest among my army
By belittling ourselves when enemies attack us.
You are a poisonous snake crouching in Langa;
You are really a hidden disaster beside me.

"What you have said means bad luck to me.
In your words, I am not even as good as an ant.
You are fawning our enemy and diminishing our morale,
I will have a coward like you thrown into the sea."

The ten-headed king became more furious while scolding,
He caught Biyasha and punched and kicked him violently.
Oh, the badly-hurt heart of Biyasha
Cringed like a scorched lotus flower.

The righteous Biyasha kept persuading his brother,
"I still have to make things clear even if you would kill me.
Zhao Langma has not invaded or harmed our kingdom.
It is you who has robbed him of his dear wife.

"Zhao Langma's troops are approaching close to us.
Our kingdom is on the verge of destruction.
Zhao Langma will be supported by gods for his justice.
How could you take the fate of our country as a game?

"Do you still remember the words from our father the immortal?
That the white monkeys in the forest shouldn't be slaughtered;
That the kindly and righteous prince shouldn't be insulted.
I think Zhao Langma is exactly the prince our father mentioned."

残暴昏庸的捧玛加,
气得胡子直立眼冒金花,
"该死的多嘴的彼亚沙,
竟敢说出这些混账话。

"就是神仙也要向我磕头,
我曾打败天神叭英,
天底下的人都得服从我,
何况一个小小的召朗玛。"

他不容分说令士兵把彼亚沙捆起,
绑在竹筏上,流放大海里,
任狂风暴雨将他扑打,
让惊涛骇浪把他吞没。

犹如笼中小鸟有翅难飞,
彼亚沙在死亡线上挣扎,
在海面上漂浮了整整三天,
经受日晒、风吹、雨淋、浪打。

狂风卷起层层波浪,
竹筏在大海里随风飘荡,
海浪没有吞没正直善良的人,
彼亚沙漂到召朗玛驻扎的地方。

召朗玛见海上漂来一张竹筏,
叫人把它拉到岩石峥嵘的岸边,
筏上躺着一个被紧紧捆绑的人,
脸色苍白,气息奄奄。

第十四章 战前　Chapter 14　Before The War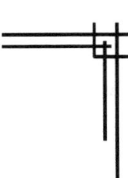

The cruel and stupid Pengmajia became so furious
That his beard stood on their end and eyes flamed.
"Damned you for having such a big mouth.
How dare you say bullshit like this?

"Even gods and deities will kowtow to me.
I have defeated Baying, the heavenly god.
Everyone under the sky follows my order,
Let alone this little Zhao Langma."

Not giving Biyasha time to explain any more,
He ordered the soldiers to tie him up onto a bamboo raft.
The bamboo raft drifted on the sea in winds and storms,
Biyasha was almost swallowed by the fierce surging waves.

Biyasha was like a caged bird unable to fly,
He struggled and tried to hold on to his life.
He floated on the sea for three whole days,
Suffering the hot sun, the wind, the rain and the waves.

The strong wind rolled up huge billows.
The raft floated with the wind in the sea.
Luckily the sea spared the life of this man of integrity,
Biyasha floated to the seaside where Zhao Langma stationed.

Zhao Langma saw the floating raft on the sea.
He had it dragged onto the beach by the side of rocks.
He saw a guy bundled and tied to the raft tightly,
Who seemed to have stopped breathing with a bloodless face.

召朗玛心中产生无限的怜悯,
亲手给他解开身上的棕绳,
把他轻轻扶进岸边的帐篷,
用泉水和食物挽救了他的性命。

召朗玛用柔和的言语介绍自己,
又关切地询问受难者的遭遇,
彼亚沙从死亡中被救活,
对恩人召朗玛深深地感激。

"我哥哥就是十头王捧玛加,
我是他的三弟彼亚沙,
他不听我忠言相劝,
反诬我是胆小如鼠的内奸。

"你们把我搭救上岸,
我发誓对你们绝对忠诚,
请收留我助你们一臂之力,
协助你在战争中取胜。"

召朗玛听了十分同情,
嘎林听了也十分欢迎,
"早就听说他心直如箭,
他也是具有远见卓识的人。

"他熟知勐兰嘎内情,
洞察十头王的隐秘,
收用他来辅助你,
我们定能夺取最后胜利。"

第十四章 战前 Chapter 14 Before The War

Endless pity surged in Zhao Langma's heart,
He himself untied the ropes for the poor man.
Zhao Langma helped him walk into the tent,
And he saved him with spring water and food.

Zhao Langma introduced himself gently,
And he asked the victim about his suffering.
Since Biyasha was saved from death by Zhao Langma,
He told him his story and expressed his gratitude sincerely.

"My brother is the ten-headed king Pengmajia,
I am his younger brother Biyasha.
He turned a deaf ear to my sincere advice,
Instead he accused me of a traitor like a timid mouse.

"Since you have saved my life from the sea,
I swear that I will be absolutely loyal to you.
Please let me stay to do something for you.
Maybe I can assist you to ensure the victory."

Zhao Langma was sympathetic at hearing this.
Galin also welcome Biyasha to stay with them.
"I heard that Biyasha is quite straightforward,
He is also a knowledgeable man of great vision.

"He knows everything about the Kingdom of Langa.
He also knows well the secrets of the ten-headed king.
If you can take him in to assist you,
We will surely be able to win the final battle."

召朗玛和彼亚沙庄严地立约发誓,
双方赤诚相待,齐心协力,
将来战胜凶暴的十头魔王,
彼亚沙就是勐兰嘎的主人。

三、漂尸

彼亚沙成了召朗玛的帮手,
十头王气得浑身发抖,
他做梦也没有想到弟弟还活着,
竟然成了自己的死对头。

诡计多端的捧玛加,
急得心里就像刁猫抓,
他想阻止住召朗玛的进攻,
气急中想出一个退兵的办法。

他把会变相换形的月雅嘎喊来,
要它变成南西拉美丽的人形,
让它装作不堪折磨跳海的样子,
让尸体顺着海水漂向猴子营地。

月雅嘎摇身变成死去的南西拉,
顺着滚滚的波浪向远方漂去,
召朗玛在海边洗澡游泳,
发现蓝色的水中漂着一具女尸。

第十四章 战前 Chapter 14 Before The War

Zhao Langma and Biyasha made their oaths solemnly
That they will be honest with each other and work together.
If the ferocious ten-headed king was defeated in the future,
Biyasha would be the new master of the Kingdom of Langa.

III Floating Corpse

Knowing Biyasha had become Zhao Langma's assistant,
The ten-headed king shuddered with great anger.
He never imagined that his brother was still alive,
And even turned himself into his deadly foe.

The crafty ten-headed King of Pengmajia,
He was agitated as if his heart was scratched by a cat.
Trying to work on a plot to stop Zhao Langma's attack,
He hit on a plan in his desperation to get enemies retreated.

He called in Yueyaga who knew the trick of transformation.
He asked her to transform into the beautiful Nan Xila,
And pretend to jump into the sea out of desperation.
Then her body would float to the camps of the monkeys.

Yueyaga transformed herself into dead Nan Xila,
Her body floated with the wavy tide to the camps.
Zhao Langma was taking a bath by the beach,
And he spotted a female corpse on the blue water.

身材像南西拉一样颀长苗条,
脸庞像南西拉一样俊俏端正,
发丝像南西拉一样乌黑光亮,
脸色像南西拉一样嫩细白净。

召朗玛顿觉天昏地暗,
恰似万箭穿过胸肺,
他把死去的爱妻抱到岸边,
号啕大哭,满脸眼泪。

"南西拉啊,我的妻子,
你为什么把眼睛紧闭,
我们到处将你寻觅,
难道就得到这个结局?

"我们穿过阴暗的森林,
我们涉过寒冷的河水,
经历了多少艰难和辛酸,
承受了多少痛苦和伤悲。

"鲜花开放的时候,
我眼前出现你的笑脸,
乌云笼罩的日子,
我心中感到你的温暖。

"历尽千辛万苦找到了你的下落,
满怀着希望与你幸福地会合,
谁知迎接我的不是你的欢笑,
竟是你被残害的冰凉的躯壳。

第十四章 战前 Chapter 14 Before The War

The slim body looked like Nan Xila;
The pretty face looked like Nan Xila.
The same dark and shining long hair
And the same tender and ivory skin.

Zhao Langma felt his world turned upside down,
He seemed to be penetrated with thousands of arrows.
He held his dead wife and put her on the beach,
He burst into loud sobs with bitter tears all over his face.

"Oh, Nan Xila, my dear wife,
Why you closed your eyes so tight?
We have been searching you everywhere,
How can things end like this?

"We have walked through the dark forest together;
We have trekked through the freezing cold rivers.
Together we have experienced so much hardship;
Together we endured all the sorrows and griefs.

"When the flowers are blooming,
I see your face among those flowers;
When the sky is covered with dark clouds,
The thought of you warmly brightens my heart.

"We finally got to know your whereabouts after so much hardship.
My heart was full of hope for the happiness of our reunion.
But how can I expect what awaits me is not your smile
But your cold body and the bitter truth of your death.

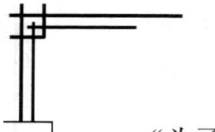

"为了你我才到处奔走,
为了你我才大动干戈,
你死了我来到还有何用,
满心的希望全成了泡沫。"

召朗玛的眼泪洗刷着尸体,
哀伤的哭声久久不停,
"他们竟然下了这样的狠心,
是不是阿努曼的鲁莽行为造成?

"他放火把允兰嘎烧成灰烬,
十头王就拿你泄愤,
把你推进海洋淹死,
用你脆弱的生命抵偿仇恨。"

阿努曼带着猴群闻声赶来,
站在一旁审慎观察,
"英明的召朗玛,
这不像你的妻子南西拉。

"南西拉曾表示要耐心等待你,
绝不会突然轻生自杀,
贪淫好色的捧玛加,
怎舍得杀害到手的南西拉。

"可能是他指使妖怪变的把戏,
来扰乱军心把你欺诈,
他妄图欺骗我们,
让我们撤离勐兰嘎。"

第十四章 战前 Chapter 14 Before The War

"I searched all over the world just to find you;
I waged the war only in the wish to get you back.
All these mean nothing now that you are dead.
My hope and dreams now evaporate into thin air."

Tears from Zhao Langma drenched the body,
He couldn't help himself but kept crying sadly.
"How could they be so brutal to make such a crime?
Or did Anuman's blunt action lead to your death?

"He set fire and burnt down the city of Langa,
So the ten-headed king took the revenge on you.
He pushed you into the sea and got you drowned,
He sought his revenge with your fragile life."

Getting the news, Anuman came with his soldiers,
He stood by calmly and watched carefully.
"Wise Zhao Langma, think twice.
This one doesn't look like your wife Nan Xila.

"Nan Xila once said that she would wait for you patiently.
She would never give up and commit suicide.
While Pengmajia is licentious and lusty for beauties,
He wouldn't kill Nan Xila who was already at his hand.

It is possible that he used a demon to play tricks,
So that you might be fooled and your army be disturbed.
He attempted to take us in with the trick,
So that we will retreat from the Kingdom of Langa."

召朗玛听了将信将疑，
请彼亚沙来占卜算卦，
彼亚沙翻开万能的天书，
立刻认出它是吃人的妖怪月雅嘎。

召朗玛还是心存疑虑，
坚持要按照古老的风俗火葬，
万一真的是妻子南西拉，
好让她的灵魂进入天堂。

猴兵把尸体放在干柴上，
火光把蓝色的海水照亮，
月雅嘎害怕大火烧毁灵魂，
随着袅袅浓烟升到天上。

这躲不过阿努曼的神眼，
它纵身跳上天空紧追月雅嘎，
月雅嘎一看难以逃脱，
回过身来同阿努曼厮打。

女妖哪里是阿努曼的对手，
阿努曼一下就抓住它的双脚，
把它从天上摔到地下，
然后对召朗玛大声说道：

"如果它是你亲爱的妻子，
如果它是美丽的南西拉，
现在我把它抓来交给你了，
你就把它领回家去吧！"

第十四章 战前 Chapter 14 Before The War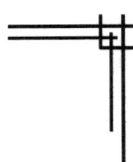

Zhao Langma was still doubtful at hearing this.
He decided to ask Biyasha to do the divination.
Biyasha opened his omnipotent prophet book,
Immediately he knew it was Yueyaga, the monster who ate human.

Zhao Langma had doubt in his heart.
He insisted on following old custom to get the body cremated
Just in case that one were really his wife Nan Xila.
Then her soul could at least rest in heaven.

The monkeys put the corpse onto the dry woods,
The roaring flames lit up the blue sea.
Yueyaga was afraid that her soul might be burnt,
Her spirit escaped and floated into the air with thick smoke.

This could not run out of Anuman's sharp eyes.
He jumped into the sky and chased Yueyaga.
Seeing that she couldn't get away from his chasing,
Yueyaga turned her back and started to grapple Anuman.

How could the female demon be Anuma's match?
All at once, Anuman caught her by her feet.
And he threw her down to the ground from the sky.
Then he spoke to Zhao langma loudly,

"If this one were your dear wife,
If this demon were pretty Nan Xila,
Now I have got her and gave her to you.
Why not take it back home with you?"

悔恨自己感情脆弱分不清真假,
召朗玛低着头说不出话,
他在大家面前感到羞愧,
回到帐篷悄悄把自己责骂。

猴子兵围着披头散发的月雅嘎,
嘲笑它以假乱真还是逃不脱惩罚。
阿努曼一拳结束了它的性命,
一脚把它踢下海边的悬崖。

四、劝降

召朗玛的大军在海边驻扎,
一个月来天天操练兵马,
一切事情都准备就绪了,
才选定日子向勐兰嘎进发。

心胸如同火烧的旺果,
手脚早已发痒的嘎林,
恨不得快点打仗,
和十头王交锋比个输赢。

胸襟宽阔的召朗玛,
一一劝说它们冷静:
"勐兰嘎已被我们围困,
神圣的战争一定要先礼后兵。

第十四章 战前 Chapter 14 Before The War

Knowing that he had made a mistake out of blind passion,
Zhao Langma lowered his head without saying anything.
He felt ashamed in front of the monkey soldiers,
And he sneaked back to his tent and scolded himself.

The monkey soldiers surrounded ruffle-haired Yueyaga,
Laughing at her for her bogus imitation and failed trick.
With one punch Anuman killed the demon,
And he kicked it off the cliff into the sea.

IV Persuasion To Surrender

The troops were still stationed by the seaside.
They had practiced marching and fighting for a month.
After making sure that everything was ready,
They chose a good day to march to the Kingdom of Langa.

Wangguo was filled with the burning fires in his heart;
Galin was so anxious that he felt his hands and feet itchy.
They couldn't wait to start the battle
And fight with the ten-headed king to see who is the winner.

Zhao Langma was a leader with great vision.
He persuaded them to stay calm one by one.
"The Kingdom of Langa has already besieged by us.
A holy war should start with appropriate etiquette.

"我们不是要侵占勐兰嘎的领土,
我们不忍心让无辜的百姓血流成河,
我要先派人去与捧玛加谈判,
再决定是战还是和。

"如果十头王把南西拉送还给我,
我们就把大军撤回本国,
如果他仍然执迷不悟,
我们再用武力惩罚他的罪恶。"

猴王嘎林赞同召朗玛的主意说:
"应派一个人前去劝他投降,
阿努曼曾火烧兰嘎城不宜再去,
再去定会惹起一场血战。

"这次去同十头王打交道,
我的侄子旺果较为恰当,
因为它的父亲与捧玛加相识,
捧玛加曾败在巴力莫的手上。"

召朗玛同意派旺果做使臣,
旺果一跃便在空中消失,
黎明时它大摇大摆走进允兰嘎的宫殿,
又用长尾巴给自己绕成一个宝座。

第十四章 战前 Chapter 14 Before The War

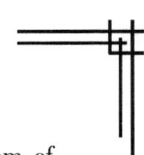

"We are not here to occupy the territory of the Kingdom of Langa;

I would rather not see blood shedding from the innocent people.

I will send my envoy to negotiate with Pengmajia firstly

Then I will decide if we should resort to force or peace.

"If the ten-headed king returned my Nan Xila to me,

We will retreat our troops and go back to our kingdom.

If he still doesn't repent and go on with wrongdoings,

We will surely punish him with our swords and knives."

The monkey king Galin agreed with Zhao Langma,

"We had better send someone to persuade him to surrender.

Anuman has set fire on Langa city so he is not supposed to go.

If he is sent, there will be surely another bloody fight.

"Who could be the one to deal with the ten-headed King?

I think my niece Wangguo is an ideal candidate.

His father Balimo was an acquaintance of Pengmajia.

Pengmajia had been once defeated by Balimo."

Zhao Langma agreed to send Wangguo as the envoy.

Wangguo jumped into the sky and disappeared.

He swaggered into the palace at dawn.

And he used his long tail to make a throne for himself.

宝座和十头王的一样高大厚实，
神气十足的旺果盘腿坐着，
捧玛加上朝时见了暗暗吃惊，
不由得对白猴厉声吆喝：

"哪里闯来的白猴子，
竟敢占据我的宝座？"
"我坐的是我的尾巴呀，
难道自己身上的肉也不能坐？"

捧玛加一时发了愣，
回过神来才又重新发问：
"你到底是来干什么的？
不说清楚可就别怪我心狠。"

旺果微微合掌：
"勐兰嘎威严的国王啊，
你曾和我的父亲巴力莫在空中作过较量，
怎么连老朋友都已忘却？

"无比神威的父王饶了你的性命，
你曾许下了做一辈子朋友的誓约，
父王临终时嘱咐我继续做你的朋友，
现在我怎能不管你的死活？

第十四章 战前 Chapter 14 Before The War

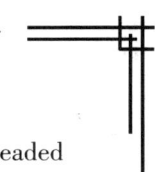

The throne was of the same height as that of the ten-headed king,

The dignified-looking Wangguo sat cross-legged on it.

Pengmajia was shocked to see him on the way to his court.

He shouted to the white monkey harshly,

"Who the hell is the intruding white monkey?

How dare you occupy and sit on my throne?"

"What I am sitting on is my own tail,

Can't I sit on my own flesh?"

For a while, Pengmajia got dumbfounded.

When he got himself together, he asked again,

"Why on earth are you here?

You'd better have a good reason or I will teach you a good lesson."

Wangguo folded his palms and bowed,

"The mighty King of Langa,

You and my father had once had a fight in the sky.

How can you forget an old friend of yours?

"My father spared your life that time

And you promised to be friend ever since.

I was told to be your friend by my father before he died

So how can I leave you alone when you are approaching death?

"勐兰嘎已被召朗玛的大军重重围困,
眼看就要爆发可怕的战争,
召朗玛派我来同你谈判,
要求你把他的妻子南西拉送还。

"我父亲的厉害你已尝过,
它也在召朗玛的箭下升上天国,
你的姑奶奶和两个表叔,
也没有从召朗玛的手下逃脱。

"你要忏悔过去的罪恶,
别再一意孤行招惹灾祸,
要是你妄自尊大不听劝说,
就会粉身碎骨自食其果。"

捧玛加听后暴跳如雷说:
"我是威望无比的十头王,
人世间没有谁能和我相比,
我怎能同低贱的猴子交往。

"召朗玛有什么力量和本事?
他还抵不上我左手的小拇指,
我轻轻放个屁,
也能把猴兵猴将冲到天边摔死。

第十四章 战前 Chapter 14 Before The War

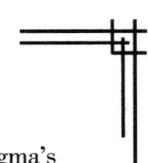

"Langa has been surrounded tightly by Zhao Langma's troops.

A terrible war is at your door step now.

I was sent by Zhao Langma to do the negotiation,

Asking you to hand Nan Xila back to him.

"You know how tough my father was.

But he was shot to death by Zhao Langma's arrow.

Your grandma and two uncles

Also lost their lives at the hand of that warrior.

"It is time for you to repent on your wrongdoings.

Stop your wanton action and don't incur disasters.

If you are still too arrogant and overweening to take my advice,

You are inviting self-destruction and will be smashed to pieces."

Hearing this, Pengmajia burst into fury,

"I am the majestic ten-headed king,

There is no rival for me in the whole world.

How can I demean myself to negotiate with a monkey?

"What tricks does Zhao Langma have to win me?

He is as little as my fifth finger of my left hand.

With just the stench from my fart

The monkeys will be blown away and choked to death.

"你竟敢在我面前说大话,
我要把你剁成肉泥,
就算你插上一百对翅膀,
今天也逃脱不了死亡的下场。"

捧玛加狠狠地咒骂一顿,
气得把宝座猛烈捶击,
高声叫来武官贡巴嘎和贡巴吉兄弟,
让他们把猴子拉出去处死。

他们架着旺果的左右手,
飞也似的跑出宫去,
他们的力气胜过十头大象,
他们架着旺果边走边商量:

"我俩把白猴子抛上高空,
让它重重砸在岩石上,
粉身碎骨成肉泥,
我们再把猴肉的滋味品尝。"

两兄弟喜滋滋地走出城门,
刚要动手抛杀猴子,
旺果冷不防甩开他们的手臂,
抓住他俩纵身飞上九霄云里。

左手举起贡巴嘎,
右手举起贡巴吉,
把兄弟俩掷下地,
两个小子跌成两滩泥。

第十四章 战前 Chapter 14 Before The War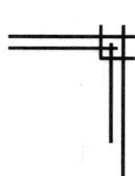

"You have guts to brag in my face.
Today I will have you chopped and smashed.
Even if you had one hundred pairs of wings
You are doomed to be executed here and now."

Pengmajia showered his bitter curses
Pounding his fists on his throne angrily.
He called in his general Gongbaga and Gongbaji, the brothers,
Ordering them to take away the monkey and have him executed.

Each of them clasping one of Wangguo's hands,
They rushed out of the palace hurriedly.
They were more powerful than ten elephants together,
And they discussed how to kill Wangguo as they walked out,

"We can toss this white monkey into the sky.
He will land on the rocks with a big bang,
And he will be smashed to thousands of pieces.
Then we can have a taste of the monkey meat."

The brothers went out the gate gladly.
Just when they were about to toss the monkey,
Wangguo unexpectedly got away out of their clasping.
And he snatched them and flew high into the sky.

Gongbaga was in his left hand;
Gongbaji in his right hand.
Then Wangguo tossed down the two brothers,
Who fell down onto the ground and turned into meat puree.

旺果乘机飞进宫殿的花园，
悄悄钻进南西拉居住的塔楼里，
它把召朗玛和腊嘎纳跨海的消息，
告诉孤独愁苦的南西拉。

勇敢的旺果飞回自己的阵地，
把劝降经过禀告召朗玛，
召朗玛见谈判要不回南西拉，
下令全军准备进攻允兰嘎。

五、劫营

两兄弟被杀死后，
十头王叫来自己的儿子歪亚拉，
吩咐他施展妖法去劫营，
偷偷捉拿召朗玛和腊嘎纳。

神通广大的歪亚拉连夜出动，
像一只老鹰钻进召朗玛的兵营，
歪亚拉念出咒语吐出黑气，
召朗玛的官兵东倒西歪昏昏沉沉。

歪亚拉抓起沉睡不醒的召朗玛兄弟，
朝远处的海岸飞去，
他把两人关在岩石上的木笼里，
洋洋得意，一阵狂喜。

第十四章 战前 Chapter 14 Before The War

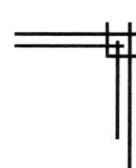

Wangguo then flew into the garden of the palace,
And he sneaked into the tower where Nan Xila lived.
He informed the miserable Nan Xila of the news
That Zhao Langma and Lagana had crossed the sea to rescue her.

The brave Wangguo flew back to his camping ground.
He reported what had happened between him and Pengmajia.
Zhao Langma knew negotiation couldn't work, so he ordered
The whole troops to get ready to attack the Kingdom of Langa.

V   Sneaking into the Camp

After hearing the news of the death of the two brothers,
The ten-headed king called in his son Waiyala, ordering him
To use his magic tricks to sneak into enemy's camp
And capture Zhao Langma and his brother Lagana.

Waiyala, who had magic power, left the palace at night.
He slipped into Zhao Langma's camp like an eagle.
Waiyala cast his spells and spat out dark clouds,
Then Zhao Langma' sentries got dizzy and fell asleep.

Snatching the tranced Zhao Langma brothers,
Waiyala flew hurriedly to the beach far away.
He put them in a wooden cages on the rocks,
And he laughed loudly with ecstasy and elation.

597

"这是桌上的肉砧板上的鱼,
我在漆黑的夜里不把他们处死①,
我现在先回王宫睡觉,
待明日再把他们扔进锅里炮制。"

当东方微微现出曙光,
彼亚沙一个人醒了过来,
全军呼呼大睡使他吃惊,
四处寻找不见了召朗玛两兄弟。

守卫他俩的人密如树桩,
左边睡着嘎林、旺果和嘎木达,
右边睡着摩米、阿努曼和玛尼腊,
统帅失踪竟然无人觉察。

彼亚沙立即卜卦,
马上看出是歪亚拉使了魔法,
只等明天海面上升起太阳,
召朗玛兄弟俩就将被煮成肉汤。

彼亚沙把全体官兵喊醒,
大家急得犹如烈火烧心,
嘎林派阿努曼立即启程,
用闪电的速度去挽救两人的生命。

---

① 傣族规矩,晚上不杀人。在晚上杀人看不清楚,怕出差错。

第十四章 战前 Chapter 14 Before The War

"These two guys are the meat on the chopping board now,
But they can not be killed in the dark at night.①
I will return to the palace to take a rest now.
Tomorrow I will put them in the pot and boil them."

At dawn the eastern sky was lit up by the rising sun.
Biyasha alone woke up and he was surprised
To see the whole troop had fallen into deep sleep.
Nowhere could he find the Zhao Langma brothers.

The sentries were allotted like thick trees around Zhao Langma.
Galin, Wangguo and Gamuda stationed to the left,
With Momi, Anuman and Manila protecting at the right side.
But nobody knew that their chief-commander had disappeared at all.

Biyasha hurried to make a divination,
Immediately he knew it was Waiyala's magic trick.
And he also knew once the sun rose above the sea,
Zhao Langma brothers would be boiled in the boiling pot.

Biyasha woke up the whole troops,
Everyone got worried as if flame burned in their hearts.
Galin asked Anuman to start out immediately
To rescue Zhao Langma brothers with the speed of lightning.

---

① The tradition of the Dai is that no one should be killed during night for fear of killing the wrong person since it's too dark to see clearly at night.

阿努曼像风一样往前飞奔,
太阳正在海面上冉冉上升,
阿努曼急忙转身扑向太阳,
扯下一块黑云把太阳裹紧。

它双手抓住太阳使劲摇晃,
迫使它退回深深的海洋,
霎时漆黑的云雾又遮盖大地,
只有星星在天上闪光。

召朗玛兄弟俩被曙光唤醒,
发现自己被紧捆关在木笼里,
突然天地又坠入一片黑暗,
两兄弟非常诧异和惊恐。

阿努曼突然跳落在岩石上,
砸开木笼替召朗玛兄弟俩松了绑,
它又返身揭开太阳身上的乌云,
太阳立即升起露出鲜红的脸庞。

歪亚拉醒来回到岸边杀俘虏,
只见召朗玛兄弟俩和阿努曼正要起飞,
他气得脸上青筋突暴杀了过去,
却被阿努曼拔起椰子树打进了海里。

第十四章 战前 Chapter 14 Before The War

Anuman flew forward as fast as wind,
While the sun started to rise to the sea level.
He turned back and rushed to the sun,
Covering it tightly with a dark cloud.

He clasped the sun and shook it with both of his hands.
The sun was forced to retreat back into the deep sea.
In a blink, the pitch darkness covered the earth,
With only the stars twinkling in the sky.

Zhao Langma brothers were waken up by the dawn light.
Now they realized they were tied up in a wood cage.
All of a sudden everything was in darkness again,
Both of them were greatly shocked and frightened.

Anuman landed on the rocks out of nowhere,
He cracked open the wooden cage and untied the brothers.
Then he returned to the sun and uncovered the dark cloud.
All of a sudden, the sun rose up with the flushing red face.

When Waiyala returned to the beach to execute his prisoners,

He only found Anuman and the brothers flying away from the rock.

He rushed forward to wrestle with them angrily,

But was swayed into the sea by the coconut tree swung by Anuman.

601

召朗玛兄弟俩遭受灾难被救回,
全靠阿努曼的勇敢和彼亚沙的智慧,
召朗玛感谢两人的忠诚,
对他们比以往更加尊敬。

第十四章 战前 Chapter 14 Before The War

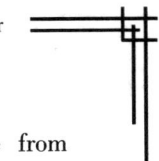

Zhao Langma brothers underwent a narrow escape from death.

It was jointly carried out by brave Anuman and wise Biyasha.

Zhao langma thanked them for their loyalty,

And he now treated them more respectfully.

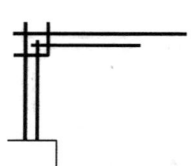

第十五章　初战

一、围城交锋

劝降等于用鸡毛拦火，
好话被当作怯懦和软弱，
十头王不但不回心转意，
反而更加狂妄、更加可恶。

只有快刀才能斩断毒蛇，
只有神箭才能征服恶魔，
要救回可怜的南西拉啊，
只有出兵一条路可以选择。

惩办凶顽的主意已经拿定，
召朗玛满怀胜利的信心，
他下达神圣的命令，
立刻向允兰嘎发起进攻。

召朗玛走出来了，
看他多么神气威风，
手持明晃晃的宝刀，
肩挎亮铮铮的神弓。

第十五章 初战 Chapter 15 The First Battle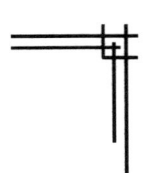

Chapter 15   The First Battle

I   The Besiege of the Langa City

Persuasion of surrender was like stopping the fire with feather
And kindness was regarded as cowardice in Pengmajia's eyes.
The ten-headed king wouldn't change his mind,
He became more vicious and haughty instead.

Only a sharp knife could slash the snake into pieces;
Only a magic arrow could conquer the demon.
To rescue the poor Nan Xila,
Launching a war is the only choice.

The decision to defeat the enemy by force was thus made.
Zhao Langma was determined and full of confidence.
He declared his orders to his troops
That the attack should be initiated right here and now.

Here marched out Zhao Langma.
He looked so prestigious and mighty.
A glistening knife was clasped in his hand,
The magic bow was carried on his shoulders.

犹如站在白云上的天将,
指挥着气势磅礴的天兵,
身边站着忠实的弟弟腊嘎纳,
眼前的兵马像无边的森林。

召朗玛亲自把兵力调配,
把大军分成四方五路纵队,
强大的兵力放在中心主攻,
进行两翼夹击四面包围。

召朗玛任命了指挥各方的首领,
详细交代了进军的路线:
"攻打允兰嘎的正中大门的任务,
交给神通广大的阿努曼。

"能卜善战的摩米做它的助手,
带足精壮的兵马数万,
一开始攻城要勇猛果敢,
犹如奔腾的洪水冲决堤岸。

"占领墙高地险的北面的任务,
交给猴王嘎林和阿哈,
迂回侧攻要快如迅雷闪电,
首先占领居高临下的宝塔。

第十五章 初战 Chapter 15 The First Battle

He looked like a heavenly general standing in the cloud,
Directing the glorious soldiers in the heaven.
His loyal younger brother Lagana guarded beside him.
The soldiers in front of them were stationed like the endless forest.

Zhao Langma allocated the troops by himself,
Dividing the troops into five sub-divisions in four directions.
The tactics was to use the main force to attack in the middle
With others to support from the flank to surround the enemy.

Zhao Langma assigned the leaders for each team.
He explained in details the marching routes,
"The task of attacking the main gate of Langa city,
Goes to Anuman, who has magic power.

"The prophet Momi will be Anuman's assistant.
They will lead thousands of elite soldiers with their horses.
The attack should be started with utmost determination.
They must attack like the rolling flood rushing out of the dam.

"The northern side of the city will be taken as a high point.
The army will be in charged by monkey King Galin and Aha.
You must attack like flash light from the flank,
The first priority is to occupy the pagoda overlooking the city.

607

"登上地势陡峻的西面的任务,
分给勇敢无畏的旺果和玛尼腊,
打通紧靠海洋的城南的任务,
交给嘎木达和腊塔。

"剩下的兵马由我和腊嘎纳指挥,
智慧的彼亚沙做我们的军师,
监视勐兰嘎的天空和海面,
防止十头王临危逃窜。

"四方五路的大军,
统一听我的号令,
行动要勇猛迅速,
要像一齐起飞的雁群。

"要在同一个时间里,
一齐围攻兰嘎城,
以太阳升起为出击时间,
隆隆的炮声就是进攻命令。"

太阳从山上升起,
炮声震撼着大地,
各路兵马一齐出动,
向宽阔的允兰嘎围去。

霎时大地一阵阵摇晃,
犹如满天的云雾翻腾,
数万威风凛凛的猴子兵,
把允兰嘎团团围困。

第十五章 初战 Chapter 15 The First Battle

"The precipice on the west side should be seized up.
This assignment goes to the dauntless Wangguo and Manila.
The south side of the city is close to the sea,
Gamuda and Lata should find a way to it.

"I am leading the remaining troops together with Lagana,
And wise Biyasha is our military consultant.
We will watch over the sky and the sea around Langa
To prevent the ten-headed king from escaping.

"All the soldiers, leaders and generals,
Follow my commands carefully.
We must act swiftly and orderly,
Just like a school of geese flying simultaneously.

"We are to act at the exactly same time
To attack and besiege the city of Langa.
The time is set at the moment of sunrise,
And the fire of gun is the signal to attack."

When the sun rose among the mountains,
The ground was trembling at the firing of the gun.
All groups initiated their attack at this moment,
They rushed forward trying to surround the city of Langa.

The earth seemed to be shaking now and then.
Dust floated like fog and clouds churning in the sky.
Tens of thousands of monkey soldiers dashed forward,
The city of Langa was being surrounded tightly.

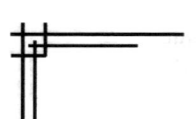

守卫允兰嘎的官兵,
急忙进宫向十头王通禀:
"就像大火烧着茅草屋顶,
战火已经烧到都城。"

捧玛加得知敌情,
迅速向全勐发布了迎击敌军的命令,
调集精锐部队投入保卫都城的战斗,
几路兵马等待着十头王的指挥。

捧玛加十双眼睛闪出红光,
命令长子英达西达出征,
由古麻帕和干塔两将辅助,
带领一支劲旅担任全军的前锋。

"你们要给进犯的敌军以致命打击,
要抓活的朗玛来见我,
我要在南西拉面前将他斩杀,
让她亲眼看见丈夫的下场。"

英达西达高傲地保证:
"父王啊,相信你的儿子吧!
我一定执行你的命令,
活捉召朗玛,杀退猴子兵。"

第十五章 初战 Chapter 15 The First Battle

The sentries guarding the city of Langa spotted the attack,
They rushed into the palace and reported it to the ten-headed King,
"Just like a flame devouring thatched roofs,
The fire of war has swept over the city."

The moment Pengmajia got informed of the situation,
He sent out an order of counterattack to all his soldiers.
The elite troops were allocated to protect the capital,
Several divisions were waiting for orders from the ten-headed King.

Ten pairs of Pengmajia's eyes glared in red flames.
He ordered his eldest son Yingdaxida to lead the troops.
With Generals Gumapa and Ganta as his assistants.
Their troops were the vanguard among the whole troops.

"You must lash the invading enemies with a fatal blow,
You must captivate Zhao Langma alive and take him to me.
I need to execute him in the face of Nan Xila.
She will witness with her own eyes the end of her husband."

Yingdaxida promised proudly,
"My dear father, please believe in your son!
I will do exactly as you have ordered,
To captivate Zhao Langma and defeat the monkey soldiers."

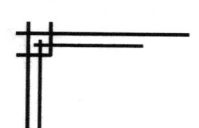

兰嘎西贺 The Ten-Headed King of Langa

三人骑着大象戴上铁帽,
举着绿绸旗幡,率领一支精兵,
风驰电掣出了城,
和召朗玛大军对阵。

所有的大路小径都严加封锁,
各个垭口洼地都栽上竹刺,
英达西达给朗玛送去木刀,
写下正式交战的通牒。

召朗玛接过木刀看着通牒,
上面写着傲慢与威胁的话:
"我父亲是威震天下的捧玛加,
我是不可战胜的英达西达。

"如果你这流浪者想活命,
就快到大王的面前跪下,
如果你胆敢同我较量,
等待你的只有死亡的下场。"

召朗玛命令兵马出阵,
一队队猴子兵冲向英达西达的兵营,
双方厮杀在一起,山摇地动,
鲜血遍地流淌,一片殷红。

第十五章 初战 Chapter 15 The First Battle

Three of them put on iron hat and rode on the elephants.

They led the most strong soldiers with green banners held high.

The troop rushed out of the city like swirls of wind,

They were to confront the Langma army directly.

All the highways and roads were barricaded,

The bamboo bayonets were buried around every valley and low lands,

Yingdaxida sent a wooden knife and an official note to Zhao Langma,

Which were the formal declaration of the war between the two armies.

Zhao Langma took the wooded knife and read the diplomatic note,

Which was full of threatening and haughty words.

"My father is the majestic Pengmajia awed by the world.

I am the invincible Yingdaxida.

"If you the wrangler want to survive,

Come and kneel down in front of me.

If you dare to fight against me,

What is waiting for you is only death."

Zhao Langma ordered his troops to start the attack,

Groups of monkey soldiers rushed into the camps of Yingdaxida.

Their fight was so fierce that the mountain and the earth trembled,

And the ground were dyed red with the blood that they shed.

英达西达和干塔拉起大弓，
射出两支神箭，声震苍穹，
阿努曼的兵马纷纷逃窜，
如同决堤的山洪。

兰嘎兵乘势紧紧追赶，
猴子兵被杀得纷纷倒下，
阿努曼和摩米见了勃然大怒，
拔起贝叶树向敌群猛打。

英达西达立即拉动大弓，
把神箭射向高高的树梢，
树叶飞落变成一根根绳索，
追上来捆绑猴子兵的手脚。

猴子兵见了慌忙逃跑，
绳索又变成椰子树粗的蟒蛇，
口吐毒舌、遍地游动，
追得猴子兵丧魂落魄。

阿努曼急中想起自己的神弓，
它射出的神箭变成遮天蔽日的巨鹰，
巨鹰的身子比老象还大，
弯弯的尖嘴把蟒蛇吃尽。

第十五章 初战 Chapter 15 The First Battle

Yingdaxida and Ganta held up a big bow,
Two arrows flew out with deafening whistling sound.
Soldiers directed by Anuman started to flee for their lives,
They rushed back like the flood out of broken banks.

Langa's soldiers took the chance to chase after them,
Lots of monkey soldiers were killed and fell down.
Seeing it, Anuman and Momi burst into fury,
They uprooted big trees and swung among the enemies.

Yingdaxida drew out his bow again.
He aimed at the top of the tree with his arrow.
The fallen leaves turned into numerous ropes.
The ropes chased the monkeys and tightened them up.

In great confusion, the monkey soldiers run for their life.
Then the ropes changed into pythons as thick as coconut tree.
They slithered all over the ground spitting out poisons,
And the monkey soldiers were chased and scared out of their wits.

The sight of this reminded Anuman of his own magic bow.
The arrow he shot turned into a gigantic eagles covering the sky.
The eagle was bigger than an old elephant,
And it ate up the pythons with its crooked peak.

英达西达的妖法失灵,
猴子兵欢呼跳跃冲进敌阵,
召朗玛指挥全线兵马,
又把允兰嘎重新包围。

嘎林和阿哈从北往南压去,
嘎木达和腊塔由南往北夹击,
旺果、玛尼腊、阿努曼在东西方猛攻,
四个战场都打得难分难解。

从北面进攻的猴王嘎林,
把一支宝箭射向允兰嘎上空,
宝箭唤来倾盆大雨,
顿时山岭、平坝爆发出滚滚山洪。

英达西达的阵地掀起波涛,
洪水的温度渐渐增高,
热流烫死烫伤敌兵过半,
残余的敌人狂叫着纷纷溃逃。

大将干塔见了大惊,
立即射出神箭飞入云层,
霎时天空卷起狂风阵阵,
把乌云吹散,热雨扫尽。

第十五章 初战 Chapter 15 The First Battle

Yingdaxida's charmed trick was defeated,
Monkey soldiers turned back to confront the enemies excitedly,
Zhao Langma reorganized all his troops,
And they surrounded the city of Langa again.

Galin and Aha moved forward from the north to the south;
Gamuda and Lata advanced from the south to north;
Wangguo, Manila and Anuman were fighting in east and west.
Armies from both sides fought fiercely in the four battle fields.

The monkey King Galin was attacking in the northern side.
He shot a magic arrow into the sky over the city of Langa.
The magic arrow brought in heavy rainfall. All of a sudden,
The flood gushed out of the mountain and down to the plain.

Waves and billows smothered the battlefield of Yingdaxida,
And the temperature of the flood started to rise sharply.
Half of the soldiers were scalded to death,
The rest of them screamed and ran for their lives.

General Ganta was shocked at the sight of it.
He shot a magic arrow into the cloud immediately.
All of a sudden, strong wind started to blow in the sky.
Then dark clouds were cleared and hot rain stopped.

狂风不停地越刮越猛,
树木纷纷响起折断声,
人仰马翻灰尘滚滚,
召朗玛的士兵寸步难行。

古麻帕乘机放出带火的神箭,
召朗玛的阵地顿时烈焰腾腾,
风助火势,火趁风劲,
猴子兵被烧得遍地打滚。

烧焦毛的猴兵边跳边跑,
猴兵的阵地开始动摇,
腊嘎纳急忙念出咒语,
天上立即降下灭火的冰雹。

冰雹变成冰凉的雨水,
滋润着猴子兵被烧伤的皮肤,
溃烂的伤口很快痊愈,
得救的猴子兵发出阵阵欢呼。

猴子兵重整旗鼓蜂拥出击,
打得敌兵措手不及后退几里,
英达西达见队伍溃败十分着急,
迅速跳上高空大施妖术。

第十五章 初战 Chapter 15 The First Battle

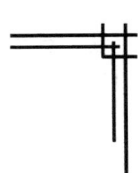

The wind became stronger and stronger.
Trees were blown broken all over the places.
Soldiers and horses couldn't stand firm on their feet.
Zhao Langma's troops were stuck on the battle ground.

Gumapa shot out his magic arrow of fire.
Flames were all over the battle field on Zhao Langma's side.
With the wind blowing harder, the fire was stronger,
The monkey soldiers were tossing and rolling in flames.

The monkeys were hopping and running with burnt fur,
The situation was out of control for the monkey soldiers.
Lagana hurried to cast his spells,
Hails were falling down to quench the fire.

Then the hails were turned into the icy raindrops.
Which cooled down the burnt skin of the monkeys.
The injuries were healed by the magic rains,
Monkey soldiers cheered for their being saved.

The monkey soldiers gathered up and charged forward again.
Their opponents couldn't hold up and had to retreat a few miles.
Seeing the withdrawing armies, Yingdaxida got anxious.
He jumped into the sky and played his magic tricks again.

顿时天上卷起黄沙，
黄沙变成刀雨从猴群头上撒落，
召朗玛急忙念出一道咒语，
千万块巨石将雨刀断成几截。

阿努曼闪电般跃上高空，
和英达西达厮杀在一起，
英达西达甩开它跃上云层，
白猴不知是计紧追过去。

英达西达拔出头发吹作长棍，
抡起棍向白猴身上猛击，
阿努曼头昏目眩跌落地上，
陷进十深的地里。

神通的摩米迅速把它救出，
用仙水灌进它的嘴里，
阿努曼像劳累时喝了凉水，
顿时苏醒浑身又有了力气。

第十五章 初战　Chapter 15　The First Battle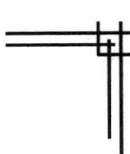

Under his spells the yellow sands appeared in the sky.

The sands turned into knives falling down on the heads of monkeys.

Zhao Langma hurriedly murmured his incantations,

Then thousands of gigantic rocks struck the knives into pieces.

Anunan hopped into the sky like a lightening,

And it started to wrestle with Yingdaxida.

Yingdaxida got rid of it and flew into the clouds;

Anuman didn't know it was a trick and it ran after him.

Yingdaxida pluck one of his hair and turned it into a long staff.

He swung the staff and hit hard on Anuman.

Anuman got dizzy and fell down to the ground.

It hit the ground so hard that it sunk into the dirt as deep as ten meters.

The powerful Momi saved Anuman out of the mud in a hurry,

And he fed magic water into Anuman's mouth.

Anuman came to life and regained his strength immediately

As if he had drunk sweet spring water and relieved his fatigue.

古麻帕向受伤的阿努曼冲来，
摩米迎面向他射出一箭，
前锋的副手古麻帕中箭死亡，
吓得士兵们纷纷扭头逃窜。

二、击毙英达西达

十头王看到初战失利，
慌忙向勐松攀和勐雅哈求援，
要两勐的兵马赶快开来，
把压境的召朗玛的兵马赶走。

两勐的队伍即时赶到，
统帅援军的是勇敢的武官干塔，
他们的利箭射死猴子兵成千上万，
召朗玛的阵地一片混乱。

摩米背来山里的草药，
把死伤的猴子兵救活，
阿努曼带着旺果、阿哈、嘎木达冲上敌阵，
敌兵在它们的刀棒前一排排倒下。

双方展开了肉搏战，
直杀得天昏地暗，烟尘滚滚，
鲜血染红了花草和树叶，
太阳和月亮吓得躲进云中发抖。

第十五章 初战 Chapter 15 The First Battle

Gumapa dashed forward to the injured Anuman,
Momi aimed at him and shot his arrow.
The vanguard assistant Gumapa was shot to death;
His soldiers got frightened and turned back to flee for their lives.

Ⅱ Yingdaxida Was Killed

The ten-headed king saw he lost the battle in the first round,
He resorted to kingdom of Songpan and Yaha for assistance,
Asking them to send their troops to help as soon as possible
So that the joined armies could drive Zhao Langma's troops away.

Helpers from the two kingdoms arrived in time.
They were led by the brave general Ganta.
They shot thousands of monkeys to death;
Battlefield on Zhao Langma's side became chaotic.

Moni carried the herbs from the mountains,
The Injured and dead monkeys were saved by his magic herbs.
Anuman led Wangguo, Aha and Gamuda to charge forward,
Rows of enemies fell down like grass under the blades.

The two sides started their one-on-one combat,
The killing lasted till the sky was covered by the dust.
Grass and flowers were stained by the blood;
The sun and the moon hid their faces in the clouds.

诡计多端的英达西达，
摇身变成天上神明的英达，
骑着宝象从天空飞下，
妄想欺骗善良的召朗玛。

"天王玛哈捧派遣我天神英达，
下凡来帮助他的儿子捧玛加，
你们出兵兰嘎丧尽天良，
定要受到天神的重重惩罚。

"我要举起神斧击出雷电，
把你们全都劈碎、轰死，
要是你们还想活命，
就赶快撤兵回勐基沙去。"

召朗玛看见这个凶恶的天神，
心中涌起了一团团疑云：
"贤明的英达为什么相助捧玛加？
我要叫彼亚沙卜算是真是假。"

彼亚沙翻开神圣的天书，
把真相看清了，告诉召朗玛：
"他哪里是什么英达，
是我的侄子英达西达。"

猴王嘎林也看清这是一个假神，
就拉开大弓射出神箭，
神箭射穿了象背上的金鞍，
金鞍被击碎成一块块碎片。

第十五章 初战　Chapter 15　The First Battle

The tricky Yingdaxida got an idea,
He turned himself into Yingda, the wise heavenly god.
He landed on the battle ground on his elephant,
Attempting to fool the kind-hearted Zhao Langma.

"I was sent here by the heavenly god Mahapeng.
He asked me to help his son Pengmajia.
You are ruthless and shameless waging a war against Langa,
So you will be severely punished by heavenly gods in heaven.

"I will use my magic axe to strike up thunders and lightening,
Each one of you will be smashed and die from them.
If you still want to stay alive,
You must now retreat and go back to Jisha."

Zhao Langma looked at this ferocious-looking god,
Doubts started to surge in his mind.
"How come the wise Yingda wants to assist Pengmajia?
I need Biyasha to divine and tell me the truth."

Biyasha opened his sacred prophet book.
Then he knew the truth and informed Zhao Langma,
"He isn't Yingda at all;
He is just my nephew Yingdaxida."

The monkey King Galin also knew this was a trick.
He held up his bow and aimed at Yingdaxida.
The magic arrow penetrated through the gold saddle on the elephant,
And it was shot broken and shattered into pieces.

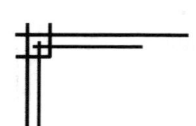

英达西达露了马脚，
慌忙掉转象头逃跑，
腊嘎纳急忙拉弓射出利箭，
三十三个头的宝象被拦腰射穿。

英达西达恼羞成怒，
跃上天空用身子把太阳遮住，
霎时电闪雷鸣天地一片漆黑，
大雨滂沱把猴子兵淹没。

召朗玛感到十分吃惊，
忙把彼亚沙叫来询问，
彼亚沙回答说：
"这是我侄儿英达西达施展的魔法。

"只有生来未接触过女性的男人，
才能瞥见在黑暗中作祟的魔影，
只有连续十二年不见女人面庞的青年，
才能用神箭把隐身的妖魔射下。"

彼亚沙说出他侄子的奥秘，
召朗玛急得半天想不出办法，
"除了在森林里修行的帕拉西，
上哪去找连续十二年不看女人脸庞的男人？"

第十五章 初战　Chapter 15　The First Battle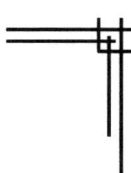

Yingdaxida knew his trick had failed,
Hurriedly, he turned the elephant around trying to escape.
Lagana drew out his bow and started to shoot,
The elephant with thirty three heads were shot into halves.

Yingdaxida felt humiliated and furious.
He jumped into the sky and covered the sun with his body.
All of a sudden the world became pitch dark with deafening thunders.
The heavy rain poured down and almost got the monkeys drowned.

Zhao Langma was so shocked at the sight of it.
He sent for Biyasha and asked what had happened.
Biyasha took a look at the sky and replied,
"That was the trick from my niece Yingdaxida.

"Only a man who has never touched a female can see
The devil hidden in the darkness. And only a young man
Who has never seen a female's face for consecutive twelve years
Can use the magic bow to shoot the hidden devil dead."

After Biyasha unveiled the secrets of his nephew,
Zhao Langma was anxious but could not find a way out.
"Except Palaxi who is practicing Buddhism in the forest,
Where else can I find such a young man under the sky?"

弟弟腊嘎纳站出来说道：
"请哥哥不必焦虑愁闷，
你的弟弟就是这样的人，
腊嘎纳可以向苍天保证。

"我们离开繁华的都城十二年，
十二年来我从未看过女人的脸。"
召朗玛听了立即反驳他：
"你说的不是老实话。

"我们离开宫殿出走一路同行，
难道忘了有你的嫂嫂南西拉？
南西拉时时在你的眼前，
我去追赶金鹿也是你守护着她。"

宝石般的腊嘎纳答道：
"不是我把这一切遗忘，
自从离开我们的国家，
我把哥嫂当作父母一样。

"每当嫂嫂在我面前，
我都是低着头做事，
只见到她的脚尖，
从来没有看过她的脸。

"弟弟坐在嫂嫂的旁边，
也从不斜着瞟她一眼，
所以十二年我没看过女人的脸庞，
弟弟的品性经得起检验。"

第十五章 初战 Chapter 15 The First Battle

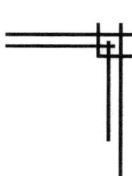

His younger brother Lagana stood up and said,
"Don't worry, my dear elder brother.
I am the one you are looking for.
And I can make an oath in the name of heaven.

"We have left our prosperous capital for twelve years.
I haven't seen the face of any female during the twelve years."
Zhao Langma retorted him immediately,
"What you have told us is not true.

"We travelled together after we left the palace.
Haven't you forgotten your sister-in-law was there with us?
Nan Xila was in front of you from time to time,
You stayed to protect her when I was away chasing the golden deer."

Jade-like Lagana answered,
"I haven't forgotten anything
Ever since we had left our kingdom.
I treated you two as my parents.

"Each time my sister-in-law was in front of me,
I always kept my head lowered doing something.
I saw only the tips of her feet.
And I have never cast one look at her face.

"When I sat beside my sister-in-law,
I have never glanced at her either. I promise you
I haven't seen the face of any female in the last twelve years.
My character stands up to any test."

629

听了这番忠实的表白,
召朗玛愁云顿开转忧为喜,
"如果是真的,你就抬头看看,
英达西达隐匿在哪里?"

腊嘎纳仰起头向天穹仔细瞭望,
看清英达西达用身子遮住红日,
他正挥舞长刀击出雷电,
撕碎了黑云洒下暴雨。

腊嘎纳用手指着告诉召朗玛:
"他正站在我们的头顶上,
顺着我的手指看过去,
就可以看到他的身影。"

召朗玛的脸贴着弟弟的手腕,
朝他指的方向仔细观看,
但召朗玛什么都没有看见,
眼前只是一片望不透的黑暗。

召朗玛只得把弓塔弩搭在弟弟背上,
顺着他的手指射出宝箭,
宝箭穿过阴霾云雾飞向太阳,
正中英达西达的身上。

第十五章 初战 Chapter 15 The First Battle

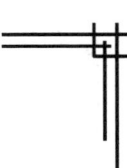

After hearing the loyal confession from Lagana,
Zhao Langma was not worried any more. Joyfully he asked,
"If what you have told us is true,
Look up and find where Yingdaxida is hiding."

Lagana raised his head and looked up into the sky carefully.
He saw that Yingdaxida was using his body to block the sun.
He was waving his long knife and striking up thunders and lightening.
The dark clouds were torn into pieces and became the pouring rain.

Lagana pointed at Yingdaxida and told Zhao Langma,
"He is standing above our heads
If you look to the direction of my finger,
You can see his shadow in the sky."

With his face close to his younger brother's wrist,
Zhao Langma looked carefully at the direction as his brother said.
But Zhao Langma could not see anything in the sky.
There is only endless darkness in front of him.

Zhao Langma could only put the arrow on the back of his brother,
He shot the arrow at the direction that his brother signaled.
The magic arrow flew to the sun through the darkness,
It hit exactly on the body of Yingdaxida.

631

英达西达惨叫一声断成两截，
从四千万约的高空掉落，
顿时云破天开太阳重放光芒，
猴子兵拍手欢呼、高声歌唱……

第十五章 初战 Chapter 15 The First Battle

With one miserable cry Yingdaxida was shot into two pieces,

He fell down from the sky as high as four thousand Yues.

Suddenly the sunlight penetrated through the thick clouds,

Monkey soldiers clasped their hands and started to sing and dance…

第十六章　破敌

一、衮纳帕出阵

大儿子英达西达丧了命，
就像断了捧玛加的右臂，
勐兰嘎的威力减少了一半，
十头王悲愤得暴跳如雷。

他纵身跳下宝座，
挥舞着宝刀大喊大叫，
他击起大鼓把众臣僚招来，
要他们赶快去把衮纳帕找来参战。

"我十头王有满腹的血海深仇，
亲人的血不能白流，
你们立刻去岩洞里把衮纳帕叫醒，
要他火速来帮我击溃敌军。"

第十六章 破敌 Chapter 16 The Enemy Defeated

Chapter 16   The Enemy Defeated

I   The Joining of Gunnapa in the Battle

The ten-headed king's eldest son was killed in the battle,
For Pengmajia it was like having lost his right arm.
The power of the kingdom of Langa was diminished by half,
Pengmajia got so mad that he stamped with rage.

He jumped down from his throne waving his sword,
He shouted loudly and pounded,
On the drum to summon his generals and officials.
They were ordered to go and find Gunnapa to join the battle.

"Now the debts are too heavy for my enemies to pay.
The blood of my family shouldn't be shed at no cost.
You must find Gunnapa in the cave and wake him up right now.
He needs to come back and help defeat our enemies."

派出的将士在岩洞里找到衮纳帕，
他还仰卧在里面昏睡沉沉，
鼾声犹如隆隆的雷鸣，
岩洞四壁震荡着回声。

人们对着他的两只大耳朵，
敲响了震天动地的大鼓大锣，
使劲吹起尖厉的牛角号，
衮纳帕纹丝不动，鼾声大作。

大家拿来一根竹竿，
插进他的耳朵内，
任凭怎样搅动拨弄，
衮纳帕仍旧呼呼大睡。

士兵们挑来四十挑烈酒，
士兵们挑来四十挑辣子，
一起灌进衮纳帕的鼻孔里，
又用烧红的铁柱杵进去。

辣酒浓烟呛得鼻子发痒，
衮纳帕猛打了一个喷嚏，
铁柱从鼻孔里喷出来，
把十几个士兵当场砸死。

第十六章 破敌 Chapter 16 The Enemy Defeated

The messengers went and found Gunnapa.
He was still in his deep sleep inside the cave.
The sounds of his snoring were like thunders,
Which were reverberating against the cave walls.

They moved in the big drums and big gongs,
Which were put near his ears and pounded loudly.
The horn trumpet was blown in high pitches,
But Gunnapa still snored and did not budge at all.

They brought a bamboo pole,
Then poked it into the ears of Gunnapa.
However hard they stirred in his ears,
Gunnapa still snorted loudly in his deep sleep.

Soldiers carried forty loads of liquor,
They carried another forty baskets of chilies.
They poured the liquor into his nostrils together with the chili;
At last they poked the hot iron staff into his nostrils.

The pungent mixture of liquor and smoke got Gunnap's nose itchy.
All of a sudden, he sneezed loudly.
The iron staff flew out of his nostrils,
And it hit and killed a dozen soldiers.

637

衮纳帕终于睁开了眼,
边伸懒腰边打呵欠:
"我刚睡下不久,睡得多甜,
才睡个半饱呵,谁给我捣乱?"

领头的武官急忙禀告:
"神圣的勐兰嘎遭到了灾难,
猴子兵已把允兰嘎严密包围,
大王捧玛加派我们来请你回去参战。

"我饿得肚皮贴着脊背,
赶快给我准备一顿美餐。"
武官说:"威武的捧玛加正在焦急万分,
等着您迅速赶回宫廷。

"今天早晨白雾消散后,
召朗玛的大军就要攻城,
召朗玛的猴子兵千千万,
你赶快去捉拿猴子充饥。"

衮纳帕听了十分高兴,
急忙起身走出岩洞,
跟着官兵回到都城,
向哥哥捧玛加请战出兵。

第十六章 破敌 Chapter 16 The Enemy Defeated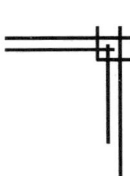

At last Gunnapa opened his eyes.
He stretched himself while yawning,
"I just laid down and slept for a while.
Who is messing around when I am still in my dream?"

The leader of the officials came up and reported,
"Our Kingdom of Langa is undergoing a disaster,
The monkey soldiers have surrounded the city of Langa.
Our King Pengmajia sent us here asking you to fight for the country.

"I am almost starved to death.
Hurry up and prepare a feast for me now."
The leader replied, "Majestic Pengmajia is in great anxiety.
He is waiting for you to go back to the palace as soon as possible.

"This morning, when the fog is cleared,
Zhao Langma's troops are to invade into our city.
There are tens of thousands of monkeys in the troop,
You can have a feast on the battlefield eating those monkeys."

Gunnapa was excited to hear that.
He hurried to get up and walked out of the cave.
Following the officials and soldiers, he came back to the capital city.
Then he asked Pengmajia to let him lead the army and fight the war.

十头王见了弟弟高兴万分,
向他详细述说了敌情,
派勇敢的苏列亚协助,
让衮纳帕率领全军出征。

九声炮响震得大地发抖,
苏列亚领兵首先冲下城楼,
召朗玛下令全线出击,
猴子兵如汹涌的波涛此起彼伏。

战斗进行得十分激烈,
苏列亚的队伍伤亡惨重,
鲜血淹没了战马的脚蹄,
到处堆积着士兵的尸体。

苏列亚率领残部退回兰嘎城,
威武凶猛的衮纳帕出阵,
他像一座黑山似地压过去,
大吼一声山摇地动海水翻腾。

他饿得肚子咕咕地叫,
径直闯进了猴子兵的阵地,
他发疯似的抓住猴子就塞进嘴,
想填饱圆鼓鼓的大肚皮。

衮纳帕的耳洞有三宽,
鼻孔像两个幽深的山洞,
吞进去的猴子从耳鼻逃出,
肚里的猴子跑得无影无踪。

第十六章 破敌 Chapter 16 The Enemy Defeated

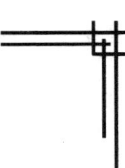

The ten-headed king was thrilled to see his brother,
And he informed him the current situation in details.
Brave Shulieya was assigned as his assistant,
And Gunnapa led the whole troops to advance into battlefield.

The nine fires of cannon shook the earth trembling.
Shulieya rushed out of the town in the very front of the army.
Zhao Langma ordered all his troops to strike out,
The monkey soldiers charged forward like surging waves.

It was another fierce battle.
Shulieya lost many of his soldiers.
The hooves of the horse were submerged in blood;
The dead bodies were lying all over the battlefield.

Shulieya led his troops to retreat back into the city of Langa.
Now the mighty and fierce Gunnapa came onto the battlefield.
He charged forward as if a dark mountain was pressing down.
His deafening roar shook the mountain and churned the sea.

He was so hungry that his stomach was rumbling.
So he broke into the line of monkey soldiers directly,
Snatching the monkeys and stuffing them into his mouth.
He just wanted to get his empty stomach full.

Gunnapa's earholes were as wide as two meters.
And his nostrils looked like two deep caves.
The monkeys in his big mouth escaped from his ears and nose,
Even those in his stomach fled and ran for their lives.

兰嘎西贺 The Ten-Headed King of Langa

衮纳帕又饿得脚软头昏，
到处找猴子虎咽狼吞，
猴子兵胆战心惊吓得发抖，
一群群向海边逃奔。

召朗玛令阿努曼去堵截逃兵，
一只猴子也不准放行，
阿努曼立刻飞到桥头，
手持宝刀威严挺立像尊石神。

溃逃的猴子兵像潮水般涌来，
它瞪圆双目大喝一声：
"衮纳帕有什么可怕的，
大家快转回去和他拼命。"

猴子兵连忙转回头，
重新集结又上阵，
它们和笨拙的衮纳帕左右周旋，
再也不到他肚里去旅行。

衮纳帕对猴子无计可施，
飞上天堂去取回他的武器，
他父亲送给他的神奇宝镖，
寄放在吉沙主拉麻尼①宝塔里。

---

① 吉沙主拉麻尼：天堂的一个地方。

第十六章 破敌　　Chapter 16　The Enemy Defeated

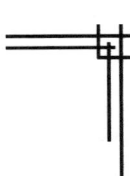

Gunnapa again felt so hungry and his legs were weak.
He kept searching for monkeys to swallow them down.
The monkey soldiers were frightened and trembling.
All of them rushed to the seaside to escape this monster.

Zhao Langma ordered Anuman to intercept the monkeys.
Not a single monkey could retreat and make one step back.
Anuman rushed to the entrance of the bridge,
Guarding with knife in his hands like an imposing statue.

The fleeing monkeys poured in like tides.
Anuman stared at them and shouted out,
"Gunnapa is nothing to be afraid of.
All of you turn back and take his life."

The monkey soldiers turned back hurriedly,
They gathered together and charged forward again.
They dodged and ducked around dumb Gunnapa
So that Gunnapa couldn't catch them putting in his mouth.

Gunnapa couldn't snatch any more monkeys,
So he flew to the heaven to fetch his weapon.
The magic flying dart was given to him by his father.
It was now stored in the pagoda of Jishazhulamani①

---

① Jishazhulamani: somewhere in heaven.

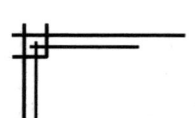

兰噶西贺 The Ten-Headed King of Langa

年深日久宝镖生了锈,
衮纳帕拿到海边去磨洗,
整整磨了七天七夜,
碧蓝的海水变得浑红如血。

站在桥头上的阿努曼,
突然发现海水由清变浑,
"海水为什么改变颜色,
这原因须要查明。"

它迅速回去报告召朗玛,
彼亚沙受命实地观察,
"有人在海边磨洗宝镖,
磨镖人就是我哥哥衮纳帕。

"宝镖是我天神父亲所赐,
还授给他十头大象的力气,
这宝镖具有无穷的神威,
他有了宝镖更是天下无敌。

"宝镖一次可杀死人无数,
飞出的宝镖还会回到他手里,
他使用宝镖和我们交战,
我军的伤亡将难以算计。

"但宝镖最怕沾上脏臭的东西,
也不能在它旁边吐唾液,
宝镖受玷污威力就减弱,
再也飞不回衮纳帕的手里。"

第十六章 破敌 Chapter 16 The Enemy Defeated

The flying dart became rusty since many years had passed.
Gunnapa took it to the seaside to wash and sharpen it.
It took him seven days and seven night to get it done,
Then the blue sea water turned into red like blood.

Anuman was standing at the end of the bridge.
He found the sea became muddy for no reason.
"Why did the water change its color?
We need to find it out."

He went back his camp and reported to Zhao Langma.
Biyasha was ordered to go and check it out.
"Someone is washing his flying dart in the water,
And that person is my elder brother Gunnapa.

"The magic flying dart is a gift from our father to him.
Gunnapai was also bestowed with the power of ten elephants.
The magic flying dart is indefinitely powerful,
Powerful Gunnapa together with such a weapon will be invincible.

"The precious dart can kill countless people each time,
And it can fly back into his hand after each attack.
If he fights against us with this weapon,
Our loss will be too heavy for us to handle.

"But the dart can never be touched by something stinking.
Even if someone spits by its side,
The precious dart will lose its magic power,
And it can't fly back into Gunnapa's hand."

召朗玛想出破敌的妙计，
叫阿努曼变成一只长蛆的死狗，
在衮纳帕磨镖的海面上漂浮，
发出一阵阵难闻的腥臭。

旺果和嘎林又变成老雕和乌鸦，
把死狗叼起来丢到衮纳帕身边，
衮纳帕闻到腥臭一阵恶心，
肠肚翻腾脏物吐了一大滩。

衮纳帕用镖尖挑起死狗，
把它抛到远远的海里，
他一边吐口水一边骂，
提着宝镖恼怒地返回允兰嘎。

二、腊嘎纳受伤

十头王捧玛加重整旗鼓，
命衮纳帕亲率大军出阵，
衮纳帕来到城外指挥冲杀，
敌对的兵马又杀得难解难分。

衮纳帕瞄准目标冲出堑壕，
把宝镖掷向召朗玛的兵营，
宝镖投中腊嘎纳的脚板，
腊嘎纳顿时倒地昏迷不醒。

第十六章 破敌　Chapter 16 The Enemy Defeated

　　Zhao Langma came up with a good idea,
　　Asking Anuman to turn into a rotted dog's corpse with worms,
　　And float around the sea water where Gunnapa sharpened the dart.
　　Then disgusting odour oozed out of the dead dog.

　　Wangguo and Galin turned themselves into an eagle and a crow,
　　They picked up the dead dog and cast it to Gunnapa.
　　Gunnapa felt nauseated with the stinking odour,
　　And he felt his stomach churning and vomited all over the place.

　　Gunnapa lifted the dead dog with the tip of the dart,
　　And he threw it out onto the surface of the sea.
　　He kept spitting and cursing this bad luck,
　　Then he went back to the city of Langa with his magic dart.

II　Lagana Was Injured

　　The ten-headed King Pengmajia rallied his troops,
　　And he appointed Gunnapa the chief commander.
　　Gunnapa and the troops marched out of the town.
　　Two sides started the fighting and killing once again.

　　Gunnapa rushed out of the dugout with his target aimed,
　　He threw the flying dart to the camp of Zhao Langma.
　　The flying dart hit Lagana on one of his feet,
　　Lagana fell down onto the ground and fainted.

647

失灵的宝镖再也飞不回去,
因为腥臭、口水伤了它的神力,
宝镖变成一棵粗壮的大青树,
把腊嘎纳的脚板牢牢钉进土里。

召朗玛把昏倒的弟弟抱在怀中,
轻声呼唤着弟弟的名字,
官兵们围了一层又一层,
有的号啕大哭,有的泣不成声。

彼亚沙大声提醒他们:
"大家要紧紧抱住宝镖不放,
假如宝镖脱离目标再飞回去,
宝石般的腊嘎纳就活不成。"

旺果、玛尼腊、摩米和嘎林,
手拉手把宝镖死死抱紧,
猴子们看到腊嘎纳脸色苍白,
哭叫声就像七月的蛙鸣。

衮纳帕以为召朗玛被镖戳死,
得意忘形回去向十头王请功:
"刚才两军激烈交锋,
我的宝镖已把召朗玛击中。"

捧玛加听了心花怒放,
高兴得不住地手舞足蹈,
他吩咐把南西拉押到前沿阵地,
让她亲眼看看死了的召朗玛。

第十六章 破敌 Chapter 16 The Enemy Defeated

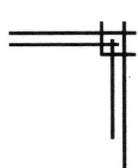

The flying dart lost its power so it couldn't fly back,
Because the stinks and spits had destroyed its magics.
But the dart turned into a gigantic evergreen tree,
And the roots nailed Lagana's feet fast into the ground.

Zhao Langma held his fainted brother in his arms,
And he called him gently trying to wake him up.
Generals and soldiers surrounded the brothers,
Some crying loudly and some weeping silently.

Biyasha shouted out to remind them,
"Everyone, hold on to the flying dart tightly.
If the flying dart flew back after it hits the target,
Our precious hero Lagana will not be able to survive."

Wangguo, Manila, Momi and Galin
Hand in hand, they surrounded and held the dart tightly.
The monkeys saw Lagana's face turned bloodless pale,
Their cries were so loud as the frogs croaking in July.

Gunnapa thought he had killed Zhao Langma,
He returned in triumph to inform Pengmajia,
"We have just had a big fight with our enemies,
And my flying dart has hit and killed Zhao Langma."

Pengmajia was elated to hear the good news.
He couldn't help but jump up and down in joy.
He order the soldiers to take Nan Xila to the battlefield,
So that she could see with her own eyes the dead Zhao Langma.

南西拉被带到阵地的土包上观望,
一眼就看见自己的丈夫召朗玛,
亲爱的丈夫还健在,
原来倒在地上的是弟弟腊嘎纳。

召朗玛没有发现远处的妻子,
他抱着弟弟痛哭流涕,
南西拉的心啊焦急万分,
为弟弟的不幸落泪伤心。

召朗玛想到忠实的弟弟腊嘎纳,
曾跟随他历尽了万苦千辛,
眼看宝镖威胁着弟弟的生命,
怎不叫他泪水纵横?

猴将猴兵爬山钻林寻找草药,
神通的摩米找来奇妙的药丸,
可是草药丸丹对宝镖不起作用,
腊嘎纳的伤势一点没有好转。

彼亚沙从哀痛中猛然醒悟:
"灵验的仙药长在干塔马塔纳金山上,
取来仙药就能治好腊嘎纳的重伤,
金山位于寒冷的北方。

第十六章 破敌　Chapter 16 The Enemy Defeated

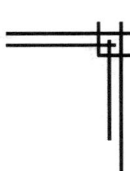

Nan Xila was taken to a small hill of the battlefield,
She picked out her husband at the first glance.
To her surprise Zhao Langma was still alive.
The one on the ground was the younger brother Lagana.

Zhao Langma hadn't seen his wife in the distance.
He was crying with his brother in his arms.
Nan Xila watched anxiously and helplessly,
She also cried for the tragedy of the younger brother.

Zhao Langma thought of the old days
When his loyal brother went through all the hardships with him.
Now watching his life to be taken away by the flying dart,
How could he not shed his tears like waterfalls?

The monkeys started to search for herbs in the mountains;
The magic Momi brought the precious pills of medicine.
But the pills couldn't work on the wound from flying dart.
Lagana's situation hadn't improved at all.

Biyasha pulled himself out of his sorrow and thought hard,
"The magic herb grows on the gold mountain of Gantamatana.
If we can get the herb, then deadly wound of Lagana will be cured.
But that mountain is located in remote and cold northern area.

651

"到那里有十万约路途遥远,
飞快的骏马从地面走也得一年,
这样仙药有如远水解不了近渴,
腊嘎纳危在旦夕生命留存的时间不到一天。

"要是今天能把仙药取回来,
腊嘎纳敷上药就能脱离危险,
否则明天太阳从东方一升起,
腊嘎纳就永远离开人间。"

猴王嘎林焦急万分,
叫阿努曼担起这个重任:
"希望你今夜把仙药取回,
时间紧迫,立刻就动身。"

阿努曼说出自己的忧虑:
"好药丑药我分不清,
药和草我无法辨认,
我怕我的无知耽误了事情。"

彼亚沙对他说:
"尊敬的阿努曼你别担心,
药名是'金色嫩叶的苏万纳帕达',
它听到你的呼唤就会答应。"

阿努曼一个筋斗腾空朝金山飞去,
到了金山开口叫喊:
"金色嫩叶的苏万纳帕达,
你们生长在哪里?"

第十六章 破敌 Chapter 16 The Enemy Defeated

"It is about one hundred thousand Yues from here.
It takes the fastest horse a year to get there.
So it is like spring water too far away to fetch for the current thirst.
And Lagana has only one day left to be saved.

"If the herb can be taken back within today,
Lagana can still be cured with it.
Once the sun rises in the east tomorrow morning,
Lagana will forever leave this world."

The monkey King was in great concern,
He asked Anuman to take the challenge,
"You have to get the herb back tonight.
Time is pressed and you should start out now."

Anuman spoke out his worry,
"I know nothing about herbs.
I can't even tell grass from herb.
I am afraid my ignorance will fuck up."

Biyasha said to him,
"Honourable Anuman, Don't worry,
The herb is called 'Suwannapada with golden tender leaves',
It will answer you when you call its name."

Anuman flew to the golden mountain with one somersault.
He started to shout once arriving there,
"Suwannapada with golden tender leaves,
Where are you growing?"

兰噶西贺 The Ten-Headed King of Langa

果然金色的仙药回答了，
从药山北面传来声音，
阿努曼跑到山北寻找，
仙药又在西面答应。

阿努曼跑到西面呼唤，
仙药又在南面应声，
阿努曼转身跳到山南，
东面又响起它的声音。

阿努曼在山东大声呼喊，
四面八方都有回声，
眼看黎明就要来临，
仙药在哪里还没有弄清。

急躁的阿努曼怒火冲天，
干脆把金山掰下一半，
抱着半个金山往回飞，
回到兵营太阳还未出山。

彼亚沙纵身跳上金山，
喊了一声就把仙药叫出，
他立即摘下金色的嫩叶，
急忙拿去熬煮。

彼亚沙又吩咐阿努曼：
"你快把金山抬回原处，
否则仙药的香味飘散开，
被我们打死的敌兵又会复苏。"

第十六章 破敌 Chapter 16 The Enemy Defeated

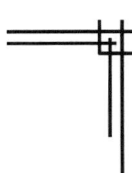

The magic herb really answered him,
And the voice was from the north side of the mountain.
Anuman ran to the north side to search for it,
The herb answered him again from the west side.

Anuman ran to the west side and called it,
It answered again from the south;
Once Anuman reached the south side,
It answered again from the east.

Anuman reached the east side and called again.
The answer was from all four directions.
The dawn was drawing near now,
He still couldn't tell where the herb was.

The agitated Anuman became more furious,
He ripped the mountain into halves.
Then he flew back to with one half held in his arms,
The sun was still hidden behind the mountain when he was back.

Biyasha jumped onto the mountain,
He called the herb once and it appeared.
He hurried to pluck the golden tender leaves,
And immediately got them boiled.

Biyasha said to Anuman again,
"Move this mountain back to its original place.
Otherwise when the scent of the herb oozes out,
The dead enemy soldiers will come back to their lives."

阿努曼抱起金山往北飞，
飞出勐兰嘎又越过海洋，
它嫌路远懒得再往前走，
把金山扔在下面一个山顶上。①

从此遍地是仙药的金山，
就留在勐帕雅龙山脉上，
人们叫它仙药山②，
从勐兰嘎走去要半年时光。

阿努曼丢下药山飞回来，
摩米已把奇妙的仙药熬好，
它把汤药在腊嘎纳的伤处擦了三下，
药汁拔毒宝镖立刻自动飞出。

阿努曼眼明手快抓住宝镖，
获得了衮纳帕这件神奇武器，
腊嘎纳在哥哥怀抱中苏醒，
很快恢复了生命的活力。

---

① 还有一种传说，阿努曼在半路把药山抛入大海里。
② 传说西双版纳遍地生长着药材，即由此而来。

第十六章 破敌 Chapter 16 The Enemy Defeated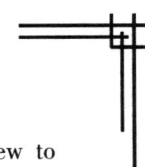

Anuman held the golden mountain in his arms and flew to north.

He flew over the Kingdom of Langa and across the ocean.

Then he felt it too far to place it back to its original place,

He dumped it onto the top of another mountain.①

The golden mountain was full of the magic herbs.

Ever since then it stayed on the range of Mengpayalong.

It was called the fairy mountain of herbs②,

It took half a year to walk there from the Kingdom of Langa.

Anuman flew back after dumping the golden mountain.

Momi had finished boiling the herb.

He wiped the boiled herb on the wound three times.

The herb got the poison out and the dart flew out automatically.

Anuman agilely caught hold of the flying dart,

Thus he owned this magic weapon of Gunnapa.

Lagana came back to life in the arms of his brother,

Very soon he was recuperated and became energetic again.

---

① Another version of the story is that Anuman threw the mountain of herbs into the sea.

② The legend says that is why herbs grow all over the land of Xishuangbanna.

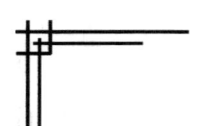

召朗玛如释重负万分高兴,
兄弟俩感谢彼亚沙、摩米医术高明,
感谢阿努曼万里艰苦寻药,
感谢大家的救命之恩。

弟弟腊嘎纳恢复了健康,
召朗玛高兴地为他庆祝,
猴子兵发出阵阵欢呼,
欢呼声震撼了森林和兰嘎城。

被押解着的南西拉看得分明,
见弟弟活转来感到欢欣,
她只能远远对着丈夫合掌,
声声呼唤丈夫和弟弟快来营救亲人。

召朗玛发现了站在远处的妻子,
恨不得冲过去把她救出敌营,
可是不能啊,鲁莽会毁掉她的生命,
他强忍悲愤呼唤着南西拉的心:

"南西拉啊,我心上的妻子,
我们久久分离,洒尽眼泪,
为了寻找你我们历尽艰辛,
现在相距咫尺却不能相会。

第十六章 破敌 Chapter 16 The Enemy Defeated

Zhao Langma was relieved and thrilled at seeing it.
The brothers thanked Biyasha and Momi for medical skills;
They gave thanks to Anuman for his endeavor in getting the herb.
And they were grateful for everyone's help in saving Lagana's life.

Lagana recovered and regained his strength.
Zhao Langma happily held a celebration for him.
The monkey soldiers cheered in chorus,
The joyful cheers vibrated in the forest and over the city of Langa.

The escorted Nan Xila witnessed everything,
And she felt relieved to see Lagana come back to life.
She could only bow to her husband with folded palms in the distance,
Wishing that her husband and brother could rescue her sooner.

Zhao Langma finally saw his wife standing afar,
He wanted so much to rescue her out of the enemy's camp.
But reckless action might only ruin her life,
He held back his sorrow and talking to Nan Xila in his heart,

"Nan Xila, my dear wife,
We are running out of tears for such a long separate.
We have gone through uncountable hardship to find you.
Now we are so close but we still can't meet.

"你别流泪啊,别伤悲,
我时刻把你挂在心内,
为了你我们才到这里作战,
誓把囚禁你的牢笼砸碎。

"但现在你在他们手中,
就像砧板上的鱼,
如果我们冲过去,
他们定会马上杀害你。

"不消灭在人间作恶的十头王,
我们团聚了还会分离,
你现在的困境不会长久了,
我们很快就会把这祸害彻底根除。

"既然敌对的双方交了锋,
不见输赢决不会轻易收场,
你暂时忍受着悲痛和哀伤吧,
我们定能打败恶贯满盈的十头王。

"你回到孤独的塔楼里去吧,
熬过这种人世间最伤心的离别,
等着迎接你的丈夫和弟弟,
正义在我们一边,我们一定胜利。"

南西拉哭着向丈夫倾诉心怀:
"夫王啊,请接受妻子下拜,
让飞洒的眼泪向你告别,
不幸的妻子就要离开。

第十六章 破敌 Chapter 16 The Enemy Defeated

"Please don't be sad, please stop crying,
Because you are always in my heart.
We are here fighting only to rescue you.
Each one of us vows to smash the cage you are in.

"But now you are in their hands,
Just like a fish on a chopping board.
If we rush forward to save you now,
You will surely be killed before we reach.

"Unless we could totally destroy the evil ten-headed king,
We might be separated again even if we got reunited.
But the plight won't last long,
Very soon we will wipe him out.

"The war has already started and last for a while,
We will hold on to it till the last moment.
Please endure the sorrows and pains for now,
We will definitely defeat the vicious ten-headed King.

"Please go back to your lonely tower,
Please hold up and face up with the torturing departure.
Please wait patiently for your husband and your younger brother.
Justice is on our side and we will surely win the war."

Nan Xila wept and murmured to her husband,
"My dear husband, please accept my bow to you.
I am saying goodbye again with my tears falling down,
Your miserable wife has to leave you again in a while.

"为什么心中的怨哀这样难以排解,
远远地见到又要远远地离开,
我就像关在铁笼里的斑鸠,
只能痛苦地望着外面的伴侣泪流满腮。

"这是一场令人心惊的噩梦啊,
还没有摸到你的手又要离别,
你和弟弟为我征战、流血,
想起来我的心几乎要碎裂。

"再见吧,亲爱的丈夫,
我就要回到防守严密的塔楼里,
但是他们锁不住我的心,
不管白昼黑夜永远跟随你。

"没有谁能挨近我的身子,
除非一刀把我杀死,
我将天天站在窗口眺望,
准备用眼泪和笑声迎接你。"

三、衮纳帕身亡

南西拉被押回兰嘎城里,
捧玛加见了产生猜疑:
"弟弟呀,你说召朗玛已中镖身死,
为什么南西拉脸上没有愁云一丝。

第十六章 破敌 Chapter 16 The Enemy Defeated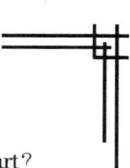

"Why is so hard to get rid of the clinging sorrow in my heart?
I can only see you in the distance and then have to say goodbye.
I am just like a caged dove
Looking at my mate outside the cage in tears and in pain.

"Everything is like a shocking nightmare.
I have to be dragged away before I can touch your hand.
You and your younger brother are fighting and bleeding for me.
The thought of this is really tearing my heart apart.

"Goodbye, my dear husband,
I am returning to the closely-guarded tower.
But they can only chain my body but not my heart.
All my heart will follow you forever day and night.

"Nobody can get close to my body,
I would die rather than being insulted.
I will stand by my window looking out from afar.
I will welcome you with happy tears and laughter."

Ⅲ The Death of Gunnapa

Nan Xila was escorted back to the city of Langa.

Pengmajia became suspicious after seeing Nan Xila.

"Gunnapa, you told me Zhao Langma had died from your dart,

Then why there is no any sign of sadness on Nan Xila's face?"

663

"难道召朗玛并没有死去,
反而让他们沟通了心思,
我有意叫人带南西拉去看,
是为了让她回心转意。

"如果让她见了活着的召朗玛,
岂不是偷鸡不着反蚀了米。
衮纳帕呀,你若欺骗了我,
我一定饶不过你。"

衮纳帕慌忙向捧玛加表白:
"我亲眼见召朗玛中镖身死,
我的每句话都珍贵如金子,
弟弟绝不敢说谎欺骗你。"

捧玛加烦躁地给他下达命令:
"现在你率领队伍再次出征,
把召朗玛兄弟的头取回来,
以后你说的话我才相信。"

衮纳帕勉强率军出城,
苏列亚跟着他当副手,
象车上飘扬着红绿旗幡,
士兵们边冲边喊"杀头,杀头"!

第十六章 破敌　Chapter 16 The Enemy Defeated

"Is it possible that Zhao Langma isn't dead

And they two have communicated with each other?

I had Nan Xila taken to the battlefield to see the death of her husband

So that she could change her mind and come to my side.

"If she saw Zhao Langma and knew he was still alive

It means double losses like wasting the rice without getting the hen.

Gunnapa, if you have deceived me,

I will surely get you to pay for it."

Gunnapa hurried to reassure Pengmajia,

"I saw with my eyes Zhao Langma got killed by my dart.

Each word of mine is as precious as gold,

I have never had the guts to lie to you."

Annoyed and perplexed, Pengmajia gave him orders,

"You must lead your troops and attack once again.

You must come back with the heads of Zhao Langma brothers

Otherwise I would never believe what you have said."

Gunnapa led his troop and marched out of the town reluctantly.

Shulieya was his assistant general and followed behind.

Red and green banners swagged on the chariots of elephants.

Soldiers marched forward shouting "chop heads, chop heads"!

兰嘎西贺 The Ten-Headed King of Langa

勇敢的召朗玛挥动闪光的宝刀，
指挥强大的猴子兵迎敌，
性情暴烈的阿努曼像一阵大风，
冲向敌人刀枪林立的阵地。

它手握衮纳帕的宝镖猛杀，
一排排敌人纷纷倒毙，
衮纳帕见到自己神奇的武器，
捋起袖子冲过来妄图夺取。

阿努曼甩开力大无比的衮纳帕，
一镖就把他的助手苏列亚戳死，
百发百中的腊嘎纳拉起神弓，
一箭把衮纳帕射倒在地。

就像大青树倒下一样，
轰隆隆震动了勐兰嘎大地，
犹如石破天惊，
好似电击雷劈。

衮纳帕流出的鲜血，
变成了一汪湖水碧波荡漾，
湖面上盛开着美丽的荷花，
潋滟的大湖隔开了鏖战的双方。

官兵们扑倒在十头王脚下，
一个个心惊胆战低首乞援：
"我们头上威望无比的捧玛加，
敌人杀死了衮纳帕和苏列亚。

第十六章 破敌 Chapter 16 The Enemy Defeated

The courageous Zhao Langma swung his shining sword.
He directed the monkey soldiers to confront the enemies.
Hot-tempered Anuman ran like wind,
Rushing into the enemies bristled with swords and spears.

Anuman held the magic dart of Gunnapa and slashed.
Rows of the enemies fell down like grasses.
Saw it was his own magic weapon in Anuman's hand,
Gunnapa rolled his sleeves and rushed to snatch it back.

Anuman threw away the stalwart Gunnapa,
Then he stabbed and killed Sulieya with one stab.
Lagana, who has never missed his target, held up his bow,
With one arrow he hit Gunnapa down to the ground.

Gunnapa fell down like a giant evergreen tree,
The rumbles trembled the land of Langa.
It was as if an explosion of a giant rock piercing the sky,
Or as if the world were struck with lightening and thunders.

The blood flew out of Gunnapa,
And it turned into a wide and deep lake.
Beautiful lotus flowers were blooming in the lake.
The wide lake separated the fighting armies.

  The generals and soldier knelt down before the ten-headed King,
  They all trembled in terror begging for more supporting troops,
  "Our majestic King Pengmajia,
  Gunnapa and Sulieya have been killed by our enemies.

"兵马混乱犹如无王的野蜂,
快派得力的武官去坐镇,
召朗玛的兵马有如乌云压顶,
他们的包围圈已经越拉越紧。"

四、智取宝棍

捧玛加对战役又作了重新部署,
分兵三路反击猴子兵的包围,
他命令撒哈沙统率大队人马正面出击,
要像大风卷落叶一样把敌人击退。

右路军由武官乾哈、苏判带领,
左路军由大将苏马里率领,
左右两路从侧翼夹击,
配合中路军反击强敌。

黎明天空乌云翻滚,
撒哈沙带领兵马出城,
层层黑云遮住初升的太阳,
顿时雷电交加大地一片昏沉。

召朗玛感到是不祥之兆,
急忙问身边的彼亚沙是何原因,
彼亚沙把即将发生的战事,
一一讲述给召朗玛细听。

第十六章 破敌 Chapter 16 The Enemy Defeated

"Our army is now in chaos as wasps lost their king.
Please assign a capable general to calm down the soldiers.
Zhao Langma's troops were swarming toward us like clouds.
Their circle around our city is increasingly tightening."

Ⅳ Getting Magic Staff by Strategy

Pengmajia allied his troops and had new strategy.
He divided his army into three parts to counter attack.
Sahasha would lead the troops to confront the enemy directly.
They should beat back the enemy as wind sweeping the fallen leaves.

The army on the right route was to be led by Qianha and Supan;
General Sumali was to be in command of the left route.
The armies of the two routes would attack from the flanks
In order to cooperate with the troops in the middle route.

The dark clouds rolled all over in the sky at dawn.
Sahasha led the troops out of the town.
The rising sun was blocked by the layers of dark clouds.
In a blink the land was ripped by the thunders and lightening.

Zhao Langma felt it was an ominous sign.
Hurriedly, he asked Biyasha by his side what was happening.
Biyasha knew what was happening and what would happen,
And he started to explain everything to Zhao Langma.

"这次攻打我们的是撒哈沙大将,
他有大象般的力气武艺高强,
他有一根叫环几拉别的宝棍,
一棍可以使很多人丧生。

"这根带火的宝棍,
能伸能缩多变异,
伸长长度有六十,
缩短短得像筷子。

"这次战前至关紧要的事情,
是用计谋巧取宝棍环几拉别,
不然撒哈沙战场上挥舞宝棍,
我们的兵马就所剩无几。"

如何才能巧取到宝棍?
召朗玛立即叫来阿努曼吩咐:
"凭你的智慧和本事,
快去把撒哈沙的宝棍夺取。"

阿努曼身披破烂的旧花毯,
身挎七通八补的小筒帕,
来到兰嘎城外的路边蹲着,
泪流满面地等着撒哈沙。

第十六章 破敌 Chapter 16 The Enemy Defeated

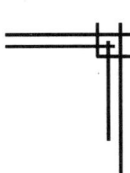

"The general led the army to attack us is Sahasha.
He is as strong as an elephant with super martial arts skills.
He has a magic staff weapon named Huanjilabie,
And one swing of it could kill many people.

"This magic staff could spit out fire.
It can stretch and shrink freely.
When stretched, it can be as long as sixty Yues;
When shortened, it can be the size of a chopstick.

"We must do one most important thing before starting the battle.
That is to get this magic staff of Huanjilabie with a wise plan.
Otherwise, Sahasha would use this magic weapon in the battle,
He could wipe out almost all of our soldiers with it."

How to get the magic weapon strategically?
Zhao Langma called in Anuman and said,
"Now we depend on your skills and wisdom.
Go and get the magic staff out of Sahasha's hands."

Anuman wrapped himself in a ragged carpet,
And he carried a Tongpa with many patches on it.
Then he squatted at the roadside outside of the city of Langa,
Waiting for Sahasha with tears all over his faces.

勇猛的撒哈沙率兵从大路走来,
见一个可怜的白猴哭着蹲在路旁,
他走上前去详细盘问:
"你是何人?为何哭得这样悲伤?"

阿努曼呜呜咽咽地说:
"我本来是召朗玛部下一员武将,
跟着他们拼死拼活,
在战争中历来英勇顽强。

"可是他一点也不同情部下,
动辄打骂,怎不令人寒心。
我不满意就被他驱逐出来,
整得我走投无路无人同情。"

"斑鸠哪能和恶鹰在一处,
黄鳝不能和毒蛇在一起,
你脱离召朗玛是一件好事,
有本事还怕没有地方效力?

"如果你真的有本事,
我撒哈沙就收留你。"
阿努曼用讨好的口气说:
"那就请你看看我的真本领。"

第十六章 破敌 Chapter 16 The Enemy Defeated

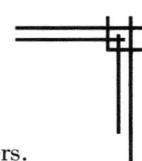

The mighty Sahasha came down the road with his soldiers.
Seeing a wretched white monkey weeping by the roadside,
He came up and examined him carefully,
"Who are you and why are you crying so sadly?"

Anuman wept and replied,
"I was a general fighting for Zhao Langma,
And I risked my life fighting for him,
I have always been the most courageous in the battles.

"But Zhao Langma is not sympathetic with his inferiors at all,
How could we not get bitterly disappointed with his daily abuses?
He expelled me just because I showed my disapproval.
I have nowhere to go and nobody has sympathy for me."

"How can a dove stay with a ferocious eagle?
How can an eel coexist with a poisonous snake?
It is a good thing that you broke up with Zhao Langma.
There is always opportunity in the world for the capable ones.

"If you are really a capable warrior,
I can keep you by my side."
Anuman showed his eagerness to please Sahasha,
"Please give me a chance to show you what I can do."

673

阿努曼冲向一块二十长的巨石,
上去一拳就把它击得粉碎,
它又顺手拔起一棵大椰子树,
轻轻一跃就在云端里来回飞。

撒哈沙见了分外欢喜:
"你别到处流浪去了,
就跟着我做我的养子,
我绝不会像召朗玛那样虐待你。"

阿努曼故意表现得有些不乐意:
"你有意收下我做你的干儿子,
你的一片好心我领情,
但我不愿再在别人手下做事。

"我的魂差点被召朗玛吓散,
我早就受不了这口气。"
"孩子啊,我不像别人不讲义气,
不要怕,跟着阿爹进城去。"

"谢谢你了,好心的义父,
但还有一件事使我担心,
我过去曾得罪过召捧玛加,
放火烧过允兰嘎的房屋。

"召捧玛加见了我不会宽容,
倘若他记仇还会杀我的头,
想来想去不如回森林的好,
父亲啊,你还是让我走。"

第十六章 破敌 Chapter 16 The Enemy Defeated

Anuman dashed to a giant rock as long as twenty meters,
With just one punch he smashed the rock pieces.
After that he uprooted a coconut tree,
And with one jump he flew back and forth in the clouds.

Sahasha was very glad to see what he could done,
"Stop wandering around like a vagrant.
You can follow me and be my adopted son.
I would never treat you the way Zhao Langma did."

Anuman pretended to be reluctant to accept the offer,
"I know you meant well to adopt me.
Thank you very much for your kindness.
But I don't want to work for anybody any more.

"I was almost scared to death by Zhao Langma.
I can't stand such thing any longer."
"My son, unlike Zhao Langma, I value loyalty.
Don't be afraid and follow me to go inside the city."

"Thank you, my adaptive father with a kind heart,
But there is another thing that is biting my heart.
I have done something terrible to Zhao Pengmajia,
I once set fire to the houses in the city of Langa."

There is no way that Zhao Pengmajia would forgive me.
If he still harbors bitter resentment, he would have me killed.
Maybe it is still a better choice for me to go back to the forest.
Please let me go, my dear father."

撒哈沙宽慰阿努曼：
"放心吧，这件事包在我身上，
我带你到国王面前去说情，
国王一定会对你宽宏大量。"

阿努曼佯装高兴的样子，
双手合十拜撒哈沙为义父，
父子俩一直交谈到天黑，
仗也忘记打，越谈越投机。

撒哈沙带着阿努曼去拜见十头王，
捧玛加见阿努曼归顺十分喜悦，
他一跃而起跳下御座，
手舞足蹈洋洋得意。

"这下我们必定能战胜召朗玛，
南西拉一定会成为我的妻子。"
阿努曼在宫廷里住了一夜，
第二天清晨加入了出征的队伍。

铓锣阵阵，号角声声，
撒哈沙率领大军出征，
他坐在战车上策马前进，
命坐在一旁的阿努曼为他握住宝棍。

第十六章 破敌 Chapter 16 The Enemy Defeated

Sahasha tried to comfort Anuman,
"Take it easy, you can count on me as to this matter.
I will take you to our King and plead his mercy for you.
The king is sure to be so generous to forgive you."

Anuman pretended to be happy about what he had heard,
He bowed to Sahasha with folded palms to be his adopted son.
The Father and Son talked and talked till it was getting dark.
They had such an agreeable chat that they even forgot the war.

Sahasha took Anuman to pay his respect to the ten-headed King.
Pengmajia was joyous to see Anuman coming to surrender.
Jumping down from his throne,
He stamped his feet and clapped his hands elatedly.

"Now we will surely be able to defeat Zhao Langma.
Nan Xila will definitely become my wife after that."
Anuman spent one night in the palace.
He joined the troops marching to the battlefield next morning.

Gongs were pounded and trumpets blown,
Sahasha led the army starting new round of attack.
He rode on the chariot and spurred his horse to gallop,
Asking Anuman next to him to hold his magic staff.

677

士兵们呐喊着奋勇冲杀,
正面左右两路将领全披挂上阵,
个个都施展出高超的本领,
决心杀退召朗玛的猴子兵。

撒哈沙从战车上跳下来,
身先士卒带着阿努曼冲锋,
阿努曼佯装十分勇敢,
从腰间拿出宝棍往前冲。

阿努曼为了保护自己的猴子弟兄,
一直冲在撒哈沙的前头,
它假装杀敌把猴子兵撵走,
撒哈沙几次砍杀都没有得手。

猴子兵气愤地向阿努曼扑来,
怒斥它临阵脱逃叛变投敌,
它们恰似一窝蜂"嗡嗡"叫喊,
涌过来要对阿努曼实行惩治。

阿努曼高高举起宝棍打下地,
宝棍席卷尘土声如雷鸣,
吓得猴子兵纷纷四散逃窜,
乐坏了勐兰嘎的将官和士兵。

猴子兵惊魂方定,
又怒吼着向阿努曼反扑:
"你这个狼心狗肺的东西,
我们要挖出你的心,剥下你的皮。"

第十六章 破敌 Chapter 16 The Enemy Defeated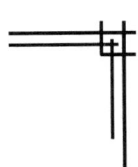

All his soldiers were charging forward bravely;
The generals from the three routes were fully armed.
All of them were trying hard to exert their fighting skills,
Determined to defeat Zhao Langma's monkey soldiers.

Sahasha jumped down from the chariot.
Leading Anuman and his soldier, he charged forward.
Anuman pretended to fight courageously,
He dashed forward with the magic staff in his hands.

In order to protect his monkey brothers,
Anuman now was running in front of Sahasha.
Pretending to kill them, he chased the monkeys away.
Sahasha could not get any chance to kill them.

The monkey soldiers dashed to Anuman angrily.
They chided him for being a traitor fighting for their enemy.
All monkeys were shouting like a swarm of wasps.
They flooded around Anuman to seriously punish him.

Anuman raised the magic staff and hit on the ground,
The hitting sound was as loud as a thunder.
The monkeys were scared and began to flee around.
Seeing this the generals and soldiers of Langa laughed happily.

After a while the monkey soldiers calmed down,
They shouted angrily and made another round of attack,
"You cruel and unscrupulous traitor,
We will dig your heart out and peel off your skin."

猴子兵把阿努曼团团围住，
勐兰嘎的士兵急忙涌上来解围，
阿努曼怕敌兵杀伤猴子兄弟，
慌忙举棍第二次捶打大地。

宝棍落地红光闪闪火花四溅，
猴子兵炙热得纷纷后退，
又一次被驱散远远逃避，
勐兰嘎众官兵见了心中大喜。

三路将领以为召朗玛的大军崩溃了，
带领官兵欢呼着跳出堑壕，
从左右两侧朝阿努曼方向狂奔，
挥舞武器穷追正在逃跑的猴子兵。

眼看猴子兵将被打垮，
阿努曼突然转过身来，
闪电般举起了宝棍，
朝勐兰嘎官兵猛扫狠打。

勐兰嘎官兵还没有清醒过来，
就被阿努曼一排排扫倒，
霎时被打死的敌人堆满大地，
苏马里、乾哈也被打死。

阿努曼又举起了宝棍，
一棍就把撒哈沙打翻，
阿努曼抱起他飞回兵营，
把人和宝棍献给召朗玛。

第十六章 破敌 Chapter 16 The Enemy Defeated

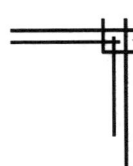

The monkey soldiers surrounded Anuman tightly,
Soldiers of Langa came forward to rescue him.
Anuman was afraid monkey brothers might be killed,
He raised the magic staff and hit the ground for a second time.

Sparks of flame flew all over from the magic staff.
The heat forced the monkey soldiers to step back.
For a second time they were dispelled and run away.
Generals and soldiers were very happy to see all these.

The generals thought that Zhao Langma's troops were defeated,
They jumped out of the dugout leading the soldiers to chase.
They rushed to Anuman from the flanks of the left and right,
Everyone was running wildly waving their weapons in the air.

The monkey soldiers would be destroyed in a moment,
All of a sudden, Anuman turned around.
He raised the magic staff with speed of lightening
And slashed to the soldiers of Langa with all his strength.

Before the soldiers of Langa knew what was happening,
Rows and rows of them were swept down to the ground.
Their bodies were scattered all over the battle field now,
Even Sumali and Qianha were killed in the chaos.

Anuman raised the magid staff again,
This time Sahasha was hit and fell over to the ground.
Anuman held him up and flew back to his own camp,
He handed Sahasha and his magic staff to Zhao Langma.

撒哈沙被打得奄奄一息,
猴子兵一伙伙来看稀奇,
召朗玛命令阿努曼,
把撒哈沙立即处死。

阿努曼提着撒哈沙到了海边,
一宝棍把他打成肉浆,
愚蠢的撒哈沙呵,
死后变成了吸血的大蚂蟥。

五、大闹祭祀场

阿努曼骗去了环几拉别宝棍,
撒哈沙和二员战将在宝棍下丧生,
召朗玛大军仍紧紧包围着允兰嘎,
武官苏判急忙逃回宫报告捧玛加。

捧玛加像热锅上的蚂蚁,
犹如暴风雨中的雷电,
好比困在笼中的野牛,
十双眼睛射出凶狠的光。

十个头张开了十张嘴,
出口的话就像晴天的炸雷,
他捋起袖子猛擂宝座,
咆哮的声音震得宫殿落灰。

第十六章 破敌 Chapter 16 The Enemy Defeated

Sahasha was so severely hurt that he was half dead.
The monkey soldiers gathered up for the rare scene.
Zhao Langma gave his order to Anuman
That Sahasha should be executed right away.

Anuman took Sahasha to the seaside.
With just a slash, Sahasha was hit into a meat ball.
Poor and foolish Sahasha,
His body turned into a big leech after his death.

V The Sacrifice Site Was Destroyed

Now Anuman had in his hands the magic staff of Huanjilabie;
Sahasha and two other generals had died under the magic staff.
Zhao Langma's troops were still surrounding the city of Langa tightly,
General Supan hurried to the palace and reported the situation.

Pengmajia now was like an ant in a hot pan,
Or the lightening in a storm,
Or a buffalo imprisoned in a cage.
Light of hatred shone out of his ten pairs of eyes.

Ten mouths on the ten faces opened widely,
His voice was like a thunder out of the blue.
He rolled up his sleeves and pounded on the throne,
His snarls shook off the dust from the roof of the palace.

兰噶西贺 The Ten-Headed King of Langa

"召朗玛呀召朗玛，
我与你势不两立，
我是天神的儿子，
难道你能不在我面前屈膝？

"我是乘坐大象的万勐之王，
你不过是树叶草尖上的露水，
露滴哪能流成大江大河，
露珠闪亮也只有一刹那的光辉。

"我要为战死的官兵们报仇，
我要为殉国的弟弟和儿子雪恨，
我要用刀箭进行报复，
我要用你们的鲜血祭奠亡魂。"

接连损兵又折将，
捧玛加找大臣来商议，
要举办一次盛大的祭祀，
祈求威力无限的神祇帮助。

大家赞同捧玛加的主意，
立即布置了祭坛，
请来祭司，备办了各种祭祀礼物，
到处点燃起熊熊的火炬。

第十六章 破敌 Chapter 16 The Enemy Defeated

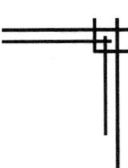

"Zhao Langma, Damned Zhao Langma,
You are my sworn enemy now.
I am a son of heavenly gods,
You will surely bend your knees in front of me.

"I am the ruler of the Kingdom of Langa riding an elephant.
You are only a drop of dew on the tip of the blade of grass.
A drop of dew can never turn into a river;
Its shine can only last for a moment.

"I will revenge for my soldiers and generals who died in the battles;
I will revenge for my son and brother who died for our kingdom.
You will die under my swords and arrows.
And your blood will be used as the offerings for sacrifice."

After so many losses and casualties of his generals and soldiers,
Pengmajia sent for his officials to give him some advice.
He wanted to hold a glorious sacrifice ritual
So that they can pray to heavenly gods for their assistance.

Everyone agreed on Pengmajia's idea,
And the alter was set up immediately.
The high priest was chosen and all kinds of offerings prepared,
Torches were lit up all over the sacrifice site.

685

允兰嘎关紧城门赶起大摆,
精湛的武术演起来,
动听的乐器奏起来,
欢乐的歌声在天空飘开。

兰嘎城里处处搭起绿叶凉棚,
祭天神地祇的供品样样摆齐,
红饭、黑饭、白饭,
香瓜、香蕉、椰子……

杀的鸭是白鸭,
杀的鸡是白鸡,
杀了黄牛、水牛和肥猪,
肉皮刮得像棉花一样白洁。

人们杀鸡把鸡血洒在大青树根,
捧玛加要大家向神祇求情,
人们把米酒滴在树根旁边,
声声念着真言呼唤鬼神。

"来吧,天上地下水里的神祇,
请你们快来吃鲜红的剁生,
请喝金碗银碗里装的肉汤,
请把杯里装的香甜米酒痛饮。

第十六章 破敌 Chapter 16 The Enemy Defeated

The gate of Langa city was closed and a fair was held.
Skills of martial arts was displayed;
All kinds of instruments were played;
Joyous songs spread all over the sky.

Lots of sheds covered with green leaves were set up in the town,
The offerings for the gods of heaven and earth were neatly arrayed.
Red rice, black rice, white rice,
melons, bananas, coconuts...

What was offered were the white ducks,
As well as the white chicken.
Bulls, cows and fat pigs were also slaughtered
With their skins were scratched as white as cotton.

The chicken blood was sprayed to the root of the evergreen tree.
Pengmajia asked everyone to pray to gods of heaven and earth.
The rice liquor was also dipped around the tree root,
Mantra phrases were chanted to call upon those spirits.

"Please come here, gods from the heaven, the earth and the water,
Please show up and enjoy the red and fresh Duosheng;
Please enjoy the meat soup in the gold and silver bowls;
Please drink up the cups of sweet rice liquor to your heart's content.

"威力无比的天神地祇,
请赐给我们无穷的力量,
帮助我们打赢这场战争,
让我们把召朗玛赶下海洋。"

十头王在宫殿前广场上主祭,
他献上宰杀了的各种牺牲,
火舌喷射,香烟缭绕,
他献上芬芳的香花和五谷祭品。

忽然乌云遮住了阳光,
雷声把宇宙震响,
电光把天空照亮,
大地刹那间变了模样。

天神地祇山鬼水鬼都来了,
他们欣喜若狂地来接受祭祀,
为了帮助十头王打仗,
他们带来了狂风暴雨。

召朗玛见云天突变十分惊疑,
他不理解天昏地暗的奥秘,
找来彼亚沙探问原因,
彼亚沙遥见城内火焰冲起。

第十六章 破敌 Chapter 16 The Enemy Defeated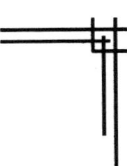

"The mighty gods of the heaven and the earth,
Please bestow us with inexhaustible power;
Please help us win this bloody war;
Please help us drive Zhao Langma into the ocean."

The ten-headed King himself performed the ritual.
He offered all the slaughtered animals as sacrifice.
Flames of the torches and the incenses drifted into the air,
And he also offered fresh flowers and five kinds of rices on the alter.

Suddenly the sunlight was blocked by dark clouds.
And the thunder shook up the whole universe.
The sky was lit up by the lightening.
In an instant the world was completely different.

Gods of the heaven, the earth and the water all arrived.
They accepted the sacrifice offerings delightedly.
In order to help the ten-headed King to win the battle,
They also brought the storm and tornado into the world.

Seeing the sudden change of the weather and the world,
Zhao Langma was surprised and could not figure out its secret.
He sent for Biyasha and asked him what had happened.
Biyasha came and saw afar the surging flames in the town.

惊慌的彼亚沙告诉召朗玛：
"捧玛加在举行盛大的献祭，
如果天神地祇来受祭帮助他，
这对我们十分不利。

"我哥哥这一招至关重要，
神祇助他将置我们于死地，
请你赶快派人前去，
秘密破坏他这一次祭祀。"

召朗玛听了大吃一惊，
急忙把阿努曼叫来吩咐：
"你趁捧玛加正在祭祀，
赶快飞到祭祀场去。

"趁黑夜行动方便好隐蔽，
把他的供桌供品全捣毁，
把关起的牺牲全放走，
使他的这场祭祀灰飞烟灭。"

阿努曼领会了召朗玛的意思，
很乐意去干这件趣事，
他带上弓箭和棍棒，
跃上高空向兰嘎城飞去。

半路上就遇见奇形怪状的神鬼，
闹嚷嚷前去允兰嘎接受祭礼，
阿努曼见了手发痒，
拉开弓箭就射击。

第十六章 破敌 Chapter 16 The Enemy Defeated

Biyasha got panic and told Zhao Langma,
"Pengmajia is holding a grand ritual of sacrifice.
If all gods came to accept the offering and provide him help,
Things will turn against us and we will be in big trouble.

"This trick of my elder brother is critical.
Gods will help him and that means the end of us.
Please send someone to damage it right now,
His sacrifice ritual must be ruined secretly."

Zhao Langma was shocked at hearing this.
He sent for Anuman and told him what to do,
"Pengmajia is performing a sacrifice ritual.
You need to fly to the site right away.

"Now it is dark and convenient for you to take actions.
You must destroy all the offering on the table,
And set free all the offering animals.
Thus his plan of sacrifice can never be fulfilled."

Anuman understood what Zhao Langma meant.
He was very glad to have such kind of fun.
With his iron staff and bow on him,
He jumped into the sky and flew to the city of Langa.

He met some odd-looking ghosts on his way to Langa.
They were heading for Langa city to accept the offerings.
Seeing them, Anuman felt his hands itchy,
And he drew out his bow and started to shoot.

几个神鬼立刻中箭而死,
其他神鬼纷纷掉头逃去,
阿努曼到祭场把祭坛供品敲得稀烂,
又放走了祭牲猪牛鸭鸡。

第二天太阳刚刚升起,
臣僚们发现祭场已毁灭,
他们慌忙向国王报告,
召捧玛加心里又气又急。

"我们关起城门利用赶摆作掩护,
祭祀天神地祇祈请帮助,
召朗玛怎么会知道这件事,
定是彼亚沙这个叛逆泄漏了机密。"

第十六章 破敌 Chapter 16 The Enemy Defeated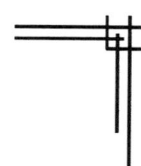

Some were shot dead right away,

The others turned around and started to flee.

Anuman arrived at the sacrifice site and destroyed everything.

And he set free the pigs, cows, ducks and hens used for sacrifice.

When the sun rose the next morning,

Officials found that everything had been destroyed.

They hurried back and reported it to the king.

Zhao Pengmajia felt furious and frantic.

"We have closed the gate and used the fair as cover-up

So that we could make offerings to gods praying for their help.

How could Zhao Langma know my plan?

It must be Biyasha the traitor who has told him the secret."

第十七章 决战

一、十头王亲征

几次开仗连连遭挫折，
官兵们伤的伤来亡的亡，
请鬼神来帮助又遭破坏，
捧玛加气得头昏脑涨。

他一拳打得宝座摇晃动荡，
决定御驾亲征不惜血染沙场，
他重新部署了攻守的兵力，
对大臣武官们大声叫嚷：

"你们不要一个个垂头丧气，
在敌人面前显得无能为力，
只要我十头王还活着，
对召朗玛就用不着恐惧。

"我要亲自带领兵马和召朗玛交锋，
明天，鬼神会来助我的威风，
天空会响起阵阵雷鸣，
乌云会像海涛那样翻滚。

第十七章 决战 Chapter 17 The Decisive Battle

Chapter 17 The Decisive Battle

I Pengmajia Taking Command of the Battle

After the consecutive setbacks in the war,
Pengmajia's troops had suffered great number of casualties.
Now the plan to ask for help from gods was also ruined.
Pengmajia got mad and his anger was beyond his control.

He pounded on the throne and got it shaken.
He decided to lead the army and fight in battlefield.
After rearranging and relocating the remaining troops.
Now he was shouting to his officials and generals,

"All of you, stop being so crestfallen.
Don't be weak in front of your enemies.
As long as I, the ten-headed King, am alive,
You do not need to be afraid of Zhao Langma.

"I myself will lead the army and fight against Zhao Langma.
Tomorrow gods and ghosts will come and assist me.
Fits of thunders will crash in the sky,
Dark clouds will be rolling like the waves in the sea.

"所有的人都要带上宝刀,
乘马骑象的要带上大弓,
各路兵马要齐心协力,
听我的口令同时行动。"

海面上微露晨曦,
允兰嘎炮响七声,
捧玛加的兵马出动了,
浩浩荡荡跨出了城门。

旗幡在队伍前头飘扬,
乐队在行列中奏乐,
前面銮铃叮当、象马嘶鸣,
后面擂起战鼓、敲响铓锣。

气宇轩昂的捧玛加,
十个头都戴上金帽银冠,
二十只耳朵吊上闪闪金环,
身披金铠银甲,肩挎弓弩利箭。

他的战象全身披金挂银,
象牙犹如两根发光的竹笋,
象头、象身、象鞍、象铃,
到处都是明灿灿发亮的纯金。

第十七章 决战 Chapter 17 The Decisive Battle

"Everyone needs to take their sharp swords.
Those who ride on elephants or horses bring their bows.
All the troops from different routes should work together,
Follow my order and take actions at the exact same time."

Morning light just shone on the sea,
After seven times of solute firing,
Pengmajia and his troops set off.
They marched out of the city mightily.

The flags and banners were waving in the front of the army;
The marching music was played by the band in the procession.
Bells were ringing , horses were neighing in the front,
And drum and gangs were being pounded in the rear.

The mighty Pengmajia showed up.
Ten gold and silver crowns were on his ten heads;
Gold earrings were swinging on his twenty ears.
He was in full armor of gold and silver with bows on his shoulders.

The elephant he rode was decorated with gold and silver.
The tusks were like the shining bamboo shoots.
The head, the body, the saddle and the bells,
Each part of the elephant was decorated with shining pure gold.

697

象背上撑着遮阳的金伞，
金伞仿照六十三种花瓣做成，
颜色比彩虹还鲜艳，
捧玛加坐在金象上威风凛凛。

有的骑着膘壮的战马，
有的坐着隆隆的战车，
有的扛着大刀、长矛，
看不见头尾的队伍风沙滚滚。

捧玛加摆好了作战的阵势，
紧紧包围了召朗玛的营地，
他指挥三面兵马发起攻击，
射向猴群的利箭如同下雨。

箭声嗖嗖、杀声阵阵，
把大地震得微微摇动，
召朗玛的营垒如同山崩地塌，
队伍和寨堡几乎被摧垮。

傲慢的十头王驱象向前，
对着召朗玛高声叫骂：
"出来较量吧，所有的猴王，
愚蠢无能的小朗玛。

第十七章 决战 Chapter 17 The Decisive Battle

Gold umbrella was set up on the back of the elephant.
The umbrella had the pattern of sixty-three kinds of flower pedals.
It was more colorful and brilliant than a rainbow.
Pengmajia on the elephant looked mighty and haughty.

Some soldiers were riding on strong war-horses.
Some were sitting on the rumbling chariots.
The knives and spears shone on their shoulders.
The endless armies marched on and on in the dust.

Pengmajia ordered his army to get ready for attack.
The camp of Zhao Langma was surrounded tightly.
He ordered the soldiers to attack from three directions.
The arrows flew to the monkey army like raindrops.

Arrows were whizzing; shouts echoed.
The ground was shaking under soldiers' feet.
Zhao Langma's barracks collapsed as mountain fell.
His troops and watch towers were almost destroyed.

The haughty ten-headed King marched on his elephant,
He showered his abuses to Langma loudly,
"Come out and fight with me, all the monkey kings,
And you, the stupid and timid little Langma.

"你还不认识我十头王捧玛加吧,
竟敢出兵来攻占和糟蹋勐兰嘎,
我要用宝刀挑破你的肠肚,
用你的血肉去祭帝瓦吾①。"

召朗玛站出来说道:
"黑心肠的捧玛加休出狂言,
我是波提亚②转世的人,
才能越过汪洋大海打到你面前。

"你罪恶滔天、怨满人间,
我们的仇恨是烧毁你的火焰,
我要亲手把你砍死,
割下你的十个头来做坐垫。"

召朗玛说完挥兵迎战,
敌对的双方拼命冲杀,
刀箭闪光、吼声如雷,
同样顽强,谁也不后退。

双方都有自己的打法,
双方都显示了自己的神威,
十头王分兵三路进攻,
召朗玛却用兵把他们分割包围。

————————
① 帝瓦吾:管海洋、土地、森林的男天神,地位低于叭英。
② 波提亚:有福气的男天神。

第十七章 决战　Chapter 17　The Decisive Battle

"You still don't know me, the mighty ten-headed King.
How dare you attack and ruin my Kingdom of Langa?
I will pierce your stomach with my sword.
I will offer your blood and flesh to the God of Diwawu①."

Zhao Langma stood forward and shouted back,
"Black-hearted Pengmajia, stop your nonsense and bluffing.
I am reincarnated from the God of Botiya②,
That's why I was able to cross the ocean to kill you.

"You have committed the most heinous crimes in the world.
Our hatred is the flame that will have you engulfed.
I will kill you with my own hands;
I will cut off your ten heads to sit on them."

After that, Zhao Langma led his soldiers to fight back.
Two armies rushed into each other fighting and killing.
Swords were flashing and soldiers shouting.
Both sides fought indomitably and no one would retreat.

Each side had their own strategy;
Each side was displaying their power and skills.
The ten-headed King attacked from three sides,
Zhao Langma intercepted the enemy and surrounded each group.

---

① Diwawu: the god who is in charge of the sea, the earth and the forest and inferior to Baying.

② Botiya: a blessed god.

召朗玛布下天罗地网，
十头王的队伍慌忙突围，
召朗玛指挥将士咬住不放，
打得敌人不能进也不能退。

腊嘎纳向捧玛加射出神箭，
箭被捧玛加一刀断成两截，
召朗玛对准他拉起神弓，
射出的利箭命中捧玛加的前胸。

腊嘎纳又乘势射中他的身子，
可是捧玛加一点也不觉得痛，
他在大象背上手舞足蹈，
拔出箭，满脸笑容。

射来的箭砍来的刀，
神通广大的十头王一点也不害怕，
他身上的箭伤刀伤呀，
就像筛子眼一样密密麻麻。

捧玛加显神威施展魔术，
放出成千只花斑猛虎，
猛虎"呜呜"吼着追逐猴群，
猴子兵乱纷纷爬上大树。

召朗玛施展帕拉西教给的神术，
放出一群凶猛的狮子，
老虎被狮子纷纷咬死，
双方又相持不下，势均力敌。

第十七章 决战　Chapter 17　The Decisive Battle

Zhao Langma got the enemy enclosed as if a net had been spread;
The ten-headed King ordered his soldiers to break through.
Zhao Langma pushed on and tightened the circling,
So that the enemies could neither move forward or retreat.

Lagana raised his the magic bow and aimed at Pengmajia.
The arrow was slashed into two pieces by Pengmajia's sword.
Zhao Langma aimed at him with his arrow,
It hit Pengmajia right in the chest.

Lagana again shot him on the body.
But Pengmajia felt no pain at all.
Moving freely on the back of the elephant,
He pulled out the arrows with smiles on his faces.

Neither the arrows nor the knives worked.
They couldn't hurt the mighty ten-headed King.
The wounds on his body were so many
That they looked like the holes on a griddle.

Pengmajia started to use his magics,
He let out thousands of vicious tigers
Roaring and chasing after the monkeys.
The monkeys were in chaos and they climbed onto trees.

Zhao Langma used his tricks taught by Palaxi.
He let out a group of more ferocious lions,
And they chased those tigers and bit them to death.
Then again the two sides were locked in a stalemate.

战斗越打越激烈，
召朗玛头部中箭昏倒在地，
十头王上前准备擒拿，
腊嘎纳大吼一声上前护卫。

阿努曼猛一下跳过来，
抱住十头王把他的铠甲撕破，
十头王惊慌失措，
顾不及捉召朗玛挣身逃脱。

敌将见十头王处境危险，
慌忙跑上前将他保护，
兵对兵，将对将，
双方相持，不分胜负。

嘎林冲向右边的苏判，
一刀把他的身子砍断，
腊嘎纳瞄准左边的嘎哈哥，
一箭把他的胸膛射穿。

阿努曼手持棍棒追击苏玉鲊，
没几个回合就把他一棍敲死，
三个敌将差不多同时一命呜呼，
猴子兵跑上去割下他们的首级。

召朗玛在弟弟的护理下苏醒过来，
拿起神弓又继续指挥战斗，
他瞄准十头王射出一箭，
捧玛加的王冠随着箭翎飞走。

第十七章 决战 Chapter 17 The Decisive Battle

The fighting continued and became more fierce.
Zhao Langma happened to be hit in the head by an arrow.
The ten-headed King moved forward to get him,
Snarling in rage, Lagana rushed to protect his brother.

Anuman jumped onto the ten-headed King.
He held the ten-headed King tightly and torn down his armors.
The ten-headed King was terrified and at a loss,
He had no choice but to turn around and escape from Anuman.

Seeing the ten-headed King was in danger,
His generals rushed forward to protect him.
Soldiers against soldiers, generals against generals,
Two sides were even and no one could win over the other.

Galin ran up to his right toward Supan,
He cut Supan into halves with his sword.
Lagana aimed at Gahage at his left side,
With just one shot Gahage's chest was penetrated.

Anuman held up his staff and ran after Suyuzha,
After several rounds Suyuzha died under his staff.
Three generals of Pengmajia were killed almost simultaneously,
The monkey soldiers ran up and cut off their heads.

Zhao Langma recovered under the care of Lagana.
He picked up his magic bow and continued to fight.
He shot at the ten-headed King in the head,
And the crown was hit and flew away with the arrow.

十头王心中暗暗吃惊,
不敢恋战慌忙撤兵回城,
他派出重兵四面严密防守,
有翅膀的雀鸟也难以飞进。

二、智取弓赛宰

召朗玛心上布满层层疑云,
捧玛加究竟隐藏着什么本领,
刀口箭眼布满他的全身,
为什么伤害不了他的性命?

召朗玛为这事惴惴不安,
他把疑虑告诉彼亚沙,
问他究竟是怎么一回事,
希望得到彼亚沙的解答。

彼亚沙心情十分沉痛,
说与不说,矛盾重重,
这件事他比别人清楚,
它关系到哥哥能否生存。

他想到自己悲惨的遭遇,
从小他对哥哥友爱、忠诚,
分担着他的痛苦,
分享着他的欢欣。

第十七章 决战 Chapter 17 The Decisive Battle

The ten-headed King got terrified but he kept it to himself.
He dare not fight any more and retreat into the town hurriedly.
And he ordered the soldiers to be on vigilant guard.
Now even a flying bird can not get into the capital city.

II Getting the Bow of Saizai by Strategy

Zhao Langma felt quite puzzled,
What magic that Pengmajia had?
He had been shot all over of his body,
Why he did not get the slightest injured?

Zhao Langma got uneasy about this.
He told Biyasha his perplexity
Asking him what's on earth going on with Pengmajia.
He hoped that Biyasha could give him an answer.

Biyasha felt so heavy in his heart.
To tell the truth or not? He was torn apart by the dilemma.
About this matter, he knew better than anyone else.
This secret meant life or death to his brother.

He recollected his bitter experience.
He had always been friendly and loyal to his brother,
Being sad when he underwent pains,
Being happy when he was joyful.

哥哥作恶他数次好言相劝,
捧玛加只当作几阵耳边风,
哥哥抢劫召朗玛的妻子,
他预料会给勐兰嘎带来灾难重重。

他劝哥哥把南西拉送回,
哥哥竟把他当作死敌,
不顾亲骨肉的情谊,
把他绑起来扔进大海里。

逆耳忠言他听不进,
竟迫害自己的同胞弟兄,
要不是召朗玛搭救自己,
彼亚沙早就没有了生命。

过去的彼亚沙啊,
他已经死去,
今天的彼亚沙啊,
已不是捧玛加的弟弟。

彼亚沙痛苦地想到这些,
就向召朗玛说出十头王的奥秘:
"我那哥哥敢这样霸道自恃,
因为天王给了他一件卫护生命的武器。

第十七章 决战　Chapter 17　The Decisive Battle

He had tried to persuade him out of the wrongdoings,
But Pengmajia only turned a deaf ear to his advice.
When his brother took away Zhao Langma's wife,
He knew this would put the Kingdom of Langa into havoc.

He had tried to persuade his brother to send back Nan Xila
But Pengmajia took him as his sworn enemy just because of this.
He disregarded they were brothers from the same blood and flesh,
And he had him tied up and thrown into the sea.

Pengmajia not only turned a deaf ear to his advice,
He even ordered to execute his own brother.
If Zhao Langma hadn't saved him out of the sea,
Biyasha would have been dead long time ago.

That Biyasha in the past,
He had already been dead;
The Biyasha living in today,
He was no longer the younger brother of Pengmajia.

Such bitter thoughts seared in Biyasha's heart.
He decided to tell Zhang Langma the secret of the ten-headed King,
"My brother has been so arrogant and ruthless
Just because god in heaven had given him a life-saving weapon.

"我们的父亲——天王玛哈捧，
在森林里送给他一副弓赛宰，
神弓紧紧系着他的生命和灵魂，
神弓可以保佑捧玛加不死。

"只有这把弓箭才能射死他①，
捧玛加死也要死在自己的弓箭下。
弓赛宰是我哥哥的命根子，
他珍惜地背在身上从不丢失。

"那次阿努曼放火烧着宫殿，
捧玛加怕大火烧毁神弓，
秘密拿到森林委托帕拉西保存，
各人留下一块刻纹的竹片为凭。

"如果有人变成捧玛加的模样，
拿着一半竹符去找帕拉西，
把神奇的宝弓弄到我们手里，
我们才能置捧玛加于死地。

"用弓赛宰射死捧玛加后，
必须立即砍下他的十个头，
但千万不能让他的头落地，
因为他死后还有害人的本事。

---

① 傣族有一种说法，凡是刀枪不入的人，只有用他身上佩戴的刀枪才可以把他杀死。

第十七章 决战　Chapter 17　The Decisive Battle

"Our father, the heaven god of Mahapeng,
He gave my brother a magic bow named Saizai,
This magical bow is tied with his life and soul,
And it blesses him with an ever lasting life.

"You can only kill him with his own bow[①],
If he was to be dead, he would die from his own arrow.
The Bow of Saizai is the root of Pengmajia's life.
He vigilantly carried it on his back day and night.

"Last time when Anuman set fire on the palace,
For fear that the bow of Saizai got burned in the fire,
Pengmajia went to the forest asking Palaxi to keep it safe.
Each of them holds a piece of bamboo slip with signs on it.

"If someone could transform into the image of Pengmajia,
He could go to Palaxi with that piece of bamboo slip,
He might be able to get the magic bow.
Then we could kill Pengmajia with it.

"After Pengmajia being shot with the Bow of Saizai,
His heads must be chopped off immediately.
Never let his heads land on the ground,
Because he can still harm people even after his death.

---

① There is another version among the Dai people. That is those who can't be killed by swords or guns can be killed by the sword or gun of his own.

711

"他的头会喷出熊熊大火,
他的血会变成滚烫的铁水,
大火能把大地烧裂,
铁水会使人类遭到毁灭。

"唯一能接住捧玛加头颅的,
是天上英达的宝簸盘子,
这宝盘藏在吉沙主拉麻尼宝塔里,
得到它人类才能免除一场浩劫。"

召朗玛知道了十头王的奥秘,
心中有说不出的欢喜,
他把聪明的阿努曼找来,
郑重地交给它新的使命。

"现在我要派你变成十头王,
到森林帕拉西处去取弓赛宰,
拔下你的毫毛变成竹符,
不要让帕拉西心中猜疑。

"见了帕拉西你要下拜,
礼貌周到、态度和蔼,
一定要用你的全部智慧,
把十头王的生命之弓取回来。"

霎时阿努曼变成逼真的十头王,
又拔下一根毫毛变成竹符,
彼亚沙验证上面有三十六种刻记,
智慧的帕拉西也不能把真伪辨出。

第十七章 决战　Chapter 17 The Decisive Battle

"His heads will spurt out flames;
His blood will turn into scorching iron liquid.
The flame will burn and blacken the land;
The iron liquid will bring an end to human beings.

"The only thing that can catch the heads of Pengmajia
Is the holy bamboo plate of the heavenly god of Yingda.
It is hidden in the sacred pagoda of Jishazhulamani.
Only with it can human beings stay away from annihilation."

Zhao Langma was more than happy
To know the secret of the the ten-headed King.
He sent for the clever Anuman,
Then he gave him a new mission solemnly.

"Now you need to turn yourself into the ten-headed King,
And go to the forest to fetch the bow of Saizai from Palaxi.
Pluck one of your hair and turn it into the bamboo slip,
Don't let Palaxi get suspicious.

"Once seeing Palaxi, you bow to him with respect.
You must be genteel, polite and amiable.
Use all of your wisdom and brains
And get back the magic bow of life of the ten-headed King."

Instantly Anuman turned himself into the ten-headed King,
Then he plucked his hair and changed it into the bamboo slip.
Biyasha examined carefully the 36 different signs inscribed on it,
Even the wise Palaxi couldn't tell whether it was authentic or not.

假捧玛加像流星一样飞进森林,
手拿竹符大大方方走进巴朗,
见了帕拉西它赶忙下拜,
把来意向帕拉西细讲。

"福气广大的帕拉西,
捧玛加向你下拜问好,
我今天匆匆来到这里,
是向你取弓赛宰来了。

"千万层云雾把太阳遮住,
灾难降临了我们的国土,
敌人进攻了神圣的勐兰嘎,
勐兰嘎像木船在海浪中沉浮。

"请你把弓赛宰还给我吧,
我要用它去拯救勐兰嘎。"
说罢拿出竹符与帕拉西对合,
帕拉西把神弓交给了它。

阿努曼得到了弓赛宰,
迫不及待地拜谢起程,
飞离森林,回到兵营,
召朗玛见了宝弓感激不尽。

第十七章 决战　Chapter 17　The Decisive Battle

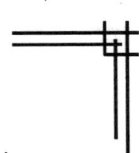

The fake Pengmajia flew into the forest like a shooting star.
He walked into Palaxi's Balang calmly and politely.
He bowed to Palaxi at meeting him.
Then he told him why he came to see him.

"You much-blessed Palaxi,
I now bowed to you paying you my regard.
I come here today in a hurry
To get my Bow of Saizai.

"Nowadays the sun is blocked by thousands of layers of clouds
And disasters befell on the land of our country.
Our enemy is attacking our sacred Kingdom of Langa.
Like a boat, the Kingdom of Langa is floating on the waves.

"Please give the magical Bow of Saizai back to me.
I need it to save our Kingdom of Langa."
After that he took out the bamboo slip for Palaxi to have a check.
Then Palaxi handed him the magical bow.

Anuman took hold of the magical bow,
And he hurriedly bid farewell to Palaxi.
Immediately he flew out of the forest and back to their camp.
Zhao Langma received the bow with much gratitude.

召朗玛又派阿努曼上天，
叫它去取来英达的宝盘，
阿努曼一个筋斗腾空，
眨眼就到达吉沙主拉麻尼塔旁边。

它向守塔的帝瓦吾跪下，
要求借用一下英达的宝盘，
帝瓦吾见它一片真心，
就把金光闪闪的宝盘交给它。

阿努曼连声道谢，
捧着宝盘从云层飞下，
在猴兵的一片欢呼声中，
它把宝盘交给了召朗玛。

召朗玛称赞它机智勇敢，
官兵们赞扬它比谁都有办法，
都说它是勐基沙的栋梁，
有了它，一定能打败捧玛加。

三、擒纵

捧玛加重新做了一项王冠，
王冠镶上红星绿星般的珠宝，
戴上它庄重、威严又美观，
头上犹如有金光万道。

第十七章 决战　Chapter 17 The Decisive Battle

Zhao Langma then sent Anuman again to the heaven.
This time he was to get Yingda's magic bamboo plate.
With one somersault Anuman flew away.
He got close to the Pagoda of Jishazhulamani within a blink.

Kneeling down in front of Diwawu who guarded the Pagoda.
Anuman pleaded to borrow the magic plate for a while.
Diwawu saw he was truly sincere,
And handed him the shining magic plate.

Anuman kept thanking him for that.
Then with the plate he flew down out of the clouds.
In the soldiers' chorus and cheers,
He handed the magic plate to Zhao Langma.

Zhao Langma commended Anuman for his bravery and wisdom.
All the generals and soldiers praised he was really resourceful,
Saying that he was the backbone of the Kingdom of Jisha.
With his help, they would surely be to defeat Pengmajia.

Ⅲ　Playing Cat and Mouse

Pengmajia ordered another crown to be made.
Jewelries like red and green stars were decorated on it.
It looked mighty, solemn and gorgeous,
It seemed to be threads of light gleaming on Pengmajia's heads.

捧玛加显得更加傲慢，
决定第二次亲自带兵作战，
他写信动员各勐的兵马，
迅速赶来助战解救危难。

十头王的命令谁敢拖延，
各勐的兵马立即来到宫殿前面，
他亲自调兵遣将发动了进攻，
带领着三方四路队伍勇猛向前。

他指挥各路队伍一齐射箭，
箭飞向敌阵如密集的雨点，
箭声嗖嗖、杀声震天，
漫山遍野的士兵向敌军席卷。

战场上的大树小树被撞倒，
原野上的房舍石头被踏碎，
起伏的丘陵土冢啊，
变成了一堆堆沙灰。

所有的猛将都出动了，
主攻是吉鲁哈、娃鲁纳、古月腊和谢米雅，
左翼是纳吉达，右翼是黑达和乾哈……
喊杀声像要把大地震垮。

第十七章 决战 Chapter 17 The Decisive Battle

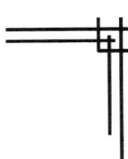

  Pengmajia became more haughty under his new crown.
  He decided to start a new round of attack.
  He wrote to other kingdoms asking for help,
  He wanted them to recruit more soldiers to rescue them.

  Nobody dared to delay carrying out his orders.
  More soldiers and horses were gathered in front of the palace.
  Then he took the command and start another round of attack,
  Leading four routes of soldiers to advance from three directions.

  He ordered all the troops to shoot arrows all together.
  The arrows flew to the enemies like tense raindrops.
  With arrows piercing the air and shouting from the soldiers,
  The troops all over the mountains and valleys swept the battlefield.

  Trees on the battlefield, big or small, were crashed down;
  Houses among the fields collapsed under the hooves.
  Even the wavy hills and rolling plains
  Were tramped into layers of sand and dust.

  All the generals joined in the attack.
  Jiluha, Waluna, Guyuela and Xiemiya led in the front;
  Najida flanked from left side, Heida and Qianha from the right…
  The earth was shaking under the forwarding troops and their shouting.

十头王捧玛加出阵了，
他骑着的大象如山一样高大，
势不可挡地向猴兵冲杀，
挺胸昂首大骂召朗玛：

"我可怜你这个小小的朗玛，
你今天必定死在我的手下，
你喜欢吃什么就快吃个饱吧，
很快你的血肉就要喂海里的鱼虾。

"南西拉是天上的仙女，
你不过是人间的一个猴王，
你还想得到美丽的南西拉，
那简直是痴心妄想。

"我留下你一条活命，
你快死了心回去吧，
别死在我的象脚下，
让自己的骨肉变成一滩泥巴。"

十头王说着驱象前进，
指挥着官兵猛冲猛杀，
召朗玛跃上马挥刀出阵，
针锋相对给了他一顿回骂：

第十七章 决战 Chapter 17 The Decisive Battle

Here charged into the battlefield was the ten-headed King.
He was riding an elephant as high as a mountain.
He advanced irresistibly into the monkey soldiers,
And with his heads high he showered his abuses onto Zhao Langma,

"I have pity on you, poor little Langma,
Today you are bound to be killed by me.
You had better eat whatever you like now.
Soon your will be tossed to the sea for the shrimps.

"Nan Xila is a fairy lady belonging to the heaven,
You are only a monkey king on the earth.
You want to get the beautiful Nan Xila?
That's only your wildest dream.

"I will spare your life
If you give up the idea and go back home.
Otherwise you will die under the feet of my elephant
And be turned into a puddle of flesh."

After that, the ten-headed King spurred its elephant to advance,
And he led his generals and soldiers to fight fiercely.
Zhao Langma jumped onto his horse and confronted the enemy.
Giving a tit for tat, he shouted back with indignation,

"南西拉有如宝石一般珍贵,
但今天我不只是为了夺回她,
我是想砍你的十个头颅为民除害,
才不辞艰辛来攻打勐兰嘎。

"你骄横跋扈、行为卑鄙,
你给人们带来灾难和泪雨,
天地不容你,人间怨恨你,
我的使命是把你的头砍下地。"

召朗玛说完冲向捧玛加,
仇敌相遇如胶粘在一起厮打,
兵对兵、将对将,
人马像赶街一样拥挤乱踩乱杀。

直打得烟尘滚滚、天昏地暗,
血水溅飞犹如密集的雨点,
只听得战鼓咚咚杀声阵阵,
尸体堆积好像一座座小山。

腊嘎纳伺机射出一支箭,
里达被射中滚下象背,
猴兵们蹿上去要割头,
被古月腊怒吼着杀退。

第十七章 决战　Chapter 17　The Decisive Battle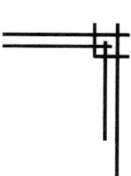

"Nan Xila is as precious as a jade
But today I came not just to get her back.
I want to chop off your ten heads getting rid of an evil for people.
That is why I took pains to attack the Kingdom of Langa.

"You are overbearing, haughty, mean and despicable.
You bring disasters and tears to your people;
The heaven can not tolerate you and people hate you.
My mission is to chop off your heads and take your life."

After the words, Zhao Langma dashed to Pengmajia,
The sworn enemies wrestled as if glued together.
Soldiers against soldiers, generals against generals,
It was in such a chaos that soldiers were tramped to death.

Now shrouded with dust, the sky got dark.
Blood flew like intense raindrops falling.
The war drums could be heard mingled with shouting;
The corpses of the soldiers were stacked high like small hills.

Lagana took the chance and shot at Lida.
Lida fell down from the back of his elephant.
Monkey soldiers rushed to cut off his head.
They were forced back by Guyuela snarling angrily.

乾哈持弓从侧面赶来助战，
嘎林跃起把乾哈和古月腊射翻，
捧玛加连折三将悲愤中跃上天空，
众将领尾随居高临下速速射箭。

双方的兵器相击乒乒乓乓，
就像锅里炒苞谷的爆炸声，
烈火似乎要把森林烧毁，
雷神好像在大地上奔驰。

召朗玛心中怀着满腔怒火，
对忠实的将士们说：
"再也不忍看遍地尸骨，
再也不忍看血流成河。

"今天我一定要飞上天空，
把罪恶的十头王亲手斩杀。"
旺果立刻变成一匹白马，
猴头马身、毛光水滑。

白净的身子套上金鞍，
响亮的金铃脖子上挂，
它昂头摆尾阵前站，
等待着召朗玛前去乘驾。

第十七章 决战 Chapter 17 The Decisive Battle

Qianha advanced from the flank up to assist Guyuela,
Then both of them were shot down to the ground by Galin.
Seeing he had lost three generals, Pengmajia jumped into the sky.
His generals followed him and they shot down from the above.

The clashing of the weapons could be heard afar.
The sound was like the popcorn in the hot pot.
Flames were burning and they seemed to engulf the forest.
It was like the god of thunder was sweeping over the earth.

Zhao Langma was full of indignation in his heart.
He said to his loyal generals and soldiers,
"I could not stand such miserable scenes any more,
With dead bodies everywhere and blood running like river.

"Today I will surely fly into the sky,
I will kill ten-headed King with my own hands."
Wangguo immediately turned into a white horse
With monkey's head and horse's body and silky fur.

Golden saddle was set up on its white body,
Ringing golden bells hang around its neck.
It vigorously galloped to the front of the troop,
Waiting for Zhao Langma to ride on.

召朗玛手持弓赛宰跨上白马,
阿努曼手托英达的宝盘,
嘎林提着衮纳帕的神镖,
一起飞上天空誓斩捧玛加。

召朗玛跃马驰骋飞近捧玛加,
仇人在天空相见立刻厮杀,
凶猛的捧玛加挥刀砍来,
召朗玛用刀格开,威力一样强大。

召朗玛拉起弓赛宰,
搭上锋利的神箭高声说话:
"凶恶的十头王捧玛加,
今天我定要把你的十个头射下。

"你的致命的弓赛宰,
已被我牢牢捏在手里,
眼看你就要死在今朝,
你还能嚣张狂妄几时?"

这一说吓得捧玛加睁大二十只眼睛,
恰似晴天霹雳震撼他的心胸,
细看召朗玛手持的弓弩,
正是请帕拉西秘藏的生命之弓。

第十七章 决战 Chapter 17 The Decisive Battle

Holding the magic Saizai, Zhao Langma mounted the horse,
Anuman held Yingda's magic plate in his hands;
Galin carried Gunnapa's dart;
They flew together into the sky to kill Pengmajia.

Zhao Langma galloped to Pengmajia,
Once meeting, the foes fought fiercely against each other.
The ferocious Pengmajia slashed to Zhao Langma,
The equally-powerful Zhao Langma fended off with his knife.

Then Zhao Langma took out the Bow of Saizai,
With the sharp arrow set on the bow he shouted,
"You vicious ten-headed King Pengmajia,
Today I will shoot all your ten heads off.

"This is the life bow of Saizai,
Now I hold it in my hands tightly.
You are doomed to die today.
Your arrogance and haughtiness won't last long."

His words got Pengmajia shocked with his twenty eyes wide open,
As if he was stricken right into the heart by a thunder.
He looked at the bow held in Zhao Langma's hand carefully,
It was exactly his bow of life he entrusted Palaxi to hide secretly.

捧玛加顿时惊恐哆嗦起来，
身子像躺在摇篮里那样晃动，
脸色突然变成像隔夜的炉灰，
胸腔似有万把火烧那样疼痛。

知道生命快要完结的捧玛加，
突然失去了往日不可一世的威风，
他向召朗玛连连告饶，
请求召朗玛恕罪宽容。

"我头顶上的朗玛王啊，
你是宽宏大量的人间天神，
饶我的罪恶，免我的死刑，
千错万错都怪我得罪了你。

"我不曾侮辱过美丽的南西拉，
让她住在漂亮的塔楼里，
我去请她来同你相见，
让你们永远生活在一起。

"勐兰嘎的海洋、山林、千百个勐，
勐兰嘎的大臣、武官、众多百姓，
我要双手拱托来奉送给你，
请你做勐兰嘎至高无上的国王。

"勐兰嘎有千千万万珠宝金银，
我将它们全部献给你，
辉煌的宫殿和美丽的花园，
一齐交到你手下统管。

第十七章 决战　Chapter 17　The Decisive Battle

Pengmajia was terrified and he began to tremble.
His body shook like a swinging cradle;
His face turned as pale as the overnight ashes;
His chest ached as if it would be scorched by fire.

Seeing the end of his life was drawing near,
Pengmajia lost his usual air of haughtiness.
He begged to Zhao Langma again and again,
Pleading him to generously forgive his sins.

"The King of Langma over my head,
You are a benevolent god living in the world.
Please forgive my sins and spare my life.
It is all my fault that I have offended you.

"I have never insulted your beautiful Nan Xila.
She is living alone in a pretty tower.
I will send for her to meet you here,
And then you can live together ever after.

"The sea, the forests and many small kingdoms in Langa,
The officials, the generals and all the people on my land,
I will hand them over to you with my great respect,
And you will be the supreme king of the Kingdom of Langa.

"All the treasures, gold and silver on the land of Langa,
I will give all of them to you.
The glorious palace and the grandiose gardens,
They all will be at your disposal.

"留下我这微弱的生命吧!
让我服侍你,
让我为你端洗脚水,
让我在你的脚下把罪孽赎回。"

召朗玛大义凛然地说道:
"我不想霸占别人的国土,
我不想在别的勐称王称霸,
更不想让勐兰嘎的百姓服从我。

"我不要勐兰嘎的宝贝珍珠,
我不要勐兰嘎的一草一木,
我们跨过大海来到勐兰嘎,
是要消除你这人间的恶魔。

"你多行不义必然要失败,
尽管你有数不清的兵马、大象,
尽管你本领高强有十个头颅,
罪恶使你逃脱不了死亡。

"既然你现在声声求饶,
愿意洗清罪恶重新做人,
你立刻把南西拉送来还给我,
表示你认罪的一点真诚。

"你要是真心实意悔过,
赶快下去跪在地上磕头求情,
向我和我的部属作出保证,
请求大家宽恕、饶你一命。"

第十七章 决战 Chapter 17 The Decisive Battle

"Please just spare my wretched life
So that I can serve you.
I will personally fetch the water to wash your feet
I will crouch under your feet to redeem my sins."

Zhao Langma answered with awe-inspiring righteousness,
"I won't take the land that isn't mine,
I won't claim the throne of other kingdoms.
I have never thought to have people of Langa under my rule.

"I want none of your treasures or pearls,
Not even a piece of grass or a tree from Langa.
We came to the Kingdom of Langa across the sea.
With the only aim to get rid of you the devil in this world.

"Your so many evils brought you the doomed destruction.
Now matter how many soldiers or elephants you have;
Now matter how powerful you are with your ten heads.
Death is the wage that you paid for your heinous sins.

"Now that you keep begging for your life,
Claiming you are to cleanse your sins and live a new life,
You should give Nan Xila back to me immediately
To prove your sincerity of confession and repentance.

"If you sincerely repent of your sin,
Now come to kneel down and plead for our forgiveness.
You should also make promise to me and my troops,
Pleading to everyone so that you can be forgiven and keep your life."

捧玛加战战兢兢地回答：
"要我下去跪在地上磕头，
这事万万不能做到，
除非高山削平，河水倒流。

"十个头只能折断掉落下来，
而不能低下来自己叩击地面，
全勐的百姓看着会耻笑，
这将丢尽一个大男子的尊严。

"我只会像大树一样断裂不会弯曲，
要是我在地上下跪，
就会损害父王玛哈捧的声威，
他的诺言比金子还珍贵。

"要是我不下跪，你就不饶恕我，
请你留给我七天的期限，
让我回兰嘎宫殿一转，
我决不逃跑躲藏、怠慢拖延。

"我要向亲人作最后的告别，
向臣僚和百姓作最后的告别，
到那一天我一定准时来受死，
有福气的召朗玛，请遂我心愿。"

召朗玛宽宏大量，
准许十头王回宫一趟，
命运注定了他即将灭亡，
放他回宫又有何妨。

第十七章 决战　Chapter 17　The Decisive Battle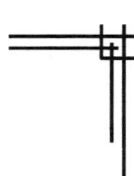

Trembling violently Pengmajia answered,
"I would never do such shameful things
To kneel down on the ground and kowtow to you.
Unless mountains are leveled and river flows backward.

"My ten heads can only be cut off down to the ground;
They could never be lowered to knock on the floor;
Otherwise I will be the laughingstock of the whole kingdom,
My honor and pride will be buried in such shames.

"I would rather be broken than be bent like a straight tree.
If I kneel down on the ground in front of you,
I will ruin my father Mahapeng's reputation.
Everyone knows his promise is more precious than pure gold.

"If you won't forgive me unless I kneel down,
Please give me an extension of seven days.
I want to go back to the palace of Langa and have my last look,
I vow that I will never try to escape or require more delay.

"I will bide my farewell to my families;
I want to say goodbye to my people and officials.
I will be here after seven days to let you take my life.
You blessed Zhao Langma, please grant my wishes."

Zhao Langma was kind and generous,
And he granted the wishes of the ten-headed King.
He was already a doomed persons approaching to death,
There is nothing to fear about his going back to his palace.

捧玛加带着兵马退出阵地，
就像一只斗败的公鸡，
看着他们垂头丧气回城去，
猴子兵的阵阵欢呼撼天动地。

贪婪和逞凶把十头王葬送，
他的生命到此告终，
到了他刚刚认识到自己的罪行的时候，
灾难已扯断了他的生命之弓。

四、妻子的劝告

生命快要结束的捧玛加，
满面愁容回到堂皇的宫殿，
同外祖父和母亲告别，
同三个妻子会面。

亲人们听说是生离死别，
一个个哭得像泪人儿一般，
哭声像七月田里的蛙鸣，
哭声几乎把宫殿震裂。

三个妻子特别痛苦、害怕，
她们苦苦地请求捧玛加：
"你快去送还南西拉，
向朗玛说说忏悔的话。

第十七章 决战　Chapter 17　The Decisive Battle

Pengmajia and his armies retreated from the battlefield,
This moment, he looked Like a defeated rooster.
Watching them retreating dejectedly back to the town,
Monkey soldiers cheered joyfully for their victory.

Greed and aggression led the ten-headed King to his destruction.
Very soon his life would come to its end.
Just when he was aware of the crimes and sins he had committed,
The disaster had already broken the string of his life bow.

Ⅳ　Wives' Persuasion

Now, Pengmajia was soon to die,
He returned to his grand palace with a sad face.
After saying goodbye to his grandfather and mother,
He met his three wives.

The families had heard they would be parted forever,
Everyone was crying and wailing.
The cries were like the croaking of frogs in July,
Their loud cries almost shook the roof of the palace off.

Three wives were most frightened and agonized.
They pled to Pengmajia in tears,
"Please send back Nan Xila to Zhao Langma as soon as possible,
And also tell Langma how repentant you are.

735

兰嘎西贺 The Ten-Headed King of Langa

"搜罗宫殿的全部珍宝,
赶着所有的大象和骏马,
配上漂亮的金座、银鞍,
一齐拿去献给召朗玛。

"老人常说宁愿失去万两黄金,
不可丢失宝贵的生命,
快把全勐最贵重的东西送去,
请召朗玛宽大饶恕箭下留情。

"你别再梦想娶南西拉为妻了,
你要体察妻子的一片好心,
人死就不能复生了,
请你可怜可怜我们三个人。

"妻子不能没有丈夫,
失去你我们的生活只有苦味,
去吧,向朗玛屈膝下跪,
去吧,向朗玛低头认罪。"

捧玛加毫不动心地说道:
"我是天王之子、勐兰嘎的国君,
我不能卑贱地向别人下跪求饶,
屈膝活着,不如挺胸挨刀。"

第十七章 决战 Chapter 17 The Decisive Battle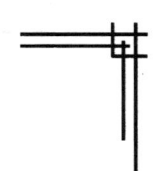

"Collect all the treasures in the palace;
Gather all your elephants and horses;
Set the gold saddles and silver spurs on them,
And offer all these to Zhao Langma.

"As the old saying goes,
We would rather lose 10 kilograms of gold than our precious life.
Please send all the valuables in your kingdom to Zhao Langma,
And plead to him to spare your life.

"Give up your wild dream of marrying Nan Xila.
You should understand our good intention.
No one could have a second life.
Please have pity on the three of us.

"A wife could not live without her husband.
Without you our life could be nothing but bitter.
Please go and kneel down in front of Langma;
Please go and confess your sin to Langma."

Without the slightest hesitation, Pengmajia said,
"I am the son of heavenly god, the King of Langa,
I will never condescend myself to kneel down and beg for mercy.
I would rather die with honor than live in shame."

737

兰嘎西贺 The Ten-Headed King of Langa

刚愎自用的捧玛加，
下令全勐举行盛大的赶摆，
他要在临死前苦中作乐，
威风凛凛地离开这个世界。

村村寨寨敲响铓锣和象脚鼓，
家家户户吹起拉响，
精通武艺和神术的人们，
显示着他们了不起的本领。

有的耍魔术玩手艺，
有的演杂技翻跟斗，
有的嘴含利箭脱下衣服跳鼓，
有的光着脚板在刀刃上行走。

小伙子穿着崭新的衣裳，
姑娘们打着红绿的花伞，
小伙子望着姑娘"嗒嗒"弹舌，
有意让姑娘看他们一眼。

宫女们迈着优美的步子走来，
她们打扮得花枝招展，
长长的筒裙一直拖到地上，
孔雀舞跳得娴熟、自然。

孔雀一忽儿向着人们开屏，
一忽儿又扇动多彩的翅膀，
百看不厌的孔雀舞啊，
吸引着多少赶摆人的目光。

第十七章 决战 Chapter 17 The Decisive Battle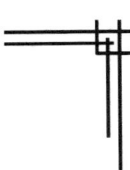

The conceited Pengmajia made a decision.
He ordered a fair to be held in the whole country.
What he wanted was to have fun before death,
So that he could leave this world in dignity.

Elephant-foot-shaped drums and gangs were hit in each village;
Music instruments were played in each household.
Those good at martial arts and magics gathered up,
They were displaying their skills to the villagers.

Some were conjuring tricks;
Some were doing somersaults;
Some dancing with sharp arrow in their mouths;
Some walking bare-footed on the blades of knives.

Young fellows were wearing new clothes;
Young girls were under colorful umbrellas.
The young lads whistled to the girls,
Trying to attract their attention.

The service maids in palace walked in grace;
They were all dressed up as beautiful as flowers.
With their long skirts trailing along the floor,
They performed the peacock dance adroitly and naturally.

The peacocks sometimes extended their tails,
Sometimes they shook their wings.
The forever-popular peacock dance,
Now again, it enchanted so many people in the fair.

兰嘎西贺 The Ten-Headed King of Langa

人们脸上谁也没有哀伤的表情，
他们为捧玛加超度灵魂，
他们热热闹闹前来参加赶摆，
是要让十头王感到高兴。

不会唱歌的人也张开嘴，
表示已经给捧玛加唱歌了，
他们唱着古老的哀歌毫不悲伤，
好像捧玛加已经脱离了死亡。

捧玛加对大臣——昐咐，
为他准备足够的米酒，
鲜美可口的剁生和生血，
香喷喷的烤鱼和鸡肉。

还有勐兰嘎香甜的瓜果，
香蕉、芭蕉、橘子、甜柚，
人们一一端到捧玛加跟前，
让他痛痛快快遂心吃个够。

在阴郁的十头王的身旁，
坐着他那三个可怜的王后，
声音哭哑了，眼睛哭肿了，
悲伤的泪水还不断地流。

此时此刻，仿佛世界上的人，
就数她们有最多的泪水淌流，
捧玛加对她们好言安慰：
"你们别再流泪，别再忧愁。

第十七章 决战　Chapter 17 The Decisive Battle

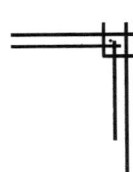

There was no trace of sorrow on people's faces.
They came here to bless Pengmajia's soul.
They came here joyfully to join in the fair,
So that the ten-headed king could feel happy.

Even those couldn't sing opened their mouths,
That showed they were singing for Pengmajia.
They were singing the old sad songs without sadness,
As if Pengmajia's soul had risen to the heaven.

Pengmajia gave orders to his officials,
Asking them to get enough rice wine ready for him,
Together with delicious Duosheng the cold dish,
As well as tasty barbecued fish and chicken.

The sweet melons and fruits from all over Langa,
Bananas, tangerines and shaddocks…
They were served one after one to Pengmajia
So that he could eat and drink to his heart's content.

Beside the gloomy ten-headed King
Sat the three poor queens.
They have cried their eyes swollen and voice cracked
And their sad tears were still running down their cheeks.

At this moment, as if among all the men on the earth,
They were the most miserable three with most tears.
Pengmajia comforted them gently,
"Please stop crying, don't be sad.

"我的灵魂要升上天国,
永远离开勐兰嘎这人间乐土,
平时你们有什么过错,
今天我许诺对你们宽恕。

"梭芭花一样的妻子们呀,
我死了,愿你们生活快乐安康,
愿疾病和灾难远离你们,
愿你们的脸孔像星星永远明亮。

"要是我闭上了眼睛,
结束了今世的生命,
请端上祭物、滴下几壶水,
祭奠我归去的灵魂。"

捧玛加说完泪湿了胸襟,
三个王后哭得东歪西倒,
母亲和宫女一起落泪,
臣僚和头人大声号啕。

所有的大象一齐悲鸣,
所有的战马一齐哀叫,
宫殿的金柱在震荡抖动,
王国的宝座在颠簸晃摇。

捧玛加在痛苦中度过夜晚,
夜里他被许多噩梦纠缠,
他梦见大象全部飞离宫殿,
三个妻子一个个离开他身边。

第十七章 决战 Chapter 17 The Decisive Battle

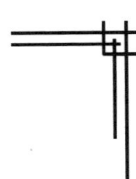

"My soul will soar to the heaven
Leaving Langa, the paradise in this world, forever.
As to the errors that you have made in the past,
I promise you today that I have forgiven you.

"My dear wives, you are like Shoba flowers in my heart,
After I die, may you live a happy and healthy life.
May illness and disaster stay away from you.
May your faces will shine like the stars in the sky forever.

"When I close my eyes forever,
When my life in this world comes to its end,
Please offer your sacrifice and splash water around
So that my soul could be pacified."

Then Pengmajia's tears soaked his clothes;
The three queens were wailing and trembling.
His mother shed tears with the service maids;
The officials and chieftain were crying loudly.

All the elephants were moaning in sorrow;
All the horses were neighing sadly in unison.
The pillars of the palace were shaking;
The throne of the kingdom was trembling.

Pengmajia spent the night in great pangs.
He was haunted by many nightmares.
He dreamed all the elephants flew out of the palace,
And his three wives left him one by one.

兰嘎西贺 The Ten-Headed King of Langa

太阳忽然被青蛙吞食，
浓雾沉沉遮住了蓝天，
宫殿的宝石失去了光辉，
宫廷变得一片黑暗。

他还在梦中看见自己，
全身泡在鲜红的血水里，
身子在污血中腐烂，
蛆虫爬满了他的躯体。

捧玛加确确实实做了噩梦，
醒来后他却不把它挂在心中，
他把不祥的预兆看得很轻，
他一点也不珍惜自己的生命。

他仍然天天吃喝玩乐，
夜夜醉醺醺睡到大天明，
他好像一点也不忧伤和发愁，
热热闹闹欢乐了七天整。

此时十头王的儿子菲玛兰敢归来，
他在外祖父龙王那里学得一身法术，
听母后讲到勐兰嘎战况和父亲的命运，
菲玛兰敢满腔怒火要拼个你死我活。

第十七章 决战　Chapter 17 The Decisive Battle

In his dream the sun was suddenly swallowed by a frog.
The blue sky was cloaked in thick fog.
All his jades housed in his palace lost their shine,
And the palace was immersed in endless darkness.

He also dreamed of himself.
He was immersed in a blood pool.
His body was rotted in the blood
And worms were creeping all over his body.

Pengmajia did have the nightmares.
But he paid little heed to such things.
He took such bad omens lightly,
He didn't care much about his own life.

　　He still indulge himself in eating, drinking and being merry every day.
　　He got himself drunk and slept in his numbness till dawn every night.
　　He didn't seem sad or worried at all.
　　And he spent the seven days jolly and nosily.

　　At that moment his son Feimalangan came back home.
　　He had learned many magics from his grandfather the dragon king.
　　After his mom told him the situation of Langa and his father's destiny,
　　Feimalangan was indignant and vowed to take revenge.

伤心的母亲南曼达苦苦劝阻，
菲玛兰敢一句也听不进耳朵，
他气冲冲去谒见十头王，
把自己的决心说出：

"召朗玛其实没有什么了不起的力量，
儿子在龙宫学的本领定比他强，
不能白白地束手等死啊，
拼它一场还不知道谁死谁伤。"

十头王本来不愿服罪投降，
儿子的回宫给他增加了胆量，
他决定展开一次闪电式进攻，
拼死拼活，决战一场。

五、十头王的惨死

七天的期限到了，
捧玛加又开始第三次亲征，
他抱着头不落地不服输的决心，
调集兵马作最后一次殊死拼命。

十头王和菲玛兰敢检阅了队伍，
兵马多得像密集的森林，
气势磅礴、威武坚强，
一个个虎视眈眈。

第十七章 决战 Chapter 17 The Decisive Battle

His sad mom Nan Manda tried to talk him out of the idea,
But Feimalangan wouldn't take in even one of her words.
He rushed angrily to see his father the ten-headed King,
And he expressed his determination to kill the enemy,

"Langma indeed is not as powerful as you thought.
I am more capable than him with the tricks I learned in the sea.
We can't just wait here to be killed by them.
Let's have another try to see who will die and who will survive."

The ten-headed King was reluctant to surrender deep in his heart.
The return of his son to the palace emboldened him,
So he made up his mind to start another flashy attack.
He was to try his last luck in the battlefield.

V The Miserable Death of the Ten-headed King

When the seven days' extension period ended
Pengmajia launched a third time attack.
He was determined never to surrender till the last breath.
He gathered all his troops to start the life-or-death battle.

He and Feimalangan inspected the troops.
Soldiers were numerous as the dense trees in the forest.
They looked mighty, brave and staunch.
And they were eager to go for the fighting.

他调派了十五员大将,
组织了八路大军,
像决堤的江水滚滚翻腾,
捧玛加的队伍涌向召朗玛兵营。

军号呜呜响彻云天,
战鼓咚咚震撼大地,
就像狂风在呼啸奔腾,
勐兰嘎士兵的呐喊响遍森林。

召朗玛见捧玛加垂死挣扎,
立即指挥全线兵马冲杀,
将士们挥刀舞棍拉弓举矛,
要把十头王彻底打垮。

捧玛加督促十五员大将往前冲,
把猴子兵的阵地杀得一片通红,
他们决心一举夺回弓赛宰,
挽救十头王的生命。

气势汹汹的阿康达连连发箭,
猴将嘎木达被利箭射中受了伤,
阿康达骑象冲杀得正开怀,
嘎林迎上去与他厮杀不相让。

摩米为嘎木达裹好了伤,
嘎木达又挥舞弩箭冲上战场,
它拉动弓弩对准阿康达射出一箭,
阿康达中箭惨死从象背滚落地上。

第十七章 决战 Chapter 17 The Decisive Battle

Then he designated fifteen generals,
And divided the troops into eight routes.
Like the rolling water bursting out of the broken dam,
Pengmajia's troops marched toward the camps of Zhao Langma.

Sounds of trumpets could be heard in the clouds;
The rollings of the drums shook the earth.
Like the gales roaring and screaming over the land
The shouting from the soldiers of Langa echoed in the forest.

Seeing Pengmajia waging his desperate struggle,
Zhao Langma immediately commanded a counterattack.
His generals and soldiers took up all kinds of weapons,
And they vowed to completely destroy the ten-headed King.

Pengmajia urged the fifteen generals to rush forward,
Then the battlefield on the monkey soldiers' side got bloody red.
The generals were determined to get back the bow of Saizai
So that they could save the life of their ten-headed King.

The aggressive Akangda kept shooting his arrows,
And the monkey general Gamuda got hit and hurt.
On his elephant, Akangda rushed toward Gamuda,
Galin intercepted him halfway and they fought fiercely.

Momi came to bind up the wound for Gamuda,
Then Gamuda returned to the battlefield with his bow.
He aimed at Akangda and shot an arrow,
Akangda was hit dead and fell down from the elephant.

猴将玛尼腊和阿哈接连射箭，
成群的敌兵死在它们的箭下，
尼腊一箭射死了纳吉达，
阿哈一箭射死了吉鲁哈。

军马战象掀起一阵阵灰尘，
飞箭撕碎一片片乌云，
灰尘烟雾把天地遮蔽，
看不见太阳、看不见森林。

阿努曼手持宝棍冲入敌阵，
遍地倒下了死伤的兰嘎官兵，
猴子兵跟着它左冲右杀，
血水染红了山冈、溅污了丛林。

菲玛兰敢见兰嘎将士死伤惨重，
口中念念有词施展妖法，
霎时树叶和沙粒变成千军万马，
手持弓箭向猴子兵猛烈冲杀。

他们射出密集的箭雨，
箭矢宛如一只只回巢的蜂子，
猴子兵伤的伤死的死，
顿时召朗玛的阵地一片紊乱。

第十七章 决战　Chapter 17 The Decisive Battle

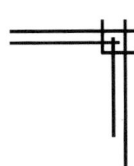

Monkey general Manila and Aha kept their shooting,
Groups of enemies died under their arrows.
With just one shot, Amani killed Najida,
Jiluha got shot by Aha and died instantly.

Dusts rose from under the feet of the elephants
The flying arrows pierced through dark cloud.
The land was shrouded with dusts and smoke,
Neither the Sun nor the forest could be seen.

Anuman fought his way in the armies with his magic staff,
Rows of enemy soldiers fell onto the ground, injured or dead.
The monkey soldiers followed him fighting all around,
Blood soaked into the land and spilled all over the woods.

Feimalangan witnessed the heavy casualties of their troops.
So he chanted his spells to perform his magic tricks.
In an instant, leaves and sands were turned into numerous soldiers,
They fought against the monkey soldiers with their bows and arrows.

They shot arrows as dense as raindrops.
Arrows flew like the bees returning to their nests.
Many monkeys were shot and injured or killed.
Langma's soldiers was in panic and chaos.

嘎林和猴将夺路冲上前来，
抵挡住兰嘎将士的反击，
发怒的阿努曼大吼一声，
如滚雷般向菲玛兰敢冲去。

菲玛兰敢迅速闪身躲过，
回过头挥刀砍向阿努曼的脑袋，
阿努曼敏捷地躲过利刀，
抓住刀柄和他厮打起来。

阿努曼想活捉菲玛兰敢，
可是他比池塘里的青苔还滑，
犹如泥巴里一条黄鳝，
滑溜溜的无法抓住他。

阿努曼边打边思忖：
"他哪里来的这套本领？
我得去问一问彼亚沙，
想办法把他战胜。"

阿努曼甩掉菲玛兰敢，
飞回营帐请问彼亚沙，
彼亚沙告诉阿努曼：
"用你的尿水搅拌泥沙。

"让泥沙粘满你的两只手，
你就能稳稳地抓住他。"
阿努曼双手沾满泥沙飞回战场，
立刻抓住菲玛兰敢像老鹰抓小鸡一样。

第十七章 决战　Chapter 17　The Decisive Battle

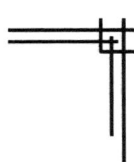

Galin and other generals fought their way in the front,
They fended off another wave of attack from Langa soldiers.
A loud yelling burst out from the furious Anuman,
Then he dashed to Feimalangan like a rolling thunder.

Feimalangan dodged his attack swiftly like a flash,
Then he turned his back and slashed toward Anuman's head.
Anuman dived agilely away from the sharp blade,
And he grabbed the knife handle and wrestled with Feimalangan.

Anuman tried to captivate Feimalangan alive,
But Feimalangan was as slippery as the moss in the pond.
And he was like the eel in the mud,
Anuman couldn't grasp any part of him.

Anuman thought to himself while fighting,
"From where did he acquire such skills?
I must go and ask Biyasha about it
So that I can figure out how to conquer him."

Anuman then got rid of Feimalangan,
And he flew back to the camp to ask Biyasha.
Biyasha told him of the secret,
"Mix your urine with sands.

"Smear your hands with the mixture,
Then you can take hold of him firmly."
Anuman did as Biashi taught and flew back to the battlefield.
Then he snatched Feimalangan as an eagle snatching a chicken.

菲玛兰敢拼命挣扎脱不了身，
阿努曼抓住他的双脚，
把他活活地撕扯成两半，
一半摔到北山，一半丢到南岭。

可是两半身子又飞回来合拢，
凶恶的菲玛兰敢又复活，
他拔起大树扑向阿努曼，
暴怒的白猴又大战妖魔。

两人又激烈地厮打起来，
阿努曼又趁机抓住菲玛兰敢，
迅速撕下他的四肢剥下他的皮，
狠狠地把他的头颅在石上砸烂。

阿努曼搬来一块野象大的石头，
把尸首紧紧压在下面，
菲玛兰敢再也不能复活了，
妖兵像风一样顷刻消散。

十头王见儿子惨死，
二十只眼睛闪着凶光，
他决心拼个鱼死网破，
带着将士气汹汹再次上场。

第十七章 决战 Chapter 17 The Decisive Battle

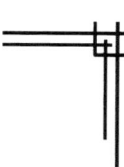

Feimalangan struggled to get away but just in vain,
Anuman grasped his feet and tore him alive into two pieces.
One half was thrown to the north side of the mountain;
And the other part to the south side.

But the two parts flew back and glued together,
The ferocious Feimalangan came back to life again.
He uprooted a big tree and threw at Anuman,
The agitated white monkey wrestled again with the devil.

Two of them glued together and wrestled fiercely.
Anuman caught hold of Feimalangan again,
He tore off all his limbs and skinned him.
He smashed Feimalangan's skull on the boulder.

Anuman moved over a rock as big as an elephant,
He pressed the rock heavily on the body of Feimalangan.
Now Feimalangan couldn't come back to life again.
The ghost soldiers of Feimalangan disappeared like wind.

The ten-headed King witnessed the miserable death of his son.
His twenty eyes were shimmered with hatred.
He was determined to drag the enemy down with him if he died.
Leading his generals and soldiers, he started fiercely the last attack.

召朗玛率领将士立刻迎上前去，
把十头王团团包围在中间，
嘎木达对准十头王射了一箭，
十头王眼疾手快一刀把它砍断。

长矛、大刀、利箭一齐杀去，
十头王的身躯到处是窟窿，
但他既不流血也不疼痛，
他毫不介意、神态从容。

十头王瞄准召朗玛连发数箭，
被召朗玛挥刀一一砍断，
十头王随即纵身跃上云天，
同众将一起居高临下射出利箭。

捧玛加的神箭在云中隆隆转了一圈，
变成一块块野象大的石头，
纷纷落在召朗玛的兵营上，
许多猴子兵被砸死砸伤。

召朗玛再也不能忍让十头王，
仁慈宽大只能使他更残忍疯狂，
召朗玛手持弓赛宰骑马飞上天去，
同凶恶的十头王作最后一次较量。

第十七章 决战　Chapter 17　The Decisive Battle

Zhao Langma led his troops to confront him directly.
They surrounded the ten-headed King in the middle.
Gamuda aimed at him and shot an arrow.
Agilely the ten-headed King slashed it into halves with his knife.

Spears, knives and arrows flew together toward the ten-headed King.
They pierced through his body and left numerous holes.
But he was not bleeding and didn't feel pain at all.
He was quite composed paying no attention to those wounds.

The ten-headed king shot his arrows at Zhao Langma,
The arrows were also broken by Zhao Langma with his sword.
The ten-headed King then jumped high into the clouds,
Together with his generals, he shot the enemies from the above.

The arrows from Pengmajia soared around the clouds,
Then they turned into rocks as big as the elephants.
They fell down onto the camps of Zhao Langma.
And many soldiers were pounded dead or injured.

Zhao Langma couldn't tolerate the ten-headed King anymore.
His clemency only invited more cruel revenge from him.
Zhao Langma flew with the bow of Saizai into the sky.
He was to fight the last battle with the evil ten-headed King.

召朗玛取出致命的弓赛宰,
用力拉动向捧玛加射击,
第一箭被他挥刀砍断了,
第二箭被他躲过避开了。

威力无比的弓赛宰箭矢,
穿透了谢米雅、朗皮塔嘎的身子,
射死了哈腊干、月哈纳,
勐兰嘎的四员大将从云层摇摇晃晃摔下地。

召朗玛见两箭都未射中十头王,
又一次瞄准他的喉管射击,
他使尽平生力气放出第三箭,
像闪电一样迅猛的神箭飞了出去。

长空突然雷声隆隆,
神箭掀起了猛烈的狂风,
捧玛加无法躲避,
霹雳一声,喉管被射中。

树干一样粗直的脖颈折断了,
捧玛加威严的十个头啊,
犹如熟透的芒果,
纷纷从粗大的脖颈上掉落。

阿努曼端着英达的宝盘,
接住掉下来的十个头颅,
迅速飞到茫茫海洋的上空,
把十个头颅抛进大海深处。

第十七章 决战　Chapter 17 The Decisive Battle

Zhao Langma took out the magic bow of Saizai.
He pulled the bow with great strength and shot at Pengmajia.
The first arrow was cut down by him with his knife.
Pengmajia also managed to dodge the second one.

But the arrows of Saizai were so powerful
That they penetrated the bodies of Xiemiya and Langpitaga;
And they killed Halagan and Yuehana.
These four generals of Langa fell down from the clouds.

After having missed two shots at Pengmajia,
Zhao Langma aimed again at Pengmajia's throat.
With all his strength he let go of his third arrow,
Which flew out like a flash toward Pengmajia.

Roaring thunder crashed all of sudden in the sky.
The magic arrow produced violent gales.
Pengmajia had no time to dodge,
With a thunderclap, he got shot at his throat.

His neck, as thick as tree trunk, were broken off.
The ten awe-inspiring heads of Pengmajia,
Like fully ripe mangoes
One by one fell off from his thick necks.

Anuman carried Yingda's magic plate,
And he caught the falling heads with it.
Then he flew to the sky above the vast ocean,
And dumped the ten heads deep into the sea.

十个头颅顿时爆炸燃起大火,
把烟波弥漫的海水煮沸,
热浪翻滚、掀起水柱,
被烫熟的鱼虾螃蟹在海上漂浮。

捧玛加的头颅变成人间的毒虫,
有的变成毒蛇和怪龙,
有的变成花花绿绿的水蛤蚧,
有的变成大蚂蟥在水中游动。

捧玛加的身子落在地上,
变成大蟒、豺狼、虎豹,
飞溅的血液和碎肉,
变成蜈蚣、虱子和跳蚤。

骄横跋扈的捧玛加呀,
最终受到了十头落地的惩罚,
勐兰嘎的王座上再也不见十个头转动,
十头王的故事从此告终。

第十七章 决战　Chapter 17　The Decisive Battle

The ten heads exploded and caused great fire,
Which boiled the misty sea water.
Hot waves rolled on the wavy water,
Scorched fishes and shrimps were floating on the sea.

Pengmajia's heads turned into poisonous creatures.
Some became venomous snakes and evil dragons;
Some turned into the colourful geckos;
Others into the leeches swimming in the water.

His body fell down onto the ground,
And it turned into pythons, jackals and leopards.
The splashing blood and small pieces of flesh,
They became centipede, lice and scorpions.

The overbearing Pengmajia got his final punishment,
Death was the price he paid for his evils. Since then
There were no more turning of the ten heads on the throne,
And that's the end of the story of the ten-headed King.

第十八章 凯旋

一、召朗玛的胜利

威武无比的召朗玛率领着猴子兵,
浩浩荡荡、威风凛凛地开进兰嘎城,
召朗玛骑着高大的白牙大象,
金鞍闪亮,金伞挡住火热的阳光。

腊嘎纳骑着金鞍银铃的白马,
彼亚沙乘着十头王的坐骑,
各猴将簇拥着召朗玛向前行,
猴兵个个喜笑颜开、步伐整齐。

年迈的前国王叭兰巴,
得知捧玛加在战场上阵亡,
领着女儿、孙媳和侍女,
战战兢兢躲进深山老林。

召朗玛走进富丽堂皇的宫殿,
里面冷冷清清、空无一人,
不见叭兰巴,不见国戚皇亲,
他立刻派人四处找寻。

第十八章 凯旋 Chapter 18 Return in Triumph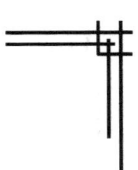

Chapter 18　Return in Triumph

Ⅰ　The Victory of Zhao Langma

The majestic Langma led the army of monkeys,
And they marched into the capital city of Langa.
Langma rode a huge elephant with an ivory and golden saddle;
A golden umbrella shielded him from the hot sunlight.

Lagana rode a white horse with gold saddle and silver bells;
Biyasha was on the elephant of the ten-headed King.
Generals of the monkey army escorted Zhao Langma;
Monkey soldiers marched forward orderly and joyfully.

Ba Lanba, the old king of Langa, got the news
That Pengmajia had died in the battlefield.
Taking his daughter, granddaughter-in-law and servants,
He hid in the deep mountain forests with fear and trepidation.

Zhao Langma walked into the magnificent palace
Only to find it was empty and forlorn.
Ba Lanba and all the royal families were not there.
He sent for his army to search for them immediately.

兰嘎西贺 The Ten-Headed King of Langa

找遍各个勐的城镇和乡村，
也看不到叭兰巴一家的踪影，
最后在深山老林找到他们，
士兵把他们带回兰嘎宫廷。

叭兰巴见了召朗玛不敢抬头，
他流着悲伤的泪水请罪：
"请英明的召朗玛开恩，
请饶恕我，给我赎罪的机会。

"我是一个年迈体衰的老人，
万万没想到会发生这场战争，
也没想到由外祖父来哀悼外孙，
年轻的死去，年老的苟生。

"兰嘎是个豪华富庶的地方，
捧玛加为王却虐待百姓，
我告诫他要恪守规诫不做恶事，
他对我的话一句也听不进。

"他把自己看得比上天还高明，
有了权力有了本领就胡作非为，
他抢劫南西拉造成你们夫妻分离，
让你们不知流了多少眼泪。

"本来我们都是一座山上的斑鸠，
本来我们都是一个湖里的游鱼，
何必你啄我的头、我咬你的尾，
可是捧玛加却掠夺你的妻子。

第十八章 凯旋　Chapter 18　Return in Triumph

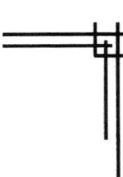

All the towns and villages were searched,
But there was no trace of Ba Lanba and his families.
At last they were found in the deep jungle,
And soldiers took them back to the palace of Langa.

Ba Lanba dared not raise his head when meeting Zhao Langma.
With sad tears running on his face, he pled,
"Wise Zhao Langma, please have mercy on me.
Forgive me and give me a chance to atone for my sins.

"I am worn out with my age.
It never occurred to me this war could have happened.
Nor did I know that I would mourn for my own grandson.
Now the young died while the old lives a miserable life.

"The Kingdom of Langa boasts for its prosperity.
Pengmajia, as the King, treated his people badly.
I have warned him to follow rules and not to do evils,
But he turned a deaf ear to what I had preached to him.

"He thought himself more powerful than the heaven.
He thought he could do whatever he liked with his power and skills.
He robbed Nan Xila and had your couples separated;
And he was the one who made you two shed so many tears.

"We are the doves living in the same mountain;
We are the fishes swimming in the same pond.
Why should we fight with each other?
But Pengmajia started it by taking your wife away.

"善良和正义啊,
犹如宝石一样,
具有磨灭不了的光芒,
就是沉到海底也会发亮。

"奸诈邪恶有时也会得逞,
就像骤雨之前滚动的乌云,
可是雨后日出天空晴朗,
遮天的乌云就被大风吹得无踪无影。

"今天你像一颗宝石降落,
兰嘎宫殿光芒四射闪闪灼灼,
你的善良和威望天下闻名,
你的胸襟比海洋深沉宽阔。

"我有棉花一样柔软的心肠,
我把王位交给了捧玛加,
希望他治理国家谨严宽厚,
对待百姓温和善良。

"俗话说爱偷鸡的黄鼠狼,
再小心也会落进猎人的网,
常吃人的贪婪的老虎,
再凶猛也终要遭到身亡。

"捧玛加像地下的蚯蚓,
活在土中还怕吃不着泥,
前面吃进去、后面泄出来,
周而复始、永无休止。

第十八章 凯旋 Chapter 18 Return in Triumph

"Kindness and justice
Are like the diamond,
They have the everlasting sheen
They still glitter even at the bottom of the sea.

"The wicked may take the upper wind for a while
Just like the dark cloud before the storm comes.
But the blue sky is still there after the storm,
And the dark clouds will be cast away by the wind.

"You are like a diamond landing here today;
Your glamour shines all over the palace.
Your kindness and reputation spread the world.
You have a heart wider and deeper than the ocean.

"I have a heart as soft as cotton.
I passed my throne on to Pengmajia,
Hoping he could rule the country wisely and leniently,
And treat his people with respect and kindness.

"No matter how careful a weasel is when it steals chicken,
There is always a day when it falls into the trap of a hunter.
It is the same with the greedy tiger which preys on human,
No matter how fierce it is, it still has its final day.

"Pengmajia is like a greedy earthworm,
Living in the earth while wanting more of dirt.
The earthworm gets the dirt in and out,
On and on without ending.

"捧玛加管天管地管海管森林,
一直管到上苍的天神,
千人朝拜、万民归顺,
还不能满足他的贪婪和野心。

"他横行霸道超越了天规地法,
直到偷劫别人的妻子,
现在捧玛加厄运临头惨死了,
这是他罪有应得的惩罚。

"请求你宽恕一个年迈的老人,
我愿把勐兰嘎的无价之宝全部献给你,
勐兰嘎的宝座请你来坐,
让我在你的福荫高照下栖身。"

明智的召朗玛不责怪叭兰巴,
不把十头王的罪行记在他的身上,
他欣然满足了老国王的恳求,
并请他协助把混乱的勐兰嘎安顿。

这时召朗玛才宣布迎接南西拉,
允兰嘎全城轰动、欢声四起,
胜利的猴兵更是兴高采烈,
犹如迎来了一个盛大的节日。

第十八章 凯旋 Chapter 18 Return in Triumph

"He governs everything from the sky to the forest;
He even tried vainly to keep the heavenly gods under his rule.
Tens of thousands of people bowed to him and served him,
But he was still insatiable due to his greed and ambition.

"He was a tyrant and violated the rules of heaven and earth;
And he even committed the crime of stealing your wife.
Now misfortune befell and he had the miserable death.
That is the final punishment he deserved.

"Please forgive me the old man,
I will offer all the invaluable treasures of Langa to you.
You can sit on the throne of the Kingdom of Langa,
Just let me have a resting place under your blessing."

The Wise Zhao Langma didn't blame Ba Lanba,
He was not held responsible for the crimes committed by Pengmajia.
He readily met the pleadings of Ba Lanba, the old king,
Asking him to help bring the chaotic Langa back to its normal track.

Then Zhao Langma announced to meet Nan Xila.
Cheers were heard from each corner of the city of Langa.
The victorious monkey soldiers were in high spirit,
As if they were celebrating a significant festival.

人们按照传统的礼仪，
热热闹闹走进御花园，
用大象和花环迎接纯洁的南西拉，
把美丽的南西拉接进兰嘎宫殿。

二、火的考验

像泪人儿般的南西拉，
扑倒在召朗玛的脚下，
心在颤抖、泪在流淌，
悲伤使她说不出一句话。

悲喜交集的召朗玛，
热泪也像喷泉一样滚出，
他有满腹的热情和温柔的疼爱，
又夹有男性的狐疑和嫉妒。

他慢慢把妻子扶起来，
对她说的话缓慢、柔和、低沉，
既像夜里月亮泻下的银光洁白宜人，
又仿佛夜空小星那样闪烁不明。

"梭芭花般的南西拉，
珍珠般明亮的妻子，
我俩相见付出多少代价，
仿佛是死后又重生。

第十八章 凯旋 Chapter 18 Return in Triumph

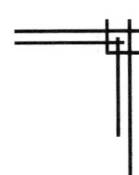

People thronged into the royal garden.
Following the traditional custom and etiquette,
They welcomed the pure Nan Xila with flowers and elephants
And they escorted her into the palace of Langa.

II The Test of Fire

With tears running like a river,
Nan Xila threw herself to the feet of Zhao Langma,
Her heart trembling and her tears shedding,
She was too sorrowful to speak even one word.

Zhao Langma was both sad and joyful,
His scorching tears burst out like hot spring.
He was full of passion and gentle care for his wife,
But he also had the suspicion and jealousy of a man.

He helped his wife up and spoke to her.
His words were slow, soft and in low voice,
Like the silver moonlight pouring down at night,
While twinkling invisibly like the remote stars.

"Nan Xila, you are like a Shuoba flower;
You are as bright as a pearl.
We have paid too heavy price for this reunion,
Now it seems that we have had a second life.

兰噶西贺　The Ten-Headed King of Langa

"捧玛加把你劫走,
使你受尽折磨吃够苦头,
现在捧玛加已被杀死,
你究竟是怎样熬过这些年头的?

"我彷徨、疑虑和不安,
我的心是多么的忧愁,
你像颗五彩缤纷的宝石,
会不会蒙上看不见的污垢?

"过去的南西拉呀,
恰似一棵叶嫩花馥的丁香树,
生长在圣洁的僻静的山坡,
没有蛀虫和黑蜂来爬过。

"过去的南西拉呀,
犹如珍珠在沙层里隐藏,
没有受过灰尘的玷污,
日夜发出锃亮纯净的白光。

"后来皎玛哈宁①被人偷走,
成了别人箱子里的宝贝,
只怕它被沾染了肮脏的灰尘,
不像往日那样闪射耀眼的光辉。

---

① 皎玛哈宁:黑宝石。

第十八章 凯旋 Chapter 18 Return in Triumph

"Pengmajia robbed you away from me,
And you have gone through uncountable sufferings.
Now Pengmajia has been killed.
Tell me how you survived those hard time?

"I feel hesitating, doubtful and uneasy.
How sorrowful my heart is at this moment.
You are like a colorful gemstone,
But could there be invisible stain in it?

"Nan Xila in the old days was like a clove tree.
It grew in a remote and sacred corner
With tender leaves and fragrant blooming flowers.
No worms or black bees have ever touched it.

"My Nan Xila in the old days was like a pearl.
It was deep buried in layers of sands,
Free from the stain of worldly dust.
She shines with pure white light.

"Later my precious Jiaomahaning① was taken away,
And became the treasure in the box of someone else.
I am afraid she has been stained with the dirty dusts,
She is not as bright and pure as it used to be.

---

① Jiaomahaning: black gemstone.

773

"我作了这么多的比喻,
是要说出我心中的疑惑和忧虑,
纯洁的宝石是否被脏手摸过?
柔弱的南西拉是否被强力侮辱?

"我相信你如过去一样的纯洁,
我相信你自始至终坚贞忠诚,
纯洁的璧玉和珠宝丢失了,
就怕被损坏污染失去原来的光泽。

"我相信失去的璧玉依然完好无损,
可是就怕别人难以置信,
现在流言蜚语到处传播,
你怎样才能证明自己的忠贞?

"开在树顶的缅桂花,
怎样证明它未被蛀虫爬过?
闪烁在高空的微弱的小星,
怎样证明它未被乌云玷污?

"如果你的心像蜡条一样正直,
你一定能用高尚的行为,
消除我心中的不安和疑惑,
也让那些多嘴的人没话可说。"

纯洁善良的南西拉紧皱双眉,
心如针刺又扑簌簌流泪,
除了宝贵的生命还有什么可以作证?
不是真正的金子就让它变成灰。

第十八章 凯旋 Chapter 18 Return in Triumph

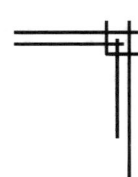

"I have used many parables
Trying to express my concerns and doubts.
Has the pure gemstone been touched by dirty hands?
Has the fragile Nan Xila been insulted by forces?

"I believe you are as pure as before;
I believe you are always loyal and faithful.
But once the precious gemstone got lost,
Her glorious sheen could be damaged or contaminated.

"I believe that the retrievable jade is still intact,
But I am afraid that the others might not think so.
Now rumors have been spread everywhere,
How can you prove your chastity and purity?

"The flower blooming on top of the clove tree,
How can it prove not being moth-eaten?
The fading twinkling star in the high sky,
How can it prove not having been stained by dark cloud?

"If you are as upright as a bar of wax,
You must be able to use your noble deed
To wipe out my worries and uncertainty
And to stop the rumor of those gossipers."

The pure and kind Nan Xila got her eyebrows knitted,
She cried out again as if her heart was pricked by needle.
Except for her life, what else she had to prove herself?
Let it be burned into ashes if it was not pure gold.

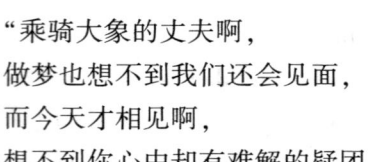

"乘骑大象的丈夫啊,
做梦也想不到我们还会见面,
而今天才相见啊,
想不到你心中却有难解的疑团。

"妹妹的心从来没有离开过你,
就像被抓在银盆里的小鱼,
天天怀念着深广湛蓝的江湖,
这江湖啊就是我的朗玛丈夫。

"妹妹被监禁在孤独的塔楼里,
受尽折磨的心变成碎末,
就像晶莹纯洁的露珠,
在林中低矮的海芋叶上凝聚。

"这露珠见不到太阳的脸庞,
永远不会闪射色彩和光芒,
它忍受着阴暗潮湿等待太阳,
这太阳啊,就是你朗玛王。

"蜜蜂和花朵情意缠绵,
大海高山不能阻止它们会面,
大树可以砍倒,岩石可以掀翻,
夫妻柔情似水的挚爱怎能斩得断?

"我们已在一起拴过线,
金丝银线拴紧两人的手腕,
我们的心早已紧紧相连,
相连的心啊,利刀也砍不断。

第十八章 凯旋 Chapter 18 Return in Triumph

"My majestic husband riding on elephant,
I had never thought we would see each other.
Now finally we got united today,
I didn't expect your heart was bitten by your doubts.

"My heart has never been away from you.
Just like a small fish trapped in a sliver basin.
I miss that deep blue lake day and night.
While you, my dear husband, are the deep lake.

"I was imprisoned in the tower alone.
My heart has been ground into pieces by tortures.
I was like the morning dewdrop,
Which condensed on the low Haiyu leave in the woods.

"The dewdrop can not see the face of the sun,
So it can never shine with every hue.
It has to bear the darkness and dampness waiting for the sun,
While the sun she is waiting is you, my Langma the King.

"The bees are naturally attracted by flowers,
Even the sea or mountains can't keep them from seeing each other.
A tree can be cut down and a rock can be shoveled away.
Can the love of a couple as tender as water be cut off?

"We have been tied together by threads,
The threads of silver and gold were tied around our wrists.
Our hearts have been connected tightly,
Even the sharp knife can't split the connected hearts.

777

"禁囚中我无时无刻不把你怀念,
白天太阳升起我托白云向你问好,
晚上明月高挂我托星星向你祝福,
我就这样天天把恋情对你倾诉。

"要是妻子无私的苦苦表白,
疑虑重重的丈夫不肯相信,
就请烧起熊熊的圣火,
我将站进去验证自己的忠贞。

"如果我的心已经变了颜色,
爱情已离开了自己的丈夫,
就当着大家的眼睛,
让大火把我的肉体烧成灰烬。"

召朗玛脸色阴沉严峻,
下达了点燃大火的命令,
他要证实妻子的话是真是假,
他要考验妻子爱情的忠贞。

南西拉坦然地请叭英作证:
"如果我对丈夫有丝毫不忠诚,
如果我献媚别人被人污损,
就让大火烧焦我的心身。

第十八章 凯旋 Chapter 18 Return in Triumph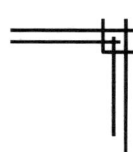

"I missed you so much in prison day and night.

I asked the sun and clouds to send my regards to you in the day;

And I pleaded the bright moon and stars to bless you at night.

In this way I conveyed to you my deep love all the time.

"If you, my suspicious husband still suspect

The bitter confession from me, your wife,

Then light up a rolling fire,

I will step in to prove my loyalty and purity.

"If my heart has changed its color,

And my love has left my own husband,

Then in the face of everyone,

Let the big fire burn my body into ashes."

Zhao Langma looked solemn and sombre.

And he gave the order to ignite a fire.

He wanted to know if what his wife said is true.

He wanted to test her wife's loyalty of their love.

Nan Xila calmly asked Baying to be the witness for her,

"If I were not loyal to my husband in the slightest way,

If I had flattered others and got myself dirty,

Let the big fire get my body and heart burned.

"如果我说的句句都是真言，
如果我的思想纯洁行为端正，
如果我对丈夫朗玛始终如一，
就请大火维护我的名声。

"不仅是我的肉体完好，
就是衣服和披巾也应无损，
一丝头发也不能烧着，
我将在圣火中生存。"

勇敢无畏的南西拉，
从容走到火堆中央，
大火越烧越旺，
她在烈焰中安然无恙。

是非分明的火神呀，
同情坚贞无罪的南西拉，
卫护纯洁崇高的南西拉，
不让烈焰烧灼着她。

犹如金子一样纯真的南西拉，
大火没有烧焦她的一根头发，
她站在熊熊的烈火中，
仿佛沐浴着太阳温暖的光华。

多少人被南西拉的行为感动，
流下了同情的泪水，
他们一齐称赞她的美德，
对她表示无比的敬佩。

第十八章 凯旋　Chapter 18　Return in Triumph

"If what I said is nothing but truth,
If I am pure in heart and dignified in conduct,
If I have always been faithful to my husband,
Let the fire protect me and my honor.

"Not only my body will not be burned,
Even my clothes and scarf would be intact,
And none of my hair will be scorched.
I will survive the holy fire."

Without hesitation, dauntless Nan Xila walked
Into the center of the burning fire.
The fire grew more and more fierce,
But she was safe and sound in the fire.

The god of fire was fair and judicious.
Being sympathetic with the innocent Nan Xila,
He protected her, the pure and noble Nan Xila
From being burned by the rolling fire.

Nan Xila was as pure as gold,
The flame even didn't get a single hair of hers burned.
She stood in the blazing fire,
As if she was bathed in the warm sunlight.

People were deeply moved by Nan Xila,
They shed their tears with sympathy.
They are full of praise for her virtues,
And she was greatly admired by them.

"南西拉的心比蜡条还正直,
南西拉的心比星星还明亮,
南西拉的心比月亮还皎洁,
谁的爱情能比她晶莹高尚?"

召朗玛亲见妻子的壮烈行为,
内心受到深深的责备,
他眼里闪着悲喜的眼泪,
心情又激动啊又忏悔。

"亲爱的南西拉呀,哥哥的心肝,
你的贞节经受了考验,
请原谅我的过错吧,
快快来到我身边。"

南西拉在大火中不动一步,
用莹莹的泪眼看着丈夫,
满腹的辛酸涌上心头,
随着执拗的话儿流出。

"丈夫啊,我不能出去了,
妻子将永远在火中站立,
要是你仍像过去把我当眼珠珍惜,
就请你跨进燃烧的火里将自己的妻子牵出。

"如果你不进来牵我,
妻子怎么能相信你?
怎能相信你爱她一辈子?
怎能相信你不再把她抛弃?

第十八章 凯旋 Chapter 18 Return in Triumph

"She is more upright than a bar of wax;
Her heart is brighter than stars.
She is clearer than the moonlight.
Whose love is nobler and purer than hers?"

Zhao Langma witnessed his wife's heroic action,
He felt truly guilty deep in his heart.
With tears of sadness and happiness in his eyes,
He was excited and also repentant.

"My dear Nan Xila, my sweet heart.
Your chastity has stood up to the test.
Please forgive me.
Please come to me."

Nan Xila stood in the fire motionlessly,
She looked at her husband in tears.
The feeling of bitterness surged in her heart.
And here came her words of stubbornness.

"I won't take a step forward, my husband.
Your wife will stand in the fire forever.
If you still cherish me as your eyeballs as before,
Please step into the fire and lead your wife out.

"If you don't step in and lead me out,
How can I believe in you?
How can I believe you will love me all your life?
How can I believe that you won't desert me again?

"如果你不敢走进大火，
如果你还是如此多疑，
你的妻子南西拉呀，
就不如永世站在大火里。"

悔悟的召朗玛听了深感羞愧，
为什么要等着她自己出来，
他毫不犹豫地走进大火中，
也让烈火考验自己对妻子的珍爱。

他在火焰中将妻子紧紧拥抱，
牵着她的手走了出来，
能熔铜化铁的烈火啊，
触到他们的身上就绕开。

人们对他们发出一片赞扬声：
"乌云抹不黑星星的光辉，
灾难拆不散忠贞的爱情，
大火又怎能烧伤两颗纯洁的心。"

两颗星星啊一对忠贞的情人，
两只金凤啊一对恩爱的夫妻，
召朗玛和南西拉在万人欢呼声中，
双双向灿烂辉煌的宫殿走去。

他们暂时住在兰嘎寝宫里，
就像太阳和月亮交相辉映，
头人、百姓向他们祝贺表达谢意，
感激他们给勐兰嘎带来和平与安宁。

第十八章 凯旋 Chapter 18 Return in Triumph

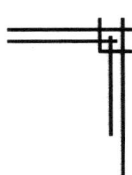

"If you dare not come into the fire;
If you still are so suspicions,
Your wife Nan Xila,
She would rather stand in the fire forever."

The repentant Zhao Langma was ashamed at hearing this.
Why should he wait for her to walk out of the fire?
So he walked into the fire without hesitation.
He wanted his love for his wife also to be tested.

He held his wife tightly in the fierce fire,
Then he took her hands and led her out.
The fire was so huge that it could melt iron,
But it kept itself away from the two lovers.

People started to sing their praise for them,
"Dark clouds can never cover the glory of stars;
Disaster can never tear apart faithful lovers,
Then how fire can hurt the two pure hearts?"

The faithful lovers were like two stars;
They were also like two golden phoenixes.
The couple went to the glorious palace together,
With cheers from tens of thousands of people.

They temporarily lived in palace of Langa,
Like the sun and moon complementing each other.
Chieftains and the people expressed their gratitude to them
For the peace they brought to the Kingdom of Langa.

接受老国王的请求和百姓的委托，
召朗玛让彼亚沙登基当了国王，
让他在年迈的叭兰巴辅佐下，
尽心竭力治理好勐兰嘎。

彼亚沙深知哥哥失败的原因，
废除了十头王制定的法规，
重新实行外祖父老国王的规矩，
遭受灾难的勐兰嘎又有了勃勃生机。

三、凯旋归国

召朗玛打算返归故里，
彼亚沙却不舍依依：
"我愿意把勐兰嘎的王位放弃，
紧紧跟随你永远为你效力。"

召朗玛对彼亚沙说：
"不讲信义即使寸步不离也没有意义，
如是肝胆相照啊，
远隔万里也近如咫尺。

"可敬的彼亚沙啊，
你不能离开自己的国家，
受了伤的人要好好治疗，
饱经灾难的勐兰嘎等着你来治理。

第十八章 凯旋 Chapter 18 Return in Triumph

Accepting the pleading from the old king and the people,
Zhao Langma let Biyasha ascend to the throne and be the King.
He asked Biyasha to get help from the old King Ba Lanba,
And to devote himself to govern the Kingdom of Langa.

Biyasha knew very well why his brother failed,
So he revoked the rules made by the ten-headed King.
He then reactivated the laws adopted by the old king,
The disaster-stricken Kingdom of Langa thrived again.

Ⅲ Return to Homeland in Triumph

Zhao Langma planned to return to their homeland,
But Biyasha was reluctant to part with him,
"I am willing to give up the throne of Langa
To follow and serve you wherever you go."

Zhao Langma told Biyasha,
"It is no use staying close when there is no trust or faith.
Being faithful to each other, we will be affectionately connected
Even when we are far away from one another in distance.

"My respectable Biyasha,
You can't leave your country behind.
Just as an injured person needs medical treatment,
The disaster-stricken Langa needs your governance.

787

兰嘎西贺 The Ten-Headed King of Langa

"你要善于辨别善恶美丑，
你要善于体察国情民心，
如果你忘记了这些，
国家就要落入最大的不幸。"

离别的时刻到了，
召朗玛和南西拉就要启程，
猴子兵云集在广场待命，
勐兰嘎的百姓夹道送行。

天空响起欢送的炮声，
锣鼓和乐器震动了兰嘎城，
一队队的兵马穿过森林，
彼亚沙把他们远送到边境。

召朗玛的大军通过石桥回到了大陆，
山风给他们送来阵阵花香，
召朗玛率领队伍继续前进，
美丽的南西拉紧靠在他身旁。

麂子金鹿在身边奔跑，
蜂群鸟儿为他们歌唱，
他们沿着蜿蜒逶迤的山路行进，
穿过了勐基沙茫茫的森林。

第十八章 凯旋　Chapter 18 Return in Triumph

"You should be wise enough to tell good from bad,
To know the current conditions of your country and people.
If you forget all of these,
Great misfortunes will befall your Kingdom."

It was time to say goodbye,
Zhao Langma and Nan Xila were to depart.
The monkey soldiers crowded on the plaza waiting for the order,
The people of Langa lined along the street to see them off.

The explosion of firecrackers echoed in the sky.
The sounds of gangs and drum shook the city of Langa.
Groups of soldiers and horses passed through the forests,
Bishaya saw them off far to the frontier of their country.

Langma's army went through the stone bridge and came to the plain.
They were refreshed by the fragrance of flowers in the wind.
The troops marched on led by Zhao Langma,
And the beautiful Nan Xila stayed close to him.

Muntjac and golden deer ran along the crowd;
Swarms of bees and birds sang for them.
They marched along the wandering ranges of mountain;
And they went through the dense forest of the kingdom of Jisha.

在一个三岔路口他们分道扬镳,
嘎林领着猴群返回勐基沙,
召朗玛把珍贵的金伞送给它,
把它称作勐基沙的叭龙帝雅①。

嘎林让阿努曼跟着召朗玛,
永远守卫在他的身旁,
召朗玛和南西拉又回到伊麻板森林,
住进帕拉西简陋的巴朗。

再说召朗玛的弟弟帕腊达,
当年哥哥出走后也不愿为王,
他在森林里修行了十二年,
如今已还俗回宫不再当和尚。

他听说哥嫂依然健在,
准备接哥哥回来继位当王,
他和弟弟沙达鲁嘎一起,
召集群臣把国事商量。

"按照过去老国王的旨意,
沙达鲁嘎当国王已经满期,
应该把召朗玛从森林接回,
让他当国王把全勐治理。"

---

① 叭龙帝雅:意思是最大的王。

第十八章 凯旋 Chapter 18 Return in Triumph

The army departed with each other on a fork of the road.
Leading the monkeys, Galin returned to the Kingdom of Jisha.
Zhao Langma gave him the precious golden umbrella,
And addressed him the Palongdiya of Jisha.①

Galin asked Anuman to follow Zhao Langma
So that he could always be his bodyguard.
Zhao Langma and Nan Xila returned to the forest of Yimaban,
And they stayed in the simple Balang cottage of Palaxi.

Let's come back to Zhao Langma's younger brother Palada.
He also refused to be the king when Zhao Langma left home.
He had practiced Buddhism in the forest for twelve years.
Now he resumed his secular life and returned to the palace.

When he heard Zhao Langma and Nan Xila were still alive,
He decided to welcome his brother back to ascend to the throne.
He talked with his younger brother Shadaluga,
Then they summoned all the officials to discuss about it.

"According to the will of the old king,
Shadaluga's term as the King expired.
We should get Zhao Langma back from the forest,
So that he can be the King and govern the whole country."

---

① Palongdiya: the greatest king.

这个主张得到群臣的拥护，
百姓们闻讯更是欢喜，
修好了桥梁铺平了道路，
准备迎接召朗玛回国登基。

帕腊达弟兄俩和三位母后，
率领着山泉一样奔流的队伍，
红绿旗幡飘扬，鼓乐震动大地，
来到伊麻板森林帕拉西的茅屋。

帕腊达拜倒在哥哥的面前，
和王后一起叙说离别的情怀：
"十二年我觉着有十二万天，
我们天天把你们盼望和惦念。

"现在十二年终于过去，
哥哥一定要回到宫里，
不要辜负已故父王的期望，
把神圣的勐沓达腊塔治理。"

随行的大臣头人一齐跪下，
同来的百姓发出声声欢呼，
多少人的请求只有一句话：
"请召朗玛回宫继位治理勐沓达腊塔。"

第十八章 凯旋 Chapter 18 Return in Triumph

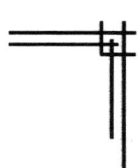

This proposal won the support of all the officials,
His people were more excited at the news.
They repaired the bridge and paved the road
To get ready for Zhao Langma to return as the King.

The two brothers and their three mothers set out,
And the troops following them moved on like flowing brook.
Colorful banners waving and marching band shaking the earth,
They arrived at the thatched cottage of Palaxi.

Palada knelt down in front of his older brother Zhao Langma,
Telling how much they missed him after his departure,
"These twelve years was as long as 120 thousands of days.
We were missing you and worried about you every day and night.

"Now that twelve years has finally passed,
My brother, please come back to our palace.
Do not forget the expectation of our late father,
And keep our sacred Kingdom of Langa well-governed."

All the escorting officials knelt down,
The accompanying people cheered joyfully.
What they wanted to say is just this,
"We need Zhao Langma to be the King and rule our kingdom."

召朗玛见众望难以拒绝，
收下弟弟手中的花盘、蜡条和鲜花，
人群响起一片欢呼声，
召朗玛关切地询问帕腊达：

"气候和雨水是不是合适？
树上的果实是不是累结？
田里的五谷是不是丰收？
百姓的生活是不是富裕？"

帕腊达听了哈哈大笑，
不以为然地答道：
"哥哥在森林里吃野果树叶，
还在为百姓的生活心焦。

"我们勐多年来风调雨顺，
百姓安居乐业丰衣足食，
现在国库里粮油充足，
还堆着无数的金银宝石。"

召朗玛紧紧皱起眉头，
想了一个主意给他教诲，
吃饭的时候在帕腊达的碗里，
装满金银宝石玛瑙翡翠。

聪明的帕腊达猛然醒悟，
赶紧上前请求哥哥宽恕：
"哥哥用金银宝石给我充饥，
使我发现自己见识的谬误。"

第十八章 凯旋 Chapter 18 Return in Triumph

Zhao Langma knew he couldn't again refuse their request,
So he accepted the wreath, wax and fresh flowers.
Rounds of cheers burst out among the crowds.
Then Zhao Langma asked Palada with great care,

"Is the weather good? Do we have enough rain?
Are the fruit trees bearing fruits?
Do we have a harvest year of crops?
Are our people living a prosperous life?"

Palada burst into hearty laughter at hearing the questions.
Without giving them a serious thought, he answered,
"Is it because you are living on wild fruits in the forest
That you worry about the livelihood of our people?"

"We have been blessed with timely wind and rain,
Our people are enjoying a good and prosperous life.
Now our national treasury is full of grain and oil,
As well as uncountable gold, silver and precious stones."

Hearing this, Zhao Langma knitted his brows,
Then he had got an idea to teach his brother a lesson.
When they had a meal together,
He put gold, jade and jewelries in his bowl.

Clever Palada understood what he meant immediately
And he hurried up to ask for his brother's forgiveness,
"You feed me with gold, silver and gemstones,
Now I know how erroneous my view was."

"亲爱的帕腊达弟弟,
普天下的人全靠五谷生存,
金银珠宝只能存在库房里,
你刚才的讥笑不是一个为王者应有的行为。

"你别以为我不问金银只问五谷,
是因为我在森林里吃不上粮食,
如果一勐之主不关心百姓的疾苦,
就不会得到百姓的拥护。"

召朗玛告别了帕拉西,
走出森林踏上了洒满阳光的大路,
山花一齐朝召朗玛吐露芬芳,
嘎兰托鸟开喉为南西拉歌唱幸福。

四、朗玛即位

离开了十二年的召朗玛回到王宫,
勐沓达腊塔沉浸在一片欢乐之中,
宫廷大臣擂响了咚咚的金边大鼓,
大臣和头人纷纷来到富丽的宫殿。

第十八章 凯旋 Chapter 18 Return in Triumph

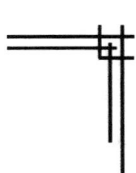

"My dear brother Palada,
People in the world live on grains and crops,
All those jewelries can only be stored in warehouse.
Your sneer just now is a conduct unbecoming to a King.

"It is not because I didn't have enough to eat in the forest
That I asked about grains and crops rather than gold and silver.
If a king does not care about the suffering of his people,
There is no way for him to get the support from them."

After making his farewell to Palaxi,
Zhao Langma walked out of the forest and onto the sun-bathed road.
All the flowers were blooming to say goodbye to Zhao Langma;
All the sky larks sang for the happiness of Nan Xila.

Ⅳ Zhao Langma's Ascendance to the Throne

Zhao Langma returned to the palace after 12 years' departure.
The Kingdom of Dadalata were immersed in joy and bliss.
The ministers of the court pounded on the gold-rimmed drums,
Officials and chieftain gathered in the magnificent palace.

他们一致推举召朗玛继承王位，
推举朗玛的三个弟弟当吾巴腊扎①，
选定了新王登基的吉日良辰，
大臣们喜气洋洋忙得手脚不停。

按照王国古老的规矩，
准备了六十三种颜色的金盘，
五朵金花、七座笋塔，
登基时吹的金螺号和遮阳的金伞。

新王登基的吉祥日子来到了，
这是万物生枝发芽的季节，
大臣和头人用芬芳的金水银水，
给继承王位的召朗玛沐浴洗礼。

吹响洪亮的金螺，
召朗玛戴上王冠穿上王服，
米花像雨一样纷纷飘洒，
他坐上了父王金碧辉煌的御座。

人们一一向召朗玛表示祝贺，
全城敲响了象脚鼓和铓锣，
有威望的宫廷大臣帕麻纳，
行使职责第一个向全勐宣布：

① 吾巴腊扎：亲王。

第十八章 凯旋 Chapter 18 Return in Triumph

They unanimously chose Zhao Langma to ascend to the throne,
And his three young brothers to be Wubalazha.①
Auspicious day was selected for the inauguration,
The ministers busied themselves happily for the ceremony.

According to the traditional rules of the Kingdom,
Sixty-three golden plates of different colors were prepared;
Five flowers of gold and seven pagodas of bamboo shoots;
And golden trumpets and umbrellas for the ceremony were also ready.

Finally came the day for the inauguration of the new King.
This was the season when everything started to grow.
The ministers and chieftains sprayed the fragrant water
To shower the blessing to Zhao Langma, the one to be the King.

Golden trumpet sounded resonantly.
Zhao Langma put on his crown and kingly garment.
Rice flowers were sprayed onto him like raindrops,
He ascended to the splendid throne of his father.

People came to felicitate Zhao Langma on his enthronement.
Elephant-foot-like drums and gongs sounded all over the city,
Pamana, the reputed minister, executed his duty
Announcing to the people all over the kingdom,

---

① Wubalazha: Prince.

"福气无边的王子召朗玛,
从今天起继承勐沓达腊塔王位,
愿新王长寿国家富足,
愿他的臣民万代幸福。"

帕麻纳代表全勐臣民,
献给召朗玛五种仪仗,
六十三把彩色的金伞,
祝新王福星高照天下名扬。

召朗玛接受了臣民的祝愿,
收纳了隆重的礼物,
收下了父王传下来的金盘大印,
开始行使国王的崇高权力。

按照王国的规矩和父亲的遗嘱,
接纳臣僚和头人的奏议,
根据弟弟们功劳和能力的大小,
召朗玛分别给他们封王封官。

与召朗玛同生共死的腊嘎纳,
担任第一吾巴腊扎,
分管北方和东方各勐的土地,
建立一座宫廷、享受王子的权力。

忠实的帕腊达担任第二吾巴腊扎,
建立一座宫廷分管西面各勐的土地,
每年向王国敬献战马和大象,
享受一个王子应有的权力。

第十八章 凯旋 Chapter 18 Return in Triumph

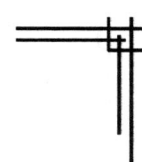

"Our Prince Zhao Langma has boundless blessing,
Today he inherits the throne to be our new King.
May our King live long and our kingdom be prosperous;
May our people live happily forever under his rule."

On behalf of all the officials and the people,
Pamana presented to Zhao Langma five types of wands
And sixty-three colorfully-decorated golden umbrellas,
To bless the new king with good luck and reputation.

Zhao Langma accepted the blessings of his subjects,
And their presents of significance,
As well as the golden round seal of his father.
Officially he started to execute the supreme power of the King.

According to the rules of his nation and the will of his father,
And also the advice from his officials and chieftains,
Zhao Langma offered official titles to his brothers
Taking their abilities and achievements into consideration.

Lagana stood by his side during all the wars
So he was assigned the title of the first Wubalazha,
He was in charge of the land in the north and east.
He would enjoy the power of a prince and his own court.

The faithful Palada would be the second Wubalazha,
He would rule the land in the west and have his own court.
He would tribute elephants and horses to the king every year
While enjoying the power that a prince deserves.

801

善良忠厚的沙达鲁嘎,
担任第三吾巴腊扎,
分管南面各勐辽阔的土地,
每年向王国敬献牛羊和马匹。

对于功勋显赫的白猴阿努曼,
召朗玛留它住在王宫里,
委任它担任王国的收税官,
同时还要管理兵马和田地。

召朗玛还颁布命令,
将全勐珠宝赏赐给臣僚和头人,
将稻谷豆薯分给穷苦的百姓,
臣民欢呼召朗玛的豁达英明。

召朗玛的床头挂着父王的弓塔弩,
宫廷中央放着父王留下的金鞋,
对于这两件祖传罕世之宝,
召朗玛和臣僚每天都要顶礼膜拜。

全勐最高的房屋要数王宫的宝殿,
全勐最亮的塔楼要数王宫的宝塔,
全勐威望最高权力最大的人,
要数国王召朗玛和王后南西拉。

第十八章 凯旋 Chapter 18 Return in Triumph

Shadaluga was kind and honest,
He got the title of the third Wubalazha.
He would be the ruler of the land in the south,
He should also tribute cattle, sheep and horses to the king.

Considering Anuman's great achievement in the wars,
Zhao Langma invited him to stay in the palace,
And he would be the tax collector of the nation,
As well as the administer of war horses and land.

The king also declared his orders to distribute the valuables
In the national treasure to his officials and chieftains,
And the grains and necessary food to the poor people.
Everyone cheered for the new king's generosity and wisdom.

On the bedhead of Zhao Langma was hung the crossbow of his father,
In the centre of the court was kept the golden shoes left by his father,
These two items inherited from their ancestors were so precious
That Zhao Langma and his officials bowed to them every morning.

The tallest building in the country was the king's palace;
The brightest pagoda in the kingdom was the one in the palace;
The most powerful and prestigious people in the kingdom
Were the King Zhao Langma and the Queen Nan Xila.

兰嘎西贺 The Ten-Headed King of Langa

成百上千的宫娥彩女，
轮流给他们跳舞唱歌，
乐队终日演奏着悦耳的乐曲，
为他们解除深宫的寂寞。

武官们喜欢到野外赛马，
百姓们忙碌着种植谷物，
他们好像鱼儿在大海里，
过着自由自在安定宁静的生活。

勐沓达腊塔像星星一样明亮，
犹如林间金湖似的平静无波，
召朗玛和南西拉在舒适的宫殿里，
幸福愉快地度过一天天。

他们享受到团圆的欢乐，
他们享受着恩爱的生活，
可是谁能预料得到啊，
灾难就要在善良的南西拉头上降落。

误解和嫉妒像一条毒虫，
咬啮着召朗玛的心田，
痛苦和悲哀犹如一团黑云，
笼罩在召朗玛和南西拉中间。

第十八章 凯旋 Chapter 18 Return in Triumph

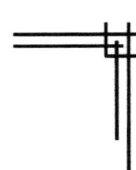

Hundreds of maids were beautifully dressed,
They took turns to sing and dance for them.
Beautiful melodies were played by the royal band
To relieve their loneliness of being locked in the palace.

Generals enjoyed themselves in the horse races in the open air,
The common people were busy with planting crops.
They were like fishes swimming in the sea
Enjoying their carefree and peaceful life.

The Kingdom of Dadalata shone like a bright star,
And it was as peaceful as the lake in the deep forest.
Zhao Langma and Nan Xila lived in the cosy palace,
Enjoying their happy lives with time passing by.

They were enjoying the merriness of their reunion;
They were enjoying the happy life of a loving couple.
But who could expect the disaster
That would soon befall the kind Nan Xila.

Misunderstanding and jealousy were like a poisonous insect,
And it was biting the heart of Zhao Langma,
Bitterness and sorrow were like the dark clouds,
And they were shrouded Zhao Langma and Nan Xila.

第十九章 冤

一、怀疑

一天召朗玛悠闲地离开寝宫，
到御花园观赏绽开的鲜花，
无忧无虑的南西拉留在宫内，
年轻的宫女们陪伴着她。

宫女们像春天的燕子嬉笑戏闹，
无拘无束和南西拉开心地闲聊，
她们想知道十头王是什么样子，
就像孩子想看到妈妈手中的东西。

"尊贵的王后南西拉，
我们想知道捧玛加的古怪长相，
听说他的头和眼不像世上的人，
请你画出来看看是什么模样。"

第十九章 冤 Chapter 19 Injustice

Chapter 19 Injustice

I Suspicion

One day Zhao Langma left the bedroom leisurely,
He was wandering in the garden to enjoy the blooming flowers.
The carefree Nan Xila was left in the palace,
And she was accompanied by the young maids.

The maids were having fun like the swallows in the spring;
They were chatting gaily with Nan Xila.
They were curious about what the ten-headed King looked like.
Just as the kids eager to tell what was hidden in mom's hand.

"Dear majestic Queen Nan Xila,
We are wondering how odd the ten-headed King looked like.
It's said his heads and eyes were unlike those of common people.
Could you please draw a picture of him for us to have a look?"

宫女们的恳求声像知了叫个不停，
南西拉难以拒绝她们的好奇心，
"如果你们真想知道十头王是什么样子的话，
拿一团红泥巴来我捏给你们看个仔细。"

宫女们去到不远的河边，
拿来了一团柔软的红泥巴，
把宫女看成妹妹的南西拉啊，
高高兴兴给她们捏捧玛加泥像。

捏出了身子、头、鼻、耳、眼，
看上去真如十头王再现，
"这么奇特、古怪、丑陋，
真是独一无二世间少见。"

宫女们叽叽喳喳讥笑着议论，
南西拉讲述捧玛加的凶狠，
就在她们嬉戏谈笑的时候，
宫殿上空出现一团乌云。

女妖姐里哈达的精灵从宫廷上空飘过，
见南西拉捏成一个捧玛加泥塑，
就化作一团云雾悄悄降落，
钻进泥像内部兴风作浪。

第十九章 冤 Chapter 19 Injustice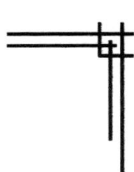

Their chatters were like the chirping of citadels,
It was hard for Nan Xila not to meet their curiosity.
"If you really want to know the look of the ten-headed King,
Bring me some red mud and I will mould a clay figurine of him."

The maids went to the nearby river side
And they got back some soft red clay.
Nan Xila treated them as her sisters,
So she began to mould the figurine of Pengmajia for them.

Body, heads, nose, ears and eyes started to take shape,
It looked like the real ten-headed King coming to life.
"He looked so different, weird and ugly.
It was true he had the unique look in the world."

The maids were laughing, chatting and teasing,
And Nan Xila told them how wicked that monster was.
The moment they were chatting and laughing,
A dark cloud appeared in the sky above the palace.

The Spirit of the enchantress Dalihada was floating over the palace,
And she saw the figurine of Pengmajia made by Nan Xila.
So she changed into a cluster of cloud descending secretly,
And she slid into the figurine to stir up troubles and evils.

精灵找到了躯体寄托,
泥塑的十双眼睛突然闪闪烁烁,
嘴巴张开哈哈大笑,
阵阵弹舌声如敲刀壳。

宫女们惊愕得目瞪口呆,
一个个惊呼着四散逃开,
南西拉吓得浑身发抖,
急忙伸出双脚又踢又踩。

泥像伸出双手抱住南西拉的脚,
南西拉大声呼叫拼命挣扎,
她使尽全力用两手拽打,
泥像还是死死抱住她。

一个宫女急中生智想出一个主意:
"快把它带到你的卧室里去,
用弓塔弩刺它的身子,
它害怕神箭也许会放开你。"

南西拉惊慌失措战战兢兢,
把泥像带进自己的卧室,
她拔出弓塔弩的神箭刺过去,
泥像惊叫一声跌倒在地。

恰巧此时召朗玛返回寝宫,
南西拉慌乱中把泥像踢进床底,
梳理一下散乱的发髻,
战战兢兢把国王迎进卧室。

第十九章 冤 Chapter 19 Injustice

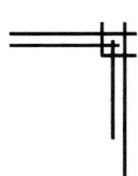

The spirit found the body to sojourn in.
Suddenly those ten pairs of eyes started to twinkle,
Mouths opened and burst into loud laughter,
Their tongues clicked crisply as someone knocking on a knife.

The maids were terrified and dumbfounded.
They screamed and scattered in all directions.
Nan Xila was trembling in terror,
And she tried to kick and stamp the figurine.

The figurines stretched its arms and held Nan Xila's feet,
She shouted for help and struggled to get rid of it.
With all her strength, she fought with both hands,
But the clay figurine still held her in its arms tightly.

At the crucial moment, one maid came up with an idea,
"Hurry up and take it with you to your bedroom.
Stab at it with the arrow of the magic crossbow,
It is scared of the magic arrow and might let you go."

Nan Xila was at a loss in panic,
She hurried into the bedroom dragging the figurine,
She drew out one arrow and stabbed at it,
The clay figurine fell onto the ground with a scream.

It was that moment when Zhao Langma returned to the bedroom.
In panic Nan Xila kicked the figurine into under the bed.
She tried to calm herself by tidying up her tousled hair,
And greeted the king into the bedroom timidly.

召朗玛像往常一样,
不慌不忙在金床上坐下,
突然泥像又弹响舌头,
用傲慢的语言咒骂召朗玛:

"召对召,王对王,
为什么你坐在我头上?
是不是你瞎了眼睛,
看不见我这威严的大王?

"我是一个蜚声于世的国王,
谁见了我都不敢怠慢,
你为何胆大到这个地步,
竟敢坐在我的头上面?"

召朗玛听了异常惊讶,
是谁在床下发出辱骂,
听声音似乎是捧玛加,
他急忙在卧室四处搜查。

召朗玛在床下发现了仇人的泥像,
顿时脸色苍白火冒三丈,
他把泥像拿到室外质问宫女:
"是谁手艺如此高明捏得这般相像?"

第十九章 冤 Chapter 19 Injustice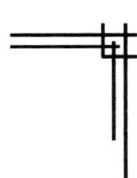

As he did in usual time,
Zhao Langma sit down on the golden bed leisurely.
Suddenly the figurine clicked its tongue,
And it started to curse Zhao Langma haughtily,

"We are both the majestic kings of great kingdom,
Why are you sitting on my head?
Are you blind or what?
Don't you see me a dignified king here?

"I am a powerful king known to the world.
Nobody dared to take me lightly.
Why are you so bold and rude
And have the guts to sit on my head?"

Zhao Langma was shocked at hearing this.
He didn't know who was abusing him under the bed.
It sounded like Pengmajia's voice,
He hurried to search all over the bedroom.

He found the figurine of his enemy Pengmajia under the bed,
All at once, he became pale and burst into a fury.
Taking the figurine out of the bedroom, he questioned the maids,
"Who has such craft and produced this lifelike figurine?"

宫女们胆战心惊慌忙下拜:
"我们从来没有见过十头王的脸嘴,
就是吃了龙心虎胆,
也不敢这样胆大妄为。"

菩提树叶般光亮的南西拉,
急忙走过去向丈夫跪下,
把事情的经过如实诉说:
"是我捏的泥像捧玛加。"

召朗玛听了满腔怒火,
举起拳头捶击宝座:
"我不听你的谎言谎话,
你心里仍然偷偷眷恋着捧玛加。"

南西拉泪如泉涌,
召朗玛的误会令她心痛,
"夫王啊,请饶恕我的过失,
请不要用这话刺伤我的心。

"我从来没有想念过十头王,
我错就错在迁就宫女的好奇心,
这着魔的泥像又得罪了你,
才使你产生了误解和怀疑。"

南西拉一声一泪地辩解,
召朗玛一点也听不进,
"你这女人的心肠真狠,
忘了我兄弟俩怎样把你救出火坑。

第十九章 冤 Chapter 19 Injustice

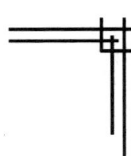

The maids were terrified and hurried to kneel down,
"We have never seen the face of the ten-headed king.
And we would never have the nerve to do such thing
Even if we had eaten the heart of dragon and the tiger."

Nan Xila had a heart as bright as the bodhi tree leaf.
She stepped forward and knelt down in front of her husband.
She told Zhao Langma the whole story and confessed,
"It was I who made this figurine of Pengmajia."

Zhao Langma exploded after hearing this.
He hammered on the throne with his fists,
"I won't listen to your lies any more,
You are still keeping Pengmajia in your heart."

Nan Xila's tears ran down as spurting spring,
Zhao Langma's misunderstanding broke her heart.
"My king, my dear husband, please forgive my error.
Please stop hurting me with such remarks.

"I have never missed the ten-headed monster.
I was wrong but I just meant to meet the curiosity of the maids.
I am sorry that the enchanted figurine offended you.
And because of this you misunderstood and doubted me."

Nan Xila explained to him with tears,
But Zhao Langma would not listen to her at all.
"You have an evil and cruel heart.
You forget how we brothers took you out of that living hell.

"为了寻找你，救出你，
我们穿越森林跨过海洋，
经历了多少人间的苦楚辛酸，
几乎丧失了宝贵的生命。

"我们流了多少血，
我们流了多少汗，
才把你从囹圄中解救出来，
谁知道你竟对我如此冷酷。

"在你回宫的日子里，
原来你心里一直怀念着我们的仇敌，
你思恋他的情意太迫切，
才把他捏成泥像藏在圣洁的宫廷里。

"你心中隐藏着卑污的泥水，
你这淫荡的女人罪该毁灭成灰，
你不配在我这个劢生存，
快去死吧，我要叫你变成鬼①"。

无辜的南西拉眼泪往肚里流，
丈夫的话儿叫她全身发抖：
"妻子头上的'主宰'，
请平心静气听听妻子的表白。

---

① 还有一种传说，召朗玛看到十头王的泥塑后，将南西拉驱逐到森林去。

第十九章 冤 Chapter 19 Injustice

"To find you and rescue you,

We had trekked through forests and crossed the ocean.

We had been through so many hardships and pains

We had almost lost our precious lives.

"How much blood we had shed?

How much we had sweated?

We tried everything to rescue you out of the prison.

I had never expected that you would be so cruel to me.

"Ever since you returned to our palace,

You had been missing our sworn enemy.

You missed him so much and so strongly

That you made the figurine of him and hid it in our bedroom.

"Filthy water is hidden in your soul,

Lewd woman like you should be burned into ashes.

You don't deserve living in my kingdom.

Go to hell and I will have you turned into a ghost①."

Innocent Nan Xila swallowed down her tears,

She was trembling at her husband's words,

"You are my husband and my master,

Please calm down and listen to your wife's explanation.

---

① Another version is Zhao Langma expelled Nan Xila into the forest after he saw the figurine.

"我对十头王的憎恶和仇恨,
我对夫王忠贞的爱情,
正直无私的天神啊,
已用烈火给我作过验证。

"今天的疑惑为什么又重新发生,
只怕是你从来不相信我的忠贞,
今天的事情妻子已如实讲明,
为什么定要让我带着耻辱丧生?

"夫王呀,看在夫妻的面上,
就算我做错了这件事,
也请你宽恕体谅,
仍让我生活在你身旁。

"要是我的苦衷得不到你的同情,
请让妻子当一名普通的宫女,
为你端茶倒水来赎罪,
我诚心服侍你一辈子。"

召朗玛对南西拉大声呵斥:
"不要多说了你必定得死,
要是你不思念捧玛加,
怎么可能把他的像捏出?

"你是心中没有了我啊,
才会做出这等卑贱的事,
王后啊,我再也不想见到你,
现在来哀求已属多余。"

第十九章 冤 Chapter 19 Injustice

"I hated the ten-headed King and took him as our enemy,
I have always been faithful to you and our love.
My hatred of him and my love for you have been tested
By fair and just heavenly god with fierce fire.

"Why you started to suspect me again?
Maybe you have never believed in my faithfulness.
I have explained to you what had happened today.
Why do you still want me to die with disgrace?

"My dear husband, we are couples.
Even if I have done things wrong today,
Please be understanding and forgiving.
Please let me stay and live by your side.

"If my bitterness can not win your sympathy,
Please give me the chance to be a common maid,
So I can take care of you and redeem my honor.
I will serve you with all my heart in the rest of my life."

Zhao Langma shouted at Nan Xila,
"Shut up, you must die today.
If you don't miss that monster,
How can you make the figurine so alike him?

"It is because you don't love me any more
That you have done such a despicable thing.
I don't want to see you anymore, my queen.
It is useless for you to beg for my forgiveness."

黑眼睛的斑鸠受到了无辜的折磨，
还可向百鸟倾诉自己的苦衷，
善良的麂子受到不幸，
还可以对森林述说自己的伤痛。

可是无辜的南西拉蒙受了冤屈，
却得不到丈夫的体谅和同情，
她流了多少泪水，
也洗刷不掉自己的耻辱和罪名。

难道就这样不明不白地诀别？
难道就这样含着冤屈死去？
南西拉心中愤愤不平，
含着泪去向母后诉说不幸。

南苏甘嫡母后知道儿媳受到委屈，
带着南西拉去找儿子，
"像麂子一样善良的朗玛，
你的心为什么会变成了石头？

"南西拉是妈妈的眼珠，
南西拉是妈妈心上的肉，
她对你无比忠诚坚贞，
她的心比露水还洁净。

"你出走去到无人烟的森林，
她跟着你受苦受难毫无怨言，
她遭劫落入十头王的掌心，
却一直对你怀着忠诚。

第十九章 冤 Chapter 19 Injustice

When the innocent black-eyed dove suffers from torture,
It still has chance to share with other birds about its feeling;
When the kind muntjac undergoes misfortune,
It can still tell the forest of its pains and suffering.

But when innocent Nan Xila was unfairly treated,
She couldn't get sympathy from her husband.
No matter how many tears she had shed,
She still couldn't wash away her shame and guilt.

Would she have to leave the world in such an indecent way?
Would she have to die with such wrongful treatment?
Nan Xila felt so aggrieved and indignant,
Thus she resorted to her mother-in-law with tears.

Nan Sugandi knew Nan Xila was wrongly treated.
She took Nan Xila with her to see her son.
"My son Langma, you are as kind as a deer,
What has turned your heart into a hard stone?

"Nan Xila is like the eyeballs of mine;
She is one part of my own heart.
She has been loyal and faithful to you as always,
Her heart is purer than the morning dew.

"When you went to the remote forest,
She stayed with you without a word of complaint.
She was taken away by the ten-headed monster,
But she has always been faithful to you.

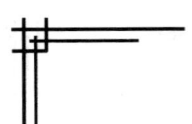

兰嘎西贺 The Ten-Headed King of Langa

"她讲的今天发生的事情,
符合情理,应该体谅,
只因宫女们缠着一再地请求,
她才捏了十头王的泥像。

"怎么能因为今天发生这点事情,
就播种下猜忌的葛藤?
怎么能因为捏了十头王的泥像,
就武断地杀害自己的亲人?

"不要把怀疑当成了真实,
不要让乌云遮住了眼睛,
一时恼怒不容她申辩,
会给你一辈子带来不幸和悔恨。

"孩子啊,你不同情妻子,
也该可怜年迈的母亲,
不能让南西拉无辜受到折磨,
更不能伤害她宝贵的生命。"

召朗玛无动于衷默默不语,
一团团黑雾在头脑里翻滚,
"我在民间暗访听到不少议论,
责怪我把南西拉领回都城。

"说什么南西拉被十头王劫走,
养尊处优住在孤独隐蔽的塔楼,
召朗玛还借兵讨伐救回来,
对别人抚弄过的明珠还爱不释手。

第十九章 冤 Chapter 19 Injustice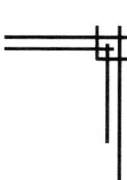

"She told me what had happened today.
What she said is reasonable and understandable.
It is just because the servant maids kept begging her
That she made the clay figurine of the ten-headed king.

"How can you plant the seed of suspicion
Just because what had happened today?
How can you be so arbitrary to have your wife killed
Just because she made a figurine of that monster?

"Don't take what you suspect as truth;
Don't let dark clouds blind your eyes.
If you deny her the chance of explanation out of anger,
You will spend the rest of your life in misery and regret.

"My dear son, if you are not sympathetic with your wife
You should at least have pity on your old mother.
Please don't let innocent Nan Xila suffer any more,
And you should never take her precious life."

Zhao Langma remained unmoved and silent.
Clusters of dark clouds were rolling in his head.
"I heard rumors during my secret visits to civilians.
Some blamed me for bringing her back to the palace.

"They said that Nan Xila enjoyed the monster's favor
After she had been taken away and hidden in the tower.
That Zhao Langma even borrowed armies to rescue her back,
And he was cherishing a peal already caressed by someone else.

823

兰嘎西贺 The Ten-Headed King of Langa

"一个男人和妻子吵架,
说'我又不是痴情的召朗玛,
我决不像他那样的傻,
再爱别人搂抱过的南西拉'。

"是我看错了南西拉,
我没有什么对不起她,
绝不能给人们留下话柄,
成为千年万年的笑话。"

召朗玛抬起头来告诉母亲:
"你去听一下百姓私下传播的流言,
我是一个勐的国王,
决不能让人们指着背脊骨讥贬。

"男子汉说过的话是砍断了的树,
做王的一作出决定就是蒸熟的饭。"
召朗玛命令弟弟腊嘎纳,
带南西拉出宫去处死。

忠厚善良的腊嘎纳紧蹙双眉,
心中涌起无限的忧愁和苦恼,
他为无辜的嫂嫂求情,
为王的哥哥怎听得进劝告。

第十九章 冤 Chapter 19 Injustice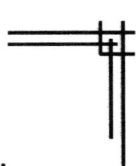

"When a husband bickered with his wife, he would say,
'I am not that infatuated Zhao Langma.
I would never make myself a fool as he does.
He still loves Nan Xila who had been touched by someone else.'

"I have not seen clearly who Nan Xila was;
I have never done anything wrong to her.
There is no way for me to become a laughingstock
And to be jeered at even thousands of years after I die."

Zhao Langma lifted his head and said to his mother,
"You can go out and listen to what rumors are spreading.
I am the dignified King of this vast kingdom,
I should never be derided by my people behind my back.

"A man's words are like a cut-down tree;
A king's decision is like the fully-cooked rice."
Zhao Langma then ordered his brother Lagana
To take Nan Xila out of palace and have her executed.

The kind Lagana frowned at the order.
Endless sorrow and anxiety were surging in his heart.
He pled to his brother for mercy on his innocent sister-in-law.
But Zhao Langma would not listen to him at all.

要是不执行哥哥的命令,
召朗玛一定会对他治罪追究,
要是把无辜的嫂嫂杀死,
天大的冤屈啊他一辈子都会感到内疚。

召朗玛见弟弟犹豫不前,
又对他下达了执刑的命令:
"你快去把南西拉砍成两段,
我等着你掏回她的心。

"俗话说淫荡女人的心像狗心。
狗心的女人最多情,
我倒是要看看这个女人,
长的究竟是颗什么样的心?"

脸色苍白的南西拉猛地站起身,
不再祈求召朗玛的怜悯,
"再见吧,勐沓达腊塔的君王,
苦命的西拉将含着冤屈离开人世。

"今天尽管你亲手割断夫妻的恩爱,
尽管你亲手葬送我们的爱情,
天地间也只有你的妻子,
最理解丈夫的心情。

"因为你珍惜爱情的纯洁,
才会这样的狠心和冷酷,
因为你憎恨邪恶和狡诈,
才会这样的果断和残忍。

第十九章 冤 Chapter 19 Injustice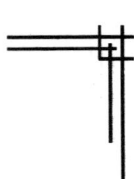

If he disobeyed the king's order,
He himself was to be punished.
The execution of his innocent sister-in-law would be so unjust
That he would live in guilt for the rest of his life.

Zhao Langma saw his brother's hesitation,
He pushed further and ordered him to carry out the execution,
"Hurry up, cut her into halves,
I am waiting for you to bring back her heart to me.

"It is said that the lusty woman's heart is like that of a dog,
A woman with a dog's heart is the most wanton one.
I am waiting to see
What kind of heart is hidden in this woman?"

The pale-faced Nan Xila stood up abruptly,
She stopped asking mercy from Zhao Langma.
"Goodbye, the King of Dadalata,
Miserable Nan Xila is leaving the world with grievance.

"You cut the bond of us as husband and wife,
And you are burying our love with your own hands.
But only me, your wife is the one
Who understands you best in this world.

"It is just because you cherish the purity of our love
That you become so ruthless and cold-hearted.
It is only because you hate the wickedness and tricks,
That you are so resolute and merciless.

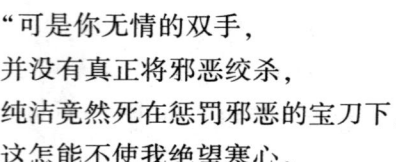

"可是你无情的双手,
并没有真正将邪恶绞杀,
纯洁竟然死在惩罚邪恶的宝刀下,
这怎能不使我绝望寒心。

"再见吧,慈祥的母后,
愿您度过幸福的晚年,
永别了,可爱的宫女们,
愿你们歌声更动听服饰更鲜艳。

"再见吧,各位大臣和武官,
召朗玛治国请你们竭力协助,
让人间的欢乐和幸福,
代替你们的不幸和痛苦。

"再见吧,南西拉洗澡的清水和金槽,
别因为主人死亡而潺潺流泪,
永别了,王宫的大象和战马,
愿你们在阳光下享受绿茵茵的青草。

"再见吧,忠实敦厚的弟弟腊嘎纳,
为了寻找嫂嫂你历尽苦难,
为了救出嫂嫂你流下鲜血,
今天让嫂嫂最后把您细看。

"我们一起住在伊麻板森林,
尽管不幸的遭遇把我们折磨,
但我们生活在召朗玛身边,
我们是既艰苦又欢乐。

第十九章 冤　Chapter 19 Injustice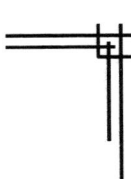

"But with your ruthless hands,
What you are murdering is not the evildoer. Instead
Purity is to be killed in the name of punishing evils.
And my heart is chilled by such absurdity.

"Goodbye, my dear benevolent mother-in-law,
May you have a very happy life in your remaining years;
Goodbye, my dear servant maids,
May you sing more beautifully and be dressed more colorfully.

"Goodbye, all the officials and generals.
Please work together to help the king govern this kingdom,
So that happiness and merriness will fill the earth,
And misfortune and hardship stay far away from the people.

"Goodbye, my bathtub and spring water,
Please don't cry for the death of me.
Goodbye, elephants and horses in the palace,
I wish you always enjoyed the green grass under sunshine.

"Goodbye, my kind younger brother Lagana.
You have suffered too much when trying to search for me.
You have shed blood to save me, your sister-in-law.
Please let me have a close look at you for the last time.

"We have lived in the forest of Yimaban together.
We have been tortured by miserable sufferings.
But since we lived by the side of Zhao Langma,
We still enjoyed our life no matter how hard it was.

"追求的幸福今天变成苦难,
这哀愁悲戚现在对谁表达?
嫂嫂尽管心中有千悲万愁,
只愿弟弟继续照顾召朗玛。"

腊嘎纳默默地拿着大刀,
领着嫂嫂走出庄严的宫殿,
人群顿时发出阵阵哀号,
哭声就像八月的青蛙鸣叫。

腊嘎纳押着嫂嫂走进森林,
悲伤的泪水暗暗流进心田,
森林啊,为何变得这般凄凉?
滴落的露珠好像也在哭泣悲伤。

聪明的腊嘎纳停下了脚步,
合掌祈求天神给予帮助:
"神明的英捧啊,
请来挽救一个蒙受冤屈的生命。

"要是南西拉的心如宝石般纯洁,
我的宝刀将砍杀不进,
如果嫂嫂欺骗哥哥心地不正,
就让宝刀结束她的生命。"

腊嘎纳慢慢地举起宝刀,
霎时地上长出无数花树,
千簇万簇鲜花卫护着南西拉,
把腊嘎纳的宝刀挡住。

第十九章 冤　Chapter 19 Injustice

"The happiness we have pursued turns into bitterness.
I don't know to whom I can express my sorrow.
Although my heart is overfilled with sadness and worries,
I still ask you to take good care of your brother Zhao Langma."

Lagana took up the knife without a word,
He led Nan Xila out of the grandiose palace.
The throngs burst into loud sobs,
Their cries were as loud as the squawking of frogs in August.

Lagana escorted Nan Xila into the forest.
He cried silently deep in his heart.
The forest seemed to have turned desolate,
With the dew dropping down from the leaves like tears.

Clever Lagana stopped his steps.
Folding his hands, he prayed to god of heaven for help,
"Wise God of Yingpeng in the heaven,
Please rescue the innocent life who suffers injustice.

"If her heart is as pure as jade
My knife will not be able to cut into her body;
If she has cheated on my brother with an evil heart,
Let the precious knife end her life immediately."

Lagana raised the knife slowly. All of a sudden,
Countless flower trees grew out from the ground.
They gathered together to guard around Nan Xila
They fended off the precious knife of Lagana.

腊嘎纳又惊又喜明了一切，
森林的花树证明了南西拉的贞洁，
这时一只黑狗闯到跟前，
他一刀把它砍成两截。

他向吓呆了的南西拉跪下，
用悲哀的声音对她说：
"洛木花一般的嫂嫂啊，
你赶快远走高飞吧！

"弟弟今天放你逃走，
望你逃向海角天涯，
愿你洁净的身躯脱离一切苦难，
望你疾病离身一路平安。"

南西拉迅速逃进了深山老林，
腊嘎纳心情沉重地回到宫廷，
他当着大臣的面向召朗玛述职，
交出一个血淋淋的狗心。

从此召朗玛猜忌的心更重，
更加痛恨卑污的女人，
他心中的怒火渐渐平息，
头脑中也慢慢消失了南西拉的身影。

二、生子

死里逃生的南西拉，

第十九章 冤 Chapter 19 Injustice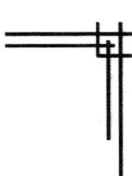

In a joyful surprise, Lagana understood everything.
The flower tree proved the innocence of Nan Xila.
A black dog appeared at that moment,
He cut it into halves with one slash.

He knelt down in front of the terrified Nan Xila.
He said to her with the most sorrowful voice,
"Sister-in-law, you are as pure as the Luomu flower,
Please leave and find your own way out of here.

"I, your little brother, let you go today.
Please run away as far as you can.
May your pure body be protected from any hardship.
May you stay away from disease and have a safe journey."

Nan Xila rushed into the deep jungle.
Lagana returned to the court with a heavy heart.
He reported to Zhao Langma in front of the officials
And he handed out the bloody dog heart.

Zhao Langma became more suspicious ever since,
And he hated more those disgraceful women.
His anger was gradually appeased as time passed by.
Nan Xila started to fade and disappear from his head.

II Giving Birth to a Son

After the narrow escape from death,

兰嘎西贺 The Ten-Headed King of Langa

忍受着无比的痛苦,
她一个人孤孤独独,
无目的地走向密林深处。

寒露把她从梦中冻醒,
仰望着星空无法再入睡,
命运使她从山头坠入黑暗的山涧,
天空啊,求你快一些露出晨曦。

黑夜终于慢慢地退去,
太阳终于慢慢地升起,
南西拉到清澈的泉边洗脸饮水,
到树丛中寻找野果充饥。

她想到召朗玛出走的时候,
他们也在这样的森林里徜徉,
那时虽然艰辛却不悲切,
因为她紧紧跟随在丈夫身旁。

今天谁来陪伴谁来分忧,
她只听见林中的虎嗥狼吼,
啊,自己一生的遭遇多么凄惨!
犹如花朵经历一阵阵风雨摧残。

白头翁突然高声喧哗,
是不是召朗玛追来啦?
也许他消除了误解原谅了她,
不,不,密林里又静寂得叫人害怕。

第十九章 冤 Chapter 19 Injustice

Nan Xila suffered from her endless sorrow.
She walked lonely and aimlessly,
And she went into the deep jungle.

She was awakened by the chilly frost.
Then she looked up into the starry night and couldn't fall asleep.
Fate brought her down from hilltop into the dark canyon.
She was begging the morning to come a little faster.

At last the darkness faded,
And the sun rose slowly.
Nan Xila came to the clear creek to wash and drink.
And she again went to the woods to get wild fruits.

She thought of the time with Zhao Langma,
They also wandered in the forest like this.
Life had been hard but they were not sad at that time,
Because she followed her husband step by step.

Who could accompany her and share her sorrow?
She could only hear the roaring of tigers in the jungle.
What miserable experiences she had gone through in her life!
She was just like a devastated flower shaking in the storm.

A pulsatilla starling suddenly shrieked loud in the tree,
Was it Zhao Langma coming to chase her?
Maybe he had cleared up his misunderstanding and forgiven her.
But no, no, the silence afterwards in the jungle made her scared.

无望的南西拉只有向英捧祈告：
"神明的天王英捧啊，
请你营救我这个无辜的女人，
让我有个地方栖身。"

南西拉委屈的呼喊传到天宫，
天宫的西腊石①阵阵摇动，
英捧举目向人间观望，
只见受难的南西拉正在林中徘徊。

英捧急忙从天上下到人间，
变成一个英俊的"国王"走到南西拉身边，
"宝石般的姑娘啊，
你的美貌果然叫我一见倾心。

"我是一个没有伴侣的国王，
听到你的不幸特到森林里把你找寻，
今天接你到哥哥的宫廷里去，
让你享受王后的荣耀和欢欣。"

黄金般纯洁的南西拉回答：
"南西拉感谢你的一片好心，
情欲在我心中已经熄灭，
我不爱你，也不爱任何人。"

---

① 西腊石：传说中的天堂巨石，能将不祥报告英捧。

第十九章 冤 Chapter 19 Injustice

Hopeless Nan Xila could only pray to Yingpeng,
"Your wise Yingpeng, god of heaven,
Please help me the innocent woman.
Please give me a place to stay."

Nan Xila's sad prays reached the heaven.
And Xila Rock① in the heaven began to shake.
Yingpeng looked down from the heaven to the earth,
And he saw poor Nan Xila wandering in the jungle.

Yingpeng descended to the earth in a hurry.
He changed himself into a handsome king and came to Nan Xila.
He said to her, "My girl as precious as a gemstone,
"I fell in love with your beauty at the first sight.

"I am a king without a mate by my side,
I heard your miseries and searched for you in the forest.
Today, I will take you with me to my palace.
You will be my queen and enjoy honor and happiness."

Nan Xila , as pure as the gold, answered,
"Thank you very much for your kindness.
The desire for love has been extinguished in my heart.
I won't love you, I won't love anyone any more."

---

① Xila Rock: It is said it was a huge rock in heaven which could report ill omens to Yingpeng.

英捧还要进一步试探,
说出的话儿比糯米饭还要柔软:
"可怜的孔雀啊,你别忧愁失望,
哥哥对你是一片真心。

"我决不会像召朗玛那样狐疑心窄,
决不会像召朗玛那样三心二意,
要是哥哥有半点假意虚情,
让天雷劈头天斧砍身。"

甜言蜜语打不动南西拉的心,
她用坚定的声音回答:
"南西拉正在遭受灾难和不幸,
就像一朵被风雨摧断的山花。

"你若是一位庄严的国王,
你若是一位善良的君主,
请同情南西拉的不幸和痛苦,
别让她受伤的心再受折磨。

"人生真正的爱情只有一次,
南西拉的爱情已献给召朗玛,
纵然由于误会他置我于死地,
但是真正的爱情刀箭不能扼杀。

"既然召朗玛已抛弃他的南西拉,
南西拉也决不再出嫁,
让天神安排我的命运吧,
从此森林就是我的家。"

第十九章 冤 Chapter 19 Injustice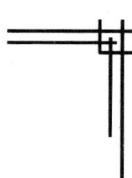

Yingpeng still gave her another test,
His words were softer than the cooked sticky rice,
"My poor peacock, don't be disappointed and worried.
What I am offering you is my heart and true love.

"I am not as suspicious and narrow-minded as Zhao Langma;
I will never be like him who has a fickle heart.
If there is any insincerity in my love for you,
I will be punished and struck by thunder and lightning."

Nan Xila was untouched by his sweet talk,
And she answered with a resolute voice,
"I am undergoing mishap and bad luck,
Just like a fragile flower in the mountain devastated by storm.

"If you were a dignified king,
If you were a kind-hearted ruler,
Please have your sympathy on my miseries,
Please don't torture my injured heart any more.

"There is only one true love in one's life.
My love has already been given to Zhao Langma.
Although he put me to death out of misunderstanding,
But true love can't be killed by knife or arrow.

"Since Zhao Langma has abandoned her Nan Xila,
Nan Xila will never get remarried.
Let god of heaven decide my fate,
The forest is my home from today on."

兰嘎西贺 The Ten-Headed King of Langa

南西拉说完向远处走去，
像一只孤零零的野鸡，
她艰难地在山道上爬行，
天地无边，森林无际。

英捧变成一条白色水牛，
脖上的铜铃发出叮当的声响，
它在前面边走边吃青草，
粗粗的花绳拴在头上。

南西拉看见前面的水牛，
不禁心中一阵喜悦，
"水牛拖着绳子在这里吃草，
森林中一定隐藏着村寨。"

她跟着白牛走了七天，
来到温暖的伊麻板森林，
幽静的森林出现一间巴朗，
南西拉回头不见了水牛的踪影。

一个衣着朴素的帕拉西走出来，
南西拉虔诚地向他下拜，
她对帕拉西讲了自己的身世，
请求帕拉西让她在这里栖身。

帕拉西说出了安慰的话语：
"可怜的南西拉，我的女儿，
你的遭遇使我同情，
你在这住下吧，这里就是你的家。"

第十九章 冤 Chapter 19 Injustice

After this Nan Xila walked into the deeper woods,
Like a lonely pheasant in the mountain,
She trekked with pains on the zigzagging path,
Under the endless sky and in the boundless forest.

Yingpeng turned himself into a white buffalo,
And the brass bell under its neck was tinkling.
While grazing, it roamed in front of Nan Xila,
A thick colorful rope was tethered on its head.

Seeing the buffalo in front of her,
Nan Xila felt so happy in her heart.
"A tethered buffalo is grazing here,
There must be a village in this deep jungle."

She followed the white buffalo for seven days.
At last she arrived at the warm Yimaban forest.
There appeared a Balang in the tranquil forest.
Turning back, Nan Xila found the buffalo disappeared.

A Palaxi in simple clothes got out,
Nan Xila bowed to him with great respect.
She told her life story to Palaxi,
And she asked if he could let her stay there.

Palaxi consoled her with gentle words,
"Poor Nan Xila, my daughter,
I sympathize with your suffering.
Please stay and make it your home here."

帕拉西为南西拉盖了一间舒适的草房,
从此南西拉安心在森林住下,
离开人世的烦忧和喧哗,
安静地度过了几个月的时光。

南西拉离开宫殿前已经怀孕,
现在分娩的日期终于到来,
婴儿从母体呱呱坠地,
生下来的是一个男孩。

孩子的皮肤白里透红,
犹如火炉里熔化的金水,
漂亮的眼睛和脸庞,
同召朗玛一模一样。

孤独的南西拉无比高兴,
把孩子当作自己的眼珠,
每当她出去采野果,
就把孩子托给帕拉西照顾。

南西拉勤快得像只母鸡,
一早就到山上寻找瓜果薯芋,
夜里她把孩子紧紧搂在怀里,
母子俩睡得香甜又安谧。

一天南西拉在密林里采野果,
见一只母猴背着两只小猴爬树,
南西拉担心小猴掉落下来,
把心中忧虑对母猴说出:

第十九章 冤 Chapter 19 Injustice

Palaxi built a thatched house for Nan Xila.
Now finally she got a place to live in the forest.
Free from the worldly noises and troubles,
She had lived peacefully for a few months.

Nan Xila had been pregnant when she left the palace.
Now it was the day when she should labour.
Then out of her body came a crying baby.
It was a boy that Nan Xila had delivered.

The skin of the boy was fair touched with pink,
It was like the gold melt in the furnace.
He had pretty face and eyes,
And he looked exactly like Zhao Langma.

The lonely Nan Xila was overjoyed.
She treated the boy as her own eyeballs.
Each time she went out to pick wild fruits,
She asked Palaxi to take care of her baby.

Nan Xila worked hard like a diligent hen,
She tried to find all kinds of wild fruits in the mountains.
Each night she held her baby tightly in her arms,
And both the mommy and the baby slept sweetly.

One day Nan Xila was picking wild fruits in the jungle.
She saw a monkey climbing the tree with two babies on her back.
Nan Xila was worried that the little monkeys might fall off,
So she spoke out her care to the monkey mother.

843

"白猴啊，你为什么这样傻，
出远门还背着自己的孩子，
爬大树，过深沟，来来去去，
难道你不怕把孩子摔死？"

母猴听了反驳她说：
"我看愚蠢的正是你自己，
你身为王后，孩子珍贵万分，
可是你一点不疼爱幼小的生命。

"你每天太阳偏西才回去，
孩子丢在家中饿奶你不心疼，
要是你的孩子突然不幸暴死了，
等你回去他已变得冰凉僵硬。

"我不像你那样不心疼孩子，
凡是出门我都带着它们，
万一发生什么意外和不幸，
死活我们母子也都在一起。"

南西拉听了不觉心中一惊，
神色不安，心情不定，
她觉得母猴的做法符合人情，
暗暗责备自己过分粗心。

南西拉匆匆赶回巴朗，
见儿子在床上睡得正熟，
她不声不响背起儿子，
返回森林去采摘瓜果。

第十九章 冤 Chapter 19 Injustice

"White monkey, why are you so silly?
You carry your kids when you are far away from home.
Aren't you afraid they would fall off and get injured
While you are climbing the tree and jumping into the ditch?"

The monkey mother retorted upon her,
"In my eyes, you are the silly mom yourself.
As a queen, you have a precious baby,
But you don't care such a fragile infantile life.

"You can't go back home until the dusk,
Disregarding your baby crying for milk at home.
If your baby died all of a sudden,
He would be cold and stiff when you get back home.

"I am not like you who don't care for your own baby.
I take them wherever I go.
If mishap or misfortune happens to them,
We are all together, dying or living."

Nan Xila was shocked at hearing this.
She became worried and restless.
She felt what the monkey did was more humane
And she blamed herself for being so careless.

Nan Xila rushed back to the Balang,
She saw her baby was sleeping sound.
Carrying her son on her back silently,
She returned to the forest to gather wild fruits.

帕拉西一觉醒来，
床上不见了小孙孙，
他就焦急地四处找寻，
里里外外不见孩子的踪影。

"是谁悄悄偷走了小宝贝，
竟敢这样伤天害理？
是林中的虎豹进来叼走，
还是作恶的妖怪把他掳去？

"恨只恨我睡得太死，
孩子失踪我还蒙在鼓里，
南西拉回来不见孩子，
残酷的打击定会使她昏倒在地。"

为了不让南西拉的精神再受创伤，
帕拉西用木头雕出一个模样相同的婴儿，
他向着木头吹了三口气，
木头婴儿马上有了生命。

阳光晒红了脸的南西拉回来了，
背着孩子高高兴兴走进巴朗，
一眼看见孩子踢踢蹬蹬躺在床上，
立刻俯身抱起来频频吻他的脸庞。

她解开胸襟把奶头塞给孩子，
嘴里不停地喃喃低语：
"妈妈的宝贝呀，饿坏了吧！"
一切同平常从森林里回来一样。

第十九章 冤 Chapter 19 Injustice

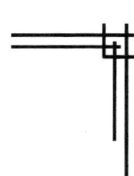

When Palaxi woke up from his sleep,
He found that his grandson was not in the bed.
He searched for him anxiously all over the places,
But still there was no trace of the baby inside and outside.

"Who came here and stole the baby away?
Who dared to do such a lawless and ruthless thing?
Was it the leopard or tiger that took away the baby?
Or the baby was robbed away by an evil monster?

"I shouldn't have slept so dead like a log,
I was in the dark even when the baby got lost.
When Nan Xila came back and found her baby missing,
This cruel blow will surely get her heart broken."

To protect Na Xila from being struck by another trauma,
He carved a doll out of wood exactly like the baby.
He blew three times of his breath to the wood,
The wooden doll became alive all of a sudden.

Nan Xila came back home with a tanned face,
With the baby on her back, she walked into Balang joyously.
Seeing the baby in the bed with its legs kicking around,
She bent over, picked him up and kissed his face.

Nan Xila untied her clothes to milk the baby,
And she kept talking gently to him,
"You must be very hungry now, my darling!"
Everything was as usual as each time she returned from the forest.

站在旁边的帕拉西惊愕得睁大眼睛,
丢失的孙子正睡在南西拉的背上,
南西拉也恍然大悟放下孩子,
两个婴儿在一起分不出两样。

她询问帕拉西是怎么一回事,
帕拉西把事情经过对她讲明:
"要是女儿不喜欢他,
阿爹吹口气就让他无踪无影。

"要是你喜欢这孩子,
就留下他给孩子做伴,
女儿你作决定吧!
一切按你的心愿去办。"

善良的南西拉温和地回答:
"你不说我还分不出来,
他们就像一对双胞胎,
这孩子谁见了不喜爱。

"两个孩子都是宝贝,
他们就像我的两个眼珠一样,
慈父啊,别毁了他的小生命,
让他和你的孙子一道成长。"

帕拉西听了十分高兴,
他要为孩子祝福取名,
南西拉的亲生儿子算作哥哥,
赠给他的名字叫洛玛。

第十九章 冤 Chapter 19 Injustice

Standing by her side, Palaxi was gasped with wide eyes,
The lost baby was sleeping on Nan Xila's back.
Nan Xila also found it out and she put down the baby.
The two babies lying together were exactly the same.

She asked Palaxi what had happened.
After telling her the whole story, Palaxi said,
"If you don't like this baby,
I can let him disappear just with a breath.

"If you are fond of him,
He will stay with us to accompany your son.
My daughter, you make the decision!
Just follow your own heart."

The kind Nan Xila answered gently,
"I can't tell one from the other if you didn't tell me.
They are just like twin brothers.
Any one who sees the baby will be fond of him.

"They both are my babies.
They are like the two eyeballs of mine.
Dear father, please don't destroy the little baby,
Let him grow up together with your grandson."

Palaxi was very happy at hearing this.
He then named them with his blessing.
The son of Nan Xila was elder brother,
So he was given the name of Luoma.

帕拉西做成的儿子算作弟弟，
赠给他的名字叫相娃，
南西拉望着两个活泼可爱的孩子，
心里感到无比的幸福。

森林的树叶黄了又绿绿了又黄，
转眼过去了漫长的七年时光，
两棵金笋虽然长在山箐里，
但他们比一般的笋子茁壮。

帕拉西天天给他们传授武艺，
还传授给他们智慧和学识，
他们精通神术和武艺，
手臂有二十条大公象的力量。

长大懂事的洛玛和相娃，
有一天向南西拉说出心头的疑问：
"慈爱善良的母亲啊，
谁是我们威武的父亲？

"他是乘骑大象的国王，
还是统率千军的武将？
他是走遍千勐的商人，
还是种田种地的百姓？"

南西拉有说不出的苦楚，
只好半真半假告诉孩子：
"你们的父亲是沓达腊塔国王，
召朗玛就是他的名字。

第十九章 冤 Chapter 19 Injustice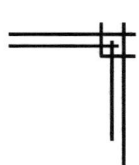

The boy Palaxi had created was younger brother,
So he was blessed with the name of Xiangwa.
Nan Xila watched these two lovely babies,
She was overfilled with joy and happiness.

Leaves in the forest turned from green to yellow and yellow to green,
In a blink seven years passed by.
Those two babies were like two golden bamboo shoots,
They grew stronger than others in this quiet valley.

Palaxi taught them martial arts every day;
He also passed them his wisdom and knowledge.
They were versed in martial arts and magics.
Their arms had the strength of twenty elephants together.

Luoma and Xiangwa now grew up and had their own thoughts.
One day they asked the question buried deep in their minds,
"Our kind and amiable mom,
Who is our mighty father?

"Is he a king riding on the elephant?
Or a general commanding thousands of soldiers?
Is he a businessman travelling around the world?
Or a farmer working hard in the field?"

With her unspeakable bitterness,
Nan Xila could only tell half of the truth,
"Your father was the king of Dadalata,
Zhao Langma was his name.

"你们的父亲已经逝世,
妈妈被赶到这里过着伤心的日子,
你们一定要苦练本领勤奋学习,
为受苦的妈妈争一口气。"

两兄弟把妈妈的话记在心里,
更加刻苦地学习知识和本领,
他们天天在森林里摘野果射鸟兽,
侍奉亲爱的母亲和年老的帕拉西。

第十九章 冤 Chapter 19 Injustice

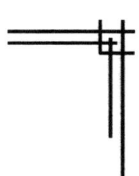

"Your father had passed away,
And I was driven out and live my sad life here.
You two must work hard and be more skillful.
So that I can be proud of you when you grow up."

The two brothers kept their mother's words in their minds.
They worked harder to acquire more knowledge and skills.
They gathered wild fruits and hunted in the forest every day,
And they took good care of old Palaxi and their dear mom.

第二十章　团圆

一、在沓达腊塔街上

洛玛和相娃聪明又勤快，
聪明得赛过垒巢的小鸟，
勤快得好像采花的蜜蜂，
他们在伊麻板种出了庄稼和瓜果。

一天兄弟俩在地里交谈起来：
"母亲说允沓达腊塔宫殿雄伟，
是我们的父亲居住的地方，
城里又有热闹繁华的街场。

"母亲说父亲早已离开人世，
是真是假我们没有看见，
生来我们没有赶过街集，
生来我们没有见过堂皇的宫殿。"

洛玛和相娃谈得津津有味，
决心到城里看看是什么模样，
他们摘下了芳香的瓜果，
动身去允沓达腊塔赶集。

第二十章 团圆 Chapter 20 Reunion

Chapter 20　Reunion

I　On the Street of Dadalata

Luoma and Xiangwa were clever and diligent.
They were more clever than the birds building their nestles;
They were more diligent than the bees gathering honey.
They now planted and harvested crops and fruits in Yimaban.

One day the two brothers chatted in the field,
"Mom said the palace in the city of Dadalata was grandiose.
It was the place where our father had lived.
There were also many crowded streets and plazas in the city.

"Mom said that Father had already left the world.
But we don't know if it is true.
We have never been to a fair since we were born,
We have never seen what grandiose palace looks like."

They were so much interested in what they were talking about
That they decided to go to the city to take a look at it.
After gathering some fragrant melons and fruits,
They set out for Dadalata to go to a fair.

他们瞒着妈妈离开伊麻板,
翻山越岭走了七天七夜,
来到了宽敞富饶的坝子,
来到了京城热闹的街市。

赶街的人群熙熙攘攘,
出卖的东西五光十色,
不同的街摆着不同的东西,
不同的摊前有不同身份的顾客。

洛玛和相娃的豆角、黄瓜新鲜肥大,
又有熟透的散发着芬芳的香瓜,
吸引着人们争先恐后购买,
忙得兄弟俩汗如雨下。

有的人不买东西也不走开,
站在那里观看相貌相同的两兄弟,
观看的人越来越多,
看不着的人又往前挤。

这时走来了税务官阿努曼,
对洛玛和相娃说出了傲慢的语言:
"我是为国王征收税租的叭龙,
快拿出你们的瓜果来上贡。"

第二十章 团圆 Chapter 20 Reunion

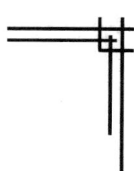

They left without telling their mother.
It took them seven days to cross over the mountains.
At last they reached the spacious and prosperous village,
And then they got to the crowded streets in the capital city.

Lots of people were trading on the street.
Thousands of items were sold here and there.
Different items were sold in different places.
Customers of different status were bargaining before various stalls.

The green beans and cucumbers of the brothers were big and fresh.
And they were also selling melons ripe and fragrant.
People were attracted and swarmed to buy them.
The two brothers were so busy that they sweated profusely.

Some people didn't buy anything but still wouldn't leave.
They just stood there looking at the identical brothers.
More and more on-lookers gathered there,
Those who were blocked tried to push forward.

Now here came the tax collector Anuman.
He said to Luoma and Xiangwa haughtily,
"I am the Balong in charge of tax collecting for the king.
Now tribute some of your melons to pay your tax."

洛玛和相娃看了阿努曼一眼,
待理不理顶撞过去:
"我们弯腰流汗种出的瓜果,
凭什么要拿给你?"

"金殿王朝的命令委托给我,
我收多收少没有谁敢说,
你俩竟敢对抗法令不交税,
我看你俩是不是不想活?"

阿努曼的话激怒了兄弟俩,
他们出口的语言像飞来的皮鞭:
"你这猴官架子十足,
想整死我们料定你不敢。

"你想多吃请到山中去,
你想多要请到伊麻板,
我们远道挑来就是要卖钱,
一切都得按照买卖规矩办。"

暴躁的白猴捋起衣袖,
一把抓起一个大香瓜,
洛玛和相娃飞起一脚,
把阿努曼的竹箩踢朝一边。

愤怒的白猴朝他们狠狠踢了一脚,
把兄弟俩踢出十远,
洛玛和相娃怒吼一声冲向阿努曼,
一人一拳把它打得仰面朝天。

第二十章 团圆 Chapter 20 Reunion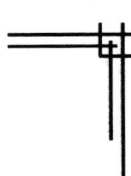

Luoma and Xiangwa took a look at Anuman,
They treated him coldly and retorted upon him,
"We did all the work in the field to harvest the melons,
Why should we give them to you for free?"

"I am entitled to gather taxes by our court,
No one dares to challenge me when I tell him how much to pay.
How dare you two violate the law and pay no tax?
I guess you two just don't want to live any longer."

What Anuman said provoked the two brothers.
Retorts from their mouth were like flicking whip,
"You, the monkey officer, are too haughty,
We bet you have no guts to take our lives.

"If you want to eat some, go into the mountain.
If you want to have more, go to the forest of Yimaban.
We have carried them here from afar to trade.
We all should follow the rules of doing business."

The short-tempered white monkey rolled up his sleeves,
And he grabbed a very big melon.
Luoma and Xiangwa jumped to kick,
And Anuman's bamboo basket was kicked aside.

The angry white monkey kicked hard on them,
The two brothers were bounced fifteen meters away.
Luoma and Xiangwa charged toward Anuman with a shout,
They bashed the white monkey down to the ground.

859

双方拳脚交加厮打起来，
整个街子乱成一团，
得到神灵帮助的洛玛兄弟，
把阿努曼打得周身瘫软。

阿努曼当众出丑羞红了脸，
它跑回宫里向召朗玛告状：
"你委任我收税从没有人敢反对，
可是今天却有两个孩子同我打起来。

"兰嘎大战我没有战败过，
今天堂堂的大臣遭打骂，
头也被打出一个大疙瘩，
不干了，我要回勐基沙。"

二、放马寻子

召朗玛听了非常震惊，
"阿努曼的神威和力量远近闻名，
天下无敌的人竟遭毒打。
这两个孩子究竟是什么人？

"我是唯一能拉动弓阿沙尖的王子，
渡海征战杀死十头王，
一百零一勐的国王和臣子，
没有哪一个敢和我对抗。

第二十章 团圆 Chapter 20 Reunion

They fought with each other kicking and bashing,
The whole street was in a total mess.
With the unseen help from god and ghost,
The two brothers beat Anuman black and blue.

Anuman blushed because of the humiliation in the public,
He ran back to the palace and resorted to Zhao Langma,
"You assigned me to collect tax, and nobody dare disobey.
But today two kids had guts to fight against me.

"I have never been defeated even in the war of Langa.
While today I, your minister, was abused and beaten.
Even my head was pounded so hard that it now lumped.
I quit and I am heading back to the Kingdom of Jisha."

II Horse Released as a Bait

Zhao Langma was shocked when hearing this.
"Anuman's magics and power were known to the world.
While today this invincible Anuman was beaten badly.
Who could be those two dauntless kids?

"I was the only prince that could pull open the Bow of Ajiansha.

I crossed the sea and killed the ten-headed monster in battles.

Among the kings and their officials of one hundred and one kingdom,

No one has the guts to disobey me.

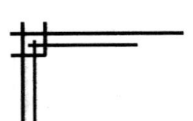

兰噶西贺 The Ten-Headed King of Langa

"两个孩子既然敢与阿努曼较量,
也一定会对抗我的命令,
听说他俩已经逃跑,
我一定要设法把他们找寻。"

召朗玛发出一个通告,
神圣的王命拴在七匹骏马的脖子上,
"谁在这土地上服从我的管理,
就乖乖地把散失的骏马送回。

"谁在这土地上敢反对召朗玛,
就请牵走我的骏马,
表示接受我的挑战,
我们就面对面比一个高下。"

七匹骏马同时从宫殿放出,
它们随心所欲、四处狂奔,
召朗玛派腊嘎纳带兵暗暗跟随,
看看谁敢违抗国王的命令。

骏马吃着青草向四面八方走去,
士兵沿着蹄印步步紧跟,
有的人表示敬意牵马送回,
有的人生怕惹祸远远躲避。

第二十章 团圆 Chapter 20 Reunion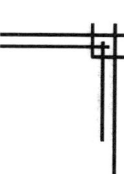

"Since the two kids dare fight against Anuman,
They must be also bold enough to rebel against me.
It is said that they have run away,
I will try every way to find them out."

Zhao Langma sent out public notices.
The notices from the King were hung on the necks of seven horses.
"Whoever is on my land should obey my rules;
Whoever has seen my lost horses will send them back to me.

"Those who dare disobey me,
You can take away the horses.
That means you accept my challenge,
And let's have a duel face-to-face."

The seven horses were released out of the palace.
They ran wildly roaming everywhere.
Zhao Langma ordered Lagana with soldiers to follow them secretly
To see who dared to rebel against the king.

The horses walked around while grazing.
The soldiers followed their footprints step by step.
Someone saw the horse and sent it back to the palace.
Some stayed away from the horses for fear of trouble.

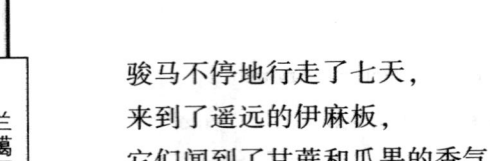

兰嘎西贺 The Ten-Headed King of Langa

骏马不停地行走了七天，
来到了遥远的伊麻板，
它们闻到了甘蔗和瓜果的香气，
闯进了洛玛和相娃的瓜园。

它们大口大口地啃吃甘蔗瓜果，
把果园菜地一一糟蹋，
洛玛和相娃前来看地，
立即把骏马拴了起来。

跟踪的武官命令士兵解开缰绳，
洛玛和相娃又要阻拦，
"马糟蹋了瓜果就得拿银钱赔偿，
你们国王的通告管不住我们。"

武官命令士兵将骏马抢走，
洛玛和相娃抓住武官猛踢猛打，
有些士兵被打得头破血流，
逃出森林报告了腊嘎纳。

腊嘎纳带着士兵急匆匆赶来，
看到两个孩子怒冲冲站在园里，
七匹骏马被拴在树下，
腊嘎纳仔细端详产生了怀疑。

"这两个硬气的孩子天不怕地不怕，
为什么长得像我哥哥召朗玛？
他们的眼睛、眉毛和鼻子，
为什么这么像我的嫂嫂南西拉？

第二十章 团圆 Chapter 20 Reunion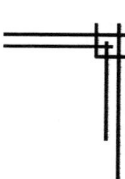

The horses strolled for seven days,
And they reached the remote Yimaban.
When sniffing the fragrance of melons and sugar cane,
They broke into the yard of Luoma and Xiangwa.

They ate the sugar canes and melons freely,
And the orchard and yard were tramped into a mess.
When Luoma and Xiangwa came to the yard,
They tethered up the horses immediately.

The following soldiers came up to release the horses,
The two brothers stopped them and said,
"You have to compensate for the damage the horses had made.
The notice of your king doesn't rule over us."

The official ordered the soldiers to take away the horses,
So the two brothers started to kick and bash the official.
Some soldiers were injured in the head.
They escaped out of the forest and reported it to Lagana.

Lagana led the soldiers and rushed in.
He saw two angry kids were standing in the yard.
And the seven horses were tethered to the trees.
Lagana took a close look and suspicion surged in his heart.

"These two stubborn brothers are dauntless.
Why they look so alike my brother Zhao Langma?
They also have eyes, brows and noses
That look so much like those of Nan Xila?

"我不能伤害他们的生命,
不能用硬箭把他们射死。"
腊嘎纳顺手采下一根草秆,
搭在弓弦上射了过去。

洛玛被草秆冲倒,
腊嘎纳忙跑过去把他扶起,
"你叫什么名字,父母是谁?
宝石般的孩子,说说你们的身世。"

相娃见来人抱住哥哥,
误认为他们要下毒手,
立即拉弓搭箭射过去,
一箭把腊嘎纳射倒在地。

士兵们吓得纷纷逃跑,
跑回宫殿向召朗玛报告,
召朗玛闻讯大为震惊,
如临大敌立刻带兵声讨。

阿努曼带着一大队人马,
把瓜园团团包围住,
就像渔网罩住水井,
召朗玛往里面看得分明。

两兄弟的面貌似乎十分熟悉,
原来他们长得和南西拉一个样子,
召朗玛站在远处大声发问,
对他们二人的身世盘根究底。

第二十章 团圆 Chapter 20 Reunion

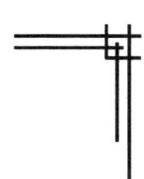

"I had better not harm their lives.
I can't shoot them with my arrows."
Lagana broke down a piece of straw.
He used the straw as arrow and shot.

The flying straw pushed Luowa down to the ground.
Lagana rushed to him and held him up.
"What is your name and who are your parents?
You little kid, tell me something about your family."

Xiangwa saw the stranger holding his elder brother,
He thought they were trying to kill him.
He pulled the bow and shot with an arrow.
Lagana got hit and fell down to the ground.

The soldiers were frightened and ran for their lives.
They returned to the palace and reported to the king.
Zhao Langma was shocked to hear that.
He took them as enemy and led the soldier to suppress.

Anuman led a large group of troops and horses,
They surrounded the yard tightly
Like the fishing net covering a well.
Zhao Langma had a close look from the outside.

The two brothers looked very familiar to him.
They looked exactly like Nan Xila.
Zhao Langma asked loudly in the distance,
Trying to get the details of their family background.

兰噶西贺　The Ten-Headed King of Langa

"是谁来查问我们的祖宗三代？
那么胆小只敢躲在森林里，
你们是哪个勐开来的军队？
是不是想来伊麻板送死？"

洛玛说完射出电鞭似的箭，
一下射进召朗玛的胸膛里，
儿子无情的神箭好像为母亲复仇，
父亲召朗玛疼得立即昏死过去。

洛玛和相娃拿过召朗玛的弓赛宰，
拾起他身上的东西奔回巴朗，
途中碰到前来援助的阿努曼，
抓住它用粗绳扎扎实实捆绑。

南西拉听到叫喊声跑出巴朗，
眼前的景象使她十分惊惶，
白猴阿努曼双手被反绑，
国王用的宝刀丢在地上。

神威无敌的弓赛宰摆在一旁，
高贵的王冠丢在地上闪着金光，
多么熟悉啊，这都是召朗玛的东西，
看到它们，南西拉心头无比悲伤。

眼泪从南西拉脸上像雨点流下，
两兄弟不理解妈妈的心情，
他们责骂阿努曼睁大眼睛，
一个劲看着妈妈使她受惊。

第二十章 团圆 Chapter 20 Reunion

"Who was there cross-examining our ancestors?
You are so timid that you hid yourself in the forest.
Which kingdom are your soldiers from?
Do you come to Yimaban to get yourself killed?"

After this Luoma let go of his arrow,
It was as fast as flash and hit Zhao Langma in the chest.
As if the ruthless arrow was to seek revenge for their mother,
Zhao Langma was so much injured that he came into a coma.

The two brothers took away Zhao Langma's Bow of Saizai.
They rushed back to their house with all his things.
When coming upon Anuman who came to rescue Zhao Langma,
They grabbed him and tied him tightly with thick rope.

Nan Xila came out of the door when hearing the noise.
She was terrified at what she saw.
Anuman's arms were tied behind his back,
Zhao Langma' sword was lying on the ground.

The magic Bow of Saizai was put aside,
The glittering majestic crown was thrown on the ground.
They are so familiar and they belonged to Zhao Langma.
Seeing them, Nan Xila's heart was filled with sorrow.

Tears fell off from Nan Xila's face like raindrops.
The two brothers didn't understand how their mother felt.
They scolded Anuman for scaring their mother,
Because he stared at their mom with his widely-open eyes.

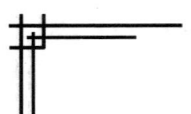

"该死的白猴不准瞪着眼睛吓人,
今天落在我们手里休想逃生,
我们要打断你的双腿,
看你还敢不敢到街上去收税?"

母亲哭着劝阻儿子:
"快快松开白猴身上的粗绳,
你们不能用恶言秽语辱骂它,
更不准伤害它的生命。

"这个白猴跟我们虽不是亲属,
可它是你父母的恩人,
它是你父亲最得力的武官,
没有它呀妈妈早就被杀害。"

两个儿子听了母亲的叙述,
立刻给阿努曼松绑赔了不是,
南西拉领着儿子走进巴朗,
把儿子杀伤召朗玛弟兄的事告诉帕拉西。

帕拉西忙向英达祈祷,
带着神药仙水跑进了森林,
他往召朗玛和腊嘎纳嘴里滴了药水,
昏死过去的两人慢慢苏醒。

三、大团圆

南西拉默默地站在丈夫身旁,

第二十章 团圆 Chapter 20 Reunion

"You damned white monkey, stop staring at our mother.
You are now at our hands and don't expect you could escape.
We are to break your legs to see
If you still dare to collect tax on the street."

Their mother tried to stop them with tears,
"Hurry to untie the white monkey,
And stop abusing him with your threats.
More importantly you should never take his life.

"Although the white monkey is not our relative,
He was the benefactor of your parents.
He is the most capable general of your father.
Without him I had been killed many times."

When the two brothers heard their mother's explanation,
They immediately untied Anuman and made apology to him.
Nan Xila took the two brothers inside Balang,
Telling Palaxi how Zhao Langma brothers had been injured.

Palaxi immediately prayed to Yingda,
Then he took magic water and rushed to the forest.
He dipped the water into the mouths of the injured brothers,
They came back to life slowly but steadily.

Ⅲ The Family Reunion

Nan Xila stood by her husband silently.

焦虑地一直守到召朗玛、腊嘎纳苏醒，
她回想起自己的痛苦遭遇，
忍不住拜倒在召朗玛前面啜泣。

苏醒后的召朗玛渐渐看清，
跪在面前的是被自己处死的妻子，
他惊愕得慌忙坐起来，
询问腊嘎纳究竟是回什么事？

腊嘎纳把经过向哥哥陈述，
召朗玛立即伸手把南西拉扶起，
内疚使他痛哭不止，
夫妻俩伤心得昏过去几次。

召朗玛想到自己太狐疑，
冤枉了善良无辜的妻子，
他忍着悲怆向妻子表示忏悔，
请求妻子原谅自己的过失。

"眼珠般的妻子啊，请把过去忘记，
误会和嫉妒已使我受到惩治，
请你告诉我这两个聪明的孩子，
可是我们亲生的儿子？"

南西拉怨愤地追叙往事，
召朗玛越听越痛恨自己，
他悔恨交加又无限感激，
他用温和亲切的语言召唤两个儿子：

第二十章 团圆 Chapter 20 Reunion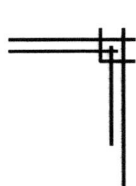

She waited anxiously for them to come round.
Recollecting all her miserable sufferings,
She burst into tears at the feet of Zhao Langman.

Zhao Langma looked around after waking from coma.
Seeing his executed wife kneeling in front of him,
He was startled to sit up.
And he asked Lagana what on earth had happened.

Lagana recounted to his brother the whole story.
Zhao Langma hurried to hold up Nan Xila.
Out of guilt he cried bitterly.
The sad spouse fell into comma several times.

Now he knew it was just because he was too suspicious
That he had treated his kind and innocent wife wrongly.
He refrained his sadness and repented to his wife
Pleading that she could forgive him for all his errors.

"My dear wife, you are my eyeballs. Please forget the past.
I have been punished for my jealousy and misunderstanding.
Please tell me,
Are these two intelligent boys our own sons?"

Nan Xila recounted her bitter experience.
The more Zhao Langma heard, the more he hated himself.
His heart was filled with both gratitude and regret.
Then he called the two sons gently and amiably,

"宝石一样珍贵的儿子啊,
快过来让父亲看看你们,
跟随父亲回到庄严的宫殿,
去见你们的祖母、叔叔和婶婶。"

两个孩子态度冷淡而生硬:
"我们生下来就没有父亲,
从来也没有亲戚,
你别来诓骗,我们不认识你。"

失掉小犊的母牛哞哞叫唤,
死了伴侣的斑鸠咕咕哀鸣,
见儿子不认父亲,
召朗玛懊恼万分。

饱尝悲欢离合的南西拉,
对丈夫产生无限的怜悯,
她用母亲的关怀和温存,
向儿子说出了真情。

"两颗珍珠啊,
你们冒失射倒的两个人,
一个是你们的王叔,
一个就是你们的父亲。"

从小没有父亲的孩子最听妈的话,
洛玛和相娃平心静气回答母亲:
"不是我们不想念亲人,
不是我们不想念父亲。

第二十章 团圆 Chapter 20 Reunion

"My dear sons, you were as precious as gemstones
Come up to your father and let me take a close look.
Please come with me back to the grand palace,
And meet your grandparents, aunts and uncles."

The two kids answered in bitter and cold tone,
"We have no father ever since we were born.
And we have no relatives either.
Don't lie to us. We know nothing about you."

When losing its calf, a cow would moo in sadness.
When losing its partner, a dove would coo in grief.
When his two sons wouldn't accept him,
Zhao Langma felt agonized in his heart.

Having herself suffered the grief at separation,
Nan Xila got deeply sympathetic with her husband.
With a mother's tenderness and care,
She told the boys the truth.

"My two pearls,
The two men you have shot,
One is your uncle,
The other is your father."

Having no father around, the two brothers trusted their mom most.
So Luoma and Xiangwa answered her calmly,
"It is not that we don't miss our families,
It is not that we don't miss our father.

兰嘎西贺 The Ten-Headed King of Langa

"我们天天盼望见到父亲的面，
就像寒夜中的小鸡盼望太阳，
只因妈妈对我们说过，
父亲的灵魂早已升入天堂。

"过去我们悲哀地天天悼念他，
又怨他死得早把我们抛在林间，
今天你又说他是我们的父亲，
到底你的话哪句是假哪句是真？"

孩子的聪明使南西拉高兴，
她把事情的真相进一步说明：
"站在面前的是你们的父王召朗玛，
他治理着勐沓达腊塔。

"你们父王的正直和勇武，
天下的国王谁也比不上，
勐沓达腊塔的光辉和威望，
就像太阳和月亮一样。

"只因妈妈做错事得罪了他，
猜疑和误会使他下错了决心，
要把妈妈处死在荒凉的森林，
多亏你王叔腊嘎纳救了我的生命。

"他把妈妈从刀下放走，
从此妈妈在森林里生存，
我对召朗玛的无情怀着怨恨，
所以才说他去见了死神。

第二十章 团圆 Chapter 20 Reunion

"We long to meet our father every day,
Just like the young birds missing the warm sunlight in deep night.
But mom, you have told us
That our father's soul has long risen to the heaven.

"We used to miss him and mourn for him each day.
We also blamed him for leaving us behind in the woods.
But today you told us he is our father,
We can't tell which part is true and which is not."

Nan Xila was glad to hear her sons' sensible words.
She explained more about what had happened in the past,
"The man standing here is your father, the King Zhao Langma,
He is the ruler of the Kingdom of Dadalata.

"Your father is a man of unmatched honesty and bravery.
He is the king of the kings on the earth.
The Kingdom of Dadalata is reputed with its glamour,
It shines as bright as the sun and the moon.

"Because I have done something wrong that offended him,
He made a wrong decision out of suspicion and misunderstanding.
He gave can order to get me killed in the desolate forest.
Only because of your uncle's protection that I got saved.

"He let me go from under his sword.
I started to make my living in the forest ever since then.
I held grievance at Zhao Langma for his ruthlessness,
So I told you that he had gone to see the god of death.

"今天他来见到了你们,
过去的事情就让它过去吧!
快去亲近你们的父亲召朗玛,
还有好心肠的叔叔腊嘎纳。"

洛玛和相娃这才走过去见父亲,
召朗玛伸出双手把儿子抱在怀中,
他从心里敬佩南西拉的坚贞纯洁,
他悔恨交织、无地自容。

"南西拉啊,我的爱妻,
沓达腊塔宫殿少不了你,
今天我要把你们接回去,
让我们白头到老再不分离。"

受尽折磨和凌辱的南西拉,
满腔的愤懑难以平息,
她从红红的嘴唇里,
说出一句句低沉哀怨的话语:

"感谢你的好情意,
感谢你跋山涉水来到这里,
请你把两个孩子接回去吧,
让他们将来继承你国王的位子。

"你的妻子早已不在人间,
她已在你的刀口下丧生,
带着深重的屈辱,
成了森林中的野鬼孤魂。

第二十章 团圆 Chapter 20 Reunion

"Today he came and met you two.
Please let the bygones be bygones.
Come up and say hello to your father,
And to your kind-hearted uncle Lagana."

The two brothers then came up to meet their father.
Zhao Langma opened his arms and held them tightly.
He admired Nan Xila's faithfulness and purity in his heart.
He was so penitent and ashamed of his selfishness and jealousy.

"Nan Xila, my dear wife.
The palace is lifeless without you.
Today I beg you to come back with me
So that we will grow old together."

Having suffered too much torture and humiliation,
Nai Xila still couldn't get her indignation appeased.
Out of her trembling lips
Were the words of sadness and bitterness.

"Thank you for your kind invitation,
Thank you for coming here from afar.
Please take your two sons back to the palace,
So that they can inherit your throne in the future.

"Your wife has long left this world.
She has died under your sword.
And she died in shame and humiliation,
She is the wandering ghost now in the forest.

879

"已经死了多年的人,
怎么能够重新回生?
被你定了死罪的南西拉知道羞耻,
怎么有脸去见大臣头人?

"拴在我们手上的线已被一刀砍断,
滚滚的江水怎么能倒流?
寂寞的茅屋就是我的归宿,
荒凉的森林将是我的坟地。"

"烈火已证明你忠贞无比,
泥像的误解却又使我产生狐疑,
可恨的猜忌使我变得冷酷无情,
妻子啊,请原谅我的过失。

"你不回去,孩子不会有快乐和温暖,
你不宽恕,我的心不会得安宁,
我的妻子南西拉啊,
你一定要跟我回到宫廷。"

站在一旁的官员和士兵,
眼含热泪向南西拉跪拜,
宫廷大臣双手捧着花盘,
南西拉不答应回宫就不起来。

第二十章 团圆 Chapter 20 Reunion

"I have been dead for so many years.

How could I come back to life?

The Nan Xila sentenced to death by you has the sense of shame.

She has no face to meet the officials and chieftains.

"The thread tying us together had been cut by your sword.

There is no way that the rolling river could flow backwards.

This lonely thatched house is my last home;

The desolate forest will be my graveyard."

"The burning fire has testified your purity.

But I doubted you again due to the clay figurine.

My suspicion turned me into a ruthless monster,

My dear wife, I am begging you for forgiveness.

"If you are not returning with me,

Our sons will never feel the happiness and warmth of a home.

Without your forgiveness, I will never have peace in my heart.

My dear wife Nan Xila, please return to the palace with me."

Soldiers and officials had tears in their eyes,

They knelt down in front of Nan Xila;

The ministers held flower plate with both hands,

Saying they wouldn't stand up unless Nan Xila change her minds.

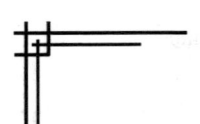

兰噶西贺 The Ten-Headed King of Langa

宽厚的南西拉比丈夫还难过，
她不愿在召朗玛的心上增添忧烦，
她不愿看到痛苦的离别，
再次把亲生的骨肉拆散。

南西拉同意了丈夫和臣民的请求，
接下了大臣举着的花盘，
召朗玛激动得热泪如注，
官兵们高兴得一片欢呼。

召朗玛邀请帕拉西也到宫殿去住，
帕拉西向他们诚恳祝福：
"我是森林里修行的和尚，
不能跟你们去城市居住。

"我祝你们白头偕老、终身幸福，
愿你们身体健康永葆纯洁，
祝你们的国家兴旺发达！
愿你们的百姓安居乐业。"

召朗玛率领亲人返回京城，
全城百姓在大路两边欢迎，
三个母后走下宫殿迎接，
一家人在金碧辉煌的宫殿里团聚。

宫廷请来了高贵的帕麻纳，
为南西拉和两位王子拴线祝福，
帕麻纳向全勐庄重宣布，
美丽的南西拉重新做勐沓达腊塔王后。

第二十章 团圆 Chapter 20 Reunion

The lenient Nan Xila was more sorrowful than her husband.
She didn't want to put more trouble onto Zhao Langma;
She could not bear the painful separation
That will tear the whole family apart.

Nan Xila granted the request of her husband and the subjects.
And she accepted the flower wreath from the ministers.
Zhao Langma was so excited that his eyes were full of tears.
The officials and soldiers started to cheer in joy.

Zhao Langma also invited Palaxi to live in the palace.
Palaxi sincerely gave them his blessing,
"I am just a monk practicing Buddhism in the forest,
I can't go with you to live in the city.

"May you live happily together till the last day.
May you stay healthy and pure in heart forever.
I wish your country to be strong and prosperous!
I wish your people to live a happy and comfortable life."

Zhao Langma led his families back to the palace.
All his people welcomed them along the roads.
The three mother queens walked out of court to greet them,
The families gathered together again in the glorious palace.

The dignified Pamana was invited into the court
To bless Nan Xila and the two princes.
Pamana declared to the whole kingdom
That Nan Xila became the queen of Dadalata again.

兰嘎西贺 The Ten-Headed King of Langa

威武的国王召朗玛，
接受人们的欢呼祝贺，
扶着贤良的南西拉王后，
庄严地登上金光闪闪的御座。

受尊敬的波涛、咪涛①，
年轻的小伙子和姑娘，
缅桂花迎着太阳开放，
我就要结束这篇故事的吟唱。

当你静静地听完最后一章，
当你诵读这长如江河的诗行，
一定会问谁提金笔把它写成，
也会想知道谁最先把它吟唱。

在浩瀚的经书和唱本里，
谁愿意把自己的姓名写上？
谁也不愿像凤凰那样显示自己，
在这里我请求傣家人原谅。

传说佛经有八万四千套，
灿烂辉煌，源远流长，
就是像《兰嘎西贺》这样长的十部，
也达不到一套的篇章。

---

① 波涛、咪涛：即大爹、大妈。

第二十章 团圆 Chapter 20 Reunion

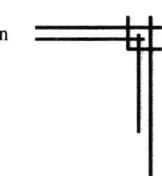

Here came the mighty king Zhao Langma
To accept the congratulations from his people.
He held his kind and docile queen Nan Xila
Together they ascended to the glorious throne.

Respectful Botao and Mitao①,
The young lads and girls,
Magnolia are blooming toward the sun,
I am about to finish chanting this story.

When you listen quietly till the last part,
When you read the lines flowing like rivers,
You will ask who wrote it with his golden pen,
You will wonder who was the first to chant it.

In the uncountable classic books and ballads,
Who wanted to leave his name behind?
No one would show off himself as a phoenix does.
Here I wish the Dai people would forgive me.

It is said there are 84,000 scripture books of Buddhism,
All of them are brilliant with long history.
And any one of these books is longer
Than ten *Langaxihe* put together.

---

① Botao and Mitao: this is used to address the people are a generation older than you.

世间的知识就如浩瀚的海洋，
《兰嘎西贺》能装上水珠几颗？
我的心情难以平静，
后人究竟对《兰嘎西贺》怎样评说？

尊敬的波涛、咪涛，
象牙般纯洁的姑娘，
《兰嘎西贺》写完了，
我庄重地把它放在金盘上。

当我放下金笔的时候，
太阳又从东山升起，
金色的光线照亮了天上的云朵，
它好像在对我热情地祝贺。

森林的百鸟一齐扇动翅膀，
从我的头上徐徐飞过，
它们用甜蜜动听的歌喉，
送给我无限的宽慰和欢乐。

此时此刻我心情不能平静，
只怕写下的诗篇落字掉音，
损伤了诗章的美丽完整，
荒废了读者的宝贵光阴。

有毅力和恒心就能成功，
这是我终生的信仰，
我希望获得全部知识，
钻进人类智慧的海洋。

第二十章 团圆 Chapter 20 Reunion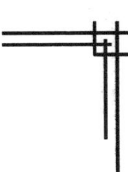

The knowledge in this world is like the vast ocean.
How many drops of water are contained in *Langaxihe*?
I felt uneasy deep in my heart wondering
What comments will the descendants have on *Langaxihe*?

Respectful Botao and Mitao,
Girls as pure as the ivory of elephant,
I have finished the story of *Langaxihe*,
Now I, solemnly, put it on the plate of gold.

When I put down the golden pen,
The sun arises from the mountain in the east again.
The golden sunlight brightens the clouds in the sky,
It seems to be expressing its warm congratulation to me.

Hundreds of birds in the forest flutter their wings,
They are flying over my head slowly.
The song they are singing is so pleasing,
It gives me boundless comfort and joy.

At this special moment I can't keep calm,
For fear that some word or sound got lost in the ballad,
Which will damage the wholeness and beauty of it.
For fear that I had only wasted the precious time of its reader.

Anyone with willpower and perseverance can succeed.
This is a faith to which I hold on for my whole life.
I wish I could acquire all the knowledge in the world,
I wish I could dive deep into the sea of human wisdom.

让我懂得文学和古拉经,
能够占卜吉凶,写出故事和诗歌,
因为我这颗破碎的心啊,
时时挂着人类的喜怒哀乐。

像初春一样美好的姑娘,
你们的青春犹如九月盛开的花朵,
当微风轻轻吹拂的时候,
鲜花的芳香就会从森林流过。

这时你心爱的人儿啊,
是不是变了心爱上了别人,
就像泉水不恋岸边的鲜花,
你就让他好好读读这篇诗文。

这篇唱诗像山中潺潺的流水,
可以把心上的污垢洗涤干净,
又可以解除欲念的焦渴,
使人变得善良、纯洁、聪明。

相爱着的年轻人,
要像召朗玛和南西拉那样忠诚,
不要怕遭受误解、折磨和分离,
才能获得人生真正的爱情。

第二十章 团圆 Chapter 20 Reunion

I wish I understood literature and Gula scripture,
So that I could divine and write stories and ballads.
This is just because I have a broken heart
Which cares for the well-beings of all the human.

Young girls, you are as beautiful as early spring,
Your youth is just like the blooming flowers in September.
When the light breeze drifts,
The fragrance of flowers will waft across the woods.

If your beloved one has changed his heart
And fallen in love with somebody else,
Just as the creek doesn't love the flower on the bank any more,
Then ask him to take a good read of this ballad.

This chanting ballad is like a murmuring stream in mountain,
It can wash away the dirt in one's heart.
It can also help relieve the anxiety brought by desires
And help people become kind, pure and intelligent.

To those couple who are in love,
Stay faithful to each other as Zhao Langma and Nan Xila.
Don't be afraid of misunderstanding, torture and separation.
You will have your true love on the journey of life.

傣家人啊，我知道你们爱听唱本，
可是我的使命到这里已经完成，
我的歌喉已因疲倦而沙哑，
我的智慧和才能已经用尽。

要是我再往下写往下唱吟，
它就会像断了线的风筝，
随风盲目飘荡，被雨洗淡颜色，
我的唱本也会不成文和失去生命。

第二十章 团圆 Chapter 20 Reunion

My Dai people, I know you love the chanting of ballad.
But here come the end of my mission.
I have had a hoarse throat due to my fatigue;
I have used up all my wisdom and wits.

If I keep writing and chanting and singing,
My ballad will be like a kite broke off the leading thread.
It will drift with wind blindly and be washed out of color by rain.
Then it will not be a complete work and will lose its life.